THE BLACK HUNTER

A Novel of Old Quebec

BY

JAMES OLIVER CURWOOD

Illustrations by Arthur E. Becher

British Library Cataloguing-in-Publication Data
A catalogue record for this book is available from the
British Library

Contents

Illustrations

James Oliver Curwood

James Oliver 'Jim' Curwood was an American action-adventure writer and conservationist. He was born on 12th June, 1878, in Owosso, Michigan, USA – as the youngest of four children.

He left high school before graduation, but passed the entrance exam to the University of Michigan, where he enrolled in the English department and studied journalism. After two years, he quit college to become a reporter. In 1900, Curwood sold his first story while working for the Detroit News-Tribune, and after this, his career in writing was made. By 1909 he had saved enough money to travel to the Canadian northwest, a trip that provided the inspiration for his wilderness adventure stories. The success of his novels afforded him the opportunity to return to the Yukon and Alaska for several months each year – allowing Curwood to write more than thirty such books.

By 1922, Curwood's writings had made him a very wealthy man and he fulfilled a childhood fantasy by building 'Curwood Castle' in Owosso. Constructed in the style of an eighteenth century French Chateau, the estate overlooked the Shiawassee River, and made for a truly picturesque setting. In one of the homes' two large turrets, Curwood set up his writing studio. He also owned a camp in a remote area

1

in Baraga County, Michigan, near the Huron Mountains as well as a cabin in Roscommon, Michigan.

Curwood's adventure writing followed in the tradition of Jack London. Like London, Curwood set many of his works in the wilds of the Great Northwest and often used animals as lead characters (Kazan, Baree; Son of Kazan, The Grizzly King and Nomads of the North). Many of Curwood's adventure novels also feature romance as primary or secondary plot consideration. This approach gave his work broad commercial appeal and helped drive his appearance on several best-seller lists in the early 1920s. His most successful work was his 1920 novel, The River's End. The book sold more than 100,000 copies and was the fourth best-selling title of the year in the United States, according to Publisher's Weekly. He contributed to various literary and popular magazines throughout his career, and his bibliography includes more than 200 such articles, short stories and serializations.

Curwood was an avid hunter in his youth; however, as he grew older, he became an advocate of environmentalism and was appointed to the 'Michigan Conservation Commission' in 1926. The change in his attitude toward wildlife can be best expressed by a quote he gave in The Grizzly King: that 'The greatest thrill is not to kill but to let live.' Despite this change in attitude, Curwood did not have an ultimately fruitful relationship with nature. In 1927, while on a fishing trip in Florida, Curwood was bitten on the thigh by what was believed to have been a spider and he had an immediate allergic reaction. Health problems related to the bite escalated over the next few months as an infection set in. He died soon after in his nearby home on Williams Street, on 13th August 1927. He was aged just forty-nine, and was interred in Oak Hill Cemetery (Owosso), in a family plot.

Curwood's legacy lives on however, and his home of Curwood Castle is now a museum. During the first full weekend in June of each year, the city of Owosso holds the Curwood Festival to celebrate the city's heritage, and in addition, a mountain in L'Anse Township, Michigan was given the name Mount Curwood, and the L'Anse Township Park was renamed Curwood Park.

Anne at last meets the Black Hunter

FOREWORD

Probably no period in the history of the North American continent offers to the writer of romance a field richer in incident or one more filled with the picturesque and thrilling life of the pioneer than that with which this novel opens, and with which it is the author's intention that other books shall deal. Yet it is a curious and interesting fact that these years, beginning with the French and English struggle for supremacy in 1755 and ending a few years before the War of Independence, have seldom been called upon, and almost never with any degree of historical accuracy, to furnish material for the writer of fiction. A period which embraced the very birth of both the American and the Canadian peoples, and was weighted with dramatic happenings which shook the greatest nations of the earth and made them largely what they are today, these years form a valley that has long slumbered in the dim and shadowy past. Their stirring and romantic events are next to forgotten by the present generation, who seldom pause to think that it was only that short time ago that France claimed all of America from the Alleghanies to the Rocky Mountains and from Mexico to the North Pole, with the exception of a few miles of ill-defined English possessions along the shores of Hudson's Bay.

The French dominion is a memory of the past, and when, as Parkman says, we evoke its departed shades "they rise upon us from their graves in strange romantic guise. Again their ghostly camp-fires seem to burn, and the fitful light is cast around on lord and vassal and black-robed priest, mingled with wild forms of savage warriors, knit in close fellowship on the same stern errand. A boundless vision grows upon us; an untamed continent; vast wastes of forest verdure; mountains silent in primeval sleep; river, lake and glimmering pool; wilderness oceans mingling with the sky. Plumed helmets gleamed in the shades of its forests, and priestly vestments in its dens and fastnesses. Men steeped in antique learning, pale with the close breath of the cloister, here spent the noon and evening of their lives, ruled savage hordes with a mild, parental sway, and stood serene before the direst shapes of death; and men of a courtly nurture, heirs to the polish of a far-reaching ancestry, with their dauntless hardihood put to shame the boldest sons of toil."

That out of these days were born the writer's own ancestors, and that the unhappy and misled Mohawk nation gave to him an Indian maid for a great-grandmother has, since boyhood memories, been a source of unending pride; and this pride, in later years, has grown into a humble yet valiant desire to write of times in which, if he had been the arbiter of his own destiny, he would gladly have lived.

For ten years both the material and the thought for these stories have been growing; foot by foot the hallowed ground has been traveled; letters written by hands dead these hundred and fifty years have been read, their spirit-people brought to life again; the ancient stones of ruins that once rang with laughter and song and tragic happenings have been made to talk; buried and yellow manuscripts of priests and martyrs have given up their secrets that have never known the ink of a printing-press, and holy nuns of the Ursulines have contributed what gentle hands placed on treasured papers in a forgotten and glorious past.

If the writer can be true to these people and their day he will have achieved one of the greatest of his ambitions. Yet, agreeing with some of his critics, he confesses to many limitations; craftsmanship may have its horizons, but there is comfort in the fact that honesty of purpose is without circumscription. And a writer of romance is not an historian, nor can he ever be judged as such, though his pages may carry more of history and truer history of a certain people and time than has been written. For, as there are times in an historical novel when fact insists upon drawing a somber cloud between romance and its fulfilment, so there are other times when the necessities of romance make permissible that "poetic license" which writers of fiction have been granted from the remoteness of the ancients, and which will persist farther ahead than we can possibly see into the future. In

"The Black Hunter," in order that a closer continuity of the story might be brought about, two historical happenings have been slightly changed. Vaudreuil has been made to appear in Quebec several months before he was actually there, and Fort William Henry plays a minor part in the story a year earlier than fact will verify.

JAMES OLIVER CURWOOD.

Owosso, Michigan, Nov. 4th, 1925.

INTRODUCING

ANNE ST. DENIS	daughter of a fighting seigneur, who sees love and glory and God in the world, and into whose life come the dramatic happenings of an heroic and stirring age.
DAVID ROCK	a son of the forests and their dangers, who carves on his powder-horn an angel in the form of Anne.
THE BLACK HUNTER	a weird and mysterious wanderer of the wilderness, a weaver of romance and tragedy, not quite forgotten even to this day.
MARIE ROCK	David's mother, in whose heart is built a shrine to bitter memories of the past, and to a love which she hides from all the world.
JOHN ROCK	Marie's husband and David's father, killed by the Indians.
NICOLAS ST. DENIS	a seigneur of the Richelieu, and Anne's father.

11

PETER GAGNON	a chivalrous young blade (and the ancestor of the greatest family of the Province of Quebec today) whose love for dueling is second only to his love for Nancy Lotbinière.
NANCY LOTBINIÈRE	a beauty and belle of old Quebec, sweet of heart and mind, with a courage which helps David rise to triumph out of hours of darkest gloom.
LOUISE CHARMETTER ANGELA ROCHE-MONTIER JOSEPHINE LA VALLIÈRE CAROLINE DE BOULANGER	Quebec friends of Anne and Nancy.
SISTER ESTHER OF THE INFANT JESUS	Anne's closest friend in the Convent of the Ursulines.
FRANÇOIS BIGOT	the last Intendant of New France, wicked and without conscience, who plots to destroy David and win Anne.
MARQUIS DE VAUDREUIL	Governor General of the Canadas, the sly and scheming destroyer of France's power in the New World, who works hand in hand with Bigot.

HUGUES DE PEAN	Bigot's chief ally, and husband of the glorious Angélique--"La Belle Amazone Aventurière"--whom he gave to Bigot for a mistress in exchange for favor and fortune.
DESCHENAUX	the serpent in man's form who paves the roads for Bigot's amours.
CADET IMBERT BREARD RIGAUD MERCIER VARIN KANON	members of Bigot's powerful "ring."
CARBANAC	the common man who changes into a god.
NICOLET	who steals Carbanac's pretty wife, and dies because of it.
PIERRE COLBERT	a friend whom David meets at the pillories.
CAPTAIN RENÉ ROBINEAU	a man of old and courtly honor, who turns like a lion at bay upon his enemies.

CAPTAIN JEAN TALON	the greatest duelist in New France, who at last meets a fitting end.
DOCTOR COUÉ	a dried-up wisp of a surgeon, who dresses wounds and loves a gallant fight in the small hours of dawn.
FONTBLEU	the little old miller at Grondin Manor, where Anne and David live.
KILL-BUCK	a loyal Delaware.
THURENSERA (DAY-DAWN)	his daughter.
MIREPOIX	French ambassador to the court of England, who loves a lady's curls.
ALBEMARLE	English ambassador to the court of France, who plays whist as he cheats France out of her kingdom across the seas.
LA POMPADOUR	mistress of a weak and dissolute king.

CHAPTER I

It was late afternoon, one hundred seventy-two years ago. The mellow softness and golden haze of Algonquin Indian summer lay over the drowsing wildernesses, and below the two who were looking out over the paradise of stillness and tranquillity ran the always mysterious Richelieu on its way to the St. Lawrence, twenty miles farther north.

Southward another sixty miles was Lake Champlain, and beyond that the hated English, the Mohawks, and the red scourge of forest brethren who preyed on New France.

All this, and much more, through weeks of painstaking effort the boy had carved on his great powder-horn in lines as delicate and finely wrought as the silken weave of a spider's web.

He was proud of his work, and the soul of an artist lay in his eyes as he revealed it for the first time to the criticism of another than himself.

He was a lad advanced into early manhood by the rigorous and uncompromising schooling of the wild Jesuit frontiers and of forests that as yet had no end. He was nineteen. He was not, to the eye, either heavy or powerfully built. His body was slender and seemed always poised for sudden swift movement. His bare head was covered with thick blond hair; his eyes were gray, very clear and steady when they looked at one, and no Indian could take in more quickly or more truly the details of a wide horizon. His name was David Rock, and in spite of the English in his name he was heart and soul of this glorious New France which he had pictured on his powder-horn.

Anne St. Denis, who stood at his side, was even more glorious than the land. The top of her head came an inch above his shoulder. A braid of gleamy dark hair as thick as his wrist fell to her slim hips. Her cheeks were flushed and her eyes aglow with happiness and pride as she held the powder-horn in her two hands and looked at the amazing work upon it.

"I can scarce believe human hands ever did this work!" she cried softly. "Oh, I am proud of you! I would be so happy—so wickedly happy—if I could show it to dear Mother Mary and all the sweet Ursuline Sisters when I return to school in Quebec and tell them that my David is the artist. It is unbelievable—almost!"

"I am glad you like it," said David, blushing, and all through he could feel himself atremble as he looked down at the long silken lashes which hid her eyes.

"It is more beautiful than the paintings on the convent walls. And—it is made with a knife!"

"Yes, with a knife," said David, "on a flinty buffalo horn traded to me by an Algonquin who took it from a Seneca he killed in a fight two years ago."

16

"Ugh!" shuddered the girl.

"That doesn't spoil it, Anne."

"No, but I will never like fighting, though there is so much of it all over the land. I would rather a Seneca had not been killed in its taking!"

David looked down on the Richelieu, and then away over the wilderness. "Turn the horn over, Anne," he said, with a little break in his voice. "Something is there—which you haven't seen."

She twisted the horn in her hands and there in the heart of an exquisite little forest of pine trees was a scroll, and in the scroll were carved two lines of letters which read, "I love you. Until I die I will fight for you." And under the letters were the initials and a date—"D.R. Sept., 1754."

"That means you," added David. "And it's true. I'd fight—all that world out there—for you!"

He was looking away from her. He was trying to make his voice steady, but away back in it—struggling to break through the man's effort he was making—was a note that was not all happiness, a suspicion, almost, of a boyish fear and weakness which he had found himself striving against of late.

The girl caught it. For a moment she had held the precious horn close against her breast. Now she dropped it to the soft green earth and turned swiftly to David. Her hands went gently to his face, and David's arms closed about her so that his fingers gathered the sweet crush of her braid as he held her to him. Her eyes shone with the love which had been theirs almost since childhood. She raised her mouth, exquisite in its beauty and softness.

"Kiss me, David!"

Unhesitatingly she rounded her lips for him. Then she drew away as gently as she had come to him, and David let her go.

"You won't have to fight for me, David. You know that. Why"—and mischief shot suddenly into her eyes—"I have had even the wicked audacity to tell Mother Mary I am anxious to hurry through school, because until then I cannot marry you! Yes, I have horrified them just that much, David—and if it were not for you I think they might dream of replacing the rich brocades and floating gossamers which I love so much with the sable robes of serge which so beautifully become a nun!"

"God forbid!" cried David, suddenly aghast.

"But I shall become a nun only if you are untrue to me, or die in some foolish way before you are grown up," consoled Anne, and she picked up the powder-horn again.

"I wish there was no school," said David, and his voice was moody and sullen.

"You mean that, David Rock?"

"I do. There is no school for me, except the forests. You do not like fighting, and yet only fighting is left to me.

There is always fighting in the forests. There always will be. We who don't have schools must fill powder-horns like that and fight back the English and the Iroquois, while up in the great city of Quebec—you tell me it has eight thousand people now!—men and women live like kings and queens of France, and boys grow into gentlemen, and girls like you become great ladies——"

"And the great ladies, of course, fall in love with the gentlemen," finished Anne. "Why not say what is in your mind, David?"

"I cannot help what is there."

"But my gentleman dresses in deerskin soft as velvet, which is the true armor of the brave knights of the Richelieu, and always will be," said Anne, gazing a bit wistfully into the red glow of the sunset.

"Yet I am afraid, and have been growing still more afraid of late," said David, and he knew that at last he was about to reveal the thing which had been eating at his heart for many months past.

"Afraid—of what?"

With a sudden gesture David pointed to his flintlock rifle which leaned against the bole of a fallen tree. "That is all I have—that and my mother," he said.

"Our mother, you mean," cried the girl with a determined little note in her voice. "She is half mine!"

Happiness trembled for a moment in David's voice. But it died out as he went on. "You know what I mean, Anne! Your father is the great baron and fighting seigneur of all these miles about us, and your home is the Big House, while ours is a log cabin away back in the forest——"

"Pish!" interrupted Anne with a petulant toss of her head.

"And you are beautiful——"

"So is the work on your powder-horn!"

"And you love rich brocades and floating gossamers——"

"On pretty girls I do!"

"And such things go well with the linen and gold lace which gentlemen wear, and are more in company with swords and cocked hats than with flintlocks and powder-horns."

"Come to think of it, I believe they are," agreed Anne.

"And—and—there is more in your life and in the great city of Quebec than I can ever hope to give you the beginning of," finished David, his heart sinking lower.

"It is marvelous how clearly you see the truth," agreed Anne again, and her eyes were lowered so that he could not see the laughter in them.

"Well——"

"Well, David?"

"And now there is a great party of young gentlemen and ladies traveling all the way from Quebec to see you, and the King's Intendant and his party are coming on their return from Montreal, and with them this man Vaudreuil, who, they say, will be Governor of all New France next year if Intendant Bigot has his way."

"A pretty party," said Anne with irritating sweetness. "Five of the loveliest girls in Quebec, David, and I know I shall be jealous of you before they are gone!"

David was silent.

"Nancy Lotbinière, with her blue eyes and hair like the sunset out there, has sworn to take you from me," she went on a bit mockingly, "and Louise Charmette and Angela Rochemontier and Josephine La Vallière and Caroline de Boulanger are mad to lay their eyes on you."

"They are all from the seigneuries down the St. Lawrence?" he asked.

"Except Louise Charmette, who is a merchant's daughter, and a great flirt of whom I am vastly afraid!" she answered. "Will you tell me more about the powder-horn, David?"

"Peter Gagnon says this Intendant Bigot is the wickedest man in New France," persisted David.

"Peter should know," said Anne, "because Peter knows everything. And the Intendant is also the most powerful man, next to the King." She raised her lashes and looked at him with eyes so deeply blue and lovely that he felt words dying in his throat. "David, I haven't been listening very closely to what you have said because I've been fighting for courage to ask you for this powder-horn. Please, may I call it mine? I would rather have it than the most priceless painting in the Chapel of the Saints!"

In an instant he felt all the work of his words undone. "Anne—you mean that?"

"I do."

"And it is not—just to give me pleasure, to make me happy, that you say it?"

Her face was flushing now, her eyes darkening until the violet-blue in them became almost black. "David, this horn and what you have carved upon it means more to me than all the schools and all the great gentlemen in the world—if the words you have put upon it are true!"

"When they are not true—then I hope God won't let me live another day!" He made no movement toward her in his great happiness, but stood with his heart beating so fast that it made him breathe quickly, as if he had been running a little.

"And I may have it?"

"Yes."

Her laugh of gladness was like the soft beauty of the ending day. "Then you must tell me all you were about to tell me when those silly thoughts of gentlemen and schools came into your head. I must know the meaning of all that is on the horn!"

Now that trouble was gone out of his heart David looked about him once more with shining eyes upon a part of the great land which he had pictured with the keen point of his hunting knife. They had climbed to the top of Sunset Hill, whose crown of black pines and golden hardwoods caught the last glow of each dying day and held it like a benediction as dusk crept up out of the valleys.

The Richelieu was narrow and slow-moving below them, stealing without sound or fanciful movement between embankments of rock and dense timber, as if it knew itself to be the one great artery of life and death that led to and from the Canadas and their enemies. Beyond that lay only a small part of the seigneury of St. Denis,[1] for a turn in the river held most of it from view; but southward and east were rolling billows and pathless worlds of forest that ended only where the sky bent down and shut out vision.

David took the horn, and Anne pressed so near him in her eagerness to miss nothing he might show her that her pink cheek rested against his arm, and her silken braid glowing with a thousand soft lights in the mellowing sunset fell over her shoulder and across his hand. And David laughed that queer, soft laugh which she had loved from their earliest childhood, and he bent down and laid his cheek and lips against the velvety sweetness of the braid for an instant before he straightened himself to point off into the blue distance of the wilderness.

"Off there are the English, who plot and pray day and night to destroy us, and who are buying our scalps from the savages like so many beaver skins, and who would turn every one of us over to the fire stakes of the Iroquois if they could!" he said, and his voice began to fill with the first words until a note of bitterness was in it that drew an anxious light into the girl's eyes. With her two hands she pressed his arm gently, for she knew that whenever he thought of the English and their Indians he saw also a vision of his father—tortured and slain by them. "And I hate them so," he cried fiercely, "that all their land I have covered with little devils, as you see here on the horn!"

"Yes," she nodded, thrilled by his passion—for to the depths of her soul she loved New France.

"And this—all this—is the Waterway," he went on, drawing a slim forefinger over the exquisitely carved detail on the bulge of the horn. "This is the one path—the one trail—between our enemies and us. That is why the King granted to fighting seigneurs like your father these lands along the Richelieu—[2] that they might block this trail to invasion and hold our enemies back. Away down here at the beginning, on this lake which we call Lac St. Sacrament and which the English call Lake George, is the first of the English strongholds—these two forts which you see—Fort Edward and Fort William Henry; and at each of these forts I have carved a barking dog, for they are always barking at us there, and biting us when they can!"

The girl shivered a little against him. "And will they—do you think—ever get up to us, and do what their barking clogs want to do?" she whispered.

"Not if your gentlemen in the great city of Quebec have the courage to fight," said David.

"Not my gentlemen, David," she chided gently. "Not my gentlemen."

"And from these barking dogs," he continued after a moment in which he seemed to be measuring her words, "we come to our own Lake Champlain; and here, where I have put the flag of France at the top of a broken pine, is the place called Ticonderoga by the Mingos, where very soon we are going to build a fort."

"You talk like—like a man who has his heart set on fighting," said the girl, seeing less now of what was on the horn than of grim visions which were rising before her out of the forest. "Why do you say 'we' are going to build a fort, David? Why do you put yourself in it at all? Won't the King's soldiers build the fort?"

"The time is coming," said David slowly, "when every rifle in New France will be needed to hold back the barbarians. That time is very near. I am not guessing. I know it. And rifles like mine are better than those of the soldiers, Anne."

"And our enemies will come from those barking dogs into Lake Champlain, and from Champlain into the Richelieu, and down the Richelieu to—to—us?"

"Yes, and beyond us to Montreal and Quebec and every home in New France unless we along the Richelieu can hold them back," said David gravely.

"You speak more surely—even—than—my father," said Anne doubtfully. "He speaks only of peace, believes in peace, and—the power of France. And so they speak and think in the city of Quebec, David!"

"The forests know different," declared David. "While your gentlemen in Quebec dance and play and grow rich those barking dogs down there are growing hard and lean and hungry. Those are not my words. They are——"

"Whose?"

"The Black Hunter's, Anne."

He spoke the words very softly, as if they carried a secret which even the winds must not hear. The girl stopped breathing for a moment, and in that moment her slim body grew a little tense against him.

"He has been here again?"

"Yes. A month before you returned from the school at Quebec he came one dark night. I was asleep, and I was dreaming that terrible dream of mine. After that I spent two weeks with him away down in the forests south, going into the very heart of our enemies' country and even to the lead mines in the valley of the Juniata. I was at Fort William Henry and saw the barking dogs, and because I was with the Black Hunter they saw no harm in me. And I saw red scalps, and many dried ones attached to the round hoops which the Indians stretch them on."

The girl had drawn slowly away from him. Her cheeks had paled and in her eyes was the frightened look which he had many times laughed at. "And your mother—let you go—freely—-without warning or fear?"

"She has not your horror of the Black Hunter, Anne."

Laughing, he took her hand. And for a moment she looked at him so steadily and with such an odd searching in her eyes that the smile died away.

Then, as if she had read a thing which he was fighting to keep to himself, she looked at the horn again and said, "You have not finished with the horn, David. You have got as far as the Richelieu, and this, I know, is where our water runs into the St. Lawrence, and here must be Quebec on its big rock, and there Montreal on its island, and all this farther north must be the lands of the Upper Canadas. But I see other things which I do not understand—down here, for instance, a shrine with two beautiful angels kneeling in prayer, and over here not so far away a most miserable-looking creature sitting with a fishing-rod in his hand. Who can it be, and what is the mystery of the angels and the shrine?"

"In that patch of woods," explained David solemnly, pointing again with his forefinger, "is a big house which you cannot see. It is the Château St. Denis, your home. And one of the angels at the foot of the shrine is yourself, but only half as beautiful—and the miserable-looking creature trying to catch a fish is myself, Anne—and flatters me considerably at that!"

"David, am I supposed to laugh or—cry? And you have given these angels most wonderful hair!"

"There never was such hair as yours, Anne."

"Not even your mother's?"

She looked up to find a glow of pride in the boy's face.

"My mother is beautiful! That is why the Black Hunter suggested another angel kneeling beside you—my mother."

"The Black Hunter! He told you that? He knew you were making this horn—for me?"

"He helped me plan it those days we were together in the south country. It was he who suggested the shrine and the angels."

At his words the girl slowly turned the horn over, and on this other side of it was the last of the carved pictures David had made—a vast and untrailed forest with a group of tiny tepees buried in the heart of it.

"That is Hidden Town," said David, turning so that he was looking south and west toward the sunset. "It is off there, no white man knows where—except the Black Hunter. It is where the Senecas have taken their white captives since the days long before we were born—the captives they do not kill but keep to become a part of their tribe. Women and babies, mostly, the Black Hunter says—and hundreds must have gone there. Some day I should like to see it. With the Black Hunter I would be safe."

The girl had come close to him again. "As long as I live I shall love the horn, David. Look at the sunset—redder than blood! And it is growing a bit chilly up here, without a scarf for my shoulders. Please let us go home or your mother won't see you before darkness comes—and there is no early moon these nights to help light your way through the forest."

[1] This seigneury of Nicolas St. Denis, on the Richelieu, should not be confused with the St. Denis seigneury on the St. Lawrence below Quebec, now known as St. Denis Bay.

[2] The Richelieu River, the "bloody waterway" between the Canadas and the British and American colonies, has since been variously named the St. John, the Chambly, the St. Louis and the Sorel.

CHAPTER II

The girl looped the buckskin thong of the big powder-horn about her shoulders and led the way down a sloping path that brought them very soon to a flat plateau of giant oaks under which the shadows of evening were beginning to gather more thickly.

The boy, for a little while, had followed closely behind her, but now he stepped swiftly ahead, and the long-barreled rifle was held readily in his two hands, while his eyes and ears seemed suddenly alive to nothing but movement and sound which the forest gloom might be hiding near them.

Anne's eyes shone softly as she followed and watched him, and listened with him. She loved to look at him when he was walking ahead of her, his moccasined feet making less sound than falling leaves and the boyish slimness of his body filled with panther-like lithesomeness. In a moment of unusual irritation her father had once called him a young panther, a cub that was growing into a beast good for nothing but the deep woods. And she was proud of that! She was proud of David—immensely proud. In a year there had come a great change in him. He was no longer just a boy and a playmate and someone she loved devotedly. He was, at moments—and in moments like these—a man!—a man who filled her with a deeper and more splendid thrill than ever her girlhood love for him had done, and who frightened her a bit, and who had set her heart beating in a new and wonderful way.

Last night, while he was smoking his big pipe after supper, with Anne perched on a corner of the table in the room which he had set aside for his study and his library, the Seigneur Nicolas St. Denis had said to his daughter:

"You are a woman, Anne. You are seventeen. I don't want to lose you, because you are all I have left of your mother. But half a dozen young gentlemen have asked for permission to pay serious attentions to you, and it is time for you to get over this silly childhood attachment for David. You can, if you will, marry into any one of the three or four most powerful families in New France. You are no longer a child. You are a woman! And now, with the Intendant and his people coming, and your friends from Quebec——"

It was there Anne had stopped him, with her two hands determinedly over his mouth, and while the grizzled old veteran made no resistance against this soft prisonment she whispered in his ear, "I am going to marry David, you dear old one-legged papa-faucheur! I am going to marry David!"

There she had left him, running to her room and laughing happily on the way; and below her, after that, she could hear her father stumping back and forth on his wooden leg, but she did not see the smile in his eyes or hear the satisfied chuckle deep down in the old warrior's chest as he looked out from his window toward the deep forest where lay the cabin home of Marie Rock and her son.

But his words she remembered, and they were repeating themselves over and over in her brain now in a kind of wild song, "You are a woman—a a woman!" And, somehow, in this dusk of the great oaks the truth possessed her suddenly and strangely. She was seventeen! And in Quebec in this year of grace, 1754, young ladies of seventeen knew the world, and were a part of it, and married, and became the mothers of children!

And David——

She touched his arm. "Why are you so still—so cautious?" she whispered. "Surely there can be no danger on Sunset Hill!"

"It is the hour for partridges and turkeys to be out," he replied in a low voice.

"You are not thinking of partridges and turkeys," she retorted quickly. "You are thinking of Indians, David. Always Indians. They are never out of your mind. They would not dare to come here."

"They dare anything, Anne. And when I look at you, and your hair—for which I would kill any man if he touched it unkindly——"

"You like my hair?"

"More than anything else in the world. Why do you ask that, when you already know?"

"Because it is time for you to begin saying nice things to me without always making it so necessary for me to angle for them. And when you look at me, and my hair, you think of Indians—and are afraid for me?"

"I think of things I have seen down in the Iroquois country, and of Hidden Town," he said. "I think of———"

"Of what?"

"I shouldn't tell you."

"But I want to know."

"Well, I think of a packet of scalps the Mohawks sent in to Fort William Henry as a gift to their English friends. There were eight of them, all of French women, with long hair braided in the Indian fashion, and they were on blue hoops with black knives and hatchets painted on them to show they were killed with those weapons, and with little tadpoles all over to represent the tears of their relatives and friends. And one of those braids looked so—so much like yours—that I was sick—and frightened———" He caught her hand and held it so tightly that she could not complain of his gentleness now. "When the scalping-knife and the hatchet come up the valley again—and the Black Hunter says they are coming soon—then I hope you will be in Quebec," he finished, as if choking the words out of himself. The grip of his hand was hurting her.

"What do you mean?"

"Maybe—nothing. I shouldn't talk like this. It will make you nervous. See, we are coming out of the dense timber and there is still sunshine left in the valley!"

The girl dropped a step behind him, her lips parted and her cheeks flushed. She liked to hear David talk as he had talked in this last gloom of the big oaks. He was taking a man's interest in her. Her hand ached where he had crushed it for a moment. His face had a grim and strange look in it, unlike the boy David. The feminine in her rose exultantly.

They came down into the level of the valley where there was still a mellow glow of dying sun. It was here the river had twisted, and about them lay the cultivated lands of the Seigneury St. Denis. Yellow fields of flax and wheat stubble hugged the edge of the stream and ran in and out of the edge of the forest. There were meadows, innumerable stacks of hay, green seas of potatoes untouched by frost, pumpkins and squash and not far from the foot of Sunset Hill an apple orchard that hung heavy with unpicked winter fruit. For miles one could see the clearings and the bluish spirals of wood-fire smoke that rose from the chimneys of the farmer-vassals of the Seigneur St. Denis. Here, as one might have viewed the prospect a hundred and seventy-two years later, were civilization and progress, a husbandry of peace and plenty.

So Anne St. Denis looked upon it. Her eyes were glorious with the pride she felt in her world—and the happiness that was in her heart. But David, looking over the princely domain, saw the other thing—the forest. The forest, reaching farther on all sides of them than white men's feet had ever traveled; the forest, meeting clouds in the distance, obliterating the rims of the sky, creeping nearer, nearer, shutting them in, hugging them, suffocating them— all but that little breathing space with the grayish spirals of smoke rising out of it! The forest, hiding things from them, laughing at them in their dreams of security, smoldering, waiting—a giant biding its time while it watched pigmies of men and women at work and at play!

Near Sunset Hill they passed a farmer's home built of flat stones, and swung back from the four windows were shutters of thick oak, and under the eaves eight loopholes through which guns might be fired.

But Anne saw nothing of these things. They had been there since she could remember, and so had grown common. But the look in David's face was new and different, and held her eyes.

She was filled with a comforting kind of happiness. Restlessness, which she had known, was gone. And David, looking at her with eyes in which the boy still struggled with the man, had never seen her so beautiful. She was a part of the ending of the day, with its beauty of sunset, its stillness and the gentle breath of sweet-scented things that came out of the forests and from the fields. She unbraided her hair to let the coolness of the air play through it, and it streamed about her slim body in a radiant warmth and color. A hundred times she had done this before, with David. It had been an unconscious intimacy of childhood, growing up with them, and without thought or purpose. But tonight David's heart choked up as he looked at it, and inside himself he was trembling again. And for the first time, too, Anne St. Denis knew that she had given this streaming freedom to her wonderful hair with a deliberate and subtle intent, because David loved it.[1]

Over their heads a million wild pigeons were flying swiftly to the forest roosting-places, so thick at times they were like a dun-gray cloud, and David and Anne could hear the purring of their wings. Out of the valley clearings came sounds of comfort and peace and well-being—a voice far away calling cattle, the musical notes of a gong summoning the men-folk of one of the stone-built and loop-holed cottages to supper, the crowing of a rooster who liked his sunset as well as his sunrise, the barking of a dog—a woman's trill of song coming to them faintly from the place they had left near the foot of Sunset Hill.

It was the girl's habit to fill her arms with flowers when they came to the cleared and half-cleared places near Grondin's Wood. Trilliums and columbines and yellow marigolds were gone, but out of the fields had sprung blue seas of autumn corn-flowers, and in the edges of the thickets were masses of goldenrod, and crimson chokeberries and creeping sweetbrier, and in places wild asters so thick that Anne knelt down to pick them, a shining goddess in the nun's-veil of her hair.

And she was kneeling in this way, laughing up at David as she added to his load of flowers, when suddenly he dropped his burden and drew her swiftly up to him and held her so closely in his arms that for a moment or two her breath was taken away from her. And never had he kissed her as she felt his kisses on her mouth now.

She gave a little cry, and struggled back, pressing her hands against him, but even in this movement of apparent protest her heart was near breaking with triumph and joy. She saw David's face and eyes aflame with the splendid passion which at last had conquered the humbleness and repression of his boyhood, and ceasing to struggle she covered her eyes with the palms of her hands and bowed her head against his breast.

A voice broke in on the immeasurable thrill of this moment which would always remain the unforgetable dawning of manhood and womanhood in their lives—a mockingly apologetic and too evidently amused laugh very close to them. It brought Anne out of David's arms in an instant, and David himself faced the sound of it quickly.

A dozen steps from them three men had appeared from behind a thicket of wild elder and sumac. It was the first, a pace or two in advance of the others, who had laughed, for the humor and the ill-concealed suggestiveness of it were still in his face, while his companions were smiling with the partly exultant and half-envious emotions of men of the world whom fortune had permitted to look upon the joyous privacy of lovers.

But no sooner had Anne St. Denis turned upon them than the smiles died and the man in advance made a swift and ghastly effort to transform the mockery on his lips and in his eyes to something like a formal and respectful greeting and apology.

"Pardieu, we ask your forgiveness, mademoiselle and monsieur," he cried, bowing low. "We did not hear you, or see you, and we thought——"

"You lie!" interrupted David, advancing a step toward him. "You did see, and you did hear, and you laughed— because you did not know mademoiselle was Anne St. Denis! And you thought—what?"

Anne tugged at his arm. "David—David—please come," she pleaded, and before he could answer or turn she had darted down a narrow path that led through the thicket to the edge of Grondin's Wood; and deliberately David picked up his gun and the flowers and followed her.

"Pardieu!" gasped one of the two men behind. "Vaudreuil, did you ever see anything half so beautiful in all your life? And you, De Pean—a pretty mess you've made of it sneaking us up on a scene like this! And that young savage! Who was he? Kissing her, by heaven! Holding her in his arms! And she liking it, if I know anything about women——"

"And what you don't know wouldn't fill two pages in my note-book, Bigot," said De Pean, brushing a bit of white mullen-cotton from his sleeve. "Did you, by any chance, observe her hair?"

"Glorious!" exclaimed Bigot. "I'd give a governorship to be in that young Indian's shoes!"

"Moccasins, you mean," smirked De Pean, still picking the cottony mullen from his sleeve. "And as for the governorship—why, I doubt if such a price would be necessary, sir. Especially if there should happen to be seriousness in your thought, and De Pean were placed in charge of the matter——"

François Bigot, last and most powerful of the King's Intendants in New France, stepped quickly to the hidden opening of the path down which Anne St. Denis and her lover had disappeared. His dark eyes had leaped to sudden fire and his almost malevolent countenance was flushed with a hunter's eagerness as he strained for another glimpse of the flying loveliness that had disappeared in the bush.

Behind him, looking over his shoulder, was the slighter figure of De Pean, a bit foppish in form and dress but with a fox's keenness and trickery in his brain, Bigot's shadow and closest associate and the man whom all Quebec knew as the husband who had traded to Bigot the favors of his beautiful wife, Angélique de Pean, in exchange for the wealth and power with which the Intendant had been able to pay him.

And still behind these two, rubbing his hands over a comfortable stomach in appreciation of the rare humor of the situation, stood the Marquis de Vaudreuil, at the present moment Governor of the King's domains in Louisiana—pompous, cheerful, happy, without a shred of conscience, proud of himself to the point of absurdity, a little cock among men always on the point of blowing up with his own egoism, and the possessor of an extraordinary executive ability which was habitually directed toward the achievement of his own ends.

And Vaudreuil, as so often happened, spoke what was in his mind—a thought inspired by the exquisite humor of witnessing the husband and the lover of Madame de Pean in an attitude such as they now held, looking with feverish interest for another glimpse of this rival beauty who had taken flight almost before they could gain a second breath.

"It is well Madame de Pean is not here," he prodded them good-humoredly, "or this double treachery would—er—undoubtedly humiliate her!" And he rubbed his fat hands a bit more briskly when he saw the red flush in the back of De Pean's neck and the fierce glare which Bigot shot at him out of his sooty black eyes when he turned.

And then Bigot's dark face suddenly filled with the humor and laughter which at times made even his enemies accept him as a friend.

"Your good fortune is your blindness to beauty in women, Vaudreuil," he bantered. "That is why you love yourself so well, and why I am anxious to bring you from Louisiana and make you Governor of all the Canadas next year—you won't be a rival in my way! And as for this girl, and the savage who was with her, I still offer a governorship for the one and something equally handsome for the head of the other."

"Am I to understand that you are commissioning me to make that offer to her father?" asked De Pean with a sly smile, though he was still smarting from Vaudreuil's stupid hit.

The smile left Bigot's face. His humor was gone. "We must return and have a laugh with St. Denis over the incident before his girl gives him her own impression of it," he said. "You were a fool, De Pean, for thinking her one of these bumpkin farmer's daughters, even kneeling there as she was in the grass and flowers."

"You have known farmers' daughters who were lovely, François—several of them," reminded De Pean with a suggestive shrug of his shoulders. "And as for this being a misadventure I think you are mistaken. It has, if you care to make it so, almost boundless opportunity for romance."

Bigot was silent as they turned back toward Grondin's Wood and the concealed manor-house.

A figure had emerged from the wood and was coming to meet them, whistling cheerily on its way.

"That prying ass, Peter Gagnon!" announced De Pean unpleasantly. "Eternally whistling and always the same thing. The more you insult him the more he thinks you love him. It is a mystery why all the girls in Quebec are crazy about him, unless they know he is so simple that he cannot harm them."

Bigot nodded appreciatively. Vaudreuil, walking with a little wheeze in his breath, made as if he did not hear. But away back in his ordinary-looking head he was thinking— thinking with an astounding directness and clearness of purpose that brought a dull glow into his eyes and with it a keener appreciation of the evening's adventure.

[1] After escaping the vicissitudes of time for more than 100 years an age-yellowed letter written by Mother Mary Boucher to Madame de Longueuil was found in the effects of one of the latter's descendants. "And of these young nymphs of our classroom," wrote Mother Mary, "Anne St. Denis is queen. I cannot but think of the beauty and sweetness of angels when I look at her, though her heart and mind are afire with youth and life. Should it ever become my duty to perform an act in consecration to our Dear Lady by shearing the glorious hair which is her pride and ours I am sure my eyes would fill with tears, for she at times makes me wickedly

feel that her loveliness is such that to change it at all would be something very near to desecration."—Aug., 1753.

CHAPTER III

In the edge of Grondin's Wood with its magnificent sweep of giant hardwoods David found Anne St. Denis waiting for him.

She had replaited her hair, and her face was aflame with the stress of her flight mingled with anger and pride and shame. When she saw David's face, hard and set and as coldly white as her own was burning red, she held out her hands to meet him and take the flowers, and tried to laugh.

"I was a coward," she cried, "but I couldn't wait for you, David—with my hair all down."

"Who were they?" he asked.

Anne turned, crushing the flowers in her arms, and from the direction she faced there came through the thin strip of Grondin's Wood sounds that were new and strange.

Faintly they heard shouting voices and laughter and the tumult of ringing axes, unusual at the vesper hour, and above all that a wild snatch of song and a whoop that put a grimmer look in David's face.

"The Intendant's party must have come," she answered him. "They were not expected until tomorrow. The dark, heavy man back there was Monsieur Bigot, and the one who apologized was Hugues de Pean, Town Major of Quebec. I have seen them in Quebec. Who the other was I do not know. But I do know that—I hate them!" And a toss of her head and a quick catch in her breath told David she was thinking of the smiling insult in the face of the man who had afterward tried to save himself with lies and an apology.

With a look down the path they had traveled she held up her lips to David. "I must hurry! Papa Long-Legs is surely in a panic with all this company, and needs me. There is the kitchen, David, and all the food to serve, and I must fix my hair and dress—and meet these people in a way that will set them right about my dignity. So—good night!" David kissed her twice, and stood watching her until the last wave of her hand was gone and she had disappeared in the direction of the big house of Grondin Manor, leaving him with a heart into which a strange and brooding emptiness began to enter as he turned toward the deeper and darker forest which lay between him and home.

He had gone but a short distance when he stopped, and a thought twisted him in his tracks and held him for a few moments listening again to the faint sounds that came from the direction of the château. Pride and humiliation flushed his face as he left the path and approached the seigneury clearing. He tried to stifle the gloom in his thoughts as he came up behind the Seigneur's grist-mill.

This mill was the first thing that had photographed itself on his mind as a child—except one. He could remember it even farther back than he could remember his mother. Sieur

Grondin had built it away back in 1690, long before the days of St. Denis, for the date was carved in a stone slab over the narrow door. He had built it in the form of a round tower, twenty feet in diameter at the base and seventy feet tall, of flat slate rock grouted with mortar in a semi-fluid state so that it was like solid rock, with the old Dutch windmill still at the top of it. He had loop-holed it for defense against the Indians—and then had gone out into Grondin's Wood one Sabbath morning after turkeys, where the Mohawks scalped him nicely and stole his bag of game.

The old mill had been the earliest playhouse of David and Anne—the mill and the great outside bake-oven, built of mortar, stones and clay, which was not far from it. And the big wheel at the top of the tower was turning in the wind, making a wheezing and moaning sound in its labor when David came out from among the last of the trees.

A little beyond the mill the bake-oven with wide-open doors revealed itself a roaring pit of flame inside. It was half as big as David's loft bedroom at home, and two negroes whose black skins gleamed in the light of the fire were feeding it with fresh resinous fuel, so that in a little while the whole mass of the oven would be heated throughout, and the ashes and coals raked forth upon the ground to give place to loaves of bread that weighed ten pounds each when done.

Baking was seldom done in this oven at night—and beyond it was other activity such as David had never beheld at Grondin Manor.

The great château, built of slate rock like the grist tower and two stories in height, with windows that were deep-set and massive, and with a great chimney of stone rising at each end, was already aglow with a hundred lighted candles in the dusk; and David could see many moving shadows against the light, especially in the long kitchen, where a dozen servants—half of them borrowed from a neighboring seigneur down the river—were in a tremendous fuss of excitement and activity.

From the front of the house, facing the river, he heard the low melody of Anne's harpsichord, the shriller notes of a cornet, and laughter. And moving to the other side of the mill he could see Anne's room, with shades drawn at the windows, but lighted, and he knew that Anne was dressing hastily to take her part as housewife and hostess below.

But it was when he looked into the twilight spaces between the big house and the river that his heart jumped a little faster. Beginning at the edge of the thinned-out trees was a smooth green meadow up which no enemy could approach in safety and which sloped down to the water of the Richelieu a fair rifle-shot distance away. On one side of this meadow was the May-pole green, and on the other the seigneury church, which had more loopholes than windows in its stone sides; and the park between these two was the playground of the Baron's liegemen and their families on all holidays, and their rendezvous before and after mass on Sundays. But it seemed to David that something beside peace and frolic had taken possession of the space tonight.

From the far end of it, where the water of the river lay shrouded under a fringe of tall pines, came laughter and song and the sound of axes which he had heard faintly in the woods. A dozen fires were blazing, and one of these was half as big as a burning cottage, with many figures moving actively about it. Without looking at the figures he could tell the Indian fires from the white men's fires, and there were seven of these to five of the others; and about these fires were half a hundred men at least, not counting those that the pines or the edge of the river itself might conceal. His eyes, inheriting their instincts from birth, and trained by the Black Hunter's experience and skill, were quick to perceive the points of the encampment even at that distance in the firelit dusk. There were a score of warriors, either Ottawas or Hurons he decided quickly, and as many soldiers, with two parks of muskets near the big fire—and the others with their fringed skin shirts and skin caps and long rifles were scouts and rangers.

He had seen such encampments before, even where there were fresh scalps and wounded men. But what he saw on the green between the hundred burning candles of the château and the twelve fires against the black shadow of tall pines was new.

Here were another score of people or more walking slowly about in little groups, as if stretching their legs after long cramping in canoes. It was not so dark but that David could see the shimmer of their swords and the manner of their dress so that he knew them to be the smart officers and gentlemen who had accompanied the Intendant's fine party up to Montreal, and who had now come with their superior ways and splendid trappings to pay their respects to the seigneuries of the Lower Richelieu.

A dull resentment filled his breast as he looked up again at the lighted windows in Anne's room. He saw a slim shadow against the curtain and his heart beat faster. Then the lights went out until there was only a faint glow in the room. Anne had snuffed the candles, all but one. She was dressed, and her hair was up, probably in that wondrous way on the top of her head, which made her look so much taller and older. Now, in a moment, she would be going down the big oak stair.

The night, it seemed to him, was troubled by sound—a strange and unusual mixture of it which did not go well with the low whisper of the wind in the tree tops or the moaning drone of the big Dutch wind-wheel at the top of the grist tower. For sound came up from the black pines along the river as well as from the big house and the green—

the chopping of axes and voices in song and now and then a whoop like that which had sent a shiver through him when he heard it first in the woods.

To these was added suddenly, close at his side, a low, cackling laugh. Little old Fontbleu, the miller, had come like a dusty ghost out of the darkness of the tower door, and he was rubbing his hands as he gave his quaint laugh and looked at David.

"A pretty company, eh, master lad!" he cried. "A brave lot, and hungry too—so hungry they are walking the minutes away to make them shorter. A messenger should have come this noon, but he didn't—lost they say, or potted and scalped on the way. And here they show up without us knowing it, eighty of them by count, all good and strong—and the Intendant gives order for twenty bushels of meal and flour to go on with them tomorrow, which must keep me fishing like an angler for every capful of wind that comes this way tonight. And the wind is weak, too weak for good grinding, master lad!" he lamented.

"Eighty," said David. "That is too many to feed. Mademoiselle Anne told me they expected forty—no more."

The little miller grimaced and shrugged his thin shoulders.

"Down at the river they fare well. See the big fire? They are roasting an ox which the Seigneur slaughtered this morning in preparedness for tomorrow, and I have sent them a grist of five full bushels of coarse meal, which with potatoes and cabbages and turnips and squash should fill their bellies to bursting until the hour they leave. But for the gentry inside, the grand monde of Quebec, master lad, there must be fowl and tender roasts and fine pastry—and in such quantities that the kitchen is much upset, having planned for one mouth where now there are two, and not expecting any of them until tomorrow. I grant you there will be no sleep in this mill or at the big oven tonight, for the Intendant has also given order for one hundred loaves of bread—and one is safer to pull the King's nose at a distance than disappoint the Intendant at close range!"

David laughed recklessly. "He looks less dangerous than some people I have crossed in the woods, and if I were baking his bread tonight, or grinding his flour, Père Fontbleu, I think I should add a little burdock bitters to it," he said. "And do these orders of the Intendant for flour and meal and bread mean that his party are leaving again tomorrow?"

"Yes, or I cannot see why they should keep me working all night," said the miller, puckering his little old face into myriad lines of disgust at this unusual task set upon him.

Suddenly he pointed up to the dull light in Anne's window and the cackling humor came back into his voice again, with the metallic quaver of something like seventy years behind it.

"Look to her now, master lad," he cried. "Look to her now, with all this gold and silver lace and these high-stepping young gallants about! She's prettier than anything that ever came from Quebec, and it won't take young eyes long to see it, and older ones too, David lad. I wouldn't trust such prettiness out of my sight too long—God bless her sweet heart!—for la belle Pompadour herself would be forgotten if King Louis were here to set eyes on our sweet Anne. She belongs here, with the flowers and this old mill and the song of birds—so watch yourself, master lad, watch yourself—and her!"

David felt a tumult rising in his heart, and before he could make answer to the ancient man at his side a hungry complaint from the creaking bowels of the tower drew the miller back into darkness as suddenly and as noiselessly as he had appeared.

Slowly and fiercely it pressed upon David that he was as good as those on the green, or better, that no woman of their kind was sweeter or more beautiful than his mother, that no man who had ever set foot within the four walls of the city on the rock was braver than the Black Hunter, that the whole world was his—while theirs was a narrow heritage upheld by rifles like his own in the wilderness!

His heart began to beat with exultation, a triumph that sent a red flush into his thin-cut, sensitive face. Man to man he could kill De Pean. He was thinking of it in that way now—man to man! The boy was gone.

He no longer made an effort to conceal himself but strode out boldly, passing the bake-oven and close to the lighted windows of the château. Not by a foot or an inch did he swerve from the directness of his line to the river.

He passed a group of three officers, who stared at him with unfriendly eyes, and came on another group of four. These halted, almost bumping into him. One was gray-mustached, with hard, cold eyes, and the butt of David's gun brushed against him.

"Pardieu! Who are you, and what are you doing up from the river?" he demanded.

"My name is David Rock, of this seigneury, and I am taking a stroll like yourself," answered David with equal sharpness, and went on without touching his cap or bending his head an inch.

"The devil!" he heard a younger man exclaim. "Shall I prick him with the end of my sword, Colonel, to see how fast he can run?"

But no steps followed behind him, and David came to the edge of the pines, his blood strangely singing and his head awhirl with the thrill of what he had done.

CHAPTER IV

Cheer and friendliness and much good humor of the kind he knew were ringed about the campfires. Frivolities of taste had not entered here to waste precious moments, where every man was his own cook and servant, or joined his exertions with others to a mutual end. The aromas of roasting and boiling things floated like an incense in the air, and hungry men looked at David as he came among them, and nodded, or spoke, or waved a hand in brotherly greeting, as though they knew him not as a stranger but as a friend.

A half of the ox, spitted like a huge fowl, was roasting on the two iron barbecue rods which St. Denis had brought from Quebec, and as men turned it with hooked poles and others dipped its dripping juices back from the big under-pan to the browning and sizzling meat, a hungering desire entered into David. From boiling kettles the perfume of the other half of the ox rose to mingle with that of the broiling mass on the spits, and between the two David knew why hard and tired men's faces were softened with good cheer and why they laughed and joked and sang bits of song as they waited for a few more minutes to pass. And he saw, propped up on pointed sticks, and spitted on others, whole halves of golden squash turning more golden and crisp in the heat; and in the edge of each of the white men's fires was a pile of ash and coals covered with damp grass in the heart of which potatoes were baking.

The men were a dun-colored and much-worn lot, most of them. The rangers, with knives in their belts and long rifles never more than a step or two away, were in fringed buckskins and wore thin skin caps from which the fur had been taken with the exception of the ornamental tail down the back. Their leggings and moccasins were ragged, their hands hard and knotted, their faces smoke- and wind-stained to the color of Indians. Beside them the soldiers in their natty uniforms and hats looked more like company for the château and the green. Aloof from the white men the Indians were gathered about their fires; twenty of them David counted, all Hurons, already engaged in their pleasant task of devouring half-done meat from spit and kettle.

Near the big fire men's faces were flaming hot and sweating as they worked the broiling half of an ox.

"Two more turns like that and we'll begin slicing the outer works,'" said one, with a ravenous but friendly grin at David. He was thin and lank and grizzled, and was evidently captaining the job. "That's the way to eat it, lad—slice it as it broils and its juices will melt it in your mouth—cook it through and its outer casing is hard as wax. And lambaste it with the juices as they drizzle out. Sharpen your knife, friend! We're almost ready!"

David thanked him, but kept on, though an inclination to remain with them was burning him up. His mother was running through his mind, and had been for an hour past. He would be late at home, so late she would worry, in a mother's usual way, even though she knew it was the sweet company of Anne that was keeping him in these last few days of her visit at home. He cut across the green again toward the château whose lighted candles made it look like a fairy castle against the black shadows of Grondin's Wood. Again he made no effort to avoid the strolling officers and gentlemen of the Intendant's party, but walked boldly on his way to the big spring at the upper end of their promenade.

This spring was one of the unusual features of the St. Denis seigneury. Where the water gushed up cold as ice, was a great rocked-in pool twenty feet in width—and the earth had been dug out and the rocks put there, so legend said, even before the adventurer Sieur Grondin came that way to build his wilderness palace for the three beautiful mistresses whose soft tresses the Mohawks took on the very day that they scalped Sieur Grondin and stole his turkeys.

There were people near when David, ignoring the wooden gourds at hand, knelt down on the rocks to drink. The barrel of his rifle clattered against a stone. His skin-dressed figure and moccasined feet were clearly revealed in the light that still remained in the open sky. And when he rose to his feet, his face wet and one doeskin sleeve dripping water, he found the cold-eyed, gray-mustached man and his companion half a dozen steps behind him.

"It is the young scoundrel who insulted you," exclaimed the same voice that had threatened to prick him in the back a few minutes before, and David saw a fiercely scowling young cub half draw his sword and take a step toward him.

"He is more than that," came another voice that sent a thrill through David, and he swung a little at the sound of near footsteps. On the other side of him stood De Pean and Bigot and Vaudreuil, and from behind these three stared the amazed and startled face of his friend Peter Gagnon.

On De Pean's face was the same detestable smile, only it was made more significant and more insulting now by a movement which he made by drawing a sleeve across his mouth, clearly intimating that David's needed wiping. Vaudreuil's fat body shook and chortled with laughter at the rare humor of his companion's pantomime.

"He is more than that," repeated De Pean, advancing a step and making David an elaborate bow filled with mockery and ridicule. "He is pretty as you see him, gentlemen— but you missed a prettier sight which our eyes beheld this evening!"

He straightened himself, and came beside David, even touching his arm daintily with the tips of his fingers, while his eyes flamed with the promise of the fun he was about to make.

"Observe him, gentlemen, observe him closely," he commanded, simulating the professional voice of a huckster on the market-square in the city. "Not a savage, as you think, though his hair is uncut and his face adrip—not altogether the silly fool he appears to be, my friends!—but a lover, an amoret, the name of whose lady-love would astonish you. Yes, this is the darling duck of her pretty eyes, the pretty eyes of the one we caught in his arms today out where the brush is thick, the pretty eyes of——"

Farther than that no power in heaven or on earth could have made David let him go. Swifter than a bar of light was the movement of his body. It turned, bent, snapped in an instant, and De Pean was caught in the snap of it. Before any man could make a cry or a move he was turned like a twisted reed and was hurled with a mighty plunge into the center of the icy pool.

Bigot was first to spring forward to stop what was already done, and again before others could intervene David had met him in all his rage, and his powerful young arms sent him in an instant close upon the floundering and splashing body of De Pean.

A cry of incredulity and horror went up from the others, and above that cry David heard Peter Gagnon's. In a moment half a dozen men set upon him. He made no effort to defend himself or struggle. He had settled with De Pean and Bigot, and the mad triumph in his blood drove out all thought of combating others against whom he bore no personal malice. He was conscious of a number of things happening at once—of men holding him, of a gleaming sword pointed at his breast, of a strap closing tightly about his wrists behind his back, of a wheezing and floundering and puffing behind him as friends pulled Bigot and De Pean from the depths of the pool.

And then, at the last, came a voice that had sent the chill of death into more hearts than one, and it said, "Take him to the house, and command St. Denis to inflict upon him a punishment of a hundred lashes on his naked back—and you, Colonel Arnaud, see to it that the thing is done, with all who would like to see looking on!"

Even that voice in its terrible hardness did not frighten David in the momentary delirium of satisfaction that possessed him. It was worth his life to have closed De Pean's mouth in the breath with which it was about to speak Anne's name. It was worth the price of a thousand lashes. He was not thinking of Bigot, the man who had condemned him, nor of his act as a crime punishable by death if this most powerful man in New France had so willed it. He was thinking only of Anne, and of that something precious between them which De Pean had been on the point of desecrating.

A hundred lashes!

They were leading him across the narrow space of green between the pool and the château, a fury of men with clanking swords and angry faces, Colonel Arnaud stalking ahead with a face as merciless as steel.

A hundred lashes!

The thought was beginning to possess him slowly. A hundred lashes—with people looking on! A hundred lashes—on his naked back!

He saw Peter Gagnon, and his friend's round face, usually as pink as the rosy side of an apple, was now as white as the dust that settled on the little old miller's shoulders at grinding time.

And he began to feel cold—the chill of something terrible that was creeping through him.

They were taking him straight up into the big hall of the château. And there, he thought, Anne would see him. She would hear the sentence—and he must not look afraid or sorry.

His face was dead white in the first candle-glow. But his chin was stiffer than the warrior Colonel's. His head was up, his hair a little wet where it had dipped into the pool.

With a clatter of feet and metal they thrust him half the length of the big hall, where the candle-lighted tables were ready for their guests. Instantly, it seemed to David, the significance of the intrusion was felt and known. Almost before the coldly furious voice of the Colonel was calling upon the servants to demand the presence of St. Denis the room had begun to fill. Voice and laughter grew suddenly hushed in the drawing-room, and faces appeared at the door; then men came through boldly, forgetting the courtesy of place and hour in the unexpectedness of the spectacle which confronted them.

Looking neither right nor left, but straight ahead, David sensed this swift gathering of amazed and curious people like one in a dream. He could feel their eyes upon him. He could hear their breath, their whispers, the sound of other footsteps coming up from the green, and in his own breast he could hear the pounding of a heart that seemed to be sending a clammy chill through the veins of his body.

Yet, staring at him, men saw no sign of shrinking or fear, except that his face was gray and bloodless in the candle-light. But it was the gray of stone, with eyes looking out that were level and straight, with the emotionless stoicism of an Indian in them. He might have been an Indian except for his blond hair and gray face. An Indian would have stood like that facing death at the hands of his enemies.

Yet his brain was reeling—reeling with words that were repeating themselves mercilessly now—"a hundred lashes—a hundred lashes—a hundred lashes with people looking on!"

And then he found himself looking straight into the face of Anne St. Denis—Anne and her father standing in the wide doorway that entered the Baron's private room.

And she was as he had pictured her when looking up through the dusk at the candle-glow in her curtained room.

She was not the Anne of Sunset Hill, nor the Anne of the bottomland thicket of sumac and wild elder whom he had dared to hold so closely in his arms.

She was an older Anne, a more glorious Anne, in a dress that was like gossamer sheen and with her hair piled up in an amazing glory on the top of her head, until her slim little body seemed almost of regal height even beside that of her tall father.

She was not his Anne as she stood there, but a new Anne who had made herself glorious and different for these people of the big city, and whose proper place would be among them when he received the hundred lashes on his naked back.

His heart seized on that thought, and his whole body and soul, until his face and eyes gave no sign of recognition or emotion as he met her frightened gaze.

Dully he heard the Colonel's implacably hard voice telling of the heinous double crime he had committed. He saw the surprise in Anne's face and eyes give way to shock, and the shock to startled horror, until every vestige of the radiant color in her cheeks was gone, and she was whiter than he had ever seen her before.

He heard in the same distant way the demand for his punishment—a hundred lashes on his naked back, with people looking on. And then he saw Anne sway as if the words had struck her a blow, and a twisted pain came into her face, and he thought she tried to cry out—but no words came.

And all the time he was looking at her in a strange and unemotional way, as if she were a stranger to him. For it seemed to him that she was no longer his Anne—not as she stood there in the doorway beside her father.

But others saw differently. Through the doorway from the green had come Bigot and De Pean, disheveled and with trickles of icy water running from their clothes, and close behind them was Vaudreuil.

It was Vaudreuil who whispered softly and quickly into Bigot's ear, "I told you it was madness to condemn him like that—if you hope to find favor with the girl! Look at her now—whiter than a lily of Artois and more beautiful than all the Graces of Quebec! If you let the thing go on she will hate you. If you do what I advise she will—almost—love you! This young savage cannot hold her. Make her your friend. Gain her favor. Do that—and the beauty you look on now will be yours in time—and—the governorship—mine!"

The whisper was also for De Pean, who added softly, as half the eyes in the room were on them, "Never has fortune placed so fair a flower in your way, or offered such splendid opportunity for plucking it, François!"

In those same moments Colonel Arnaud was repeating in a voice clearly heard by all, so that the Seigneur St. Denis could not possibly misunderstand, "One hundred lashes,

Baron, no more and no less, all on his naked back—and in the open green for the public to see. I offer you the responsibility, sir, of guarding the prisoner until morning, when no doubt the punishment will be given."

A rough hand had gripped David's shackled arms, but now a lighter one rested upon his shoulder, and Bigot's voice followed it close at his side. The Intendant was smiling. A friendly glow lay in his eyes. And De Pean, behind him, was bowing with cheer and friendship written over his damp countenance, while Vaudreuil chuckled audibly with his hands crossed in their favorite resting-place over his stomach. At the same time one of Bigot's hands pinched Colonel Arnaud's arm in a manner most significant to that officer.

"Mademoiselle, we humbly beg your pardon," said Bigot in a voice which he could make as soft as music at times. "I am afraid Colonel Arnaud has carried our little joke too far. This young man is not to be whipped, sweet Mademoiselle Anne, but is brought here in this fashion that we may all have our little play and at the same time do him proper homage as the most courageous youngster in all of New France. De Pean and I have both had a proper ducking at his hands for making thoughtless fun of him at the pool, and he has so proved his mettle, and I like him so much for it that—if he will forgive us our frolic—we pledge our friendship to him from this hour on; and should he adventure to Quebec, where opportunities lie in the way of bold and fearless blood, I shall see to it that the Intendant he has so thoroughly baptized this night takes proper care of him. And now if you will excuse us while we change into dry clothes which we are fortunate to possess, and if you, Anne, will grant us your forgiveness for taking the color from your pretty cheeks—why, this hour will be a pleasant one to be remembered all my life!"

An inner triumph warmed Bigot as he saw the effect of his words. Every passion in a soul darkened by dissipation and fed by unlimited power had centered itself in Anne. Her young beauty possessed him wholly. Her sweetness and innocence were like the spur of drink in his blood. Vaudreuil, shrewd and plotting, had seen the birth of this passion; Bigot himself now experienced the unguessed force of it as he played his clever game. Standing beside her father like a white angel in whose face life was beginning to paint itself in color again, Anne St. Denis was worth the risking of a kingdom.

Yet to no eyes but those of Vaudreuil and De Pean did the Intendant reveal a visible sign of what had become a consuming fire in his breast. Even his exultation he concealed. He had been insulted, the crime of lèse majesté had been offered against his person, and he was inspired by the knowledge that St. Denis and his daughter knew this and had trembled at its consequence. Yet no suspicion of mockery or of anything but frankness and friendship was in his attitude or his words. He was offering his hand and his grace where, to any other living man, he would have given the gallows or the whipping-post. And he looked at Anne, and smiled into her eyes, and watched the color return into her cheeks as he gave back life where he might have given death.

He advanced and took her hand and bowed over it as reverently as he would have made obeisance to the Queen, or to la Pompadour, the King's mistress, whose pet and protégé all New France knew him to be.

"May good fortune and happiness always follow you two," he said to Anne; and the meaning of these words, which she alone knew, sent the flush more swiftly into her cheeks as she looked starry-eyed at David.

But the boy had turned, freed quickly from behind of his bonds. Men stepped aside as he stalked to the door. Someone placed his long rifle in his hands. He did not look back and did not hear the low crying of his name which came from Anne's lips before she could stop it. He had found his place again—in the darkness outside.

CHAPTER V

The cool air of evening blowing gently from the river came as a comforting stimulant to David, and it seemed to him that for the first time in many minutes he was breathing freely as he saw the rim of fires along the edge of the pines.

He paused outside with the château a blazing glow of candle-light behind him. He heard movement and the rattle of scabbards. Someone laughed and the laugh was like the touch of fire to a powder-fuse. A voice bantered De Pean and he heard the Seigneur St. Denis making a relieved announcement to his guests that in another ten minutes the supper would be served.

His thoughts were swift flashes filling him with a fierce glow of exultation, a fire which quickly consumed itself in the passion of his youth and inexperience. He had defended Anne and had shown his contempt for the grand monde against, which he had been nursing his resentment for many weeks past. This filled his mind, overriding all else in the first moments.

And then came a gloomier reflection of the other thing. He had been dragged in with his hands tied behind him. His gun had been taken from him and he had been threatened with a hundred lashes. Only Bigot had saved him, and he had seen Bigot bend over Anne's hand and raise it to his lips—and for an instant had seen her eyes filled with the light of stars!

His breath came unevenly in the conflicting emotions that possessed him as he retraced his steps around the end of the château. He could never forget Anne as she had stood in the doorway beside her father, dressed for the officers and gentlemen from the big city. A world had put itself between them then. She had not come to his aid as he would have gone to hers. She had not spoken to him and had not raised her voice in protest.

Yet there was something of exultation remaining in him which no depression could kill. It was like a song which kept repeating itself in his heart and which lifted him above the hopelessness that had struggled to possess him. With the thrill of youth in his blood was also the glory of achievement, and something was telling him that tonight he had lifted himself above the David Rock of yesterday—that he was not the same, and would never be the same again, and that somehow the change was a thing which he would not barter for Bigot's kingdom, yet could not tell himself why.

He found himself passing the oven, roaring with its fire; and in front of the black door of the tower the little old miller was standing, more ghostly than before in the faint illumination of a million stars.

"You have seen them, David, all these fine first-fiddles of the land?" he greeted. "You have seen Bigot, the great

Intendant and master-lover, the protégé of la Pompadour and the pet of the King?"

"I have seen him," said David, "and have stood beside him with his hand on my arm in the big hall."

"What—you! David Rock, that comes of having Anne St. Denis for a sweetheart, for Bigot's fingers touch by choice only velvets and satins, and if he petted you like that, I say— it was because of Anne!"

"I think it was," said David truthfully. His blood was growing cooler. He looked at the château's lighted windows and his face had in it a softer light.

"And what does Bigot think of our Anne?" asked Fontbleu with his cackling laugh and queer rasping of thin hands.

"That she is beautiful, of course."

"Yes, of course," nodded the miller; and of a sudden he grew very quiet, so that after a moment or two David said good night and went on his way.

The miller looked after him and shook his head, and muttered dubiously to himself, "Yea, yea, David, she is beautiful, too beautiful for you, and that is why Bigot and some of his fine crowd will not go on with the others tomorrow. Mark that, lad, and see if old Fontbleu is not right! Yea, David," he added more bitterly as the other went out of hearing, "I'd give these two worthless hands of mine if she and her beauty could change shoes with Papineau's girl or some other like her with freckles and a pug-nose, for you two have grown up with me and this old mill, and it will break my heart almost as much as yours to lose her!"

David, looking back from the edge of Grondin's Wood, saw him standing in the starlight. And at the same time he heard the stir of a stronger wind in the tree tops and the coolness of it in his face, and the droning of the wheel at the top of the tower took on a louder note, as if talking to him as he stood there. It was the old miller, years ago, who had first told him and Anne that the ancient wheel could talk, and that it was always lonely for someone who could understand. And what tales had come from it through Fontbleu's lips—stories of love and Indians and mad fighting and weird ghosts and of the adventurous Sieur Grondin and his lovely mistresses, whose spirits were abroad each night of the thirtieth of September, starlight or storm, seeking and crying for the scalps they had lost! Through the years David and Anne were growing up together, the mill and its talking wheel had been their third playfellow, and no matter whether the day had been black or filled with sunshine there had always been comfort and cheer in its company.

Its comfort and comradeship crept into David as he stood looking back at Grondin Manor. He was not thinking of the stories Fontbleu had told them, or even very much of the mill itself, but was picturing Anne beyond the lighted windows, smiling and courtesying and very beautiful, and somehow he was less afraid for himself and for her than he had been when he first walked across the green. And the droning voice of the tower wheel kept at its work until David at last sensed the fact that it was rising softly and persistently above all other sound, and he looked up to the sky where its huge wings were drinking in the wind as it wobbled and twisted heroically against a background of stars.

For many minutes he stood in the darkness of the trees thinking of Anne and readjusting himself as the torments in his blood died away. It was then he saw a figure running, between the big oven and the mill, and Fontbleu, the miller, came from the shadow of his door to meet it. In another moment the figure was hurrying over his trail, and before it reached the blackness of the woods he could hear it puffing and knew it was his best friend—next to the Black Hunter and his mother and Anne—Peter Gagnon, whose titled father ruled the adjoining seigneury.

He almost called out in his gladness, but caught himself and remained silent. He loved Peter Gagnon—Peter the Plump, as Anne called him, with his round, rosy face, his love of pretty girls and good food, and his immeasurable optimism and cheer.

Not until Peter was about to plunge bravely into the darkness of the forest did David reveal his presence. Peter gave a gasp of relief as he seized upon his friend.

"Sancta Maria, but I'm glad!" he cried. "All the devils in the woods would have been at my heels if you had made me follow you through that pit of ink to your home!"

"It would have been easier in the morning," suggested David.

"But not with Anne St. Denis threatening me with death and destruction unless I saw you tonight!" averred Peter, drawing in a great gulp of wind.

David's heart gave a joyous throb. "She asked you to find me?"

"No. She didn't ask me. She commanded me, and said that if I failed her she would devote the rest of her life to making every pretty girl in Quebec my enemy, and would consecrate herself to hating me. That's how much she thinks of you, David!" And Peter gave another great gasp for wind.

David made no answer, and Peter, getting down to his normal breath, went on, "When you went away like that, as if every person in the room was your enemy, it didn't take her half a minute to get a signal to me, and we got off by ourselves long enough for me to tell her what had happened. David, you should have seen her eyes and heard her heart beating. Yes, I heard it! And then she made me promise to find you, even if I had to feel my way through these spooky woods, and tell you that she was happier and prouder of you than ever before in her life. And she wants to know why you

72

stalked away like that and paid no attention to her when she called your name."

"She must have whispered it," said David, even as he struggled with himself to keep back the excitement roused by this wonderful message from Anne.

"But she didn't," defended Peter with some heat. "I heard it clearly and so did half the others in the room!"

"Then it could not have been spoken when I was facing her, or when the Intendant was kissing her hand," muttered David. "There was opportunity then."

"She was dumb, like all the others about," agreed Peter. "So was I. I was never so frightened in my life. While Colonel Arnaud was commanding you to be whipped the sweat was running down my neck. And did you observe the Seigneur? His face was mottled like a sick man's, and I never saw anything so white as Anne. We all had a vision of you out on the green, stripped to the skin, with the lash falling on your back. And to think that it has all turned out so handsomely after the scare that froze our blood so horribly, and especially Anne's!"

"I can't see that it has been so very fine," reflected David, "unless you call it handsome to escape with a skin that was whole this morning and should naturally be so tonight."

Peter gave a gasp of amazement. "Do you mean you are not going to take advantage of the Intendant's friendship?" he demanded.

"What friendship?"

Peter's plump hand closed tightly on David's arm, "You are daft," he exclaimed. "No wonder you didn't hear Anne! And do you mean to tell me also that you didn't hear Bigot offer you his friendship if you should come to Quebec?"

"Yes, I heard that. It is not my intention to go to Quebec."

"Then you are hopeless. When the Intendant of New France offers you an apology, and with the apology makes a promise such as that, it means your fortune is made. A word from him and you are next to the King himself. He never makes a promise he doesn't keep, wicked as he is—at least a promise of that kind. Everyone back there knows it. There were different looks in their faces when you went out, and I heard Bigot telling Anne there wasn't a figure in Quebec that would make a finer showing than your own within a year if you accepted his invitation. That was what he called it—his invitation. And you should have seen the look in Anne's face! It made me jealous of you!"

For a space David stood clicking the metallic cover to the flint-box in the butt of his rifle.

"There is nothing in Quebec I want," he said then.

"There are riches and fame—and Anne," retorted Peter. David was silent, except for the fingering of the flint-cover. "And so many pretty girls," urged Peter, "that your eyes grow dizzy in following them." A note of placid joy in his voice made David laugh.

"You would marry all the pretty girls in the world if you had your way, Peter. You love them all."

"Every one!" agreed Peter warmly.

"And fly from one to the other like a fat hummingbird from flower to flower."

"But I always return," defended Peter, "because they are so many and so beautiful that I cannot set my mind on one and keep it there. In spite of my fat I think they would all marry me if I asked them—except Anne, of course. Her head is too full of you."

"And you think she would have me give up the forests and go to Quebec?"

"I am sure of it. She loves the city and the life there."

David laughed softly. "You are wrong, Peter. She loves the forests as much as I and in one more year she is coming back to them for good. She told me that today on Sunset Hill."

It was Peter's turn to remain silent.

"Besides," continued David, "there is greater work to be done in the forests, work which the Intendant and his people seem to be forgetting in the great town of Quebec, where it is all dancing and play."

"And making money and name—and love," corrected Peter.

"But there is no fighting——"

"Plenty of it among the gallants, where you would soon be, Monsieur David. Fighting with pistols at twenty paces, if you like it that way, or with rapiers at the cock of dawn or in the moonlight. And hangings to see in the market squares, and beheadings now and then, and every day pilloried rascals to laugh at, or whippings to look upon, if you are so bloodthirsty; and at night music and song and dancing, both in the lower town and the upper, and the prettiest girls in the world to kiss if you are lucky—and—everything else in the world worth living for!"

"Yet I care nothing for it," retorted David scornfully. "There is clean living and more honorable fighting in the forests, and of the last there will be plenty before another year goes by."

"Honorable!" puffed Peter, continuing an argument of varying merits which had never died out between the two. "Is it honorable to run a knife around another's head and take away the hair? Pooh!"

"I am not a scalp-hunter, and never will be," said David. "But it seems to be the habit of the land, with French and English as well as Indian, and as long as our Governor in Quebec and the British down below continue to offer bounties for human skin and hair, whether it be of man, woman, or unborn child—why, it is a habit which is bound to grow, I will confess. And when I see women's long hair on the hoops, or a child's, as I did at Fort William Henry—hair as long and soft as any you know of, Peter—it makes me feel like staying here where the door opens and shuts on the deadliest of our enemies."

Peter's hand grew suddenly gentle on David's arm. "I know it, David—you're always right, and sometimes when I hear you talk I wish I could stand in another pair of moccasins just like yours. But the only Indian I could fight would be a dead one, because of my fat and lack of wind. I hate 'em—the Indians, I mean—and I do love Quebec, and I also can shoot a little with pistols, as you know."

In the first pink of dawn the light-hearted and optimistic Peter had already bored holes into three rival beaus of Quebec, and withal so cheerfully and with such jolly good nature that the town loved him for it.

"But just the same," he added with grim finality, "I'd like to see you go to Quebec—for Anne's sake if not for your own."

"With the British and their colonists preparing to come up from below?" asked David. "And with the Mohawks, the Oneidas, the Onondagas, the Cayugas and the Senecas sharpening their tomahawks with their eyes on the Canadas, urged and encouraged by unlimited prize money for French hair? And with a dozen other tribes sneaking in the woods like wolves, picking up scalps here and there, even on the banks of the Richelieu? No, there isn't a long-rifle in the forests that can be spared, Peter. Not one."

"Even for Anne?"

"She will be coming back in another year, unless things have changed and where we stand now is a shambles."

"Pardieu!" exploded Peter. "You think such a thing is possible with the King and all France behind us!"

"You study and think too little in this big town of Quebec, in spite of your wise men and your schools," bantered David. "If you could have teachers like the Black Hunter——"

"And he says?"

"That there are less than seventy thousand Frenchmen in all the Canadas to a million and a half of our enemies in the English colonies."

"But we Frenchmen are in the lap of the world and seventy thousand of us here are as good as millions down there," replied the optimistic Peter.

"And Sir William Johnson has finished his survey of Indians south of the Canadas, and he says there are thirty-five thousand warriors, and that twelve thousand of these are prepared to take French scalps as against our own forty-three tribes that have dwindled to less than four thousand fighting men," added David.

"All of which is good evidence that you and I should be in Quebec when they break loose," volunteered the irrepressible Peter. "Our people will surely have ample warning so that they can follow us. And then we'll come out with a French army and drive them back, as happened at Fort Necessity, where this fellow George Washington surrendered to us recently, and as happened again at Fort Duquesne."[1]

Darkness hid the grim look in David's face. "That is just what won't happen, if the Black Hunter is right," he said, looking up again at the big wheel spinning against the stars in the sky. "It's going to come just as suddenly as it came on Sieur Grondin years ago, and there will be no warning—here or anywhere. Fire and the tomahawk are always ahead of that. So I'll not go to Quebec, Peter. Will you come home with me and have a late supper that has been waiting an hour or more?"

"I promised Anne to bring her word if I found you and I don't like the woods at night. Ugh! What you see in them with all their ghosts and tricky places makes me wonder at times if you are sane. I'll see you tomorrow, David. And please give my good word to your lovely mother, whose kindness of heart and grace and beauty it is a shame to keep hidden in the deep wilderness."

"Thank you, Peter. Good night!"

"Good night!" said Peter, and for a long time after David had gone he stood like a shadow in the night staring into the deep gloom that had blotted out his friend.

Then he turned back, and muttered to himself as he went, "You and the Black Hunter are right, David. But I'd have you go to Quebec for all that—for if you don't the Fates tell me you are going to lose Anne."

The sound of the harpsichord came to him, and with it Anne's voice—singing.

[1] Washington, impetuous and lacking judgment at twenty-two, suffered himself to be beaten and captured by the French at Fort Necessity in 1754, and so disastrous was this blow to the English that, in the next year, nearly all the Western tribes drew their scalping-knives for France.

CHAPTER VI

The voice of the old tower wheel, the sudden coming of Peter, and Anne's unexpected message of love and pride gave a final triumph to David in an adventure which had begun gloomily and with a galling bitterness in his heart. Like the day, which had opened with chill and cloud and had ended with blazing sun, the night with its somber beginning was sending him home new born. He felt and thrilled at the change but did not analyze it. He knew that tonight he had stepped forth from things that had shackled him and had stood level shouldered with men.

Darkness shut him in, darkness unlighted by the stars that were still too faint to send their rays through the forest top. It was like a sable robe about him, making of the world a black pit through which his feet followed instinctively the narrow trail. But brighter than the sun was the angel of his inspiration in that darkness. For Anne he would climb to those stars hidden beyond the tall roof of the forest! And in whatever fight he made she would be proud of him!

But it would not be in Quebec with such men as Bigot and Vaudreuil and De Pean and those others back at Grondin Manor. It would be here in the forests he loved, far from the trivial beginning of things—in the heart of a great world that was in the making. In a little while Anne would understand, when the hordes of their enemies came up from the South. It was then her heart would beat as his own was beating now, with the wild thrill of achievement about to come, for even more than her own life, David knew, she loved New France.

And now he found himself exultant that Bigot and his companions had come upon him with Anne in his arms.

The forest itself seemed to be whispering in that exultation. In the tree tops was a little wind that set them talking among themselves, as if David's coming had stirred them to life and in friendly way they were hiding the sound of his footsteps below them.

David himself was a silent shadow as he passed, for even as he thought of Anne and visioned her in a hundred sweet and wonderful ways he was also thinking of that undying caution of the wilderness which the Black Hunter said would in the end mean either life or death for him. No padded foot of beast could have fallen more lightly in the trail than David's, and the muzzle of his gun was pointed ahead, with the center of its weight in the hollow of his arm, and his forefinger and thumb resting lightly against hammer and flint.

Out of the unending pockets of gloom about him came occasional sounds, and not one of them David missed though his mind fought with De Pean or pictured again the glory of Anne as he had swept her into his arms that evening in the last sun glow of the flower-strewn bottomland.

He heard the snapping of a twig that meant a living thing abroad, a strange and creeping sigh that might have been human, a ghostly movement in the air. And he knew the twig was broken by a porcupine or a bear, and that the sighing was the plaint of one tree rubbing against another, and that over his head a great owl had passed in the seeking of its prey. But with every breath he drew he was thinking of Anne.

Once he stopped in the darkness, and it seemed to him that a mighty force was pulling him back so that he might tell her of what had come to him since they had walked through the edge of Grondin's Wood together.

But he went on, and paused again in the edge of a strange clearing that for as long as men could remember had been known as the Red Open. In this open neither trees nor grass nor flowers ever grew, and birds never sang about it, for the place was grimly accursed. In the center of it were scattered a number of great rocks, one of them half as large as a house. It was here the Mohawks had brought their prisoners from Sieur Grondin's place and had burned seven of them against the face of the huge boulder, which still bore the fire-scars of that horrible day. And in this same place, as their victims were tortured, they had hung up on triumphal poles the streaming tresses of the three beautiful mistresses whose bodies lay near Sieur Grondin's in the woods.

The place was haunted. There could be no doubt of that. The Indians held away from it in superstitious fear. During storm it was always over the Red Open that the thunder crashed loudest and the lightning struck hardest; and at night, though it was in the glow of the full moon, one could not see a hand before his eyes or a candle lantern ten feet away—at least, so it was said and believed by many up and down the river, even though the powerful priests from Three Rivers had tried to drive the troublesome spirits away with holy water and prayer.

But David as he paused was not thinking of ghosts or of men screaming in the torture of flames. He was judging how long it would be before moonrise. An illumination a little stronger than that of the stars lay in the east, and he quickened his pace with more eager thought of his mother.

A few minutes later he came out of the edge of thick woods into another clearing larger than the Red Open. In it were seven arpents, or nearly twelve acres, as he had measured them, and every foot of it he had cleared himself and put to crop, with the help of Kill-Buck, the old Delaware who had been with his mother since he was a child, and Thurensera, his daughter, whose Indian name meant Day-Dawn.

Corn-shocks were thick over a half of the fertile plot, and at the far end of it he could see the dim candle-light in Kill-Buck's cabin, and nearer, in a group of maples and oaks left for their beauty and shade, was a larger and more brilliantly lighted cottage, which was his own and his mother's. He stopped again, knowing that somewhere in the shadows the old Delaware was waiting as quietly as one of the night-birds for his return. Sometimes David wondered if Kill-Buck's eyes ever closed in sleep, for always, even in times of peace, he seemed to be watching for danger and guarding those he loved against it.

As he came out into the open he uttered a bird-note scarcely louder than the musical ripple of the spring-water creek which ran through the clearing, and a little later Kill-Buck rose as if produced by magic in his path.

Even under the stars one could see that Kill-Buck was not young, though he was tall and straight and thin and his head still had its warrior's poise. In his wampum belt he bore a hatchet and a knife which had been his companions on bloody trails long before David's time, and in his hand a gun.

The two conversed for a moment in the Delaware's native tongue, then David hastened toward the cottage.

It was built of stone, like the one under Sunset Hill where he and Anne had heard a woman's voice singing, and through the stone peered the same dark loop-holes for guns, and at the windows were the same heavy shutters of oak.

And a voice was also singing here, a sweeter voice than that in the cottage under Sunset Hill.

All his life David had been in love with his mother. He opened the door softly and looked in. He was proud of his mother's youthfulness and it gave him a pleasant thrill to see the picture she made as she knelt on a bear-rug before a mass of red coals in the fireplace, turning the crane on which he knew his supper was waiting. She was slim and tall and looked like a girl in the candle-glow, and her coiled dark hair which Anne averred was many times more beautiful than her own was a gleamy jet mass in the soft radiance of the room.

She rose quickly at David's greeting from behind her. Marie Rock was on the shadowing side of forty. In December would come her birthday. But years and tragedy and the loneliness of the wilderness had left small imprint in a face that had suddenly filled with pleasure at the sound of David's voice.

There was something loverlike in the way he kissed her and put his arms around her. "That is what keeps me young," she had told him many times. "It is you, David!"

David set up his gun in the corner.

"It's Anne again," he said laughingly. "Her fault!"

"Of course," agreed Marie Rock, turning quickly to the crane. "But tonight even these pigeons have grown discouraged for the flesh has fallen from their bones no matter how patiently I tended them. If the potatoes have hardened in the ash I shall scold you!"

"Yet you were very happy when I came up, mother. You were singing the Black Hunter's song."

He was preparing to wash himself and did not notice the length of his mother's silence.

"What makes you think of the Black Hunter to-night, son?" she asked at last.

"I think of him always," replied David, and buried his face in cold spring water.

A little later they sat across from each other at the table, with a supper between them of roasted pigeons and potatoes and brown bread and a pudding made from flour and maple syrup and fruits.

As they ate David told of many of the things that had happened, leaving out chiefly the unpleasantness of his own adventure at Grondin Manor. But he did talk of Anne as frankly as he always talked to his mother, and before the meal was over she had guessed at more than one thing truly, and knew as well as he what had come to pass in his life that day.

A candle had burned half its length and he had described in detail the unusual doings at the château before it suddenly came upon him that the flush was still in his mother's cheeks and that it could no longer be caused by the fire; and that also there were velvety pools in her eyes so deep he could not fathom them, and that about her was something which did not seem to be entirely a part of her as he had expected to find her.

"Something has happened to make you glad," he guessed. "What is it?"

"Your coming, David. I am always happy when you come."

"But tonight—you are like Anne was this afternoon near the sumac thicket in the bottom. And I wonder—I have been wondering more today than in all my life before—and I want to know——"

"What is it, David?"

"You are always happy when the Black Hunter comes," he said after another moment's hesitation, "and so am I. Today Anne asked me why, and so differently and in such a strange way that the question has been with me every hour since then. For I couldn't answer it, except that I am happy when I am with him and terribly lonely for him when he is gone. Why is it?"

"Because he has been your friend, and mine—and loves you."

David walked restlessly to the door and looked out. The moon was rising but he scarcely saw the clear beauty of it because of what was brewing in his mind.

"But why is he our friend?" he persisted. "And why has it been such a strange and secret friendship, with the Black

Hunter coming and going as mysteriously as a ghost, so that not another soul but you and I have ever set eyes on him in all this seigneury of St. Denis?"

"He is a strange man, David, and strange thoughts and desires have run in his mind," answered his mother.

"Such questions Anne has asked me and now it is time for me to answer them," he went on. "Until lately I have seen little of the Black Hunter, yet I feel he has been here many times that only you and maybe Kill-Buck know of. Why is it that all up and down these leagues of wilderness between the Canadas and our enemies he has no other name than the Black Hunter? If he loves us as you say, and as he seems to show, why is it that we cannot know his name?"

"I do know it, David. I have told you that, and also that I have kept it secret only because it seemed to mean so much to him."

"And there is a reason for hiding it?"

"He has thought so all these years. And has Anne asked you so many questions today?"

He nodded. "Yes. And I have been asking them of myself too. I think there has been talk at the manor which has not come to us. Anne trembles when I speak of the Black Hunter and she is filled with horror when I tell her of our adventures together. She asked me for the powder-horn this afternoon, and I gave it to her. Only when I told her it was the Black Hunter who had suggested another angel kneeling beside her at the shrine—yourself, mother—did she soften a little. I have tried to make her think of him as we think of him, but I cannot do it. She is afraid."

"Afraid of one who visions angels kneeling at a shrine?" asked his mother, and there was an odd little trill in her voice which David's youthful ears failed to catch.

But he did see that her eyes were glowing again as she looked up at him quickly from her task of brushing the crumbs from the table with a turkey-wing.

Then David laughed, and before she could move away from the table he put his arms about her slim body.

"No wonder he thought of you as the second angel," he cried. "You're the most wonderful mother in all New France, and Anne loves you as much as I—and tomorrow you must talk to her about the Black Hunter and answer some of the questions she has asked me. Will you?"

"I will, David."

Then he noticed that down over her wrists had fallen little clouds of snowy lace which until a moment or two ago had been safely tucked up out of sight. And beyond her in a corner of the room his eyes fell upon something which set his heart suddenly beating faster.

"I am blind and stupid," he said, holding her so that her face was turned away from him, and trying hard to make his voice as natural as it should be, "or I would have known you have on the dress which you wore at the Seigneur's party, with the lace which I love. And your hair is so smooth, and you look so fresh and pretty and were so glad when I came up to the door——"

"Because I knew you were coming," she interrupted.

"And Day-Dawn wasn't here to help you, and she hasn't been here to clear away the dishes——"

"She was tired and I sent her to bed."

His arms closed more tightly about her. "And you were singing the Black Hunter's song when I opened the door, and now—over there in the corner—I see a gun which doesn't belong to me—and it doesn't belong to Kill-Buck, mother—and it doesn't belong to anyone in the seigneury of St. Denis! I wonder——"

He stopped, and his mother was silent.

"Mother——"

"Yes, David."

"It is a rifle—all black. That is why I didn't see it. Everything about it is black."

For a space they were both very still.

Then he whispered close to her ear, excitement breaking a little in his voice, "Mother, has he come again? Is the Black Hunter here?"

"Yes, he is here, David. He came this afternoon while you were with Anne on Sunset Hill!"

And he saw the turkey-wing trembling in his mother's hand.

CHAPTER VII

In a room which they had built up together and which was like no other room in all the wilderness of New France Marie Rock seated herself in a great armchair and talked with her son. It was a room almost as large as the one in which a few minutes before they had sat at supper, and in it was a fireplace in which a slow oak fire was burning.

The room, in short, was Marie Rock herself, and one entering it knew that its mistress was a lady of gentle thought and mind and breeding, a flower strangely set in a little castle in the heart of a great woods. There were here more books than could be found in the great house of the Seigneur St. Denis, pictures on the walls that were unlike any others up and down the Richelieu, and a spinet whose polished keys gave forth their music to the soft touch of Marie Rock's fingers each day. The books, all gathered on three long shelves built of oak, were worn and some of them were ragged and ready to fall from their covers, and more were written in English than in French. Among them were a grammar and an arithmetic and a book on penmanship, and another on religious instruction, and a set of five booklets from the Ursulines containing pastorals and dramatic dialogues and complimentary apologues for anniversary occasions, and a set of rules for the development of gracefulness of manners and mind.

The room was not only a part of David and his mother, but also of Anne, for it was here that she, along with David, had first learned the mysteries of reading and writing and many other things. When she was a little tot David had reveled in showing her the precious pictures in the books, and little by little the treasures of the room had increased as the years went by. In the end, before Anne went away to the Ursulines, she could read and talk English as well as David and could play her harpsichord as well as Marie Rock could play her spinet.

It was a softly comfortable room and everywhere bore evidences of what had passed in their lives. But strange whispers seemed to be creeping about its walls tonight, and the air David breathed was heavy with portentous mystery as he stared into the face of his mother sitting in the big chair.

"Did Anne tell you she was here this morning?" she asked.

"No," said David.

Marie Rock smiled, and something was behind the smile which touched strangely at David's heart.

"Of course not. I asked her to keep the visit a secret between us. She came when you and Kill-Buck were down the river, and she was very much upset, David, and I think a bit angry at me. It was about the Black Hunter and you. She loves you devotedly, so truly that I thanked God for it when she was gone. But she is afraid. She fears the Black Hunter will in the end take you away from her, and she begged me to do what she has been unable to do—estrange you from him."

David's eyes clouded. "She need fear him no more than I fear Quebec," he said a little grimly.

"And I could confide in her no more than I have in you," continued his mother. "Then he came, and this afternoon we talked together while you were with Anne on Sunset Hill, and I told him that your child's love had come at last to be the love of man and woman—and he freed me from my promise. I am going to tell you who the Black Hunter is, and tomorrow you may tell Anne."

She bowed her head a little, as if searching for a place to begin, and in the silence David held his breath, and then said, "It cannot be so terrible. Anne will understand."

"A long time ago," said Marie Rock as if she had not heard him, and was looking far back into the past, "I met your father, who was an Englishman, in Louisburg; and in spite of the enmity which had long existed between our countries I ran away with him down into the colonies where we were married. Of course you know all that, David, and that I turned English for his sake, and went with him from frontier to frontier in his adventurous wanderings, and that at last we settled for good in the beautiful valley of the Juniata in Pennsylvania. There you were born. One other family was with us, and we prospered and were happy and became friendly with the Indians. The other man was Peter Joel. I loved Betsy Joel, his wife. She was older than I and as sweet to look at as she was good, and she was good, and she had two little daughters, who were pictures of herself, and a son just your age, David, lacking seven days."

David saw a shimmer of tears in his mother's eyes, but she did not brush them away or look aside.

"Peter Joel worshiped his wife and children, David. It was pretty to see, and I have always been a better woman because of Betsy Joel. She was a mother as well as sister and friend to me. And Peter—Peter Joel—he is the man you know as the Black Hunter!"

She waited a moment, looking straight into David's staring eyes.

"Then came that terrible night." Marie Rock shivered in the big chair. "I have always lied to you a little about it, David, for I have thought it best for you not to know that the dream you have is not a dream at all, but a horrible thing that actually happened and which burned itself so terribly into your childish mind that you recall it now and then in that way. It was night and you were four years old when the Huron war-party came. They were returning empty-handed from a raid on the Senecas, and angels could not have stayed their hands. Your father was sick, and Peter Joel was watching in the light of the moon at a salt-lick two miles away for a piece of young venison. I cannot seem to remember just how it all happened, except that I saw your father killed in his bed, and it all seemed to be over very quickly and the cabins in flames. It was what happened outside that I shall never forget—what I saw in the light of our burning homes. I have tried to bury it deep—I have fought to wipe it from my memory—and now I am bringing it all to life again for you, because the hour has come when it seems necessary!

"You were in my arms, so close it is a wonder I did not smother you, and it happened we were not killed because we had become the personal captives of the leader of the party. It was not a large party, numbering not more than eight or ten, I think, but all of the warriors except this chief were quarreling for possession of Betsy Joel and her children. And then I saw Betsy, so near that I cried out to her and tried to reach her. She was naked and her long beautiful hair flamed like gold in the firelight as it streamed about her. I saw her boy, your age, snatched from her and killed with a tomahawk. I heard the dying screams of the two little girls. And then the monster who stood beside us leaped toward Betsy. I couldn't close my eyes. I couldn't move. He caught her hair as she ran toward her children. I saw her twisted backward, saw his hatchet rise and fall—and then she was on the ground with that monster kneeling on her naked white body, and as I looked he rose with a screech that was like an animal's, and I saw Betsy's long hair streaming from his bloody hand between me and the flames."

Marie Rock's eyes no longer shone with the glimmer of tears. They were wide and staring, and consuming fire seemed suddenly to fill their depths, as if David himself had died out of her vision and in his place had come again the horrible spectacle of a night years ago. David made no movement nor uttered a word in the moment's pause that came when his mother looked beyond him into a past filled with monstrous memories.

"You saw it all too, David," she went on, looking at him, yet still seeing far beyond. "You were screaming, and never has that night died out of your dreams. It is a wonder I did not kill you, for I was crushing you close to me in my effort to hide you against my breast. I think in another moment I would have had strength to turn and run, and then the red beasts would have killed us as they had killed Betsy and her children.

"But something happened. Out of the night into that pit of murder and fire came Peter Joel, a raving, shrieking madman, coatless and hatless and with a great club in his hands in place of his gun, and the chief who was waving Betsy's hair in the firelight scarcely moved before his head was knocked from his shoulders like a pumpkin from the top of the post. Oh, it was terrible, and I smothered your face then, for Peter Joel was mad, stark mad, and his shrieks were more terrible than any sound I had ever heard come from an Indian's throat! And the Indians knew he was mad, and fled for their lives, making no effort to harm him, which is the Indian way in the face of disordered reason. But even had they stood to fight him as many would have died as fell under his club in their flight, for nothing could have stopped Peter Joel in his hour of vengeance. With the terrible club he killed three and after that, until day came and the cabins were only smoldering piles of embers, he sat with his wife and children in his arms, rocking back and forth and crooning to them, until I thought that I too would go mad.

"During those hours he took not the slightest notice of us nor seemed to know who we were. But with dawn he let me dress Betsy in a part of my clothes, and that morning we buried her and the children in one grave near the burned cabins. When it was over and the earth covered them a strange, quiet look came into his face and he picked you up in his arms and called you his boy, his boy, his boy—and repeating that over and over he walked straight into the forest with you, and I followed him.

"That was the beginning of a wild and unbelievable journey which continued for many days. Peter was no longer the Peter I had known, but each day his madness was tempered more and more by a strange, returning sanity, for he found us food, and picked our way with caution; yet in all those days that it took us to come from the valley of the Juniata to the lower waters of the Richelieu not once did he talk with me, nor could I get answer even to the questions that I asked. And every step of those wearisome miles he carried you, David, and not once would let you out of his arms into mine when we were on the trail.

"At night you slept in his arms, though mine ached for you—and during those fourteen days and fourteen nights of our flight, for it seemed to me one endless flight, I know that Peter Joel's eyes did not entirely close in slumber. So we came at last to a French camp on the Richelieu, and Peter Joel left us when it was in sight and despite my efforts to hold him turned back into the deep forests alone. The French hunting-party belonged to the Seigneur St. Denis, and in it also were Kill-Buck and his little daughter, both of whom I nursed back to life when all had given them up as dead from the plague that struck us three months later. But Peter—Peter Joel—seemed to have gone out of our lives forever."

Marie Rock drew herself back out of the horror of a grim and buried tragedy with a convulsive shudder. Her eyes were seeing David then, and she smiled at him with a wistful tenseness as she said, "So—it was the Black Hunter who carried you all that distance, and saved our lives, David, though he was not the Black Hunter then, but only poor, mad Peter Joel. And that is why you love him, though it all happened when you were so very small; and that too is why Peter Joel loves you."

During his mother's recital of the Black Hunter's relationship to himself it had seemed to David that every drop of blood was throbbing in his heart. Now it was an effort for him to speak.

"But he was mad, you say? And I did not see him again for so many years! And the Black Hunter—why that?"

Marie Rock drew a hand over her eyes as if to wipe away a shadow. "Yes, he was mad—but strangely mad," she answered him. "It was five years before I saw him again, or even knew that he was alive. During those years I saw to the welfare of the Seigneur's household and little Anne. It was in those years that all the wilderness between Pennsylvania and the Canadas began to hear of the Black Hunter, and then more and more of him, until the mere whisper of his name brought with it a strange and terrible thrill. He roamed the forests and the valleys like an uncaged tiger, the most formidable foe that ever crossed the red man's path. Yet he was not a murderer, and soon it came to be known that it was not vengeance that inspired his deeds almost unbelievable but a desire to save white women and children from the tomahawk and the scalping-knife of the savage.

"He came and went like a weird black ghost in the winds—armed with a black rifle and dressed in black deerskin and sometimes with his face painted black— The winds themselves seemed to give him knowledge of the Indians' plots and secret doings, for a hundred times he brought mysterious warning to the border settlements, and a hundred times his rifle and his alarm saved the homes and lives of lonely settlers until at last a word from the Black Hunter or his strange cry of warning in the middle of a night became along the frontiers like a word spoken from the Bible. You know all that, David, for so it is to this day.

"Various were the plans and stratagems resorted to by the Indians to capture or kill him, but they all proved unavailing, and in the end the savages came to look upon him as possessed of a spirit of death that was not of flesh and blood and that could not be killed or put in bonds. Among the white people he was known as the Black Rifle, the Black Protector and the Black Hunter, yet only now and then was there man or woman or child who could truthfully say they had laid eyes on him or heard his voice, and none knew his name or whence he came or where he lived. Fear and love—a fear that was terrible and a love that twined itself closely in the hearts of men and women and children—went with his name and his presence up and down the borders. And it was this man, David, who found you lost in the woods years ago and brought you home. Peter Joel was the Black Hunter!"

Marie Rock's eyes were shining. Where tragedy had dwelt a few moments before lay now the glowing fire of a splendid pride. For the space of a moment or two there was stillness in the room, and in that stillness David heard the old clock ticking like a wooden hammer beating on a mellow drumhead.

His voice sounded almost as strange to him as the ticking of the clock when he spoke. "But you said he was mad, mother, and never have I heard a twisted thought come out of his head from that day I first knew him until this! I have never known a man like the Black Hunter, either for wisdom or courage or gentleness that at times makes me think of a woman. Yet what else could have made him pledge you to secrecy in the simple matter of his name or filled him with the strange desire to come and go like a phantom of the woods—even here where there are no savage enemies to fear and all are his friends?"[1]

"Not madness, but—a strangeness which perhaps you and I cannot understand," said his mother. "Peter Joel buried himself with his wife and children that morning in the Juniata, and for five years he remained buried heart and mind and soul while he haunted the borderlands. Then he came to see you, and found you in the woods; and after that he came again, and still again, and more frequently as the years went, but it was not always that you saw him or even knew that he was here. That much we kept a secret between us because he wanted it so. And today my hopes and my prayers have seen their fulfilment, for the Black Hunter is no longer the Black Hunter. He is Peter Joel—to you, to all the world."

Still there was a matter in David's mind which was not clear. "But why do people fear and dread him?" he asked. "If he has been so faithfully the friend of women and children and of settlers on both borders, why is it that Anne has this horror of him? Why do they not love him, and watch for him, instead of dreaming and thinking and talking about him as if he were a monster—as I am told that many people do, even among those to whom he has so strangely dedicated his life?"

A wistful smile softened Marie Rock's face. "Because, David, even we who have all our lives been sane are at times more darkly unreasonable than Peter Joel ever was in his madness. The Black Hunter, through all these years, has known no breed or creed but one—to protect and warn his own blood, whether English, French or Dutch, against the savages who so cruelly robbed him. He has never raised a hand for the English against the French, nor for the French against the English, and never will. In a hundred French homes, as well as in a hundred English, his name is blessed even as the little children shiver there when it is mentioned, and elders look over their shoulders in the dark when they know the Black Hunter is near. And you ask me why these, his very friends, should have this fear and dread of him? This is an age of deceptions and superstitions in which you and

I do not believe, David—of demons and spirits and restless ghosts like those which are said to wander in Grondin's Wood and the Red Open. And Peter Joel, even in his early madness, seized on these weaknesses of the human mind to make his work among the Indians surer and more deadly.

"So swift and sudden were his comings and goings, so strange his dress, so unbelievable the things he did, that even those he saved or warned, both English and French, came to regard him as unearthly and spectral, and possessed of powers which made them afraid. So it was that talk and rumors began, spreading like a fire through the forests from cabin to cabin and from settlement to settlement, until women turned pale when it was whispered that this half-devil-and-half-man protector of their homes was near. And the more terrible these stories of his prowess and superhuman power, the more was the Black Hunter achieving his ends. Such stories as these Anne has heard, David, and though she is not superstitious like so many of the others, and does not believe in demons and imps, I can understand her fear and horror when she knows that Peter Joel is so close to you."

David bent over his mother and touched his lips tenderly to her shining hair where it was drawn back smooth as velvet from her white brow. And Marie Rock reached up and took one of his hands in both of her own and pressed it against her cheek as she gazed steadily into the glowing heart of the slow-burning oak fire.

"I understand now," he said. "And Peter Joel—he is coming back soon?" he asked.

"Yes. He has gone to look for you at Grondin Manor."

"And you are glad he is here, mother—as glad as I?"

"It may be, David. I have known no other friendship like his—even though it be the great Seigneur's."

"Yet you have seen him so little, counting time in days and weeks and months."

"Those fourteen days and nights in the forests were so many years. Every day of my life I have lived over again how tenderly he cared for you and for me in those terrible day-years of what I thought was his madness. My heart holds a warm place for him, David, next to your place there."

Softly David stroked her hair with his lips. Then he said, "Little mother, something strange has happened to me since morning. I understand more than I did. I think this day has been a year for me just as each of those fourteen days and nights was a year for you. I understand more about Anne, and myself, and you, and the Black Hunter—who is Peter Joel. And I am sure I understand now why he wanted me to carve a second angel kneeling at the shrine on my powder-horn!"

Until the door closed behind him and he was gone in search of Peter Joel, Marie Rock sat with her eyes upon the fire. A little later she heard the sound of the door opening again and thought it was David returning, until her ears caught the strangeness of a step which she knew did not belong to her boy. She turned then, with the red glow of the oak fire behind her, and a voice spoke her name softly from the outer room.

In another moment a man stood with bared head in the light of the fire and the burning candles. One would first have shuddered at the stark somberness of him. He was like a part of the night that had come in from a pit of its deepest shadows, and among those shadows he could have stood or moved or run unseen even where the moonbeams played, for out of that night, he was built and made except for the tanned whiteness of his face and hands. From throat to toe he was clothed in soft deerskin dyed a sooty, velvety black. No thread or mark of other color broke the swart sameness of a form that had a panther's litheness and seemed taller than it was. Powder-horn and bullet pouch, knife-sheath and belt and the cap in his hand were the same, until, if one looked no further than his raiment, the man seemed a figure of death in the door.

But above this ominous darkness rose a head and countenance which held the eye last and longest. The head was set like a stag's, as if years of playing at odds with death had trained it to alertness every hour of night and day; and in strange contrast with this was a face in which there was no single line of suspicion or unrest, one filled with a nobility of thought and mind that spoke the soul of the man.

His hair at first appeared to be gray, but this impression was given chiefly by a streak of silvery white that ran like a widow's-cap from the middle of his forehead back. This silvery strand, which was no wider than two of Marie Rock's slim fingers, together with the clear and steady gray of the eyes beneath gave to the thin, strong face a character which no man or woman could forget who had ever looked on the Black Hunter as Marie Rock was looking at him now.

Such was the man, no taller than David but with thews and sinews like tempered steel, in his forty-ninth year this September of 1754 yet bearing no mark of age with the exception of the streak in his hair—the man of mystery, of heroism and of strange and tragic deeds along the borders, into whose soul only Marie Rock and David had looked since the day fifteen years before when Peter Joel the pioneer had begun the winning of another and more terrible name—that of the Black Hunter.

[1] For fifteen years Peter Joel, the mystery-man of the borders and the terror of the Indians, was known by no other name than those of The Black Hunter, The Black Rifle and The Black Protector.

CHAPTER VIII

Out of her window Anne St. Denis looked upon a world flooded with moonlight. Her cheeks were still hot from her experiences below, and her eyes were brighter than the gold and silver radiance which transformed a wilderness night into soft paradise.

Floating up the stair came laughter and song and the clinking of glasses, for the Seigneur, her father, had dug down into his cellar for the oldest and ripest of his wines—rare Muscat at twenty-four francs a dozen, and Priniac, Modena, Malaga and Lisbon claret at from twelve to seventeen, crisp and lively on delivery from any port in France but mellowed now by many years of cherished care on the Richelieu.

The feasting was over, and the drinking, Anne knew, would continue into the night. Yet both hunger and the overflowing flesh-pots which came to satisfy it had not dulled the eyes or the senses or the ready tongues of the gay and martial company below; and Anne's ears had not ceased to tingle with the hundred pretty things that had filled them, nor her blood to run more warmly at the low-spoken words which had come to her alone in soft and secret whispers, and the glances which she had been powerless to avoid.

Now, looking from the window to her mirror, she saw reflected the amazing beauty which had stirred the hearts and brought to her feet the strongest and most powerful gentlemen of New France. It would have frightened David, and a little bit it startled Anne. Never had she seen herself like that before, her piled-up hair a radiant mass of chestnut glory, her eyes twin pools of starry brightness and her cheeks lovelier than the crimson hearts of the Queen's roses that bloomed in the June splendor of her garden. It was no longer a girl but a woman of flushed and palpitating loveliness with a crown of sudden years and knowledge set upon her head, who looked at her from the glass.

Thought of David turned her to the window again, a sudden frown of vexation gathering in her forehead, her lips curled slightly as she listened to the banter and song and sound of voice from below, and one hand swept her cheek, as if it might wipe away the radiant color, of which, as she thought of it now, she grew ashamed. For the color had been put there by pretty compliments she had no right to hear, or should have laughed aside without such silly flushing; and this was not true to either David or herself.

Until now she had been given little time in which to think of David alone, or of the courage and skill it must have taken to plunge both the Intendant of New France and his prime minister into the pool. And he had done it because of her! That in itself, she reflected, might have helped to keep her cheeks so shamefully flushed and her eyes so bright. It gave her a gratifying sense of pleasure to think of it in that way. For Bigot had told her frankly and with friendly humor in his eyes of the bantering remarks which had brought about the affair at the pool, though he told it in such a way that De Pean did not suffer much. "A foolish lad but a brave one," he had said of David. "De Pean meant no harm and his words were a compliment to you."

She liked Bigot. His courtly way, his interest in David, and the good-humored chagrin with which he had accepted the ridiculous misadventure to himself gave her an immense and satisfying confidence. Somehow words which had come from his lips had not seemed like the compliments of the others. When he told her that her hair was the most beautiful in all New France, and she had replied that David's mother had still prettier, she had felt a tingling thrill of pleasure. For Bigot had a way of saying things that stripped his words of any possible harm or effrontery and filled her with the sense of listening to one who, by a wonderful turn of fortune, had become her friend and David's. Tomorrow, Bigot had promised her, he would see David's mother, and talk with David, and urge him to come to Quebec.

No wonder her cheeks were flushed and her eyes so wide and bright they startled her. For not even the King of France could do for a man in the Canadas what François Bigot could do!

Out in the moonlight Anne's shining eyes saw the marvelous city of Quebec on its impregnable rock; and she saw David there, no longer in homespun and deerskin, but a splendid gentleman of New France; and suddenly she caught up a shawl and flung it over her shoulders, and passed to the door.

Quietly and, as she thought, unseen she made her way to the cool, crisp air of the shadows behind the château, where there was least chance of discovery by any guests who might be strolling in the moonlight. Fragrance of fresh-baked bread came from the big oven, and up against the star-filled sky the old mill-wheel was droning mournfully, as if protesting against work in hours when it should have been asleep.

In his door, a pale and ghostlike figure against a setting of black, stood little old Fontbleu, the miller.

Like a sylph made out of the golden alchemy of moonbeams Anne stood suddenly before him. Fontbleu rubbed his eyes. Then he saw who it was.

"Is it you, little lady?" he gasped. "I thought at first it was——"

"Was who?" smiled Anne, putting a hand on his flour-dusty arm.

"The spirit of your mother," said the ancient miller before he could stop the words behind his tongue. "God forgive me, but you look like her this night!"

"My hair again," said Anne softly, and Fontbleu saw a misty light gather suddenly in her eyes. "You knew my mother many years, Fontbleu."

"And loved her," nodded the miller.

They stood silent a little, and it seemed the millwheel high above them had a livelier and more cheerful note in its voice.

"You are grinding late, père Fontbleu."

"Until morning, little lady."

"And have you by any chance seen David?"

"Not since two hours ago when he went home this way."

There was another silence, and Anne looked up, for the old mill-wheel was insistent now and was surely calling her.

"Père Fontbleu——"

"Yes, little lady——"

"I am going to take David away to Quebec!"

The miller stared, and Anne did not look at him.

"I am going to take him away to Quebec," she repeated. "Away from the woods, and the Black Hunter, and Indians, and fighting. I have been afraid for him, and now I am happy. The Intendant has given me his promise to favor him."

She looked at the miller now, and it was the miller who was looking at the wheel. And, strangely in that moment, the cheer went out of the old mill-wheel's voice and it gave a plaintive wail.

"Oil," muttered Fontbleu.

"What did you say?"

"I said the old wheel needs oil."

"But I was talking about David."

"Pardon. I heard you, little lady. You said David was going to Quebec. When he does that, and this François Bigot gives him favor, then will come——"

"Honor and fortune for the young man," interrupted a voice so near that Anne gave a startled cry, and the Intendant of New France himself stood before them, and he bowed low as the miller drew slowly back into the sepulchral gloom of his door.

In spite of herself again Anne's face flushed suddenly hot. "Monsieur!" she gasped. "I thought I was alone with père Fontbleu!"

"I love the moonlight, and I came away from that clatter of tongues to get my fill of it," lied Bigot with gentle softness. "When I saw you, Anne, like a beautiful fairy passing through it, I could not resist the temptation to follow. I overheard what you said about David and I am glad you feel that way. And I like the old miller's name for you! Will you walk a few minutes upon the green with me, little lady?"

It seemed to Anne that before she had made a movement of her own Bigot had found her hand and put it in his arm, and with a heart that jumped fiercely, and a wild thought of David, she was walking closely at his side out into the moonlight.

The little old miller peered like a fierce-eyed gnome from the darkness of his door.

"The monster!" he cried chokingly, a breathless note of hatred and despair in his voice. "The monster!" And high up over his head the ancient tower wheel moaned and wailed as its rusty bones caught a fresh puff of the wind.

And Bigot was saying, still holding the warm tips of Anne's small fingers as they walked, "Your love for this David lad must be very great, Anne?"

"It is," said Anne.

"Greater, even, than wealth and glory and the queenly honors some other man might give you?"

"So much greater that I have never thought of those things at all," replied Anne.

Over her head she did not see the flame which burned for an instant like an evil fire in the Intendant's eyes. But with that flame his voice was filled with a deep and musical sympathy which seemed to bring him nearer to her than even her father had ever been in the matter of her love for David.

"Today when we came upon you down there among the flowers I envied him," he said, "and if the God we love and are fighting for in this glorious New France of ours should sometime reward me with the love of a woman, I hope she will be one like you, Anne. For such a love I would gladly barter all I have!"

A note of unutterable loneliness came into his voice, and Anne did not withdraw the fingers which in another moment or two she had meant to free. A few steps they walked in silence.

"Honor—honor and love—those two things can lift a soul to heaven," mused Bigot.

"They must go together," said Anne. "Without honor love will die."

"And David is honorable—that is sure."

"His heart and soul are as clean as this bright night, monsieur."

"And you are proud of him?"

"More than words can fitly tell!" A note of pride rang like a silver bell in Anne's low voice.

"I think," said Bigot—and his soul was like a creeping serpent stealing on its prey—"I think your love for David is too beautiful for even dishonor to destroy. Forgive me, Anne, if I have looked too deeply into your heart. But I want to see you happy, and David too, and no power I have shall rest as long as it can make your happiness greater. So much a part of you is this love of yours, I am sure, that no dishonor David could ever bring upon himself would change your heart. Is that true, little lady?"

"My heart, possibly—but my will it would change," said Anne, and if she had looked up quickly she would have seen a flash of triumph in Bigot's eyes. "But such a thing with David is impossible. He would sooner die than see himself dishonored—and so would I, monsieur!"

Bigot sighed as he gently released the fingers that were withdrawing from his own. "I shall make David one of the first gentlemen in Quebec," he said. He felt a little quiver run through Anne. "I shall take him under my personal care," he went on, smiling gently when he knew Anne's straining eyes were on his face, "and give him very soon a lieutenancy and a commission as aide-de-camp to the Governor."

An amazed and joyous cry broke from Anne. "You will do that—all that?"

"Why not?" smiled Bigot. "Horrible things have been said of me, chérie, the bitter and jealous lies that always follow in the paths of great achievement and success—but in my heart, if even my enemies would fairly look, is the desire to bring happiness and prosperity to this land and its people.[1] And why not to you and David, most of all? For when I saw you two down there among the flowers, you in all your glorious beauty and David in his proud young manhood, two lovers such as I have never seen before, you crept into my heart and filled a big and empty place that was there. It is not all for you, little lady. I am selfish too. In your happiness I shall find some happiness, even though it be but a dream-reflection of your own. And it may be that out of the fulness of your life and David's you will love me a little for what I have done."

"We will love you for your goodness," she whispered. "Both David and I. In all our dreams we have never pictured such good fortune coming to us!"

"And it may be," meditated Bigot, as if forgetful of Anne for a moment in the abstraction of his thought, "that a little later we shall have some favor conferred upon him by the King."

"Oh!" gasped Anne.

"You would like that, sweet little lady?"

"Next to our Dear Mother I love this country," replied Anne devoutly. "And the King is France!"

Bigot's lips trembled a little in the moonlight. "Then your words imply you have a love even greater than your love for David," he made hazard.

"So different there can be no comparison, monsieur."

"Country first! I honor you for it, Anne. Mother, father, love for man or woman—all must be sacrificed if necessary to the loyalty and love which New France demands of us. It is strange that I should confide secrets of state to you, little lady, but I know you will hold them close in your heart, and no other ears will ever hear. Even now I am quietly fighting black treachery in our midst, a slowly growing, infectious humor which if allowed to persist will mean our ruin."

"Treachery!" breathed Anne, aghast. "You mean———"

"That the English in some way learn of every move we plan before it is made," said Bigot. And then he added, as if the thought had come to him by chance, "David's father was English, was he not?"

"Yes," said Anne. "He was killed by the Indians when David was a little child. But David's mother is a Frenchwoman, and they both love New France as much as I."

"And this man they call the Black Hunter, and with whom I hear David is so close—he too is English, and spends much time among them, I understand."

"Yes," nodded Anne, and it was difficult for her to speak the word.

They had turned, and the lights of the château shone dimly through the moonlight. Bigot looked down at the beautiful head so near his shoulder, and bent without Anne's consciousness so that his lips faintly touched her shining hair.

"Treachery——that is why I need glorious young strength and integrity close at my side, and David has these, and you to urge him on," he said. "He is one who will not sell his soul or barter his country's life; and because he is as you believe him to be he shall have confidences entrusted to him which will mean his honor—and also yours, little lady, for it is because of you that I have unbounded faith in him."

"We will not betray it but will make it stronger, monsieur."

Anne drew her shawl more closely about her for the air was growing chill. She looked up at Bigot and in spite of the chill her eyes and face were aflame with the wonders this night had brought to her. Bigot smiled at her, and Anne smiled back from the sheer joy of what was in her heart, for in Bigot's face she saw nothing but truth and gentleness and that honor of which he had so reverently spoken.

"You are the most beautiful flower I have ever seen in this world," he said, and reverence was even then in his voice. "David must be prouder of you than Louis of his kingdom!"

He drew a step away from her, and they walked a little apart until Anne said good night to him, and Bigot bowed like a courtier in the edge of the shadows back of the château.

Scarcely was he turned toward the green again, alone, when his countenance changed. All he had held back, all he had fought to control in moments when his blood was racing like a current of fire through his veins revealed itself swiftly in his face, and where in Anne's presence there had been an almost noble gentleness and restraint now leaped a passion and triumph which transformed him. His body trembled and his hands were clenched. Never had beauty and purity so roused the evil desires of a soul that had already plumbed the lowest depths of lust and seduction, and with these desires came for the first time in his life the amazing truth that at last fate had caught him in an uncontrollable maelstrom—and that for Anne St. Denis he would not only give favor and fortune, but sacrifice everything that unlimited power and the indulgence of Pompadour and the King had placed in his hands.

His face still bore its exultation when Vaudreuil saw him approaching through the moonlight and came forth to join him. The Governor of Louisiana was chuckling and twiddling his thumbs over his stomach.

"What have you to say now of my eyes and watchfulness?" he demanded in his smooth and oily way, wheezing with good humor as he spoke. "Moonlight, a beauteous maid—and opportunity! What more could one ask, even you, Bigot?"

The Intendant seized Vaudreuil's arm and his fingers hurt the other's soft flesh. "I thank God you saw her stealing down the stair," he cried in a low voice. "Vaudreuil, I promise you this night that the governorship is yours just as surely as Anne St. Denis is mine!"

Vaudreuil's fat and inscrutable smile did not change. "It happened, then?"

"Yes, just as you said it would happen! My God, she was so close to me, with her hand in mine, that I had to make a tiger's fight to keep from taking her in my arms out there! If I had done that I would have lost. But now she is mine! She is afire with the pictures I have painted for her. She trusts me. She believes. I could feel her faith tingling through her little finger-tips into mine. All that is necessary now is to get this young savage to Quebec, exalt him, and then——" Bigot's naked teeth gleamed with the passion of words unspoken.

"Of course," nodded Vaudreuil. "There is no other way. And it must be done thoroughly, by a man of cleverness and skill." He bowed complacently at the compliment to himself.

"Yes, more thoroughly than anything like it has ever been done before," agreed Bigot. "As long as this forest clown holds her love all the powers on earth cannot win her. That love must be destroyed and its demolishment made so utter that contempt and hatred will fill its place. If I can hold myself against her beauty and restrain my madness for her until that time—why, this treasure you so aptly called a lily of Artois will come to me, if not willingly then in another way!"

"She will come willingly, only too gladly when all is over, François," assured Vaudreuil. "She is young, almost a child. Her pretty head is ripe for the seed you planted tonight. I predict that her whim for this David Rock will change, and quickly too, for my eyes told me this afternoon that environment and too intimate association in these woods have brought about this child-sweethearting between them. It is not so much the lad as her father whom I see standing in our way."

"The father will be cared for," assured Bigot with a cryptic hardening of his lips. "David Rock is the mountain to be moved, and no such simple thing as death can be employed in doing it. The other way is the only way."

"And far more interesting," added Vaudreuil, turning to look at the moon. "François, did you ever see a night of greater splendor?"

[1] At this time François Bigot was already deep in the treacherous plottings which in 1759 lost to France forever her splendid empire in the New World.

CHAPTER IX

Anne had made only a pretense of entering the château when Bigot left her. Every nerve in her was demanding that she see David even if she had to call on Peter Gagnon to escort her through the forest to Marie Rock's home.

That David might not see with her eyes and that the spirit of his beloved forests might still be stronger than anything greater the world could offer him did not occur to her in these first wild moments of her happiness. She believed that he would join in her joy and exultation. That very day on Sunset Hill they had talked of their heroes of this glorious new world, of Cartier and Champlain and De Roberval, of Frontenac and Charlevoix, of noble and heroic men who had paved the way to glory for France—and the way was opened to David now to take his place among such men as these! Pride and faith in him made her sure.

Next to David she wanted to see Marie Rock, and the thought came to her thrillingly that there was always a place for her in Marie Rock's own room where she had slept many times, and that this was the night of all nights when it would most fittingly welcome her.

An adventurous resolution began to possess her. The forest did not frighten her. A hundred times she had followed the trail through the Red Open, and its blackness would be scattered by the moonlight now. She would not need Peter Gagnon. She could go alone.

Someone came out of the kitchen door, and in a moment she had made her decision. "Chloe!" she called softly. "Chloe!"

The black slave stared at her.

"Chloe, it is I, Mistress Anne," she called scarcely above a whisper. "Go to my room and bring my red cape to me, and let no one see what you are doing."

She waited, keeping in the shadow while the servant was gone. She could see the dim glow of Fontbleu's candle deep in the pit of his mill. Once she saw Fontbleu standing in his door looking up at the sky. He had disappeared when Chloe returned with the cape.

Anne flung it over her shoulders. "Now find my father and tell him I have gone to Marie Rock's to sleep tonight. Tell him I am tired and do not wish to be kept awake by noise and song, and that David will bring me back early in the morning. Say that I miss his good-night kiss, but could not bring myself to seek him out among his guests. Carry those words to him, Chloe—and nothing more."

She waited until Chloe and her inquisitive eyes were gone before she darted out from the shadow of the château and into the shelter of the first great oaks of Grondin's Wood. Her breath came tensely as she plunged into the forest, and her eyes grew wider as they strained to penetrate the mysteries of the deep shadows and pools of moonlight which gathered like living things about her. Behind her she saw the last of the smoldering fires along the river. Sounds from the château, which at first had been distinct, became faint and distant and died away altogether.

She came to the little open where the path from Sunset Hill met the trail leading to David's home, and where David had kissed her in parting that evening.

The open was flooded with moonlight and Anne was about to cross it when she stopped with a startled catching of her breath. In the middle of the open a lone figure was standing. It was facing her as if halted suddenly by the sound of her footsteps from behind. With a glad cry she ran out, for she saw it was David.

He did not move toward her as she came. His face was almost as she had seen it when he stalked from the manor-hall that night, pale and hard and grimly set. But he dropped his gun and took off his cap and waited for her, amazement in his eyes.

"You knew I was coming, David?" she asked breathlessly, scarce believing it could be chance alone that had brought her to him like this.

"I know only that you were walking a long time with Monsieur Bigot; and though he is the Intendant I do not like it after what happened in the bottomland this afternoon!"

"You saw us, David?"

125

"I was so near when you passed me, in the shadow of the big elm tree, that I could see your hand on his arm and hear him asking you something about the queenly honors which some other man might give you."

Now Anne knew why David stood without movement or tenderness toward her, his face so white and grim. She dropped her head for an instant as if he had caught her in something of which she was ashamed, and then looking up at him with a mischievous smile and the moonlight dancing in her eyes, she said, "Were you not pleased with my answer, David?"

"I heard no answer."

"But there was one—so straight from my heart that I remember each word of it."

"I did not hear it."

"You saw only my hand on Monsieur Bigot's arm?"

"Yes, and he bending over you, smiling."

"Then I am glad you saw no more, for at that very moment he was holding my finger-tips," said Anne, and suddenly her low, sweet laughter trilled in David's ears, and she put her arms about his shoulders and kissed him, and laid her head on his breast.

"David, dear, I am so glad you feel that way toward me!" she cried softly. "If you were not a little jealous of me I would be unhappy. And I am proud of you for not turning savage again when you saw me with Bigot. You are stronger than I, for if ever I catch you alone like that in the moonlight with Nancy Lotbinière I shall tear out her eyes and never speak to you again!"

Then she pulled him to what she had so often called their drumming-log in the edge of the open, and seated him, and herself beside him, and told him all that had happened that night from the time he left the manor-hall, and repeated word for word what had passed between herself and the Intendant.

Not once did he interrupt her, but a flush gathered slowly in his face and a look came into his eyes which turned them at last away from Anne.

"David—it means all the world for us," she whispered tremblingly when she had finished. "What do you think of it?"

"I am thinking—most of all—how small and shameful I am for the thoughts I had when I saw you with Bigot," he said.

"I am glad," said Anne. "It is proof you love me——"

"More than all that Bigot and the King of France can give me, and because of that I see no reason for these other things which Bigot holds out so temptingly—for a reason which I cannot clearly understand."

"Because he has taken an interest in us, David."

"Yes, an interest."

"And he knows that you are braver and nobler than any man at Grondin Manor tonight."

"That I doubt."

"He needs you, David, because New France needs you. You have not forgotten what we talked about on Sunset Hill this afternoon—of the men who have made this land out of its wilderness?"

"But they were a part of the wilderness, Anne, and so am I."

"They came, most of them, straight from the court of the King," said Anne. She pressed his hand against her breast, and he could feet her heart beating under it like a prisoned bird. "David, the times have changed. Quebec and not the wilderness is now the heart of all this world. It is from there New France will vanquish all her enemies—or there New France will die. And sometime, David, when there is no longer the menace you have pictured on my powder-horn, we can come back to all this which is so close and dear to us."

"You are not ashamed of me, Anne?"

"Never! It is because I have been in Quebec and know that men like you are needed there."

"You would leave the forest doors open?"

"There are others who will watch those doors. When the time comes, if fight you must, I would see you at the head of men and not simply one among them."

"You are painting a pretty picture, Anne. You would have me leave my mother?"

"She will come a little later and will be as proud of you as I." Anne bent her head. "David, you will go?"

"I have no heart for it. It frightens me to change our lives as you are planning."

Her soft palm pressed against his cheek. "I will bargain with you. Go for my sake, and if you do not like it by the time my year of school is ended I will come back with you—and remain here always."

"You promise that, Anne?"

"I promise it."

"Then you leave me not an inch to stand on. I will go!"

With a glad cry Anne sprang to her feet and stood before him in the moonlight. "David, I love you more than ever in my life!" she cried.

Before the words were out he had her in his arms. "And always will?" he demanded.

"Always."

"Even if I fail to become what you have dreamed?"

"Yes, even if you fail."

David laughed as he had laughed once before that day on Sunset Hill, and held her away from him, then drew her quickly back.

"You are no longer a boy," she whispered. "You are a man!"

"It has been a long day," he answered. "A day filled with years."

"And have I grown older, too?"

"So much so that at first you frightened me."

"And now——"

She held up her mouth and David kissed her.

"I am afraid of you, like that," he said, and kissed her again.

Then she drew herself out of his arms and told him of her desperate resolution to go to his mother's home alone.

"I think angels must have put the thought into your head, Anne, and then made me stop here in the open until you came. She has something of importance to tell you—and I want you to meet the Black Hunter."

"The Black Hunter!"

"Yes. He came again this afternoon while we were on Sunset Hill." He could see the old fear leaping suddenly where happiness had filled her eyes, and he took one of her hands and held it closely, as she had held his own a moment before. "Anne, I have granted all you say about Quebec, which deep in my heart I dread. And now I ask you to grant a little to me in the matter of Peter Joel, whom you have always heard me speak of as the Black Hunter. And I too will bargain with you. If at the end of that same year you do not love this man you have such fear of now, I will never adventure with him again, no matter how short a distance away from you the journey may be."

Anne, tense-faced, saw for herself—as David had seen—no inch of ground for her to stand on.

"Yet I fear him—for some reason which I cannot explain I fear him more than anything else in the world," she said, as hand in hand they left the open and went into the forest trail.

"And I love him," said David, "as you will before that year we have pledged is gone. If it had not been for the Black Hunter——"

Then his whisper died into nothing, and he held her hand more closely as the endless aisles and moonlit caverns of the deeper woods opened mysteriously and in silence on all sides of them. And again Anne could not hear the fall of David's feet, so lightly they trod the earth, and now, as always, she strained to make her own as noiseless, and only half succeeded. It was this attitude of David's when in the forest that puzzled her and sent strange chills up her back sometimes, for he seemed always watching for a danger which she could not understand. If they had laughed and talked or lifted their voices in song as they went, she would have forgotten the forest entirely; but now its great shadows seemed to stir with life and its stillness to tremble with whisperings of fear and omen.

They came to the Red Open and Anne drew in a first deep breath. It was here that David's distressing caution always came to an end. "Sometimes I think you are afraid of the ghosts in Grondin's Wood," she declared with an unrestrained gasp of relief. "I would rather come through that wood alone than with you David, and I shall hereafter if you persist in frightening me with your—I don't know what to name it!"

"I am sorry," said David.

Her hand caught his arm in sudden agitation. "There is a figure in the Open! See!—near the first great rock—standing out clear in the moonlight where we have never seen anything stand before!"

"I saw it, and so stopped in the shadow here where we are unseen," replied David very quietly.

"It moved!" whispered Anne, a breaking catch in her voice as she clung closer to him. "It is alive—and blacker than night—and taller than any living thing I have ever seen!"

"It is the moon which, gives it that appearance, Anne."

"But it is black—black, and not gray, or—or white—as a ghost would be!"

"It is black," said David, and he was smiling.

"David, what is it?"

He answered with a soft bird-cry which was not much more than a chirping note in the air, and in a moment the note came back like a drifting echo, and Anne could hear the thump, thump, thump of her heart in her breast.

With the smile in David's face was a sudden flash of joy and understanding. "It is the Black Hunter waiting for us," he said. "Twice we have missed each other tonight!"

He felt Anne's fingers stiffen in his hand, but even he could not guess the coldness of fear that ran through her as they stepped forth into the Red Open. She sensed the thrill of eagerness in David even as she struggled against her own foreboding. She could feel it running through his body and into her fingertips, and she saw it when she looked quickly at his face. His eyes were afire with gladness while her own were hiding their fear. It was now she understood how the superstitious felt about the restless spirits of the slain who dwelt in this ghastly open, for it seemed to her that the figure ahead was an evil spirit that had come out of the heart of the rock itself, and all the time she was telling herself that she did not know the reason why. But it was strangely a part of her, woven of her very being—a prophetic warning of impending menace and misfortune to her and David, through the black art of this weird wanderer of the borders, of whom she had heard such frightful whisperings and tales.

The trickeries of the moonlight vanished as they advanced, and a few steps more Anne saw a man where the tall specter had been—a man bareheaded and with his hands reaching out—a man whose face was filled with the gladness she had seen in David's, and with a silvery streak of white in his hair.

She clutched at the throat of her cape while the two stood a long moment with their hands clasped tightly with not a word between them. And then, over David's shoulder, the Black Hunter looked at her.

David turned. "This is Anne," he said. "My Anne—of the powder-horn."

"Our Anne of the powder-horn," corrected Peter Joel, and he bowed until Anne could see the white, smooth streak in his hair from end to end. Bigot himself could not have made the act more chivalrous or filled it with greater dignity, yet Anne felt still greater dread as she remembered her pledge to David and held out both her hands.

The Black Hunter took them for a moment, with almost a reverent gentleness, then let them go.

"I have heard so much about you that it seems as though I know you almost as well as I know David," he said; and from his voice Anne knew that her pallid face and the tremble of her hands had revealed to him some of the chill that was in her heart.

"I am glad of that," she said bravely, though a consciousness bore heavily on her that the words were a shallow lie. "Your friendship is an honor to me if I can believe a half of what David has told me."

A whimsical smile played for an instant about the corners of Peter Joel's mouth. "If you can think kindly of me, only a little, I am more than satisfied," he said, and the feeling that he was reading her thoughts made her shiver. But Peter Joel did not wait to see, for he had turned his head toward David. "Meeting you here is an accident, lad. I stopped in this empty open to view the moon."

He nodded, and smiled at Anne again, and this time she was sure the whimsical, half-sad light was in the eyes that for a moment or two looked at her steadily. "I love the moon," he said, "and a moon like that fills me with the thick-coming fancies of an Alnaschar and strengthens my faith in God. I am afraid I have lost many minutes here staring at it, and building flying visions of what lies beyond. It is late. David must hurry on with you."

"This happens to be a night where time has little meaning for us," replied Anne, scarcely knowing how she spoke. "Won't you return to Marie Rock's with us?"

"I must see the Intendant," answered the Black Hunter, and his words were for David as well as for her. "Only a duty well impressed upon me could make me forgo a pleasure such as your invitation holds, Mademoiselle Anne."

She went a little ahead and for a few moments David and Peter Joel were alone. Then, taking his long, black gun from the side of the rock and covering his head with a close-fitting cap, he said good night, and bowed again to Anne, and walked away toward Grondin Manor, his somber, death's-color figure growing strangely taller as he went.

Now Anne shuddered, and made no pretense of hiding it from David. "I am cold—cold as ice inside," she said. "I did not expect to see a man like that, David—one who acts and talks so fine—yet the dread in me is greater than before."

"You were sweet and good to him, Anne. I thank you!"

"And he talks of God! That is sacrilege in one whose hands are drenched with blood."

"I have seen him pull a stick from a fire because there were living ants on it, and I have known him to go hungry that he might feed a dog," countered David.

"And he speaks like one who has lived in books, and not in deep forests where only witchcraft could give him such words and thoughts!"

"I have often told you that in his pack is always a book, Anne, and such as only the finest scholars read."

"And he dresses like that—like one whose soul is so dark it must be hidden in a devil's hood!"

"I have seen your fine gentlemen dressed in black. What difference should the forests make?"

"Ugh!" shuddered Anne again.

"It is strange. Why should you dislike him? Why should you be afraid? No act of his was ever a dishonorable one."

"Even believing that, as I must and shall, the thought grows stronger in me that he is a shadow between us and happiness. Don't ask me why, or even wonder why, for it is a mystery even to myself. Long before our year is gone I have no doubt the foolish fancy will have worn itself away."

"Yes, even before the night is gone," said David mysteriously, and hurried her faster along the trail.

"You are anxious to rid yourself of me," she accused him, "so that you may run back to him!"

"Not half so anxious to join him as to get you where you must listen to what my mother has to tell you."

"I hate riddles," retorted Anne, and closed her lips so tightly that not another word came from them until she saw the mellow glow of candle-light in Marie Rock's windows ahead of them. Then she said, "You may leave me now. Nothing can carry me away between here and the door."

"Leave you—for what?"

"For the Black Hunter, of course. Isn't it in your mind to return to him?"

"If it will not displease you, Anne——"

"Displease me! Isn't it also a part of my bargain to send you back to him?" And she tilted her chin and walked straight away from him, and David stood half doubtfully until he saw his mother's door open and then close behind her.

That night a candle burned late in Marie Rock's room. It was burning when the rest of the house was dark. It was burning when the Black Hunter and David returned and stole with the quietness of thieves to their beds in the loft.

And when the candle at last went out Marie Rock and Anne St. Denis still lay wide-eyed and awake.

In the heart of one was wonder, and happiness, and fear—a fear that persisted like a grim and ugly shadow though she had heard from beginning to end the story of Peter Joel the Hunter.

In the heart of the other was despair that grew darker through hours of yearning sleeplessness.

CHAPTER X

Days that followed were the first mile-stones David had ever seriously marked in his life. His whole world was changing, and it seemed to him that everything in it was changing, even to his mother, and Anne, and the Black Hunter, and the very forests themselves.

Events passing swiftly had left within him the impress of years. It did not seem to him that yesterday or the day before he had done such childish things as to lie grimacing at himself over the edge of a pool, while Anne had laughed at him like another child for doing it, or that he had run a red squirrel up a tree for her and had climbed that tree to let her see it jump into another. He was older, so much older that some of the buoyant lightness was gone from his feet when he went into the forest, which now was dark and filled with chill and gloom for him.

This was his world, this open freedom which seemed to frown and draw away from him now that he had given his word to leave it. In it were his splendid boyhood castles. It was his heart, the breath that had given him life, the soul that had made him look ahead into the wild and glorious imaginings of days and years to come. And he tried to hide from the others the leaden fear that oppressed him as he replaced these things with visions of another world that was to take its place. He did not confide this fear to his mother. He spoke no more of it to Anne. This much older he had grown in a single day and night.

The great city of Quebec had at last claimed Anne. It had dragged her from their forests, from this sun-filled valley, from everything on earth he cared for or ever would care for.

Brooding conviction settled itself firmly in his heart as one day followed another. He struggled against it but without avail, and with each of those days he set himself more grimly for the fight ahead—the fight to make himself as Anne wanted him to be, the fight to become a part of that gay and courtly life which her beauty and desire would fill, and in which he knew that he was bound to fail miserably.

It came to him now with sickening import why her cheeks had flushed and her eyes had sparkled when she had talked to him of the gay soirées in moments when he thought she was teasing him—telling him of fêtes and festivals and of gay dances that lasted all the night through, of l'harlequinade, la chinoise, la matelote and others, and of the stately courtesyings and finger-tipping of the minuet, where every gentleman and lady was like a king or queen. And his face grew hot, even as his heart was cold, when he foresaw the shame and failure ahead of him.

The day after his long night of grinding, Fontbleu, the miller, had his hour of gloomy triumph when he saw his prediction to David come true. Bigot's party left Grondin Manor for the lower Richelieu and the St. Lawrence before noon. It went with a wild whooping and singing of voice and a gay display of flags, but Bigot did not go with it. Nor did Vaudreuil, nor De Pean, nor half a dozen high-spirited young officers of his retinue.

Fontbleu oiled the old wheel, and doused it well. "You'll sing no more, if I can help it," he growled. "You're a fool, and so am I, and David the biggest fool of all to dream the things we have! She's going away, and she won't come back like she's ever been, and David won't have her in the end." And Fontbleu cursed in a thin, cracked voice as his bones creaked in sympathy with his feelings.

That same day word came up the river by an Indian messenger that Anne's Quebec party were at Three Rivers when the messenger left and would be following him within a few days.

With a face that was paler than yesterday Marie Rock worked the finishing touches in a new and beautiful suit of deerskin for David. In the afternoon the Seigneur St. Denis came to see her, and with him were Bigot and the Marquis de Vaudreuil.

Bigot whispered when he could get a word alone with Vaudreuil, "She is almost as lovely as Anne!"

The Black Hunter, who had gone away at dawn, came back again at dusk. From that hour and through all the others that followed it seemed to David that every soul at Grondin Manor was bent on his going to Quebec, except Fontbleu, the miller.

"Fortune has come your way, my son," said his mother, "and it would be folly for you or me to turn it aside no matter how difficult the parting may be." She told him of the visit of Bigot and Vaudreuil, and of their pledge to her to send him back with honor and fortune made.

"In Quebec beats the heart of the nation," said Peter Joel, with something that was far away and strange in his voice. "Go, David, and feel the pulse of it."

"In Quebec beats the heart of the devil, he means," mocked Fontbleu, the miller, when David repeated the words to him. "Go, David lad, and see what that devil will do with you!"

All about him David marked a swift and growing change. First, in his mother, from the night she told him the story of Peter Joel. A tired look was in her eyes and darkness lay under them, and suddenly she seemed to have lost something of the girlish joy and comradeship which she had always held for David. Then in Peter Joel, who, from that same night, fell into hours of silence and aloneness, and left at last, without letting David know, for the Isle of Montreal.

Elsewhere the change he saw and felt was different. Bigot had lost no time in letting it be known that David was his protégé, and all because of the amazing happening at the pool. A youth of David's pluck and daring was the kind that Bigot loved, the story went, and soon there was not a soul but knew each detail of the adventure from one end of the seigneury to the other, and in two letters, pages long, Peter Gagnon sent the tale to his father and to gossip-lovers in Quebec.

The cottage folk regarded him with envious eyes, anticipating the greatness which lay ahead of him. The young officers, jealous in their hearts, welcomed him among them, and twice Bigot stood with a hand affectionately on his shoulder while he related with ever increasing pleasure some new humor of his baptism in the pool. He called him David, and so did the Governor of Louisiana, and each day—two proud and splendid gentlemen!—they went to call upon his mother.

De Pean he began to like for his gentlemanliness and the regret which he so deeply felt for words spoken in moments of careless levity. And the Seigneur St. Denis, with a gleam of pride in his eyes, told him that he had brought honor to his house.

But it was Anne, sweet Anne, who swept the world from under his feet, for when she met him now she made him a low and dainty courtesy, sweeter even than those she gave to the Governor or the Intendant, for with their prettiness was love-light in her eyes when it was David who looked into them.

No matter how valiantly he struggled to keep it back the blood flamed hot in David's cheeks each time.

"You must stop it, Anne," he entreated. "I feel like a fool when you courtesy to me like that, as if I were a king."

"You are—my king," she retorted. "And I shall not give to others what I cannot give to you."

"But they must be laughing in their sleeves to see such play before a clown like me, who can neither smile nor bow nor say a clever word in return for it."

"Simply because you are frightened——"

"Yes, frightened."

"And clumsy, David, so dearly, bravely clumsy, like an Indian who won't unbend. You need a teacher, and I shall be that teacher and not once give a chance to the billing and cooing blandishments of Nancy Lotbinière, who would love to steal you from me with just such courtesies as I am giving you so happily now, and always, with a kiss besides—when we are alone."

"I will need much teaching."

"Indeed you will—so much that my time will be greatly taken up when we reach the city."

"It is too much taken up now. We no longer have our hours together in the woods and on Sunset Hill."

"I cannot go, David, with all this company demanding me as hostess and our party coming so soon."

So the days passed slowly for him, but swiftly for Anne and his mother, who were working furiously to get Grondin Manor ready for the guests from the city. He was not always alone, for sometimes Bigot and De Pean walked with him, or Vaudreuil puffed along at his side. He missed Peter Gagnon, who had gone to meet the party from Quebec.

One day De Pean helped him to harvest the last of his corn, while the Intendant sat near them, making such fun of his helper that David himself was filled with the humor of laughter. While they were at this work Anne and his mother came in from the manor-house trail, and in that very moment Bigot himself was carrying a great load of fodder.

"Sancta Maria!" gasped Anne, astounded at the sight. "The Intendant of New France carrying corn with David!"

Bigot saw them out of the corner of his eye, and again he blessed the subtlety and cunning of Vaudreuil, who had learned that Anne had planned to accompany Marie Rock to her home that afternoon.

It was Anne's first visit since the night when David had brought her through the Red Open, and she made no effort to hide the pleasure and joy at the scene which met her eyes. As David hurried to meet the two, De Pean, who was sweaty and prickly, cursed softly at Bigot's side.

145

"It will take a half of your next ship to pay for this," he grumbled. "I wouldn't do it a second time for God or the King!"

"There will be no reason for a second time," murmured Bigot, smiling and wiping his face. "It is done. Observe carelessly and see how proud even the mother is because of this amazing spectacle."

"David, David," whispered Anne as he came to her, and she could say no more. But her eyes were glowing. And there was a look in his mother's face which thrilled him with its pride.

And in her heart Marie Rock was saying, "Such men as these surely cannot be the danger I have heard!"

Later, with gentle courtesy and friendliness, Bigot asked David if he might have the pleasure and honor of escorting Anne back to her home. The request was like the prick of a knife to David, for at first sight of Anne his mind had leaped to the thought that he would be going back to Grondin Manor with her. But he bowed his head a little—he had learned that much of the courtly fashions at the château—and replied that such an honor from the Intendant could not be denied.

Only Anne herself knew the crushing disappointment inside him when he found opportunity to make known Bigot's request, and a little frown gathered in her face.

"I came this way with the intention of walking back with you," she said.

"But when he asks—can you refuse?"

Perplexity grew deeper in Anne's eyes. "It would be—discourteous, David. Still, if you desire it——"

"No. He means well. I have little doubt of his friendship now. Yet I cannot understand it. I try, but I cannot."

"If you had my eyes you would," whispered Anne, and the soft loveliness in them as she looked at David made him almost kiss her where she stood, in sight of all the others.

Until the time for Anne's return Bigot seemed absorbed in David's mother, and the gentleness and delicacy of his attentions sent a mocking smile into De Pean's face when his back was turned. De Pean remained behind when at last Bigot and Anne turned homeward. From the far end of the clearing Anne waved her hand at David. He was smiling, but inside his breast was something that choked and smothered him.

"You are a lucky man," said De Pean, laying a friendly hand on his arm, "for you have the heart of the loveliest being I have ever seen, and with it the friendship of François Bigot. Together they should lift you to the clouds. And I, poor Hugues de Pean, Town Major of Quebec, sometimes think you should love me, David, for giving voice to those so fruitful words at the pool!" After that, faithful to the master who had given him wealth and power second only to his own, De Pean continued to help David with the fodder.

In the forest, mellowed and warmed by the sun that was descending in the west, Bigot walked for some time, almost in silence, beside Anne. A humor of sadness seemed to have come upon him, and out of this he brought himself suddenly with a little laugh, and caught her hand and placed it on his arm, as if he had neglected her.

"Forgive me, Anne," he said. "What can you think of one who allows dreams to drag him away from such sweet loveliness at his side, if only for a moment or two? It is strange that when I am with you I want to dream. Can you guess why?"

"No," said Anne, a bit fearfully.

"Because, to me, you are the heart and soul and the living breath of New France. Your beauty, your purity, your love of country which exceeds all other love—these things call my mind to the visions I have built of the glory which it is my one desire in life to make this land of ours achieve. And you—you seem to breathe those very thoughts and inspirations, Anne. A country that is great and pure! A country triumphant, yet merciful to its enemies! A country rising like your own white beauty out of a wilderness of blackness and doubt! For that hour, if I could bring it, I would gladly lay down my life."

In his moments of supreme acting Bigot's voice was filled with a richness of pathos and sincerity that reached the soul; and in Anne's breast was a throbbing response as she felt the greatness of the man at her side, and the passion of sublime emotion which seemed to set every living force in his body athrill.

For the arm on which Bigot had placed her hand, and whereon she let it rest, was trembling. In those moments Anne forgot herself, and her nearness to the one whose soul she saw on the altar of New France. She was unconscious of the loveliness which Bigot was fighting to keep himself from momentarily desecrating—only that he might possess it entirely in the end. The black hypocrisy in the man's heart fell upon her ears softly, like white truth, and stirred her with a responsive thrill. That his hand found hers again, and rested gently on it, she scarcely knew. And that his eyes, looking down into the glory and riotous colorings of her sunlit hair, were aflame with a thought that would have terrified her, she could not see. For Bigot raised his eyes when she looked at him, and the fire she saw in them she took for another thing.

And Bigot knew this—knew that youth and purity at his side believed in him, and trusted him. "For God and King!" he was saying, as if for another moment he had forgotten her. "What more in this world can one ask to fight for, until the last curtain of night falls over us? That—or monastic life, holy, angelical, blessed! What matters if poisonous tongues work their ends? For there are many who forget what the Apostle says of himself, that the world is crucified to him, as he is to the world, and yet that he super-abounds in joy. Such will be my joy, Anne, if in the end I can die knowing New France is safe. And it is you—you who have given me new inspiration to go on!"

"If that is true, I am glad," trembled Anne.

"It is true—so true that François Bigot will see nothing in this world come between you and happiness, and that great and holy part which one like you can play in making my dreams for New France come true. It is because of the truth of it that I disappointed David today, and asked to bring you home. My heart urges me to confide in you a matter which I am almost afraid to reveal."

Anne was silent. No words did she dare to utter, for the Intendant's voice bore in it an almost tragic hint of something unusual impending.

"If I speak, will you listen?"

"I will," said Anne.

"And forgive me if I hurt you, and believe in the depth of my sincerity, no matter what I say?" Bigot did not wait for the answer which he knew it might be difficult for her to give. "You are loyal and true, Anne. I have faith in you almost as I would have in our dear Mother of the Incarnation. And just as she has separated herself from all that the world holds dear and delightful, that she may be acceptable for her sublime vocation, so I know you would sacrifice self, if necessary, in the cause of God and country. Because of that, and the open-mindedness with which you will receive my words, I am going to speak to you about David—and what I fear for him."

"Fear for him!" cried Anne, a little chill running through her at the softly ominous note in Bigot's voice. "If he is endangered——"

"He is," interrupted Bigot, looking straight ahead, and speaking in a slow and thoughtful way. "Not because of himself, Anne, so do not let me frighten you. But he is very young, and susceptible to a clever schemer, and I have a shadowing misgiving that seeds have been planted in his fine young mind which I would have you help me wipe away before they come to life. I am referring to the dark and sinister influence of the man you call the Black Hunter. This man, born and bred among our enemies, a shifting and homeless wanderer of the borders, I do not trust, and I have foreboding thoughts of him in these hours when a mysterious and unsolved treachery is eating at the soul and honor of New France. I suspect the Black Hunter."

"Monsieur!"

"I have asked your forgiveness, Anne, for being so painfully frank with you. But it is for David's sake, and I have spoken to none but you of my suspicion. I believe the Black

Hunter to be not so much a traitor—for he has no drop of French blood in him—as a spy whose wicked cleverness it is impossible for us to unmask. I know you love him because of David, but——"

"I—I——" cried Anne, and stopped.

Bigot's fingers pressed her hand again. "And David is not only young, but he is English too." His voice was caressing in its gentleness even as the devil in him sent up its sly insinuation. "As the twig is bent so the tree may grow, and we must not let this sly impostor bend our David."

"Dear Mother of Jesus!" Anne breathed almost to herself. "You would mistrust——"

"No, no—not David!" exclaimed Bigot. "I believe his heart to be as pure of fraud and deceit as my own, and because of that faith in him, and his courage, I love him. But see, Anne! There outside our path a step or two is a patch of poisonous ivy, turning yellow and gold with the beauty of the autumn! Let it touch even such pure and unsullied hands as your own and the mark of its infection remains. In such a way, I fear, might the poisons of a soul like the Black Hunter's work on the credulity and faith and love of youth."

He looked down and saw that the blood had left Anne's cheeks, and he laughed gently in his triumph, with one of those swift changes which had helped to make him the most dangerous man in New France. "I have frightened you, little lady, and I am sorry! It was cruel of me to let such thoughts escape my lips. For with you at his side, and with François Bigot as his friend, a thousand Black Hunters cannot harm our David. Listen to that thrush singing in the brush—a little friend who soon will be going south! That, and this bright day, are both omens of the happiness and good fortune ahead of us. Am I forgiven?"

"Doubt has only added to doubt," said Anne; and even the craftiness of Bigot did not gather fully what she meant.

But later, when he had left Anne and was talking with Vaudreuil alone, he said, "The trap is now completely set. Vaudreuil, with a bit of romance added to your skill you would have been a magnificent lover!"

CHAPTER XI

Even Bigot could not have guessed the depth to which the germs of his Judas-like apostasy had sunk in Anne's mind. She went to her room worried and distressed, innocent of the baseness to which she had been subjected, and with the darker shadows of her suspicion and fear of the Black Hunter drawing more closely than ever about her.

For the first time in her life a moment of doubt swept through her mind as she thought of Marie Rock and her long and mysterious association with the man whose story she had told a few nights before. Swiftly as it had come, Anne tore the doubt from her with a bitter cry against her own faithlessness, for no matter what knavery the Black Hunter might have in his heart David's mother could never for an instant have been a part of it.

Only because of her loyalty to David, and her promise to him regarding the Black Hunter, had she stopped the words which would have told Bigot of her own brooding thoughts, which had eaten at her happiness and peace of mind since her return from the convent of the Ursulines. At no time had she given to these thoughts a definite form. Least of all, had the suspicion come to her that Peter Joel was what François Bigot had so clearly intimated—an agent of the deadly enemies who were bent on the destruction of

New France. And the Intendant's subtle innuendo, carrying with it the whisper of a suggestion that Peter Joel might be working through both David and his mother, and that David himself might in time be made to incline toward the race of his father's birth, shocked her as no imaginings of her own had ever done.

She clutched at her breast to still the terrible thoughts which came in spite of her. She loved Marie Rock as dearly as she could ever have loved her own mother. She loved David. They were so much a part of her life that without them she would want to die. And suspicions like these were monstrous!

She did not see Bigot again, or any of the officers who had remained as guests, but excused herself from supper under the pretense of fatigue and a headache, and remained in her room.

Before she went to bed she opened a small teakwood casket on her dressing-table, and brought forth a letter. This letter she had read so many times that it bore the impress of wear. Next to her Bible, Anne had found its words a solace and consolation when she was filled with doubt or unrest.

It was from her best-loved friend in Quebec, Sister Esther of the Infant Jesus, who, on the day the letter was written, had begun the achievement of her sublime ambition by passing through the probation of the white veil.

And dearest of this gentle Esther's wishes, and most devout of her prayers, was that Anne St. Denis might join her as a nun in the service of God.

"It is my pleasure, my honor, henceforth to seek to live for God alone," were the words which Anne always read. "I trust myself to one who does not change; in Him I shall find a remedy for my own inconstancy. Here, as the author of 'The Imitation of Christ' promises, I am excited to good by example, and warned from evil by admonition.... Here, as St. Clement and St. Basil tell, one is able to pray for me to God, another to console me when sick, another to teach me what is useful to salvation. Another will correct me with kindness, or consult together with me like a friend; and all will love me truly, without guile, without flattery. O sweet attendance of friends! O blessed ministry of comforters! O the faithful services of those who fear only God! O the true simplicity which is incapable of falsehood! O the honorable labor which is in obedience to God, to please God! No tongue can express the sentiments of love which I feel for thee, no voice can depict the joy with which thou dost fill my heart! ... Thus, dear Anne, falls the curtain of each night around the peaceful cloister, while each one, according to the attractions of grace, enters into the recess of her own conscience; and there, finding all at rest, all passions hushed, who can tell the deep feeling of security and thanksgiving that sweetly fills the soul, rendering that humble cell an image and an anticipation of Paradise?"

This letter, holding forth its promise of what was the chiefest of all glories to the young womanhood of her day, was to Anne a benediction. It had worried David. It brought peace to her. To it she added her own prayer, and went to bed, confident that tomorrow, and each day after that, would point the way to fulfilment for her—and also for David.

Scarcely had the sun begun to flush the east the following morning when a messenger came for David. The envoy was from Anne, and David was to attend upon her at once.

Suspense that was half curiosity, and the other half alarm, sent him hurrying to her. He found her waiting for him in Grondin's Wood, at the edge of the May-pole green. Her eyes were dancing and her cheeks were pink with excitement, and as David came up, a little breathless, she crossed her red lips with a finger which warned him to caution and silence, though Grondin Manor was a rifle-shot away, and all in it were asleep except the quietly busy servants.

"Be quiet, David, and hold your breath, or the wonderful excursion I have planned will be spoiled! Our party leaves Contrecoeur immediately after breakfast and should be here by mid-forenoon. We are going to meet them!"

There was a freshness and sweetness about her that reminded him again of Sunset Hill as she gave him her hand and they skirted the green together; and once out of sight

157

of prying eyes she stopped and told him it was time for him to remember something, which David did, kissing her red mouth and her smooth hair so tenderly and so many times that Anne found herself blushing in a way that was delightfully new and thrilling to her.

After that, as they went down to the canoe which a servant had prepared for them, she felt singularly like a child beside him. And truly she might, her eyes told her. For this morning David's head was high, and he seemed taller, and something about him was a little different, stirring her oddly and pleasingly, even though it made her feel smaller beside him. In the canoe, facing him, she watched the easy and rhythmic swing of his lithe young body, and the supple play of his naked forearm muscles, with an unconscious sense of exultation. No wonder he had thrown both Bigot and De Pean into the pool with such little effort! She smiled, and then, in a moment, the little frown which she employed when mentally perplexed gathered in her forehead—for a sudden thought came to her of Nancy Lotbinière, the prettiest coquette in all Quebec.

David smiled back as he steadily plied his paddle. "You smile at me, and then you frown," he said. "First you see something about me which you like, and then something of which you disapprove."

"I see about you so much to like that I am thinking again of that shameless Nancy Lotbinière," she confessed honestly. "If she sees in you what I see, and betrays a single sign of rapture over you, there will be trouble, David. I hope she will think you as graceless as a baboon, as sour as vinegar, and as dull as a bookful of blockheads! To all the others, even Louise Charmette, I want you to appear as the most wonderful Prince Charming in all the world. But to Nancy Lotbinière, whom I love as a friend but will hate as a rival——"

And Fate, sitting back, contrarily twisted the happenings of the day so that it was Nancy Lotbinière whom David saw first, and in such a way as to deepen the frown in the middle of Anne's white forehead.

She came like a goddess in the first canoe, with Peter Gagnon sitting behind her, and a swart riverman in the stern. In the morning sunshine she had given wild freedom to her hair, and it streamed about her like a raiment of golden fire; as they came near she sent it cascading over her arms and in the wind, until even David, who had no eyes except for Anne, stared at it in speechless wonder. Before he could stop his foolish tongue, he had said, "She looks like one on fire!"

"She will be, some day, unless all holy teachings are a lie!" snapped Anne.

At this day, a few months past her twentieth year, Nancy Lotbinière, daughter of the seigneury where now stand the villages of St. Pierre Bequest, St. Antoine and St. Croix, was undeniably the belle of Quebec, and half a dozen hearts already lay at her feet. A product of the Ursulines, educated in its gentleness and culture, accomplished in many ways, rich, beautiful, and with a mind whose clearness of vision and keenness of wit were unexcelled, she was one of the fairest, if not the fairest, of the daughters of New France.[1]

"Who but a brazen minx would come with her hair like that?" demanded Anne in a fierce little voice as she smiled sweetly and waved her hand in greeting to the approaching vision of loveliness. "Who, I say?"

Nancy saved David, for she called from a distance, with a voice as pretty as herself, "Bless your sweet heart, Anne St. Denis! Unless these canoes travel faster I shall jump in the river to get my arms about you!"

And Anne called back, in a voice even sweeter, "You are in no greater haste than I!" But for David she said, still smiling as if her happiness were brimming over, "If she doesn't put up that hair I'll pull it out!"

A little appalled, and completely bewildered, David maneuvered his canoe as the riverman was doing, and the two craft came together so that Anne and Nancy kissed each other over the side, and so fondly that Peter Gagnon gave an audible sigh of misery.

"Love's labor lost," he quoted gloomily, "while here sit I, richly deserving, and receiving nothing!"

Anne filled her hand with Nancy's glowing tresses, and David shivered and almost cried out in his alarm. "But see how she has rewarded you, Peter!" she exclaimed, and tossed the tresses to the wind. "Nancy, dear, this is David Rock— my David Rock!"

Never in his life had David blushed as he found himself blushing now, and the more he blushed the bigger fool he knew himself to be, and because he felt himself a fool the blood came still hotter in his face. Nancy's eyes and lips were smiling at him, but not by the flicker of a silken eyelash did she let him know that she was conscious of his discomfort. But he could feel the daggers in Anne's blue eyes!

"I am proud—proud and happy to know Monsieur Rock!" she cried, and made him a little courtesy from the canoe. "I have been listening to most delightful stories about you, sir, and will be second only to Anne in welcoming you to Quebec when you come." Then, softly and almost pleadingly to Anne, "May I call him David, Anne?"

"Of course," answered Anne, but she leaned forward as she spoke, secretly untying a shoelace that it might be tied again, and so did not see the friendly smile of pleasure which Nancy shot at David.

The two canoes drifted apart, and now four others came around a bend in the river, and a chorus of joyous voices rose in greeting.

"The hypocrite!" breathed Anne. "I hate her!"

"Then why did you have her come?" blundered David.

"Because, until this minute, when she set you blushing so disgracefully, David Rock, I've always liked her!"

She turned and waved a handkerchief at the gay flotilla coming rapidly up the stream. Each canoe, decorated with flags and flowers and green balsams, bore three occupants, and quickly David counted ten in the party, including Peter Gagnon. One after another, he was introduced to them all, and now he held his heart so tightly that not a drop of blood escaped it to show up blazingly in his face, though never before this day had he looked upon so much beauty and lively youth together, or even dreamed there could be for him so many smiles from pretty lips and sparkling eyes. His fame had gone ahead of him with Peter, for the young gentlemen, politely groomed, and inspired by the contagious flutter and excitement of their lovely charges, shook his hand when they could reach it, and paid as much attention to him as to Anne.

From then until their landing below the manor-house David felt himself at home, for with the paddle there was none who could beat him up or down the two big rivers.

It was when they landed, and Bigot and De Pean and the smart young officers came down to meet them in their finest raiment, that David began to feel himself out of place. On foot, the young ladies and their escorts seemed vastly different to him—so exquisitely neat and trim, such courtly young beauties and such thoroughbred young blades, exchanging bows and courtesies with the Intendant and his party, lowering lashes, smiling, dimpling—then all off at once in gayest chatter, while he, stupidly, stood looking on, with Anne breathing tensely for him a step or two away.

Bigot, whose shrewd eyes quickly saw the confusion and misery of his protégé, came to his relief, and Anne could have thrown her arms around him for his gentle tact and gallantry, and the amazing words which he spoke.

Straight to David came the Intendant and laid a hand affectionately on his shoulder; the other he held out to Anne. "I claim this place of honor," he cried, "with Anne St. Denis on one side of me, and Lieutenant David Rock on my other—Lieutenant Rock, sweet ladies and young gentlemen, whom I have promised a place on the Governor's staff when he comes to us in Quebec!"

"A commission!" gasped Peter. "What luck!" He was squeezing the hand of Nancy Lotbinière, who had twisted her hair into a crown of golden coils.

"See how he takes it!" whispered Nancy, giving his fingers a pinch. "White as dust—and Anne is ready to cry in her joy."

"A commission," breathed Peter again, as if he could not yet believe his ears. "Commission—and a place on the Governor's staff!"

A little later Bigot had a moment alone with Anne. With tears shining in her eyes she thanked him.

"And now," he asked, half seriously, "do you love me a little for my 'goodness,' as you have promised?"

"I do," she whispered tremblingly. "Yes, I do!"

Then she saw a strange light in Bigot's eyes. "Anne," he spoke tensely, "it can do no harm to speak a thought that is pure and holy in one's heart, and all my life it will give me joy and make me stronger and better if you know the truth. I love David, and shall do these things for him, because I love you!"

And then he left her, so quickly that she could neither move nor answer, and for a space her heart stood as still as death.

A week of the liveliest gaiety, filled with music and dancing and song, followed the arrival of the party from Quebec. Even in the old days of Sieur Grondin and his lovely companions the four walls of the manor could never have contained so much color and beauty and fashion, for close after the flotilla of canoes had come larger craft bearing, in David's eyes, amazing loads of apparel, and great boxes of millinery and toilet things. In the afternoons one might have imagined that the beau monde of St. John Street had moved to St. Denis's May-pole green, and that up and down the smooth trails and paths promenaded the Vanity Fair of St. Louis and St. Paul, with all its breeding, decorum, and punctilio. Then came hours of sport and fun, with still different dress; and in the evenings the blazing halls were filled with such splendor that David felt his heart sinking lower and lower.

He came only once to the grand affairs by candle-light in the manor-house, in spite of Anne's pleading, but each day he mixed a little with her guests, in the green or on the trails, or in his canoe, and always wore his soft suit of new deerskin.

One evening, when he was buried in deep shadow near the old mill, he was startled by voices coming suddenly close to him. He recognized Peter Gagnon and Nancy Lotbinière, and a moment later the voice of Louise Charmette, and also that of her escort, the son of a rich merchant in Quebec. The four paused less than a dozen steps away from him, and before he could make up his mind to draw quietly away, or to disclose himself, Mademoiselle Charmette's sharp little tongue was saying:

"I wonder where Anne's young Indian is? He amuses me so greatly that I miss him. Did you observe him standing like a block of wood today, for a full half-minute with his foot on my dress, until I asked him to let me go? I could feel Anne blushing for him, for she saw his clumsy foot all the time, and was trying to get his eye."

"While I was passing tea," said the merchant's son. "I turned away so he wouldn't see me laughing."

"Very considerate of you, Philip," said Nancy's sweet voice, and there was a stinging note in it that cut the darkness like a knife.

"Very considerate!" snarled Peter Gagnon.

Louise laughed lightly. "Poor Anne!" she lamented, with mock tears in her voice. "What will she ever do in Quebec with this looby trailing at her heels? And what can be in Monsieur Bigot's mind when he tries to make a gentleman out of a rustic? A pretty mess I foresee——"

"If you please, Louise, will you keep this unkindness for someone who will appreciate it more than I?" asked Nancy Lotbinière, turning with Peter toward the château. "I am a friend of David Rock's. I like him, and it is not difficult for me to see how Anne can think of him as kindly as she does!"

"Bravo!" applauded Peter Gagnon.

From that hour, next to Anne and his mother, David loved Nancy Lotbinière.

At last the day came when the young Quebecers were starting home, in company with Bigot and his attendants. David had had his final hour alone with Anne, who was going with them, and no one would have guessed from the calmness of his face and the steadiness of his eyes how dead his heart had gone.

Nancy Lotbinière found an opportunity to have a word alone with him. Her eyes were mistily tender as they looked for a moment with silent understanding into his.

"You will be coming to us soon, David, and next to Anne I want you to think of me," she said. "Never shall I be more happy or more proud than when you call on me in Quebec. Please, do you believe me?"

For a moment it seemed to David that he could not speak, and then the words came. "I was in the shadow of the mill that night when Mademoiselle Charmette made fun of me, and I heard what you said to her. Yes, I believe you are my friend, and if chance should ever come that I may fight for you—why, I too shall be happy, mademoiselle."

"You mean—Nancy. That is what I prefer to have a few of my nearest and dearest friends call me. And no friend shall be truly mine who is not yours, David. That I swear."

"You are kind to me."

"And you will come to me when you reach Quebec?"

"You will be the first I shall want to see, after Anne."

Nancy's lashes drooped like shimmering veils over her lovely eyes.

"Good-by, David!"

"Good-by——"

"Say it, David. It almost came. Say 'Good-by, Nancy!'"

"Good-by, Nancy—and may God be good to you as well as to Anne!"

So, after a little, they went; and Anne was last, coming from her father's arms to David's, and twice she kissed him on the mouth before all who might be looking, and then, with a sob, went to the canoe that was waiting for her.

Half an hour later, from their sacred trysting-place on the top of Sunset Hill, David looked down on the Richelieu and saw them pass. Unseen, and with a heart that was breaking, he watched them until they were gone. And as they went they were singing!

[1] The biographies of the Ursuline nuns have enabled us to observe that the young convent girls of fifteen or sixteen, in the middle of the eighteenth century, were able to give proof of a maturity of judgment and a decision of character, which, at the present day, we hardly expect under twenty-five. The phenomenon may not be easy to explain, but it must be admitted.

CHAPTER XII

News traveled swiftly through the forests in the late autumn of this year of 1754. Couriers, white and Indian, sped over the wilderness trails and waterways, and at times it seemed as though the winds themselves carried rumors and wild stories of excited happenings, so quickly they came.

From Montreal the Black Hunter brought news which was added to that flying steadily down the Richelieu. It had been a splendid year for France along the far frontiers. Washington had surrendered at Fort Necessity, and Villiers was triumphant at Fort Duquesne. Not an English flag now waved beyond the Alleghanies, and Celeron de Bienville had completed his magnificent task of marking the boundaries of French possessions down through the heart of the United States of today, attaching metal plates bearing the arms of France to trees at certain intervals. French arms and Indian diplomacy were triumphant along the Ohio and westward to the plains. In the English colonies Dinwiddie was at his wit's ends, and the Quaker Assembly had refused to resist their enemies in the North and West. The policies of the British Royal Governors were alienating their Indian allies, and in spite of their million and a half population, as against sixty thousand in New France, Dinwiddie had frantically called upon England for help. In response England was sending General Braddock.

This was the news that thrilled David, as the day drew nearer for his departure for Quebec. He wrote Anne fully of happenings in the South, as he heard of them on the Richelieu, and ten days later a reply came from her, in which she pleaded with him to hurry his preparations and come to Quebec.

"These matters you have written me about are unimportant compared with the larger events which are bound to come in our history," she assured him, "and when those events arrive, David, you must be ready to take the splendid place which I am sure fate is preparing for you. Surely there cannot much longer be a reason for delaying your departure for Quebec."

All of her letter, which was of length and filled with everything that was tender and fine, he let his mother read. She believed that David would be pleased to know the Intendant had twice taken her for a drive on the St. Foye road, with the beautiful Mrs. de Lery and her husband, and that he signally honored her with his courteous attention whenever he had that opportunity. "And do not worry about happenings in the South," she told him. "It is common talk in the city that the King of France is planning to send an army to the Canadas, and at its head one of the greatest generals in the world. And when they come, my David, I want you in Quebec."

"Anne is right, lad," said the Black Hunter. "You should be going. You are leaving nothing neglected here. The Intendant has most surely set his eyes on you, and, if a French army comes, the further your advancement has gone the better position you will be in to seize opportunity and glory in its campaigns. I have decided to go to Quebec with you, and from there into the English colonies by the Chaudière."

David's eyes brightened at thought of the Black Hunter's company, then in an instant clouded with uncertainty and disappointment. "I had hoped you would be near my mother," he said.

The Black Hunter placed a hand tenderly on his shoulder. "She will be watched and guarded carefully, though I am not here, lad. No hour of day or night will she be alone, though you and I are many miles away. That I have prepared for."

"You mean—the four Delawares who have come to visit Kill-Buck will stay?"

The Black Hunter nodded. "Yes, until the end. Each man of them is sworn to me, and is as brave as a panther. Your mother knows, and I told the Seigneur this morning. He too will watch and care for her. So you need have no worry about your mother. The time has come for you to go."

"And you—you want me to go?"

"I think it is best," said Peter Joel softly, "even though my own heart, like your mother's, will be empty and lonely without you."

"You want me to go—why?" demanded David. "Why is it that you all urge me, when my heart and all my desires are here? I have no yearning for this glory you speak about, and even dread what the Intendant has promised me. I want only these forests—and to fight the English and their savages back when they dare to come our way!"

"Your tongue speaks only a part of what is in your heart, David, and the smallest part. More than anything else you want—Anne."

David slowly bowed his head. "That is true."

"And for Anne you must go to Quebec," continued the Black Hunter so gently that David could almost fancy it was his mother speaking to him. "You have guessed the truth, boy, for many times of late I have seen it in your eyes and heard it in your voice, though you have made a man's fight to hide it. Nothing in this world is sweeter or more glorious than a woman's love, and Anne loves you. But the city has claimed her, and her desire for it is as strong and as natural in her blood as your own love for all this beautiful forest world about you. Some day you will bring her back with you, and she will be glad and happy to come. I know that will happen, lad, just as surely as I know we are standing here now. But before that time you must fight—not for her love, but for the freedom and the glory of the wilderness against the splendor and the gaiety of the city. And you will win. When you have achieved those things which Anne has pictured for you, then—mark me, lad!—she will be glad to return to Grondin Manor. For just as surely as it is a habit for the sun to rise and set, so it is true that a woman wants the man she loves entirely to herself when the world and big events begin to drag him from her. I have spoken clearly, David. Am I right?"

"I have dreamed, and thought, and have sometimes been afraid, but never have I seen quite so clearly as I see now," answered David. "Yes, you are right."

"And you will fight, fight like a very man, with strength and honor, until you bring her home?"

"That I will do."

"And will not let the city beat you?"

"Never."

"And always, every hour, will keep inside you the cleanness which is a part of these forests of ours?"

"Yes, always."

"Then God will be with you, lad, and Anne will come back happy and true to Grondin Manor!"

The gray month of November, 1754, hung like an unhappy spirit of ill omen over the fair land of New France. Not once during that dread month, as written by Mother Mignon of the Nativity, did the sun shine with promise or cheer. It was a month of oppressive gloom and winds that seemed to hold the clammy chill of death; yet no snow came to brighten with its carpet of white the melancholy somberness of the earth.

Clouds filled the sky, and scudded low, and through the gray and dismal world beneath these clouds the wild geese sped southward, silent specters in the air, their voices hushed, no musical honkings floating down to cheer the coming of winter. Birds were gone. In the forests were ceaseless moanings of wind in the tree tops; and dawn came late, and darkness early, and the twilight of night never seemed entirely gone between the two.

The air was difficult to breathe. It filled men's souls with heavy doubt, women with a shuddering restlessness, and in the seigneurial churches masses were said, and prayers sent up, that the sun might shine again and calamity not descend upon the land.

Through this chill and gloom the canoe bearing David and the Black Hunter sped on its way down the Richelieu to the St. Lawrence and Quebec, passing beyond the limits of the country David knew, and into the powerful seigneurial world of New France which lay between the seigneury of St. Denis and Quebec.

More than a hundred parishes, ruled by a hundred lords of the manor, made up this impregnable bulwark against their enemies, and gave to the King of France the power and wealth of his empire in the New World.

With the depression of David's leave-taking there was a warmth of pride in his blood because he belonged to the warlike race of the Richelieu. Here it was that Talon, greatest of all the intendants, had followed the imperial colonization scheme of the Cæsars, when the Roman Empire was beginning to give way before the encroaching barbarians of the North, and had induced the Grand Monarque to give these lands, incessantly threatened by fire and sword and Indian massacre, to the bravest fighting men in New France.

One after another, David and Peter Joel passed the ancient baronial strongholds, in which generations of brave-hearted men and women had lived and died. Here, all along, was preparedness for war. A glacis here, a banquette there, palings and field-work and palisades, block-houses encircled by great ditches, and everywhere cottages and baronial halls and tall stone mills loopholed for guns.

And, with these, thriving farms stocked with cattle, planted with fruit trees, and yielding fine harvests of grain— acres so broad that at times the eye could not see the end of them, giving wealth and power and comfort, while behind the dark rims of the forests that hemmed them in lurked a never-ceasing danger.

"This narrow strip of Richelieu country is the land that has made brave men," said the Black Hunter. "For a hundred years they have stood in this path of danger. And you are one of them, David. Always remember that when in Quebec. I have never heard of a Richelieu man turning his back on death, or growing faint-hearted when there was a fight ahead."

The second day, paddling swiftly with the stream, they entered the St. Lawrence where it widens among the islands of Lac St. Peter.

Now, in spite of the sunless gloom which filled the world, a new emotion possessed David, stimulating him with a slowly growing mental excitement and an increasing eagerness to see what was ahead. Along the great river, up and down which the picturesque adventurers of two centuries had passed before him, the mighty forests which had made up his world from babyhood were falling farther and farther back, until in places it seemed to him there were no forests at all, but only vast open spaces which reached to the dark walls of the somber skies. And when they came to such great opens, the homes of the vassal-farmers of the seigneurial monarch who owned them were so close together along the river that he could easily have thrown a stone from one to another.

The third day they passed Nicolet and came to the splendid demesnes of the rich and powerful lords between Three Rivers and Quebec.

The fourth day was still heavier with gloom. A gray cloud seemed to have spread itself over the earth. Not once did a glow of the sun break through its armor of dusk. With this darkness the air was strangely quiet, so that sound traveled great distances and one could not judge its direction.

Late in the afternoon the Black Hunter ran the canoe ashore beyond Sillery Wood. Not until they had landed did he tell David that he had planned to accompany him no farther—that he had a good reason, which was a private matter, why he should not continue with him to the city.

An hour later, alone, bearing his possessions in a ranger's pack on his shoulders, and armed with his long rifle, David caught his first glimpse of the great city on the rock.

Following the trail worn smooth by lord and vassal, black-robed priest and savage warrior, he continued close to the river under the frowning cliffs where a few years later Wolfe was to stab at the heart of France, and came, all at once, to the curving shore beyond which lay the city. And on this day, with its forbidding gloom and melancholy chill, there was little of the glory of Quebec to greet him. The beauty of Cape Diamond, the loveliness of the panorama in the glow of sunshine, the fairy-like glisten of cupolas and minarets, the welcome of church spires, the silvery St. Charles, and the purple haze of distant mountains—all were lost in a sinister, frowning mass of rock that had no form or shape, hiding its colossal head in the murk of the heavens, monstrous and repellent, more like the ugly fastness of fiends and demons than the home of those he had come to seek.

Never had David felt such a creeping at his heart as while he stood for many minutes and gazed at the ramparted heights which Anne and his mother and the Black Hunter had described to him as the most beautiful city in the world. Of its detail he could see nothing, except that it was alive. For suddenly there came through the chilling dusk the sullen booming of a gun—a sunset gun where there was no sun.

Then, before he had moved, there followed that ominous sound a distant pealing of golden-voiced bells so sweet that in an instant they seemed to lift the weight of darkness from the earth. The music came to his ears like nothing he had ever heard before, falling from the distorted ugliness of the rock and its city in a sublime melody. It trembled in the air over him, about him, and beyond him, until the whole world seemed filled with its sweetness, as if not one voice, but many, were joining in the chorus. Her bells—welcoming him in this grisly darkness of coming night! Anne's voice speaking to him, calling to him, telling him that she was waiting for him in the heart of that pile of gloom! The bells of the convent, of the cathedral, of the Jesuits and the Recollets—all hers, she had said, because she loved them so!

He bowed his head until the last whispering sounds of them had died away. Then he went on. Night came so quickly that the city became nothing more than a great shadow against the sky. There were no lights which he could see. A bitter wind rose off the river and with it a biting sleet of hard snow. They brought him no discomfort. He was warm inside. His eyes were straining through the darkness, and he forgot everything but Anne and her city.

He could almost fancy a voice in his ears, coming from the mighty rock ahead, whispering to him, "I am the soul of the nation. I rule from the eastern ocean over four thousand miles of wilderness to Mobile and New Orleans, from the Alleghanies westward to the farthest waterways of the Mississippi. I have won a continent, and hold it by right of man and God. My enemies are as countless as the leaves of the trees, my friends are sixty thousand. Yet I triumph. When I fall, New France dies."

A miracle of change swept through him. Aspects which had chilled him as grim and forbidding became now the glories of strength and resolution. The monster had transformed itself. In him rose a kind of adulation where there had been fear and dread and the dark thoughts of prejudice and suspicion.

Lighted windows began to break the cheerlessness of the night, and he found himself suddenly in the edge of Lower Town. It was the hour of early evening when few people were abroad, and as he wandered through Sous le Fort Street, Dog Lane, and the Sault-au-Matelot their desertion made him think of forest trails, so narrow he could almost span them with his outstretched arms. Behind curtained windows he could see a glow of warmth and light. Through thick stone walls sound came to him faintly, laughter, children's play, a song, and out of the mystery of the gloom ahead of him a watchman's voice crying the hour of the night and a warning to evil-doers.

"Six o'clock, and all well! The city is at peace—and law reigns in the name of the King and the people!"

He trembled at the note of majesty in the lonely cry. It came again, nearer, and the watchman met him on his patrol, and held his lantern in his face.

"Ho, brother!" he hailed. "A long rifle and a tight pack. Freshly in from fort or post?"

"From the Richelieu," replied David.

"Then God be with you, for you are a man," exclaimed the guardian of the night, and went his way.

David's heart was singing. A man passed him, walking swiftly, with a burden in his arms. He heard a clank of metal, and two soldiers brushed his sleeve. Then he came to a window from which a child had drawn the curtain, and paused for a moment to gaze upon the scene which met his eyes within. A dark-haired woman was rocking a baby in her arms. Beyond her was a table on which supper was waiting. The little girl at the window, he thought, was listening for the footsteps of the father, and she pressed her pretty face closer to the glass as he passed.

A larger light greeted his eyes ahead, like the glow of a fire. With it came roistering voices filled with good-humor and cheer, a burst of merriment from so many throats that he hastened his steps and came out suddenly into the little square in front of the church of Notre Dame des Victoires. Here a crowd had gathered, and on three sides were great lamps burning huge candles, and on a mound of earth and stones a fire of pitchwood was burning. A sickly glare illumined the space, and in this glare he saw a platform raised even with the heads of the people standing about it, and on this platform were a man and a woman, facing each other on their knees, with their heads thrust through the pillory-blocks. The woman was a sharp-nosed hag, and she was cursing her tormentors shrilly. And the man was cursing the woman!

David's heart stopped for a beat or two. "What is the meaning of it?" he asked of a round-faced, jolly-looking youth who was roaring with laughter.

"A family quarrel!" answered the other. "Old Dame Guerin stole a silver spoon, and her husband sold it for her.

There they are, both of them—and there they'll be, each blaming and swearing at the other, until the watchman cries ten o'clock tonight. And they're lucky, I tell you, for the spoon was stolen from a private house, and the law might have hanged them for it!"

On the farther side, close under a big lamp, David saw a group that was apart from the crowd—three officers laughing and enjoying the sport, and with them three young ladies richly dressed, holding silken masks before their faces. He drew near them, fascinated by their likeness to the friends who had visited Anne; and one of the three men, a haughty and supercilious-looking fellow with a face of saturnine darkness, caught him staring.

"Now, who the devil are you, and what do you want?" he snapped in ugly humor.

Caught thus uncomfortably in his gaze, David replied, "I am looking for the Convent of the Ursulines, and will thank you for telling me the way."

The man turned his back on him. "Fresh from the gutters of the woods, and he knows no better," he apologized to his feminine companions. "If the stench of his blood would not annoy you I would prick him for staring at you so."

The females tittered.

David made a step forward, his blood boiling. A hand caught his arm, a friendly hand, but firm and strong.

"Hold, friend," spoke a voice softly. "I will show you the way to the Ursulines." And before he could remonstrate the hand had drawn him into the edge of the crowd. "If your blood is rottener than Captain Jean Talon's then I'll say it's pretty poor," continued the same voice. "I know, because I'm from Montreal, where he has sucked the fount of wickedness dry. He has killed six men, and wouldn't hesitate to kill another, friend—just to amuse his pretty companions, who have come down with him from the Upper Town to view this spectacle, which many find so amusing. My name is Pierre Colbert, and I respect the Long Rifles from the borders."

"Thank you," said David. "I am David Rock, from the seigneury of St. Denis, on the Richelieu."

"A fighting man," said Pierre Colbert, and again David's heart beat faster in its pride. "I am a buyer of fur and a trader with the Indians in the Upper City. Come with me. It is a dark and devious way, though short, from this little square to Mountain Hill, up which we must climb to reach the Ursulines."

For some reason he took his cap from his head as they passed under the last of the big lamps, and David was ashamed of the startled exclamation that fell from his lips. Beginning just over the man's ears was a scar that completely encircled his head, and above this scar was no sign of hair, and the skull itself seemed almost naked.

In spite of this disfigurement, Pierre Colbert's well-fed face, with its twinkling blue eyes and ruddy color, was one that commanded both respect and a friendly comradeship, as he said to David, "A sign of the times, ami! The Senecas got me a dozen or so years ago, and lifted my hair, but they couldn't kill a man as good as I. I came to life, and here I am, with no resentment at all against them, for they've saved me a lot of combing and brushing. I carried a long rifle myself in those days, and always go out of my way to welcome one when it comes to Quebec. Ah, here is where we turn up the hill! Never been to the city before, I take it?"

"Never," replied David.

"And it is—pardon me, lad!—a little unusual for you to ask for the Ursulines, and especially at this hour of the night. It isn't a place where they welcome men, you know."

David's face flushed in the darkness. Then he said honestly, "I only wanted to look at it. Mademoiselle St. Denis, whom I am to marry, is going to school there."

"Oh!" said Pierre Colbert, and David could hear him beginning to puff as they climbed the hill. But he managed to ask, "Do you know any people—here?"

"Yes. Intendant Bigot, and the Marquis de Vaudreuil, and Hugues de Pean, and Peter Gagnon, and—and Mademoiselle Nancy Lotbinière."

"The devil!" said Pierre Colbert.

He was winded at the top. David could see nothing, except the yellow glow of street lamps on their high posts, and in every direction he turned his eyes it appeared to him he was looking either up a hill or down. They came to a turn, which seemed half of a winding circle, and suddenly, still farther up and straight ahead, he saw the lights of a building many times larger than the Château St. Denis, like yellow stars in the night.

"The home of your friends, monsieur," said Pierre Colbert with a jerk of his thumb and the slightest suspicion of cynicism in his voice. "There they are, feasting before business—and play. This is Monday, and the Superior Council is meeting tonight. Those are the lights of the state residence of the viceroys of Canada, the Governor's Palace, and at this minute Duquesne is sitting at table, with the Bishop on his right and the Intendant on his left, and the Councilors in the order of their appointment, all with swords but the man of God. Have you a mind to call on them, Friend David?"

"The Castle of St. Louis!" breathed David, unmindful of the doubt and incredulity growing stronger in the other's tones. "No, I won't trouble them tonight!"

Pierre Colbert drew in a deep gasp at his companion's ingenuous simplicity. "God fend me," he cried, "but you've the coolness of any ten Richelieu men I ever knew! Come. The Ursulines is over here and down there a step, a twisting two minutes of walk—and I have a supper waiting for me down in the Rue des Pauvres, in the shadow of the statue of St. John the Baptist. I'd invite you to it, but what would a friend of royal governors and intendants and kings' favorites do in my humble abode?"

"He'd be very happy," smiled David, beginning to catch the other's good-humored misgiving as to his veracity.

"Then you'll come?"

"If I may, and you will humor for a little while such a liar as I seem to be."

"I'm beginning to love you!" averred Pierre Colbert. "I'll swear you have tales to tell, young as you are, that will beat any of mine! And here we are, so look your fill of whatever you can see—a bunch of gloomy shadows, shuttered windows, a few lights burning dismally, the home of the holy Ursulines, and of your sweetheart, oh, my Lord!"

David found a sudden little lump in his throat. "The boarding-school, monsieur?" he asked. "Can we see it?"

"Yes, where the lights are, of course, and they'll be out before the watchman makes another turn. Ho, wait a moment! Who comes there, right out of the pit of the convent gloom—with two attendants bearing lanterns? And a carriage in the dark on our right f Let us draw nearer. See! Skirts, and the gleam of a sword. A pretty voice too. A special dispensation of the Mistress-General, God fend me—or a lark on the quiet, or maybe an elopement! What!"

The whispering voice of Pierre Colbert grew husky. David gave a stifled cry. A lantern had been raised, and they saw the faces of the two who were entering the carriage.

"Monsieur Bigot, Intendant of New France, as I love my life!" gasped Pierre Colbert. "And with him——"

"Mademoiselle Anne St. Denis," said David, as the carriage drove away. His voice was calm, but his heart was like a weight of cold clay. "Monsieur, you have been kind. I ask one other favor of you, and will repay it some day if I can. It may be, after all, that I shall go to the Castle of St. Louis tonight, or to the palace of the Intendant. But first, if you will, I beg of you to show me the way to the home of Nancy Lotbinière!"

CHAPTER XIII

Pierre Colbert made no answer as he conducted David through darkness, up an inclined street for a few moments, then sharply to the right on St. Louis Street, with the many lights of the Governor's Palace at their backs.

There he stopped, and began counting on his fingers.

"I will go no farther," he said, when he had finished, "It is the tenth house, on your left. Don't make a mistake and go to the sixteenth, for that is the home of Madame Angélique de Pean, wife of the man you know, and chère amie of the Intendant. She too was a pupil of the Ursuline nuns. The Town Major is evidently at home!" With this remark he gave a jolly laugh, and pinched David's arm. "When you are done, and you still desire warmth and a bed and a full belly, inquire of anyone for Pierre Colbert's place, near the statue of St. John the Baptist. And if you don't come, but should need a most ordinary friend tomorrow, or the next day, remember that I was scalped by the Senecas and have a soft spot in my heart for the Long Rifles. Good night, friend!"

"Good night, Pierre Colbert!" said David.

He listened to the other's hurried footsteps down the cobblestoned street, and not until they were gone did he move. Then he faced the Governor's Palace, and came out very soon into what he knew was a large square, though it was so dark he could see nothing but the glow of the big lamps about it.

A sharp wind beat in his face here, so cold and penetrating that he believed he must be on the very summit of the rock mountain which he had seen earlier in the evening from the depths of the river. He turned right once more, on the edge of the square, and came up suddenly against an obstruction, and a cry half of horror escaped his lips.

A vast and terrible pit had opened under him, and the object his hand gripped in amazement and fear was the cold iron of a railing. Hundreds of feet below him he could see little pools of yellow light, where the lamps were burning, seemingly miles away; and the square of Notre Dame des Victoires lay almost under him, lit up out of sheer blackness by its burning pile of pitchwood, with a crowd about the pillories, like pigmy ghosts. He heard a screech, as old Dame Guerin shrieked her anathema, and a burst of merriment rose up faintly to him from those who were teasing her.

The cold, the wind, the sleety snow, the bottomless pit with its ghostly lights and impish torture, the emptiness of the night, its loneliness and strangeness, added to the deathlike chill that had entered his heart when he saw Anne leaving the convent with Bigot. Where had she gone with the Intendant? How did it happen that she was leaving the convent at night, when she had so often told him that such things were proscribed by the holy nuns? A special dispensation! Just what had Pierre Colbert meant?

He turned at the sound of wheels grinding in the street. The swift resentment that had entered into him when he heard Anne laugh, and saw Bigot help her into the carriage, urged him to approach the vehicle when it stopped. There too was a lantern, swung low in the hand of the driver. Two men got out. He could hear the rattle of their swords. But there was no woman.

He stopped again, gripping his rifle, and listened to the challenge of a soldier at the palace gate. He followed boldly until the guard barred his way.

"Easy, garçon! Why so fast? And what is the meaning of that long gun you carry, almost at the door of the Governor's residence?"

"I am just in from the Richelieu, and am looking for Intendant Bigot. Has he come?"

"It may be. I am not here to tell you. Move away, if you please!"

"But if he is here, and Mademoiselle Anne St. Denis is with him——"

The guard interrupted him. "If Monsieur Bigot has the company of Mademoiselle Anybody he has better judgment in the matter of pleasure than to bring her to the castle when the Superior Council is in session. So that is why he has failed to come to the meeting tonight, garçon? Well, good luck to him! Now, move on. Thirty seconds by the ticking of a watch is the limit for a suspicious character at this gate."

David had no desire to argue, or defend himself from suspicion and insult. His heart was sick. His blood ran hotly. He wandered through darkness, and heard the Upper Town watchmen calling the seventh hour. He passed the convent again, and saw the lights were out, as Pierre Colbert had predicted. His lips tightened grimly. In his heart was a growing determination, born in the moment when he had asked Pierre Colbert to help him find the home of Nancy Lotbinière.

A few minutes later he was back on St. Louis Street. He began counting the houses on his left, and stopped before the tenth.

It was a tall, stately-looking edifice, set back from the street, with steps leading up to it. A hammered iron lamp burned over the door, illumining a half of the front. Curtains were drawn at the windows, but light glowed through them. He heard voices and his heart suddenly leaped with hope. They were youthful, laughing voices like Anne's, and Nancy's and Louise Charmette's—and a man's was among them. It was possible that Bigot had brought Anne here!

He walked up the street steps into the glow of the lamp. In the same moment the door opened, and through it came three young ladies followed by as many men, dressed for the ill weather of the night. The door had closed behind them before they saw David. He was strangely white in the dull lamp glow and he stood as stiffly as the wooden Indian which Louise Charmette had once called him. For he saw that Anne was not of the company—and more. The three men he recognized as those he had encountered in the pillory square, and Nancy Lotbinière, when she saw him, had her hand in the arm of Captain Jean Talon!

In an instant she had given a little cry. It was not a cry of surprise or shock, but of joy and greeting—a cry that ran through him like the warmth of a fire; and in that instant she left Jean Talon's side and ran to him, her eyes shining, her lovely face greeting him as he had dreamed of the greeting in Anne's. She caught his cold, wet hand in both her own small, gloved ones, and held it closely to her as the others stared in their amazement—with the exception of Captain Jean Talon, whose dark face went darker still as he recognized the one he had insulted in the light of the pitchwood fire in Lower Town.

"David!" she cried. "David Rock! It is you—after my dream of last night, and all my thoughts of you through this gloomy day! Oh, I am glad you have come—glad you have kept your promise to me! To think that a minute more I would have been away—away when you came——" She turned suddenly to her friends. "This is David Rock," she said to them. "Lieutenant David Rock, whom I have told you so much about." One after another she introduced them, but not a name of the five did David store away clearly in his mind, except that of Captain Jean Talon.

It was Talon who said, with a sneer on his lips which only David saw, "Lieutenant Rock, you say. Of what company, sir?"

"That is a little secret between us—just now," Nancy Lotbinière answered for David. "And you, Captain, must surely excuse me tonight, as you see. Lieutenant Rock is my guest, and I am excited to hear the news he brings from my dear friends on the Richelieu. David, I am going to take you in instantly, and warm you, and feed you, and make you as happily comfortable as I can."

Captain Talon cursed under his breath.

David smiled squarely at him. "I am afraid you are making Captain Talon unhappy, Nancy," he ventured, and spoke her name with a grim satisfaction as he saw the thunder in his enemy's eyes.

"Captain Talon must nurse his unhappiness," she said with pretty finality. Then, turning her joyous eyes on him again, "Your hand is cold as ice, David, and you are wet and tired. Forgive me for keeping you here as long as I have when I should run with you to a fire as quickly as I can." And before he knew it she was leading him to the door, speaking her final apologies to her friends at the same time. The door opened—and he saw scowling hate in Talon's face; it closed, and he found himself in a paradise.

The heavy door opened into a wide hall, and this into two rooms in which huge fires were burning. A wealth and luxurious comfort such as he had only dreamed of burst on David. Without letting him pause, Nancy drew him into one of these rooms. It was almost as large as the hall at Grondin Manor. A red glow, like a sunset, filled it with soft light, coming from silken-shaded candelabra. A thick log burned in the fireplace; under his feet were soft rugs; on the walls hung great paintings whose human figures seemed breathing with life as he entered. Nancy Lotbinière, with sweet tact, was bustling about him, giving him a few moments in which to accustom himself to the delights of an environment so new to him. She called for someone, as her own gloved fingers busied themselves at the thongs of his pack. Two negro servants entered. They had his gun, his pack, his outer coat and cap almost before he had got a free breath, it seemed to him; and all the time Nancy was talking to him, and giving them instructions, and last of all piled her own hat and coat and gloves in the servants' arms, and then stood in front of David, with both his hands again in her own.

Never, even in that unforgetable sunset in the bottomland when he had caught Anne St. Denis in his arms, had he looked on a vision of sweeter loveliness. Nancy's head was a gleam of golden curls, and her eyes were alight with such starry brightness that his heart beat faster from the sheer thrill and pleasure of looking into them.

"David, I am so glad you have come that if it wasn't for Anne I would surely kiss you! And, it may be—unless you forbid me—I will!" And then, before he could either think or blush, she stood suddenly on her tiptoes, and held up to him a mouth so round and soft and sweet that David kissed it, and would not have refused if death had been its penalty.

"Oh, I promised myself I would do that, David Rock!" she cried, drawing away from him with a face that was gently suffused with color. "I had to, all on account of my dream last night—though I have given my mouth like that to only one other man in this world. Are you disappointed in me, or shocked, or distressed?"

"I would not give it back if I could," said David, and he was thinking of Anne and Bigot.

It surprised him to find how calmly he was looking into the beautiful eyes of Nancy Lotbinière. He spoke quietly and very steadily, and Nancy saw in his face something which had escaped her before. Her own eyes grew a bit troubled.

"David, you have something to tell me. Let us draw up here in these two big chairs before the fire, while the supper I have ordered is being prepared. And please begin at the beginning, with your dear mother, and the Seigneur, and the Black Hunter, and queer old Fontbleu, the miller—and don't hide away from me what I see in the back of your mind. You are unhappy, in spite of the kiss I have given you."

"Why did you kiss me?" he asked suddenly.

"Because I like you so very much, David."

She was gazing steadily into the fire, with her chin in the palm of her hand, so that he could see nothing of her face.

"And not because you were—sorry for me? Because I am a rustic looby, as Mademoiselle Charmette rightly said?"

"You are the manliest man I know, David—except one," answered Nancy Lotbinière softly. "That other is Peter Joel, the Black Hunter."

"You know—him?" cried David, half starting from his chair.

"I loved your mother. I think she loved me a little. I think she saw deeper into my heart than anyone has ever seen. That is mostly why I kissed you, David. You seem very near, because of your mother. She crept into my heart, and has kept her place there, and always will. She told me the story of the Black Hunter, and I love him because of what he has done, and because of what he is."

For a yearning instant, in his wild gratitude, he wanted to press his face to the golden head so near him. "It is different with Anne," he said. "She fears him, distrusts him, hates him."

"She should love him, for your sake," said Nancy. "Those fourteen days and nights, with you in his arms——" She stopped herself with a little shiver, and looked up at him

196

suddenly to catch his wide eyes filled with the flaming light of the fire as he looked at her. "But you are not telling me the news, David," she smiled. "Please begin, and do not miss anything, right up to my very door!"

His heart as well as his body was warming. It was not difficult to talk to Nancy. In a few minutes, unrestrained by the presence of others, she seemed to have made herself a friend whom he had known for a long time. If she had achieved a reputation as a coquette, her friendliness and sincerity blinded him to the fault. If her beauty had laid her open to the jealous gossip of rival tongues, he disbelieved their talk. That her hand had rested in the arm of Captain Jean Talon did not prejudice him, and her kiss, warm on his lips, left no suspicion of thought or intention. He felt as if, with her, he had reached a haven of refuge, a place where not only the chill and the discomfort of the night were wiped away, but where the ache in his heart grew less, and hope and courage revived.

He did not speak of his coming, or of Anne, at first, but went back—as Nancy had asked him—to Grondin Manor. Her eyes and face marvelously reflected his own emotions. Her sympathy and understanding inspired him with a happiness which made the shock and disappointment of a little while before seem trivial and unimportant. She gave him confidence and courage, and raised up again the faith that had stumbled when he discovered Anne leaving the convent in Bigot's company. Once she interrupted him to get a letter which his mother had written to her, and read a part of it to him. Marie Rock had said, "Something tells me that you, who know Quebec so well, will watch and guard my boy for me, and see that no evil befalls him. You are so much older than Anne, who will be under the careful guardianship of the nuns, and you can be a blessing to David if you will. May dear God reward you for it."

"So you see, David, you belong a little to me," said Nancy. "I am like Anne. I haven't had a mother since I can remember. But I am going to mother you—along with Peter Gagnon."

Then David told of his meeting with Pierre Colbert, and of what they saw together in the lantern-light at the convent.

"Where could Anne have gone with Monsieur Bigot?" he asked. "I think, now, that I was a fool for not calling to them."

"Yet I can understand why you didn't," said Nancy slowly, looking into the fire. "It was unusual, the hour—and Bigot. I don't like Bigot, David. I confess that, in spite of the fact that Peter laughs at me for it, and always repeats the wonderful things which the Intendant has promised to do for you, I distrust him. But Anne had a purpose in going with him, and most surely a good one, which you will undoubtedly learn about tomorrow. Of that you may be quite sure."

A long time she was looking into the fire, keeping from David what was in her face. Then, with sudden brightness, she smiled at him.

"David, I have waited all this time—keeping a secret from you. I am going to shock you. I no longer have any of Anne's confidences. We have quarreled!"

In his amazement David stared.

"And mostly about Bigot—and you," continued Nancy. "I despise and distrust Bigot. Anne likes him and has a faith in him so deep that it shocks me. I know what he is; she believes he is the soul of New France. I stated my opinions to her, she resented them; I advised her to take you back to Grondin Manor, she told me I was jealous; I assured her it was my solicitude for her happiness that made me speak, she said I had set my cap for you that very day I let my hair down in the canoe; I told her I hadn't seriously thought of you in that way, but maybe I would now—and she went into a fury. That's all, David. It is a beautiful quarrel. When we meet we are so sweetly lovely that it is worth much to see us together. Such lavender-scented and rose-tinted barbs we let fly at each other! Yet, the odd part of it is this, David: deadly enemies though we are, I love Anne more than ever, and I am just as sure that she loves me. Isn't it a pretty complication, when I have promised to be a mother to you, and am determined to have my way about it?"

What David might have answered was interrupted by the sharp rattle of the metal knocker at the door. Nancy rose from her chair, as if expecting someone. A moment later a servant opened the door, received something, and entered the room with it. Nancy took a small square envelope from her hand.

"For you, David," she said in surprise. "This is interesting! Will you pardon me while you are reading it? I will see if our supper is ready."

She was gone before he could answer. With clumsy fingers, excited and fearing, he opened the envelope.

Then, with a heart that seemed to rise up inch by inch within him, he read the lines enclosed.

Monsieur David Rock, (it began.) I am writing these few hurried lines informing you of the pleasure it affords me to know you are spending your evening in Quebec with my very dear friend, Mademoiselle Nancy Lotbinière. If you should care to call upon me at a time when I have no other engagement I will endeavor to let you know more fully my changed opinion of you because of the amazing spectacle I beheld when I happened to be driving past M. Lotbinière's house with Monsieur Bigot. When the kissing performance is repeated, which I have no doubt is most frequent, please accept the advice of a friend, and do not stand between a curtained window and a strong light.

And the letter was stiffly signed, Mademoiselle Anne St. Denis.

Weakly David dropped back into a chair. The fire itself was a blur, the walls were a blur, he could see nothing for a moment or two—but clearly, very clearly and sweetly, he could hear Nancy singing.

And then the iron knocker at the door was rattling again.

CHAPTER XIV

What happened during the following two or three minutes was hazy and indistinct to David. It was as if someone had struck him a numbing blow without hurting him physically. The shock of the letter—its alarming evidence that Anne had seen him kiss Nancy Lotbinière, the swift certainty of what that discovery meant, the cataclysmic sinfulness and unfaithfulness of the act itself, all swept upon him with an effect that temporarily left him palsied and scarcely sensible of his environment.

He had sunk into a chair facing the door, and was conscious of the negro servant opening it, and of Nancy coming into the hall, her singing suddenly at an end. For a few moments everything seemed a kind of pantomime to him. He was not surprised when he saw it was Peter Gagnon who had rattled the knocker, nor did Peter's very evident excitement and haste stir him greatly. Because he sat so lifelessly, without movement or sound, clutching Anne's heart-breaking letter in his hand, Peter did not see him.

Nancy had stretched out both hands in the same glad greeting she had given David, a radiant smile on her lips, when Peter's appearance made her pause.

Peter had been running. He was breathing heavily. His coat was buttoned askew, he was cravatless, and his eyes were flaming with a desperation which went well with his general appearance of dishabille.

He glared at Nancy. "Where is David?" he demanded.

David rose from his chair as Nancy indicated his presence. In a moment Peter was at his side, his eyes still glaring. He saw the crumpled letter in David's hand, and with a grin that had nothing of friendliness in it, but was almost diabolical, held out another page of paper identical with that which David had received from Anne. "Read that!"

There were only three lines, addressed to Peter himself. David read:

Dear Peter. I am dying. Come quickly to Angela Rochemontier's. Anne St. Denis.

The paper fell from David's nerveless fingers. Anne— dying. His very blood turned cold. Peter was picking up the message. He snatched the other paper from David's hand, and thrust them both into Nancy's. She read first the letter to David, and then the message to Peter. And to David's horror she gave a merry little laugh.

"What is she dying of, Peter?" she asked.

"Heart-break—crying!" exclaimed Peter furiously. "When I got there she sent me off post-haste to overtake the messenger and not let David receive that letter. She was sorry the instant it was gone. She is a game little thing, that's what she is! And you——"

"I am sorry, Peter," apologized Nancy sweetly. "She should not have been looking in at my window. Besides, how does she know it was David?"

"She saw him when you were out there with Talon and the others."

"Oh!" There was the slightest inflection in Nancy's voice. "And then, of course, Bigot stopped, or drove past again, to see what might happen?"

"I don't know. She didn't keep me long enough to tell me. She wants David. Where is his cap and coat?"

"But he has not had his supper, Peter, and I want him to meet my father, who will be here in half an hour I know. A little crying will do Anne good. It is delightful for the eyes!"

She was smiling adorably at Peter, whose throat seemed to be swelling as she looked at him. Then she turned to David, and her two warm hands pressed his cold fingers. "You are anxious to hurry to Anne, David?"

"Yes, I must go."

"And you do not feel unkindly toward me?" In her eyes was a gentle light which Peter could not see.

"You have been an angel. I am only sorry——"

Nancy's eyes grew even softer as he hesitated. She seemed to have forgotten Peter. "You will not be—some day, David," she said. "You will not be sorry I kissed you, nor will you be sorry that Anne saw us through the window. In a little while you will confess that to me yourself. You will be glad. And meanwhile I want you to have a great faith in me, for I told you the truth when I said I had never kissed another man like that—except one." The last two words she spoke very clearly, as if she intended them for Peter's ears more than for David's. "I would not take it back if I could, David. Not even now!"

Then she turned to Peter. "Dear Peter——" And in spite of the glare in his eyes and the fury which he was fighting to make coldly dignified she raised suddenly on her tiptoes, just as she had done for David, and kissed him quickly, and then was tripping up the big oaken stair. The last they heard of her was a note of song coming trillingly and sweetly down to them as a wide-eyed, breathless servant gave David his belongings.

"Good Lord!" gasped Peter as they went out into the night. Beyond that explosion he uttered no other word on their way to Angela Rochemontier's home.

In front of the lighted house, he said, "Angela will send a servant with you to my lodgings when you are ready." With that he was off, leaving David without a farewell, just as he had met him at Nancy's without a friendly greeting.

Angela herself was watching for him. Her nun-like face was pale and filled with deep concern when she opened the door in place of the servant. David's pallor was ghostlike.

Angela's gentle voice, a soft whisper from the convent itself, was reassuring even though it trembled with a break of emotion.

"I am glad you have come," she said. "I don't know what is troubling Anne, but it must be something terrible. Thank God, it is early, and my family are dining down in Buade Street, or there would be questions asked. She is in my room and refuses to budge an inch. You may see her there. It will be all right."

Angela Rochemontier was a slight, tall, fair-haired girl whose angelic tranquillity of countenance already gave full promise of the devoted and beautiful years to follow, when she was known as Sister St. Genevieve of the Infant Jesus; and as David followed her graceful figure up the stair he felt about him an indefinable atmosphere of serenity and faith that gave courage to a heart almost bursting in its dread and misgiving. At the top of the stair Angela nodded toward a closed door, and with a word of direction and encouragement to David descended to the lower part of the house again.

For a few moments David stood without moving. What had been alarm and misgiving pressed on him now in a grimmer kind of terror. The intense stillness within the house added to it. He could hear no one moving, no sign of life. His own heart thumped audibly. He could almost hear the blood trickling through his veins as he stared blindly at the closed door. The door grew slowly into a thing of horror for him. It barred him from Anne, just as his own faithless act had barred him from all future happiness. He was not thinking of forgiveness, or the possibility of it, but of Anne, outraged, betrayed, hating him now—and of himself, shameful, unworthy, meriting the punishment that was ahead of him.

His skin seemed touched by fire, prickling with a feverish, moistureless heat. He moved silently to the door, and stood for another moment hopeless and afraid.

His hand rose mechanically and tapped at the oaken panel. He tapped again. Three times. A fourth before an answer came, and then he heard only a smothered sobbing sound.

He opened the door gently, pressed it back an inch or two at a time, until his head and shoulders were in the room. It was lighted by two tall candles. There was a bed just ahead of him, with a snowy white coverlet and silken canopy, and a golden crucifix at the side of it where Angela knelt when she prayed.

Then he saw a great, scarlet-covered chair of royal velvet, a fauteuil so capacious that it could have held both Angela and Anne between its wide, curved arms. Crumpled in a heap on the floor in front of it, with her head buried in it, was Anne. She was sobbing. Her slim little body was quivering, so that David, in his anguish, almost let out a moan. Her long hair had fallen from its coils and pins and lay disheveled about her. Out of its confusion, as David entered, came a small, pathetic voice.

"Has he come, Angela?"

David tried to speak, but his throat was without vocal power. His breath, the first since he had opened the door, was a gasp. Anne heard the sound. She raised her head, and for a brief moment, an eternity to David, seemed to be staring at the red back of the chair.

"Angela!"

"It isn't Angela," said David humbly. "It is—me."

In an instant, it seemed to him, she was on her feet—a beautiful little fury beside the huge red chair! Grief, if her sobbing had been that, had not left its story of tears in her eyes. They were dry—dry and magnificently dark and flaming. Their blue was gone. Fire of a thousand diamonds was in them.

"You!" she demanded. "You—in here! In Angela's bedroom! How dare you, David Rock?"

"Angela sent me," mumbled David, his brain reeling.

"I don't believe you," cried Anne, her small hands tightening until they were little fists. "Angela wouldn't desecrate this room—with you!"

A courage finally born of abject despair came over David. "I am sorry, Anne," he said. "Sorry it happened. Sorry I ever came to Quebec. I am sorry I saw you and Bigot and Nancy, and sorry I have brought you this grief——"

"Grief?" interrupted Anne, flinging back her hair with a sudden fierce little movement. "David Rock, do you think that you could break my heart? That you could even hurt it, now that I know what you are? I am not hurt, monsieur. Oh, no, I am not hurt—that way!"

She came a step nearer. "It is the humiliation," she blazed at him. "The humiliation of knowing that Nancy Lotbinière has done what she said she would do, though she made me think it was a pretty joke at the time. I am glad—glad—glad she has done that, for she has proved how cheap you are in spite of the way I have tried to think of you. But the humiliation! It drives me mad! What will Bigot say? What will everybody say? Oh, I hate her! I hate that red hair of hers, which caught you first! I hate everything about her! And you—you—I hate you too, and I never want to see you again——"

And then an amazing thing happened, even as David's world was crumbling into ruin under his feet. Anne was flying at him. Blindly he waited for destruction, expecting it and hoping for it, and a cry that voiced his own grief broke from his lips. But the hands that came to him were not striking. Arms went around his neck. A head was pillowed on his breast. And the arms tightened as Anne burst into sobbing—like one whose heart was really broken.

"David, David, forgive me," his amazed ears heard. "Oh, I don't hate you, I don't, I don't! I love you! And it is my heart, and I don't care what people think or say or do—as long as I have you! But—David—dear—if you care for Nancy Lotbinière———"

Power of speech in the fulness of a tide undreamed of came from David. What he said he did not know. No word or sentence could he have remembered afterward. With his face pressed to Anne's, his arms crushing her close, his soul raised suddenly out of the blackness of despair to the heights of Paradise, he unburdened himself in a way that brought both the blue and the happiness back into the eyes hidden against him. He kissed her, and was half sobbing with her, and tried to explain—telling her of his thoughts when he saw her with Bigot, and of the spark of bitterness that it had inflamed in him until he had unhesitatingly kissed Nancy Lotbinière. And there, at that point, Anne kissed him, and kept her mouth so closely to his own that, when Angela came up to the door and knocked, there was silence in the room.

In that silence the announcement of her soft voice was almost a shock. Monsieur Rochemontier and his wife would be returning any minute now. Under the circumstances it was quite advisable for David to go.

Anne clung to him. "And you promise—you swear on your very honor—that you will never kiss that shameless witch again, and never have a thought for her that should be mine?" she whispered, at the last.

"Yes, I promise."

He looked back at her from the bottom of the stair, but he saw only the bright cloud of her hair as she went into Angela's room again. In her gentle and saintly way Angela said good night to him, and gave him into the care of the servant who was to conduct him to the lodgings of Peter Gagnon.

These were in Sainte Ursule Street, not far away. But before he had gone half the distance, with the storm thrusting at him from behind, and the servant showing the way with a lantern ahead, it suddenly occurred to him that not a word had Anne said which might explain the mystery of her night affair with Bigot. The thought forced itself unpleasantly upon him. That her plans, and Bigot's, whatever they may have been, were interrupted by the unexpected discovery of himself in the light of the Lotbinière house was a suspicion which came easily, in spite of the relief with which he had left Anne a few moments before.

In his own penitence and self-reproach he had forgotten Bigot. He had forgotten the leaden agony that had entered his heart when he saw Anne get into the Intendant's carriage and drive away. He had forgotten Pierre Colbert's words, and the look in Nancy Lotbinière's face when he had told her about it. And Anne had let him forget. He had come to her in supplication and penance. She had explained nothing.

He almost stumbled over the servant, who had stopped before a door very close to the street. He could see that the building to which this door belonged was of grouted stone, like the cottages on the seigneury. Its windows were closely shuttered. One's shoulders might have touched them in passing.

A rattle of the knocker brought a servant from within, who took David's things, conducted him the length of a gloomy hall, and through another door into a large, lighted room. The servant drew back quickly and closed the door behind him.

Instantly David would have known it for Peter's apartment even if Peter had not been there. The wall he faced in entering held an arsenal of small arms, and the big room was filled with the careless luxuriousness which was a characteristic of his friend. But Peter was present. And the moment David's eyes fell upon him his heart missed a beat, then pounded a little faster to make up for it.

Peter was pacing back and forth with a long dueling pistol in his hand, and the smile with which he greeted David held in it more of snarling menace than of friendly pleasure. His hair, still wet from the storm, was rumpled about his head, and his round pink face bore signs of a wrath which he had been nursing with some violence. He was an alarming contrast to the plump, jolly, lovable Peter of the Richelieu; and suddenly David believed everything he had ever heard of Peter's bloodthirsty prowess with the small arms hanging against the wall.

He held out his hand, in token of their old friendship, but Peter scowled over it into his face.

"So, so, so," he said, putting a drawling sting into his taunting voice. "Nancy's lover, eh? Fast work you made of it on the Richelieu, didn't you? And we all as blind as pine-bats while it was going on! Well, what have you to say? I can't call you out and shoot you, because of your mother. But I should, for Anne's sake."

There was no uncertainty about the passion brewing inside Peter's breast. Eyes usually placid and kind scintillated with a pale, steely flame in his face, his voice was tremblingly hard, and his hand was white and tense with the fervor with which he gripped the dueling pistol.

Dropping his extended hand slowly, David stared at his friend. "Peter!" he gasped. "It is a mistake. I have not——"

"A mistake!" Peter interrupted him, his voice rising. "A mistake!" With a furious movement he flung his pistol the length of the room. "I must get rid of it, or I will let go at you with powder and ball! A mistake—kissing Nancy Lotbinière like that! A mistake—base disloyalty to Anne and villainous treachery to me! And she has only kissed one other man as she kissed you, Monsieur Rock? I heard her say that. A couple of lovers—and you the last! Stealing up there like a thief, and discovered only by chance——"

"Peter!" David's face had gone white. With a swift movement he caught the other's shoulders. "Peter, you lie!"

He flung him back a step or two, and folded his arms, like an Indian. "You lie!"

Peter, his mouth half open, stared at David. His lips closed and his eyes narrowed until they were glittering points. "I have shot three men for less than that," he said coldly.

"Shoot me if you want to," replied David. "But I still say it. You lie!"

It was a new David standing before Peter. With a few years added, and a white streak in his hair, he might have been the Black Hunter.

"I kissed Nancy," he said. "I kissed her because she seemed to be the only friend I had in this place which I am beginning to hate. I went to the convent first, in the darkness and storm. A man named Pierre Colbert took me there. We saw Anne come out and drive away with Bigot, laughing with him, so happy that something happened inside me. I asked Monsieur Colbert to show me Lotbinière's house then. After a time I went there, and though Nancy was about to leave with friends she took me in, and was so kind to me that—it happened. That is all. Next to my mother and Anne there is one other woman I will fight for, because she has been good to me, because twice she has stood for me against others. She is Nancy Lotbinière. If there are angels in Quebec, as you have so often told me, she is one of them. She is as good as Angela Rochemontier, with all of her saintliness. I will not turn against her, not even for Anne. And I won't hear you insult her. If you think she is bad——"

"Bad!" roared Peter. "Who said she was bad? Do you infer that I said it, David Rock?"

"You were hinting strongly——"

"I hinted nothing. Why——" Peter ran a distressed hand through his tousled hair. "Insult her!" he cried, beginning to walk back and forth again. "I would die first. And I will kill the man who speaks a word crosswise about her. She is an angel."

"I have been trying to tell you that, Peter," said David, bewildered.

"She is lovelier than a dozen Annes, and twice as intelligent," declared Peter wiping his heated face with a handkerchief as he walked. "But—she kissed you! Now why the devil did she do that?"

"I think she pitied me," said David.

Peter halted, and his face was calmer as he looked at David. "That is it, pity," he said grimly. "She pitied me too, didn't she? Kissed me, and then ran upstairs—kissed me for the first time in her life, and so quickly that I could not tell whether it was a feather or her lips that touched mine. Kissed me because she felt sorry for me, by heaven! But it was not the way she kissed you, if Anne tells half the truth. Maybe I am excited. I have a right to be. I guess it is not so much what she did to you that has stirred me up, but what

215

she said afterward. That 'other man' she has kissed! Where is he? Who is he? What is his name?"

"I thought it was you—after what happened."

"Me?" Peter laughed despairingly. Then suddenly he held out his hand. "David, I have shown poor greeting to a friend. It is a little late, but forgive me. I am simply mad over Nancy. I shall die without her. I have been kneeling at her feet for two years, and never once has she let me touch her lips. Then—to kiss you, of her own free will and accord, giving freely after a few weeks what I have yearned for vainly for ten times that long—why, it has upset me, and I have henceforth but one great thing to live for. I am going to hunt down that other man she spoke about, take him out with pistols, and kill him."

His fingers were closing about David's. Suddenly his eyes lighted with inspiration. "Could it be Captain Talon?" he demanded. "He is rated the best shot in New France, and it would afford me pleasure to send a ball through him."

"Impossible!" exclaimed David, relieved at the sudden change Peter's temper had taken. "I would sooner believe she would give such favor to a viper."

Peter gave him a searching look. "Yet she was with him tonight."

"And so was Anne with Intendant Bigot."

"But she has explained to you——"

"No. She has explained nothing. And the more I think about it the less I like it."

The two lovers looked at each other in silence. In that stillness, each measuring the unrest in the other's eyes, a bond of sympathy wove itself between them.

"David, I am sorry I acted like a fool toward you. But you need have no worry about Anne. I am willing to swear there was good reason for her going with Bigot."

"And with equal assurance I am willing to swear Nancy Lotbinière had good reason for going with Talon, and, also, for kissing me," replied David, a note of scornful skepticism in his voice which the other could not fail to catch.

"Damn!" said Peter, and clenched his hands. In a moment he asked, "What happened when you saw Anne?"

David told him briefly and added at the end, "Of course, you know that Nancy and Anne have quarreled?"

"Know it?" fumed Peter. "I have been the butt between the two for the last month. They have worn my nerves to rags. One hates Bigot and fears for you—the other trusts him next to the Good Mother herself, and believes implicitly in his promises. One pulls him down lower than the gutters, the other exalts him to the heavens. One believes him to be the curse of New France, the other regards him as a great patriot who will lead the country to glory. Why shouldn't they quarrel, when there is also the matter of jealousy between them—which I don't like, on Nancy's part?"

David put a hand on Peter's arm. "And which of the two is right?" he asked quietly.

Peter hesitated, then said, "Both."

"You mean——"

"The Intendant never breaks a promise like that he has given to you and Anne. For some reason he has taken a great liking to you. In time he will put you in the way of both fortune and glory. Of that I am sure, and you would be a fool to neglect the opportunity. Anne has a right to that much of her faith. But in the other matters Nancy is nearer the truth. Bigot and his ring have the heart of New France under their feet down in the Intendant's Palace. Bigot is so clever that a half of the people are for him, and only a half against him. I told you once he was the wickedest man in Quebec. My opinion is unchanged. He belongs in the gutters morally. Nancy knows it. I know it. Anne does not. She refuses to believe what she calls the 'shameful gossip of jealous people.' But that fact has nothing to do with your future. You can rest happily, while I—knowing that Nancy has given her preference to another man——"

"You are sure of that?"

"As sure as I am that Anne has never let Bigot take something of yours from her lips."

The words, bearing Peter's faith, were like a dagger-stroke at David's heart.

Peter went on. "When Nancy told you that she had kissed only one other man like that, she was not speaking the words for you, but for me. I could feel it. And then she mocked me by touching her lips to mine in that insulting fashion, and running away. And all on account of——"

"What?"

"My uselessness," groaned Peter. "For two years she has been telling me that I am of less account than the gulls that fly over the rock—that I am shiftless and lazy, and have grown fat because of those things; that I think only of luxury and myself; that if all men were soft and short-winded and ambitionless, as I am, the English would come up and sweep us away with brooms. Yes, she has been telling me all those pretty things, but it was not so bad until she saw you. Since then she has sometimes grown furious at my ease and comfort, and everlastingly dangles you before my eyes as an example of what a man ought to be. And then she kisses you—and brazenly says there is one other man besides—and—and—by heaven! I'm going to make her repent it all!"

Peter's face was flushing with a wild thought.

"I am!" he cried, his voice ringing. "From this night the old Peter Gagnon is dead! With God's help I'm going to do something more than shoot with a pistol. Damn Bigot! Damn his whole tribe! But I am with them until death if they will give me action and get rid of this fat. I will go on the

219

Indian trail with you, David. I will fight. I will swim. I will run. I will have a commission, or bring about a revolution. I will show Nancy Lotbinière. As a beginning I am going to hunt down that lover she boasts of, and shoot him out of the way!"

In his excitement he flourished his arms, and picked up the dueling pistol from the floor, gesticulating dangerously with it as he faced David again.

"You have been right all along," he went on. "Why didn't I go to Fort William Henry and the South Country with you and the Black Hunter? Why have I not been working for something, instead of playing? Strike me dead if I live this way any longer! From this hour I am on the war-path for fame, glory, achievement—and vengeance on Nancy Lotbinière! Will you help me, David?"

Peter was not acting. His face was ablaze. In these few astonishing moments his almost feminine softness had disappeared. He was not the immaculate, duel-loving, gentlemanly dandy of the fashionable walks and drives. His jaw was set. His eyes burned with a fire which David had never seen in them. His hands, gripping David's, had lost their gentleness. The spirit of dead generations of fighting Gagnons had risen in him, hardening his body, tightening his muscles, transfiguring him until David scarcely knew that it was Peter who stood before him.

In his own joy David forgot Bigot and Anne and Nancy. A sense of having won something tremendous overwhelmed him. This was what he had dreamed since their boyhood— that Peter, his beloved Peter, would some day stand shoulder to shoulder with him in the ways of the wilderness, that they would adventure together, fight together, feel the magnificent thrill of life together.

More closely their hands gripped. A smile came into Peter's face, a triumphant exultation into David's. For half a minute they stood looking at each other, without speaking. A thousand things passed between them in those moments.

Peter drew a deep breath. "God rest the soul of Granddaddy Peter Gagnon," he said then. "At least one drop of his blood is left in me. I can feel it stirring."

David had a swift vision. "And also may God bless— Nancy Lotbinière," he said.

They had not heard the opening or closing of the outside door. Now there came a knock at their room. Peter answered it. A voice drew him into the hall, and the door closed behind him. He was gone for several minutes.

When he returned he bowed low before David, a whimsical glitter in his eyes.

"You are still supperless, Monsieur Adventurer," he said, "and the night continues to call you. At the door, waiting for you, are a voiture, and a man. The carriage is that of the Intendant of New France, the man is Monsieur Bigot himself. He has personally called to take you to the palace, and requests your immediate company. This is an honor beyond my power of comprehension, and my humble bed must not detain you."

Under his breath, Peter added, "Good Lord, what can it all mean!"

CHAPTER XV

François Bigot, thirteenth and last Intendant of New France, royal cosset of fortune and petted favorite of La Pompadour, had never been more justified in believing that the gods of luck were with him than during this gloomy day and night of November thirtieth, 1754.

Several things had happened to mark the ascendency of his power. Endowed by the proclamation of the King with the enormous authority of absolute superintendence over the departments of Justice, Police, Finance, and Marine in America, he had still been, until this thirtieth of November, officially inferior by one degree to the Governor General of the Colonies. But today, in the affairs of the Sovereign Council, had come the change which marked the supremacy of his despotic rule, and heralded the first page in the tragic and pitiable story of a doomed New France.

On this day the King of France lost a continent, and the greatest battle ever won by England was trivial and unimportant compared with its aftermath.

Bigot had scored a mighty triumph, a triumph that was destined completely to change the history of the western world. He had torn the Governor General, the Marquis Duquesne de Menneville, down from a pedestal that had reared itself above the Intendancy for generations. There was no longer a doubt in the minds of those admitted to the inner secrets of the affairs of state. In January the Marquis de Vaudreuil-Cavagnal would be Governor of New France, placed there by Bigot, made subservient to him, and, as a few of the elect well knew, his tool and associate in the colossal crime of plundering a nation.

Bigot, cleverer than Satan, conscienceless as a serpent. Vaudreuil, puffed up with self-glory, a thumb-twiddling, egotistical fool.[1]

So it was that saner minds regarded them, then and during later years—minds like those of Montcalm, De Longueuil, De Bougainville, La Corne, De Beaujeu, Taché, De Léry, De St. Ours and others of the Honnêtes Gens, the great souls of New France, over whose honor and strength Bigot and his plots ran at last like a destructive Juggernaut.

Hereafter the destinies of New France would be guided, not from the Castle of St. Louis, but from the splendor and wassailing luxuriousness of the palace of the Intendant.

But this was not all that the day had held for Bigot. A glutton for wealth and power, he was ruled by a still more absorbing passion—his love for women. And for the first time in his life one woman had made him forgetful of all others, and his desire for her burned more fiercely than the fires roused by his political triumph. The night, as if to add to the completeness of the day, had brought Anne St. Denis so nearly into his possession that even his triumph over Duquesne and the Honnêtes Gens seemed trivial.

So he was thinking as he waited for David. Sheltered from the unpleasantness of the storm by the leathern sides of the carriage, he was smiling in the darkness. A glow almost beneficent warmed his body. Good nature and amiability stirred his soul. For the gods were with him. He could almost believe that God was with him. Otherwise how could it be that he and Anne, through miraculous accident, should be brought to look upon David in his moment of faithlessness?

He hummed a little tune to himself as he waited, a king waiting for a victim, and visioned pleasantly what that act of faithlessness had meant for him. It would not be difficult to make Anne believe, after that, when the right hour came.

The hour!

He could feel his arms closing about her, feel her soft body crushing against him, feel her yielding to him—in these moments of his passionate sureness. What did the Intendancy of New France mean, what did anything mean—after that? Catherine of Louisburg, beautiful Angélique de Pean, the glorious Charlotte—all were forgotten in his exotic and inextinguishable dreams of Anne.

He could feel Anne beside him again, in that moment of her horror, when they had seen David. He could feel her trembling body when he had dared, for an instant, to put a comforting arm about her. He had not gone too far. Link by link he was welding the chain. Anne was growing nearer to him. The Fates were with him. All it wanted now was—the hour.

But he must be patient. His possession of Anne must be total and complete, even more absolute than his possessorship of Charlotte or of Catherine of Louisburg had been. This thought seemed to be humming itself with the tune on his lips as Peter Gagnon's door opened and David came out into the night.

He sprang from his vehicle and embraced David in the yellow light of a servant's lantern. It was as if his dearest friend had come after a long absence, someone he had missed and whose unexpected presence gave him immeasurable pleasure. In spite of what had happened he made David feel that. The lantern lighted up a face smiling and friendly. This Bigot, this man without guile, this lord-paramount over five million square miles of a continent, this anointed seigneur facing storm and darkness to welcome a friend could not be suspected!

"To think of you arriving in Quebec alone, on a night like this!" he exclaimed. "I would have sent an escort to meet you on the river trail if I had guessed your coming. And such an adventure at the very beginning! Our poor little Anne was shocked out of her pretty senses, but I have no doubt you will make it up with her tomorrow. Always look to the shutters, David, when anything like that is going on. You are out of the woods now." And Bigot chuckled good-humoredly.

There was no inflection in his voice which David could resent, no suspicion of anything but jovial fellowship. He did not make David uncomfortable in the way he said the thing.

"I must explain," he went on. "I had an appointment with the Bishop tonight, and wanted Anne to meet him, so that you might first receive his favor through her. That funny little devil we call fate took us past Mademoiselle Lotbinière's as you were standing out there with the others. I thought for a time that our little lady had turned into a chunk of ice. She insisted on going back, when she was herself again, and we returned just in time to catch you kissing Nancy. Oh, it was fine—if I had not envied you so much! Glorious Nancy—a rival of Anne herself in beauty and sweetness! You are a fortunate lover. But the shutters! Why were you so forgetful?" He laughed softly again, as if what had happened was a pretty bit of humor, and not a tragedy.

"I did not intend to go to Nancy's," began David, his heart beating with happiness at Bigot's explanation of Anne's presence with him. "I——"

"Yes, yes, I understand. Of course you did not intend it to happen. But the effect was the same—and Anne insisted that I take her immediately to Mademoiselle Rochemontier's, where I have no doubt you will find her in the morning."

"I have already seen her," said David. "She sent for me."

"The devil!" said Bigot. "And did she forgive you, or tear you into pieces?"

"I told her how it happened, and believe that she understands."

Then Bigot seemed to forget the incident. He asked about Marie Rock and affairs at home, as they went down the slippery mud and cobblestones of Palais Street. He did not say how he had discovered David at Peter's lodging, nor did the question occur to David.

They descended a long slope into a second lower town, near the river St. Charles, and David saw the frowning shadow of the impregnable wall which inclosed the main city as they passed under the gloomy arch of the old Palais Gate. A sentry flashed a lantern and challenged them as they drove through into that part of the ancient town known as St. Roch's.

Then, it seemed to David, they came into a little town of great, dark buildings, all by itself, twenty if he could have counted them, three of which stood out massive and vast above all the others. This was the stronghold, outside the fortress walls, of the Intendants of New France.

In a few moments the storm had abated. The sky was clearer. Bigot thrust back the leathern curtains, and with that note of pride and boastfulness in his voice which only at rare intervals disclosed itself, he said, "It is from here that the King governs New France, David!"

There was something sinister and a little awesome in the heavy gloom weighted with its huge, unlighted shadows. Bigot named two, first the Royal Storehouse of the Crown, already well on its way to infamy, and after that, the prison.

A minute later they turned out of a pit of darkness and were facing the palace.

Its vastness was marked by lighted windows. Built of grouted blue-slate rock, two stories in height, nearly three hundred feet in length and seventy-five in depth, it was the greatest abode of French power and sovereignty outside of the King's palace at Versailles.

The entrance, with its two flights of steps and great inset door, was illuminated by half a dozen lamps, and in their illumination two armed guards in the Intendant's uniform were pacing back and forth.

Bigot said nothing now. He alighted from the carriage, and David followed him. They entered through the door. Instantly the thick walls gave sounds of life. It crept into the great entrance chamber, murmured through the long, gloomily lighted halls. Here was nothing of the splendor and magnificence which David had dreamed as a part of the establishment of the Intendant of New France. There was something dungeonlike and chilling about it all. Under his feet, unknown to him, were the real dungeons—a score of huge arched vaults and grouted caverns, with guarded doors and corridors, secret, mysterious, hiding their deadly menace to French rule in America, opening their locked and bolted chambers only to ships that came and went stealthily in the darkness of night—and separated from David now by three feet of solid rock and mortar.[2]

The oppressive spirit of these dungeons seemed to breathe into the upper corridors. It made the air heavy and oppressive, in spite of the ghostlike murmur of life that stirred it. The lights were few. Their illumination was ghastly. One entering the place at night, filled with hope, might quickly feel the restlessness of fear. The walls were dark and grim. The doors were like closed prison mouths, black, bolted, barred with iron.

Then David knew that it was from behind some of these doors came the murmur of life.

Bigot, slyly, looked at him and saw the effect of the almost malevolent environment. He smiled gently. This too was triumph. In his own heart he never tired of gloating over the sinister success of his scheme to make these public halls and offices of the palace grimly forbidding, terrifying to those who might come with courage and resolution in their souls, hinting of pitilessness, inexorable power, of the executioner even.

Facing these solid rock walls, in dusk, or at night, the resolution of his enemies, or of those who came to petition and plead, turned to water. Even the Honnêtes Gens, gentlemen of honor who occasionally came there, shivered under their breaths.

For the Bishop, the Church, the members of Bigot's council, his friends—there was another and more carefully guarded way of entrance.

For his women, a still more secret one.

They passed a guard, a huge, dark, thick-lipped giant who might have been a devil of the Inquisition. A second came out of the gloom, so tall and thin and cadaverous that he looked like a specter.

Bigot's cleverness was not cleverness alone. It was art.

"The halls of justice," he said, and his voice was repressed and low, as if doomed ears might hear him if he spoke louder. "Tomorrow, if you wish, you may see an execution. A traitor is about to die."

David shivered. So new and strange was the environment that his face could not hide its effect. Punishment! How the thought of it had burned itself into his soul since that night, weeks ago, when he had been led, condemned and bound, before Anne and her father! A hundred lashes on his naked back! If he lived until the world was gray those words could never be wiped out of his memory. Punishment, physical, slavish, brutal, as a soulless man might punish a dog—not the stinging pain of it, not the burning agony of lash or rope, but the soul-searing, man-destroying defilement and degradation of it! Better death by inches than that—death at the Iroquois fire stake, death by bullet or knife, starvation, anything!

The somber walls pressed the thought deeper in him. Threat of punishment, monstrous and shameful, had preceded Bigot's friendship; the pillories with their cursing victims had greeted him in his first hour in Quebec, and now here—smothered between stone walls—Bigot had told him that tomorrow a man would die!

If the day had been one of amazing fortune in his life, this hour, the last of all, filled Bigot with a culminating satisfaction, as his clever brain sensed the gathering emotion behind the pale, tense mask of David's face. He saw his plans developing more swiftly than he had dreamed. He was measuring David, grasping quickly his opportunities. The psychology of the hour, its dramatic and providential timeliness, rose uppermost in his mind. Battre le fer quand il est chaud. And he would do it. Strike the iron while it was hot! Carbanac, who was to be whipped through the streets at the tail of an ox-cart on the tenth of December, should be whipped tomorrow. And the pillories should be filled!

The first of December should see justice rampant in both the Lower and the Upper Town. And David, unenlightened, unknowing, would be reading the handwriting on the wall.

His hand pressed David's arm. They entered a narrower, darker corridor. There was no sound now, except that of their feet. They passed through doors, three of them. Then another corridor, like a dungeon passage. Up a grouted stairway after that—so narrow their sleeves brushed its sides—and at the top of the stair through a door, then a second, which Bigot unlocked with a key, and suddenly into the hidden and softly lighted magnificence of the palace.

The suddenness of the change caught David's breath. From gloom, chill, depression they had emerged into a great chamber, richly carpeted, luxuriously furnished, warm with the fire of burning logs, its walls hung with tapestries and paintings. Open doors leading from this salon revealed other chambers, smaller, but lighted, luring. One was filled with a red glow, another with pale gold, a third with amber light. So the last of the intendants, prince of wassailers, scourge of women, kept them always at night, ever ready for the fair company who too frequently graced his private quarters.

Now there was sound different from that which David had heard below. It came to them faintly, as if through thick walls, but it was of cheer and jollity. In it was a song and laughter. Bigot smiled genially as he took off his coat and gave it to a black servant, who had come softly out of nowhere, it seemed to David. Then he helped David.

"Home at last," he said, with a comfortable shrug at the sound of hail beating on the metal roof brought from France. "A devilish night, but fairly pleasant here, David, though we lack the sweet welcome of a Nancy and an Anne. Here you shall be my guest until tomorrow, if in that small way I can make up for the unpleasantness of the first hour of your arrival. Besides, this is an opportune time for you to meet some of those men who will be your stanchest friends, if you are not too tired after your day's journey, or too much upset over your little adventure in St. Louis Street."

"I am neither," replied David, the warmth and glow of his surroundings pressing upon him pleasantly.

He felt himself rather oddly at ease. There was something in him, which he was unconscious of, that did not prostrate itself before greatness and splendor. He was not embarrassed or awed, as Bigot might have expected. Certain of his senses had been shocked below, but here he felt himself a man, along with Bigot. The Black Hunter would have shown the same unaffected ease. Bigot noted it, and was pleased. He liked courageous men. Their fall was greater, their demolishment more complete when it came.

He picked up a little glove from a table, and played with it as he smiled at David. It was a woman's glove.

"I shall introduce you tonight and henceforth as Lieutenant Rock," he said. "Did our little lady speak to you about the commission?"

"No," said David.

"Of course," nodded Bigot. "Too much upset to remember it, you rascal! But she has it, properly signed and vouched for, all scented in the fragrance of rose and myrrh, I'll swear—a surprise bouquet for you."

David bowed his gratitude. Even then, atremble inside, his blood running faster, he received Bigot's words calmly.

"You will make a splendid officer," complimented the Intendant. "Tomorrow you will begin military training. It will be quite private, and not difficult. I have appointed Captain René Robineau your instructor. Officially, you have been commissioned because of extraordinary services we expect to receive from you, pertaining to the wilderness and the frontiers. I personally have great need for you and do not wish to delay your military education longer than is necessary. First, the tailor, then a view of the city, and after that two hours a day with Captain Robineau, who is the crack disciplinarian of the garrison. Does it sound agreeable to you?"

"I am anxious to begin," declared David.

Bigot tossed the glove upon the table, crumpled into a round ball. He seemed to reflect for a moment, and a louder echo of laughter coming from beyond his luxurious chambers decided him.

"Yes, it is a good time," he mused. "Meet them at play, David—the men who help me to rule the four great departments of New France. Cards and a little wine. They must have their relaxation, l'esprit de corps, you know, and out there is what we call our lieu de réunion, a rendezvous of good cheer and sociability where matters of state may be discussed informally, and the gossip of the hour passed around with wine. Much that is priceless in value and importance comes to our ears through such consociation. Men who achieve great things are men who must have their merrymaking, as you will quickly discover in Quebec."

Through two open doors which, if closed, would have shut out all sound, he preceded David, and then at right angles down a carpeted hall to a third, of massive oak, bolted inside.

Before he spoke again he had ushered David into the gambling and drinking quarters of that remarkable group of men, not yet at the height of their success in 1754, whose frauds were so extraordinary in every way, and were later perpetrated with such consummate effrontery and skill that they will always take rank among the very best specimens of historic crime.

In this hell-hole of knavery, as David entered, was assembled most of that infamous political power which Bigot had gathered about him—a band of plunderers on a colossal scale, men bent on the betrayal of both King and country in the pursuit of their own selfish desires, and who, only ten days before, had deliberately drawn their plans to create universal destitution throughout New France in order that their chief might requisition help from overseas, and thus add, through a long campaign of well-planned and audacious robbery, to fortunes that had already grown huge.

These were the men, not Wolfe, who slew Montcalm on the Plains of Abraham. These were the men, carried by the very momentum of their crimes beyond the bounds they had reckoned, who bled New France of its courage and manhood and strength, and replaced prosperity with a horrible plague of poverty and starvation, until the English victors were welcomed as saviors.

These men, with Bigot at their head, had already gone far toward changing the map of the world when David came into their midst through the oaken door.

Yet New France itself did not dream of their perfidy. Even in Quebec the Honnêtes Gens were in such minority that their voices were lost. It was the Intendant and his associates who gave the magnificent balls, the gay soirées, the royal entertainments that had made a second Versailles of the city on the rock. Fashion, wealth, power were drawn by the lure of princely splendor like moths to a candle. Bigot was not only the protégé of La Pompadour. The King himself, blind and cheated, was his friend. Bigot was France.

In this second salon which David entered were a dozen men. It was larger than the first, but about it was no hint of the extreme luxuriousness which characterized Bigot's private quarters. There were a number of tables in it, lounging-chairs, several couches, carpets, and pictures. The whole, if one looked closely, bore unusual evidences of its usage. There were stains on the floor. Tables and chairs were marred, a couch was broken. An overhead candelabra was partly loosened from the wall.

These signs of questionable carelessness David did not notice. It was an age of brilliant uniforms, bright costumes, wigs of flowing locks as well as of natural hair. Soldiers and officers of state ruled the streets. Officers clanked their swords at dance and card games, and while priests came and went in raiment of somber black, ecclesiastics of higher rank wore robes of princely richness. Women, with curls shining in their own brightness, or coiffures powdered white, wore drooping hats and sweeping plumes and costumes of picturesque grace and beauty. Environment, no matter how crude, was softened with an exquisite charm by the color and grace, the wit and liveliness of conversation which had come to the new world from Fontainebleu and Versailles.

This atmosphere, this color and picturesqueness, filled the gambling salon of Intendant Bigot, and blinded David's eyes to the other and smaller things which he might have observed. There was no woman present. But the vivid flashings of uniforms, the gleam of swords, the clink of glasses and scabbards, the cavalier-like wigs and ribboned perukes, the laughter and conversation, filled his eyes and ears with a colorful and pleasing effect. Political plunderers and brigands though they were, conscienceless and pitiless in their methods, regarding women as playthings and legitimate prey, these men were still gentlemen according to the social law—gentlemen whose wit and courtliness of manner were aped by younger generations on the ballroom floor, and whose sense of "honor," paradoxical as it may seem, was easily touched and as quick to show resentment.

"The flower of New France" was the quixotical name by which Bigot called his band. And here, this evening, were its chief lieutenants—Cadet, Mercier, Varin and Breard, and after them, Vergor and Kanon, and Rigaud, the brother and understudy of the Marquis de Vaudreuil. And, finally, at the far end of the room, as if they had just entered it, Vaudreuil himself, De Pean, and a third person in a military uniform, Captain René Robineau.

Bigot's eyes lighted up with pleasurable satisfaction when he observed this last group. His messengers had done quick work. He had scarcely expected them to answer his summons so soon.

De Pean saw them, and ahead of his companions came quickly across the room, his countenance livening with pleasurable greeting, as if sight of David was an inspiring surprise. He had David's two hands, pressing them warmly, and was expressing both amazement and joy at his friend's unexpected presence, when Vaudreuil and Captain Robineau came up. Vaudreuil, with a freshly curled, glossy wig of unusual beauty, seemed equally sincere, if less enthusiastic, in his welcome.

It was Robineau whose attitude was a puzzling one. He smiled, but the smile was forced. His eyes, for a single instant, seemed to be reading into David's heart. He was of slight build, considerably under middle age, and in his pale and emotionless face was the settled look of a person who had become the victim of a permanent unhappiness. Not until the following day did David learn that Robineau was the last of an illustrious line of gentlemen and fighting men, noted through many generations for both their courage and their honor.

"This is luck," cried De Pean. "If it had not been for Monsieur Vaudreuil's new wig we surely would not have been here. He was mad to show it off, and this is the liveliest place we know of on a dull and stormy Monday night."

Vaudreuil placidly twiddled his thumbs, and then turned slowly in the light to better display the lustrous gloss of the curls that fell luxuriantly about his shoulders.

"English hair, David," he explained proudly. "What a glory it must have been on the woman who wore it! The Ottawas sent it in, with a dozen other scalps, as a present to their White Father over the sea. But I needed it more than Louis, and got it, thank God, by winning three out of five at cards with my worshipful friend Bigot. Do you like it, lad? Did you ever see a more glorious color?"

"Good Lord, to think of wearing a woman's scalp!" exclaimed De Pean, as if horrified. "Lieutenant Rock, what do you think of the vanity of a man who will do it? The woman, yes; but her hair, torn from her head by a savage's knife——"

"Or a white man's," countered Vaudreuil softly. "There are now many hair-hunters of your own sweet color, Monsieur Town Major, just as there are many gentlemen in this city who are wearing ladies' scalps, as you have so playfully called them. Is it not so, Robineau?"

"Quite true," agreed Robineau, in a dry, hard voice that seemed far away. His own hair was scant, and tightly queued.

David's lips were as dry as Robineau's voice. "The taking of women's and children's scalps is a horrible practice," he said, "and will continue as long as our governors and those of the English pay money for human hair. I have seen the scalps of Frenchwomen, Monsieur Vaudreuil, at Fort William

Henry—one of them as beautiful as that you wear. I don't like to think of it gracing an Englishman's head!"

Bigot chuckled delightedly. "A righteous rebuke, Lieutenant," he commended. "And especially timely because of the streak of abominable luck which made me lose this treasure which Vaudreuil prizes so highly."

After this, one after another, David met the men in the room—Deschenaux, the Intendant's secretary, clever planner and confidant of his master's liaisons; Cadet, the Commissary General, whose share in the plundering of New France amounted to more than twenty million francs, and who, years later, partly paid for his dishonesty and treachery in the Bastille; Imbert, Treasurer-General, and Breard, the Naval Comptroller, twin souls of that combination of treason and corruption which was dreary and cruel in its squeezing of taxes out of the people, elaborate in its swindling of the soldiers and the government, wicked beyond words in its profits made out of food withheld from the starving masses, and complete in its crippling of Montcalm's military efforts.

These, and the others, David met as polished gentlemen, who welcomed him as a brother officer, with no reservation on account of the wilderness garb he wore; and before he was half through with their declarations of pleasure and friendship he knew that Anne had written him even less than the truth, and that Bigot had truly prepared the way for him by dressing him with an importance which, in his own heart, he was certain that he did not possess.

He would never have dreamed that Brassard Deschenaux, so suave and gentle and exquisitely correct, was born the son of a poor cobbler, nor that Cadet was the son of a butcher, and in his youth had minded the cattle of a Charlesburg peasant.

It was Cadet, who would soon have a nine-year contract for furnishing supplies at ruinous prices to the hundred and twenty French forts and posts between Gaspé and the Ohio, who appealed to David most. Cadet, the arch-swindler of all time, whose ill-gained fortune even exceeded that of his master, Bigot, was, quite strangely, a prime favorite with the populace of the town as well as the province. So pleasing was his personality that, after having disgorged six million francs as a fine and served a term in the Bastille, he was released, purchased a splendid old estate in France, loaned the Government itself thirteen million francs of his stolen fortune, and lived prosperously in the country he had helped to cheat out of an empire.

Open-handed and generous in his dealings with friends, possessed of an optimism that never clouded, even when his wife deserted him for Sieur Joseph Ruffio, kindly and gentle of nature, and lavish to excess, he was liked if not loved by all, and later was regarded by many as only an amiable victim of misfortune.

He impressed himself on David, giving him a full-hearted and generous welcome that did much to lessen the strangeness of his environment.

"You must see me often, friend," he said, laying a kind hand on David's shoulder. "I love my people of the outlands, where all my posts and forts are, and you know much about them that will be useful to me in making them happier."

De Pean, the cynic, smiled again. He knew that Cadet was bleeding to death these outlanders he loved so much! He could smile in that way, with a sort of grim pleasure, even when he thought of his own beautiful young wife, Angélique, whose favors rendered to Bigot had already netted him a million francs, and were bound to get him more.

An hour later, tired from his day's exertions, his mind traveling incessantly from his present environment to Anne, David was glad that Bigot suggested they retire to his own quarters, where he was given a room. And still later, lying in a bed such as he had never rested upon before, he let his mind wander over the happenings of the most eventful and amazing day in his life.

His heart yearned for Anne. He felt a great loneliness creeping over him. Drowsiness came, and he closed his eyes to dream of her, of kings and queens and mighty adventures in which he was to play a part, of Bigot and Vaudreuil, of the settled grief in Robineau's face, and of a woman's hair worn by a man.

His last wandering thought, before he fell into these dreamings, was the consciousness that, after all, he had gone supperless to bed!

[1] The Marquis de Vaudreuil-Cavagnal of this story should not be confused with a preceding Marquis de Vaudreuil, his estimable father, who was also Governor of New France in 1705.

[2] Today what is left of these ancient vaults and dungeons, with their romance of mystery and crime, and the almost forgotten story of the part they played in the fall of an empire, is used as storage cellars by the Boswell Brewing Company.

CHAPTER XVI

Te Deum was sung in many of the churches of New France on December first, 1754.

Following a night of storm came morning with a glory of rising sun. Like a patient arising suddenly out of a dread sickness the earth awoke, filled with new hope and cheer. Weeks of gloom and melancholy depression were swept away in a single hour, and from dawn until darkness a clear sky, an unclouded sun, and an air which was like a tonic in the lungs of both man and beast, inspired the people of the land.

The bells of the churches and the convent roused David, and he saw the red east before the sun had burst through it. The melody of the bells, with God's painting in the sky rising like a benediction to greet their music, was a startling change from the ugly dream in which he saw himself at the tail of an ox-cart, like Carbanac, who was to be whipped that day.

He rose with a shudder, which was turned to a song in his heart. He believed, like his Christian mother and the Black Hunter, in omens—and surely the welcome of the bells in darkness and storm last night, and their music again this morning, together with a glorious sun, must be taken as an omen of what lay ahead of him and as a blessing from the omnipotent power that was guiding his destiny.

His first thought was of Anne. It seemed to him that he wanted to open one of the windows of his room and call aloud to her. His heart and eyes were filled with the sunrise as he dressed. And Anne was greeting that same light, stirred by its happiness. His tragedy of last night appeared strangely trivial this morning. Anne had understood. She had forgiven him. And she would understand still more clearly today how it had come to pass that he had kissed Nancy Lotbinière, when every resolution and desire in his heart was to kiss only her.

It was Captain Robineau who came to have breakfast with him. He did not see Bigot, or any of his friends of last night. And Robineau, when they were alone, became more interesting to him. He was unlike the others. He was not talkative, and the beauty of the day seemed to add nothing much to his cheer. But what he said one listened to. There was a quality in his quiet voice which demanded attention.

Their morning was taken up mostly with a fashionable tailor who lived in Buade Street, with hatters and shoemakers, and a jeweler and an armorer, but when Robineau suggested a visit to Vaudreuil's favorite peruke-maker David voiced a determined objection.

"I shall wear my own hair until the Indians take it," he said, "and after that, if it happens and I live, I shall be satisfied with a bald pate like Monsieur Pierre Colbert's."

It seemed to him that a fortune was being expended on his personal requirements, and he said as much.

"Bigot will attend to that," explained Robineau. "The Intendant and the Governor expect the officers in their service to maintain their stations like the gentlemen they are, and they provide liberally for it. It is different in the army where every man's needs must fit his pocketbook."

After their trading, Robineau took David to the citadel, ramparts and the upper wall of the town, and for the first time he began to realize something of the strength of the French stronghold in the western world.

While for a considerable period the French and English, with their Indian allies, had been bitterly fighting in America, their activities extending from raids and massacres to extensive and well-planned campaigns, the mother countries had not actually declared war, nor did they do so until May and June, 1756, a year after Braddock's defeat, and ten months after the bloody battle of Lake George, between Baron de Dieskau and Sir William Johnson.

But, so far as America was concerned, the Seven Years' War had already begun, in fact if not officially, and Quebec was alive with the thrill of excitement and the martial activity of a city engaged in the picturesque and sanguinary drama that was destined to change the history of the world.

Soldiers and officers crowded the main streets. Citizens wore their swords. Gay uniforms, flashing side-arms, the quieter dress of forest rangers and traders, the waving plumes of Indian chiefs, the dark visages of warriors and scalp-hunters met the eyes wherever one looked, in both the Lower Town and the Upper.

Anne St. Denis and David Rock

The town itself had never been richer or more prosperous, for fire and sword and massacre in the outlands meant greater fortunes here. Rich and powerful seigneurs had come to the city with their families and retinues. Never had the social life and magnificence of Fontainebleau and

Versailles come nearer to exact duplication in Quebec than during this autumn and winter of 1754 and 1755. A round of social pleasures swept the city. Balls and parties with elaborate suppers were of almost nightly occurrence, oriental in their splendor. No mandarin or pasha could have excelled Bigot and Cadet in their efforts. Even the King would have hesitated at Cadet's expenditure of two hundred thousand francs on a single ball in September, and at the favors of rare jewels which Bigot distributed among his favorites at the palace.

And this day of sunshine, after weeks of gloom, brought the city's life into the streets. David was like one in a dream. The miles upon miles of magnificent terrain which he could see from the citadel, the distant villages, the spires of churches, the two great rivers under him, the purple haze of the far-away forests, struck him with awe and wonder; but it was the city itself, its people, its great buildings, its mighty wall, its grim fortress and batteries of huge guns that thrilled him most.

He realized now the pride and faith that had inspired Anne when she had told him that the war-dogs of the English might bark and snap, but that Quebec—the soul of New France—would always drive them back.

He marveled at the batteries, guarding every point of Quebec's wonder-world—great two-ton guns that would send a solid shot a mile and a half, and ten- and thirteen-inch mortars which would fire one-hundred- and two-hundred-pound shells five thousand yards.

Surely the fleet was never made and the army never lived that could shake this heart of New France from its rock!

He voiced this thought, and Robineau startled him by saying:

"We are sleeping. The English are awake. Unless we rouse ourselves, this city, which so many believe to be impregnable, will fall."

Sleeping! David opened his eyes wider. Could this be sleep? A life so vibrant that it seemed to set atremble the very rock it walked upon?

He looked at Robineau, quiet, impassive, a man of deeply buried secrets, of mysterious gloom—and believed him. For the Black Hunter had spoken that same warning.

It was noon when, following his instructions, Robineau returned with his charge to the palace. A surprise was awaiting David. As he came into Bigot's drawing-room, with Bigot at his side, even more affable and friendly than last night, Anne sprang up to meet him. She was radiant. If grief and doubt had torn at her heart she betrayed no sign of it now. She gave David her hands, and her bright eyes told him that Bigot had already informed her of his royal welcome at the palace. She did not offer to kiss him. It was because of Bigot's presence, he thought. There were certain reservations which they must live up to now.

Then he observed that in one of the hands he held was the crumpled glove which Bigot had tossed on the table last evening. Its color, the myriad little crinkles which Bigot had put into it as he had stood twisting it in his hands, left no doubt.

A great calmness swept over him. He revealed no evidence of the shock the discovery sent through him.

Bigot was regarding them with the benignity of a father looking on two beloved children. The hand he placed on David's shoulder was affectionate.

"A little dinner for just us three, David," he explained. "I have almost wrecked the Mistress General's faith in me by asking for another half-day's absence for Anne. Twice in so short a time is beyond all their reason and rule, and I think we owe much—not to the influence of my humble self—but to the good favor of Angela Rochemontier with the Superior of the Convent."

"And also to—David," added Anne. "I have told Mother so much about him that she is sweet and good to me on his account, and is very anxious to have you come to her, David, as soon as you can."

Bigot laughed softly. "So that she may tell you what an adorable treasure you have, David, and see for herself if you are fit to possess it," he said.

Anne blushed, and her fingers squeezed David's. "Monsieur Bigot has been splendid." And the light in her eyes as she looked at the Intendant troubled David as much as the glove. "He has brought us all happiness. I pray God will reward him."

Bigot's face was swept by a flash of melancholy sadness. "Sometimes I think God has forgotten me," he said, and then caught himself with one of his quick, rare smiles. "Come! Dinner is waiting for us. And if I can believe Robineau, David must have worked up an appetite this morning."

Again, for an hour, David found himself under the spell of the Intendant. Not by an act or a word could he have criticized the wholesome friendliness, the warm human sympathy, the unadorned simplicity of Bigot. The Intendant took a special interest in every detail of the morning's happenings, and in all of his talk never seemed to tire of referring to David's mother, her beauty and sweetness, and of his hope that she would ultimately join David in Quebec.

Anne's face was beautifully flushed before the meal was half over. Her eyes, it seemed to David, never left Bigot's face when he was talking. In spite of the foment of unrest, of misgiving almost, that had begun to stir in his blood, he could not blame Bigot for Anne's attitude toward him. The Black Hunter himself could not have carried himself more completely above suspicion. At times Bigot seemed utterly oblivious of Anne's interest in what he was saying, and directed his talk almost entirely to David. And especially when he was talking about New France, its welfare, his hopes and ambitions for its people, its Church, its mighty future. But with these things, coming like inspirational prayers and prophecies from the lips of the Intendant, and given a sublime depth and feeling by a calm, quiet voice fitted by nature for such acting, there kept drumming through David's head words spoken to him by Peter Gagnon, "One hates Bigot, the other trusts him. One pulls him down lower than the gutters, the other exalts him to the heavens."

Peter was right, and Nancy Lotbinière was right. There had come a change over Anne in her attitude toward Bigot since she had left the Richelieu. Anne was not less kind to him, yet he was glad when the meal was over. A moment came to him, just before the end, when he thought again of the Black Hunter. It surprised him to find how much like him he had grown to be. He could take things calmly. Bigot had noticed that. And it suddenly came to him, with a sort of grim satisfaction, that he was not sorry he had kissed Nancy Lotbinière.

Bigot, measuring the situation adroitly, excused himself after accompanying them to the salon. "I have some important matters which will take up an hour," he said. "That hour will be short time for you to visit in. Then we will take a carriage and drive about the city." His hand pressed David's arm. He held Anne's hand for a moment, in a familiar, paternal, cleverly caressing way. He was immeasurably sincere, deeply concerned for their happiness. Anne's eyes glowed softly.

When he was gone she turned a little hesitatingly to David, expecting something. Her lips were ready for it. But David made no movement. He was looking after Bigot. David seemed to have grown taller in the past weeks, more self-possessed, older. She had not observed these things in the excitement of last night. He was changed, even since then, changed in the moment the Intendant of New France left the room.

"David!"

He turned toward her slowly.

"Pardon me, Anne," he said, in a way so quiet and steady that it carried a chill into her heart. "I was thinking how distasteful the touch of Monsieur Bigot's hand is getting to be—to me!"

He made no movement to kiss her, as she had expected.

For a moment she stood speechless. "I don't understand——"

"And I don't understand myself—quite. But I think I shall, very soon."

"David, you must explain. Something in your voice frightens me. Why do you stand like that, and look at me like that? Why do you not kiss me, as I want you to?"

"Because I have made a strange discovery very suddenly. And it would be unfair and dishonorable to kiss you now when I feel that you may hate me a little later."

"Dear God—David—what do you mean?"

"Nothing—nothing that I can explain to you now. But two voices came to me strangely as Bigot went through the door. The voice of Fontbleu, the miller, and the voice of the old mill-wheel."

"David, are you mad?"

"No. I was nearer that when I saw you leave the convent last night with him, in darkness and storm, and with happier laughter on your lips than I have heard since I came."

"Dear Heaven, I thought nothing of the hour or the storm, David, because I was thinking of you. We were going to the Bishop's, and Monsieur Bigot had given me your commission that day, and I was happy—happy——"

"I perceived that fact, Anne, and I thought I was happy until I discovered the glove which Bigot was fondling in this room last night was yours."

"I left it in the carriage. He brought it here." Her eyes suddenly flamed with fire in a face from which every vestige of color was gone. "David, you mistrust me? Is that it? You believe that I——"

"I believe nothing wrong of you, Anne. I would sooner lose faith in an angel."

"Then it is——"

"A voice, two voices, coming to me strangely."

"It is Monsieur Bigot!" she cried, her voice scarcely above a breathless, angry whisper. "His little attentions to me, his kindness to you, his—his——" Her small hands were clenched suddenly at her breast. "David, David, can it be such a pitiable thing? Have you been listening to the jealous gossip of his enemies? The foes of this one man above all others who would die for France, the one whose every impulse is for good, the one who has gathered your happiness and mine so closely to his heart? Is it—is it—the poisonous tongue of Nancy Lotbinière?"

Even then David was amazed at the calmness with which he could look into Anne's eyes and answer her.

"No. It is because of a strange and unaccountable instinct rising in me to call Bigot a liar, a hypocrite, the clever scoundrel in truth which his enemies account him to be."

She drew a step back from him in horror.

"And this instinct may itself be a lie," he added. "If that is true, Anne, and I will know soon, I will ask your forgiveness on my knees. But until then——"

He did not tell her that in the moment when Bigot had held her hand, and her eyes were glowing into his, he had caught a sudden swift vision of a face at an open door—a face that had hesitated for a moment, De Pean's face, smirking, suggestive, exultant, betraying in that careless instant only what the lightning-quick eyes of the Black Hunter himself might have detected—the secret of Bigot's soul, stark and naked.

Bigot sensed a change in the room when he re-entered it half an hour later. Anne's face was vividly flushed. David's was calmly pale. He drew swift conclusions, wrong ones. They had been quarreling over Nancy Lotbinière. Anne, judging by her color and the haughty tilt of her chin, had been the aggressor. David had not crumbled before her attack. His face was so grimly, quietly strong that it roused the Intendant's admiration.

Bigot's tact was faultless. He appeared to observe nothing, and began telling David that he had just received a request from Peter Gagnon asking that his friend might quarter with him, as his lodgings were ample for two and he wanted companionship. Then Bigot gave a huge red rose which he held in his hand to Anne. Glass-grown blooms were rare in Quebec, and his gift might have delighted a queen. Anne's color deepened. She thanked him. Her voice trembled a little.

Bigot, still tactful, seated himself next to David in the carriage. He was surprised when Anne asked him to drive her to the convent.

"What, you are going to spoil my little party?" he reproached her playfully, yet with real disappointment not unhidden in his voice. "Is it possible, Anne?"

"I am sorry," said Anne.

David said nothing, but looked straight ahead, and Bigot did not urge the desire which lay in his mind. After all, he could ask for nothing better than this beginning of a breach between Anne and David, though he had made an erroneous guess as to its cause.

Anne could feel the rigidity of David's body at her side. She could see his hands. She had always thought them fine-looking hands, not large, but filled with a lithe, supple strength, so unlike Bigot's white soft ones. They seemed harder now. Marks of the wilderness were on them. And they were very steady and calm as she stole her look at them from under drooping lashes.

David helped her from the carriage as he had a hundred times helped her from a canoe. She did not give him the soft squeeze of her hand which had always been his reward, but only the tips of her fingers. And David made no effort to take more. He bowed, and smiled, and said good-by.

She flashed up a quick, warm smile at Bigot. "I shall treasure the rose, monsieur," she said, and left them.

Bigot laughed reassuringly as they drove away. "Don't take it to heart, David," he consoled. "Because you kissed Nancy Lotbinière is not a crime Anne will hold up against you for long, though she may never get out of the habit of holding it as a sword over your head. Pardieu, these women!"

He did not seem to miss Anne, and, as they drove down Mountain Hill to see if the scaffold was ready for the execution which was to occur at sunset that evening, he told the jolly story of Jean Rathier, the executioner. It was an epic, Bigot thought, something which should never die out of story or history, though history would probably forget it soon enough. Jean had killed a girl of eighteen—Jeanne Couc, almost named after him, it would seem, by fate itself. Rathier had been tried, and sentenced to have his legs broken with an iron bar, and afterward to be hanged. Judgment had been confirmed when an unforeseen obstacle arose. The official executioner died. It was then the officers of justice overcame the dilemma by tendering Rathier, in lieu of death, the little-envied position of hangman. Rathier, of course, accepted.

But that was not the joke, as David should see. A little later the wife and daughter of Rathier were accused and found guilty as accomplices in a robbery. The daughter, as the receiver of the stolen goods, was sentenced to be whipped, but in private, by a nun at the General Hospital—la Maîtresse de Discipline. But the mother, wife of Rathier, was to be whipped publicly in the streets of the city. That was the good part of it, for as Rathier was executioner the citizens of Quebec beheld the unusual and ludicrous spectacle of a man whipping his own wife, and doing it so well that she was almost dead, at the tail of an ox-cart—the same kind of cart Carbanac was to be whipped behind today![1]

But Carbanac, he added, was to be whipped by a negro.

David felt the old, indefinable horror burning in him again, the horror of punishment that was low and degrading. He regarded the finished gibbet without emotion. To be hanged was not bad, if death had to come. To be broken, legs, arms, and back, could still leave a man, a man. But to be whipped—ugh!

They returned up Mountain Hill, and near the Upper Town Market were suddenly confronted by a surging, boisterous crowd. Bigot had timed himself well. He drew the carriage close to the buildings, and halted, as if surprised. Then an illuminating smile flashed over his face. He remembered.

"Oh, Carbanac!" he said.

The scene was unforgetable. It seemed to burn away a little corner of David's brain. The ox was a great, slow-moving hulk of a beast, swaying cumbrously as it walked. The cart creaked and bumped. And Carbanac! His head up. Hell in his eyes. A tall, blond, powerful man. David could see his white teeth, steady and gleaming, as the four-tailed lash fell. He was stripped to the waist. His back was not white, but red. Blood was running from it down his legs to the cobblestones. The man was not flinching. One could not have told from his face that leathern thongs were cutting his skin into ribbons. No cry came from him. No moan. He was magnificent.

And then, suddenly, his shoulder almost touching the carriage, he looked up. It must have been a powerful instinct that drew his eyes from straight ahead. He saw Bigot. His lips parted. His eyes seemed to start out of his head.

"You—you murderer—fiend——"

His voice was not excited or sobbing. It was not loud, but cut like a knife. It was for Bigot alone. Man to man, without any desire for the crowd to hear.

Then he was gone. The crowd filled the narrow street after him, men, women, children, dogs; some of them voiceless with horror, but most of them laughing, crowding their neighbors, joking, jeering.

"A painful spectacle," sighed Bigot. "But necessary, David, and about the mildest form of punishment justice allows us to give." He left David in front of Peter Gagnon's house.

The Black Hunter was in David's heart now. He could have told Anne the rest of the truth. He hated Bigot!

He entered Peter's door, halted, and turned back the instant Bigot was out of sight. He caught up with the crowd again, and the negro, his task finished, was freeing Carbanac from his bonds. He gave him his shirt and coat. Carbanac put on the coat but rolled the shirt under his arm. He uttered no word, gave no sign of pain. But he swayed as he walked away. The crowd dissolved. It was accustomed to such sights. A few small boys followed Carbanac.

And David also followed him. He waited until the small boys had fallen away, and Carbanac was well on his way into Lower Town. Then he overtook him. "Monsieur Carbanac," he said.

Carbanac turned. At sight of David's deerskins, and the pale, grim sympathy in his face, the resentment which had flashed in the man's eyes died out.

"I saw you whipped," said David unhesitatingly. "I am David Rock, and if you need a friend my address is Eleven Sainte Ursule Street. I heard what you said to the Intendant when you passed him. Why did you say it?"

Carbanac clenched his great hands slowly. "Why?" For the first time his emotion escaped him in a half-mad laugh. "Because—he and Nicolet, his rich friend, the merchant, have stolen my pretty wife. I threatened Nicolet on the street. Then they trumped up a charge against me of stealing a bottle of wine. They had witnesses—liars. And this is the result!" In a fury he tore off his coat, as if David had not already seen his bleeding back.

David helped him to replace it, and gripped one of the man's big hands. "If you need a friend will you call on me at Peter Gagnon's lodgings, in Sainte Ursule Street? And—meanwhile—take this, and see that your back is cared for."

Carbanac looked into his great palm. It was money David had put into it, more than Carbanac had seen for a long time.

"I can afford it," said David, reading the look in his eyes.

He left Carbanac standing in amazement. Once he looked back, and waved a friendly hand. Then he hurried to Peter's rooms, his own home from now on. But for how long? He asked himself the question as he walked. A powerful impulse urged him to turn back that very day to the Richelieu. His suspicion of Bigot was no longer an uncertainty. It was a deadly, terrible fact. De Pean's gloating face had first opened his blinded eyes. A hundred things now gave him further vision. Bigot, who was offering him name and fortune, who had won Anne's trust and faith, whom she regarded as a great and honorable gentleman, was the scoundrel his enemies had painted him to be. The overwhelming conviction seized upon him and held him. It demanded no proof. It filled him utterly.

He reached Peter's lodgings, and Peter was not there. Back and forth he walked from end to end of the big room, until he grew tired. A fire burning slowly in him at first grew into a consuming heat. A sullen, fighting resolution came with it, driving back his desire to return to the Richelieu, crushing it entirely. If Bigot was all that, if he was tricking Anne, if he was what Peter and Nancy Lotbinière had said he was, if he was as foul as Carbanac had cried out in his passion—then David would be a coward to run away. For such an act the Black Hunter would be ashamed of him.

A bitterness came with the fighting instincts gathering in his blood, a resentment because of the attitude which Anne had taken. Peter's terrible words kept repeating themselves in his brain—"the other exalts him to the heavens." And he had seen the proof of it. So great was Anne's faith in Bigot that his own suspicions, instead of arousing a sympathetic doubt in her, had caused the first tragic breach of their lives. Choosing between him and Bigot, Anne had elected to attach her loyalty and faith to the Intendant.

Almost unconsciously his fingers had picked up a roll from the table. It was parchment, tied with a blue ribbon. The ribbon stirred the thought in him to undo it, and with eyes that seemed to burn in his head like coals he read his commission as a lieutenant.

Anne had sent it by a messenger. There was no note, no word from her. Nothing but the parchment, which crackled like dry corn-husk in his hand. The thing seemed alive, with something repellent about it as he dropped it back on the table.

His pulse beat steadily, loudly, each throb of his heart as measured as the stroke of a club.

Bigot was fulfilling his promises. Why?

Tomorrow, the next day, sometime—he would find out, even if the discovery cost him his life—and Anne.

He was glad when he heard Peter's footsteps in the hall. Peter came in. He seized David's hand without a word. Then he went to the wall and took down the long dueling-pistol which he had flourished on David's arrival the preceding evening. He placed it on the table beside the parchment.

His eyes were filled with a cold glitter as he faced David again. "I have found the other man," he said. "We fight at four o'clock in the edge of the woods beyond Saint Roche."

[1] The whipping of Rathier's wife, as described above, was administered on Saint John, Saint Anne and Saint Louis Streets, and ended at the Upper Town Market.

CHAPTER XVII

Peter's announcement did not shock or alarm David. If Peter had said, "You are to fight another man at four o'clock," he would have been equally calm. He was ready to fight. The Black Hunter had told him that at times there comes into a man's life a passionate desire to fight. That desire was in him. And Peter's fight was his fight.

Peter unlocked a drawer in the table and produced powder and ball and wadding. "I am glad you are here," he went on. "I feared I would have to pick up a second at the coffee-house. I have had a furious time with Nancy. A damnable time!"

"Who is the man?" asked David.

"I don't know, and I don't care—only I hope he can shoot, for I am going to kill him and I don't want the matter on my conscience afterward. I am praying that it is Jean Talon."

For the first time David expressed his surprise. Peter laughed. His hands were devilishly steady as he prepared his pistol.

He saw David's commission on the table. "So it has come?" he interrupted himself, bending over it for a moment. "Congratulations, David. I told you Bigot would keep his word, even if he is headed for hell. We must give credit to Anne. She is a clever little schemer, and must love you enormously. You are a lucky dog. Haven't I also told you that once before?"

David explained nothing. His eyes were on the pistol and Peter's steady hands. "But this man you are going to fight——" he began.

"Will be buried tonight," said Peter confidently. "I have assured Nancy of that. We had a horrible quarrel and I never knew a woman could get so white-hot with fury. She accused me of being every kind of coward under the sun, and said that when I came to face my man I would drop my pistol in terror and refuse to fire a shot. That is why I am convinced it is Talon. He is the best shot in the Province and boasts of never having missed. Well, neither have I!" He hummed a little tune as he finished the pistol.

"But if you haven't seen the man, how can you fight?"

"Nancy has guaranteed he will be there at four o'clock. Oh, but she was furious! In her excitement she confessed to me that she had kissed him not only once but a thousand times, and she is so confident of his triumph, and of my cowardice, that she exacted a most humiliating pledge of honor from me. It is preposterous, but shows the depths to which a woman's madness will sometimes go. If I refuse to fight, if I show the white feather, I am to make public announcement that never again will I fight a duel. Imagine such a thing as that, when all Quebec knows I would rather exchange a pair of friendly shots than eat!"

David was silent. Fear for his friend, at last, was entering into him. He said, "Peter Joel, the Black Hunter, has often told me that to act in a moment of passion is a hazardous and unworthy thing to do. I believe him. I feel it in myself. If you wait until tomorrow——"

"And be the laughing-stock of the town?" sneered Peter. "And have Nancy, forever after, pointing a finger of shame at me in the streets? Bah! Where is that red blood you talk so much about in the forests?" In another minute he was ready.

The sun was still well up, and they walked by way of the Côte d'Abraham, and then strolled riverward in the direction of the woods opposite the two islands in the St. Charles. Peter, as on every previous occasion of this nature, was in the highest of spirits, and bantered David because of a nervousness that was beginning to possess him as they drew nearer to their destination.

They entered the woods, and after a little came to an open which was familiar to Peter because of a dozen different affairs, in three of which he had been the principal, and in the others a nearest friend. Not until then did his countenance fall. No one was ahead of them. And it lacked only five minutes of four o'clock. Peter himself liked to be the latest arrival, and was never more than that much ahead of time.

Scarcely had they settled themselves to waiting when they heard voices coming from a slightly different direction. As they drew nearer David could hear laughter and cheery conversation. Undoubtedly those approaching were merely chance strollers, for no man or his friends would be coming to deadly combat in such high good humor. He was immensely relieved. This unexpected interruption would delay the duel, and in delay there was hope for reflection and reason. He looked at Peter to see how he was taking it.

A louder laugh rose above the other voices of those approaching. It was an outburst of real merriment, a gaieté de coeur without guile or hypocrisy, and most apparently not intended as a stimulus to the courage of someone who was advancing, or as a deception to inspire nervousness in another who might be waiting.

Another laugh joined the first, a thin, high, cracked laugh. That, too, was real.

A scowl gathered in Peter's face. "Doctor Coué," he said. "He loves these little differences of opinion between gentlemen, but it appears to me he is a bit too friendly with my enemy. Well, he will have work to do in another minute or two."

There were a few moments of silence then, broken only by the crackling and swish of underbrush, and shortly four figures advanced into the open from behind a screen of bushes. Two of these halted, but the other two, seeing Peter and David, came to them immediately.

One was small, thin, and smiling, a little old man who reminded David instantly of Fontbleu, the miller. He carried a surgical case, and Peter introduced him as Doctor Coué. His companion was a middle-aged man of stern military bearing, their enemy's nearest friend on the field.

Peter had glanced casually at the two who had halted. David stared at them. They stood not more than fifty paces away, facing them. Both wore long capes, and both were heavily masked. Something about them sent a cold chill through him. The taller of the two, especially, was not one to lend him confidence. He stood with ease and assurance, his arms crossed upon his breast, looking calmly in their direction. So much of dignity and high resolution was in his bearing that David's blood went still colder. The smaller man was slight in build, almost boyish. But the poise of his head, the utter confidence of his attitude, the pride and calmness in the directness of his gaze made one instantly forget the smallness of his stature.

Which of the two was Peter to fight?

Colonel Taschereau, their enemy's second, touched his arm. "Pardon me, Lieutenant Rock," he said coldly. "The declining sun makes our light none too good, and we will discuss the details. Of course you know that my friend, as the challenged party, has the privilege of choosing his own weapons, distance, and manner of exchanging shots. We shall use pistols. The distance, in order that no more than two shots may be necessary to end the affair, shall be only ten paces. Because of his social and official position my friend will fight incognito."

"Afraid to take off his mask," sneered Peter under his breath. "Another insult added to the others."

Colonel Taschereau gave no evidence that he had heard him. "Each man will stand facing his opponent. Three will be counted with an interval of five seconds between each count. As the word 'three' is called, both men may fire. I think that is all. Are you ready, gentlemen?"

David's lips refused to speak. Peter answered for him. "We are ready, Colonel."

For a few moments David felt a sickness at his stomach. It was worse than an execution. If it were someone besides Peter—himself even———

Colonel Taschereau was already pacing off the ground, marking each end of it carefully. Doctor Coué was on his knees getting his surgical instruments ready. Then Taschereau raised a hand. The taller of the two men advanced from the edge of the open, and David's heart went dead within him. He looked at Peter. To his amazement a pleasant smile was on Peter's lips. He chuckled softly as he placed himself and took the pistol from David's hand.

"We will see what is behind the mask after he is dead, David," he said.

David stepped back, half blindly, and stood beside Taschereau, who already had his watch in his hand.

"Are you ready, gentlemen?"

"Ready!" answered two voices.

"Very well. We will begin. One!"

Tick—tick—tick—— David could hear the watch in Taschereau's hand. And with that ticking of the watch his own heart was beating like a drum in his breast.

"Two!"

Simultaneously with the count the tall, masked man swiftly raised a hand and tore the mask from his face. His cape and hat fell off. It all happened in two of the swiftly beating seconds of the watch.

"Now, monsieur, you may see my face!" he cried.

Startled, David looked at Peter. In those last precious seconds he saw a swift and alarming change in his friend. A terrible shock had apparently stricken from him all power of action. His jaw had fallen, his eyes were bulging, his pistol arm hung lax and lifeless.

"Three!"

Like the roar of a cannon the fatal word boomed in David's ears. Still Peter stood without movement, his face, smiling a moment ago, now white with horror.

He would be murdered where he stood!

With a sudden wild leap David was between the two.

In that moment he saw the pistol fall from Peter's nerveless hand, and Peter turned—as Nancy Lotbinière had predicted that he would—and walked toward the forest, hurrying at last until he was almost running when he disappeared into it.

David, amazed, a little dizzy, faced the others. A cool-eyed, gray-haired, splendid-looking man was smiling at him. Doctor Coué was laughing in a delighted, cackling way. The grimness had gone out of Colonel Taschereau's face.

The man who had been masked held out a hand to David. "I am Nancy Lotbinière's father," he said. "I hope you won't seriously mind our little joke on Peter, who was so tragically set on fighting that other man whom my daughter has so often kissed. Well, I am he. If my daughter says so, it must be true. Can you forgive us for the trick we have played?"[1]

"I thank God," said David.

And now, with only his own eyes turned toward that part of the open, he saw the slim young man at the edge of the woods frantically waving him a signal. At first he believed he must be mistaken. The stranger could not be beckoning to him. Then the gestures were repeated, more emphatically than before. Simultaneously, the smaller man, who had approached no nearer than the edge of the open, disappeared into the woods.

Monsieur Lotbinière had made the last of his apologies to David and was laughing with Colonel Taschereau. David interrupted them.

"I fear I am a poor second," he said. "I have forgotten my duty, and if you will pardon me I will make an effort to overtake Monsieur Gagnon."

He hurried into the forest, and had scarcely taken a score of paces when a figure darted out of its concealment toward him. The long cape was thrust back and the mask was gone. The golden head was hatless.

David stopped in amazement. "Nancy!" he gasped.

The girl was white and trembling when she came to him, yet even with that she was smiling, and a radiant light was in her eyes.

"I was never so frightened in my life!" she cried, a sobbing break in her voice as she reached out her hands to him, as if needing him a moment for support. "I didn't know it was going so terribly far! I told my father to unmask the moment he faced Peter, and he waited until the frightful two was counted! I almost screamed. If it had gone a moment longer I think I should have died! But was not Peter magnificent— until he saw it was my father?" She did not wait for him to answer. "Come quickly, David. I want you to go with me."

He followed, with Nancy a step ahead of him, dodging the bushes with her golden head, laughing now with a joyous thrill in her voice as she led the way. They came to

275

two carriages. Into one of these she pulled David after her. Not until they were on their way over the winding trail out of the woods did he draw in a full breath. It was so deep and sincere, and filled with such an immensity of relief, that Nancy looked up into his face with eyes full of laughter and triumph.

"Poor David!" she sympathized. "You were even more frightened than I."

"I think I was," he agreed.

"And Peter!" exulted Nancy. "Standing there with that smile on his face, when most men would have been white. Oh, it was splendid! He will hate me for a time, but I have won. He will never fight another of those horrid duels I have dreaded so."

"He told me of his pledge," said David.

"And he will keep it. Peter is a man of honor. That is why I love him." She spoke the words quietly, looking straight ahead, her cheeks brightly flushed. She knew David was looking at her, and in a moment her glowing eyes met his.

"It is true, David. I want you to tell Peter that for me. Say to him that I loved him for a long time, but that the passion of respect which I want him to have with my love could never be given as long as he lived only to fight duels and do nothing. And—also—David, you may tell him it is true that you and my father are the only two men I had ever kissed until I kissed Peter himself that night. And I am so happy—now—that I am almost on the point of kissing you again, David!"

"One kiss has already helped to ruin me," said David gloomily. "Yet I am so desperate, Nancy, that I would chance another, if for no other reason than I might take it to Peter along with your wonderful message."

Nancy laughed merrily. "You will be one of the gayest cavaliers in Quebec within a month. You are progressing marvelously."

"Backwards," said David; and before they reached Monsieur Lotbinière's home he told her of what had passed between Anne and himself, and of his growing suspicions and dislike of Bigot.

"It has been my prayer each night that you be not blind until it is too late," replied Nancy, her face tensely serious when he had finished. "David, I must tell you the truth, no matter how deeply it burns, now that you have guessed a part of it. I am afraid for Anne. There are two things for which she would willingly give up her life—her religion and her country. They are really one in her soul, inevitably woven together. And nothing, I fear, can blast her faith in Bigot as the human god whose every thought and instinct is to labor for the glory and triumph of the Church and New France. Bigot is wicked, terrible. I could understand his attitude toward Anne if it were not for his apparently great interest in you. That is incomprehensible. I cannot understand it. Peter does not understand it. My father, one of the noblest of the Honnêtes Gens, cannot understand it. That is the mystery for you to solve, David, and I know you will. But for Anne I am afraid. She loves you. That I know. But Bigot's influence always has been, and always will be something so far-reaching and sinister that it must have the power of devils behind it. David, does it hurt you when I tell you this?"

"No," he said, his face a trifle paler. "It strengthens me in a matter which has been growing in my mind."

They had come to her home.

"You do not mean—you are going back to the Richelieu?" she asked anxiously.

"No. Never that."

"I am glad. Peter has his secret, David, and I am going to betray him. He urged you to come to Quebec, not for your own sake, but for Anne's."

"You think——"

"I think nothing—nothing I dare put into words except that I believe Bigot is false and dishonorable, and that I cannot understand his strange friendship for you. And I am glad you are not going to run away. Anne needs you. She will know it soon. Will you come in and wait for my father?"

"I am going to find Peter," said David, trying to smile. "Such a sweet message as yours must not be delayed, Nancy."

"And, David, you will see me often?"

"Yes," said David positively.

After that he hurried to Sainte Ursule Street, and found that someone had preceded him to Peter's apartment. It was Carbanac.

He scarcely recognized the man at first. His face was sweaty and covered with grime. He was hatless. His thick hair fell over his forehead. His lips were bloodless, his eyes wild, his great hands gripped the side of the chair in which he half sat, and half crouched, like a huge beast. David closed the door and stood before him in amazement.

Carbanac rose from the chair. His smile of greeting was terrible. "I have come quickly," he said. "You told me to, if I was in trouble. I went home, when you left me. I found Nicolet there with my wife. Think of it, while I was being whipped through the streets of Quebec! I surprised them—my wife, who was good until Bigot and this merchant saw her prettiness one day, and her lover! See!" He held out a pair of hands, hands that were twitching as if each individual muscle in them had a life of its own, hands with red stains on them. "I couldn't get the blood off. I hadn't time. I killed Nicolet—like that!"

And the powerful hands grew convulsed, like rending talons.

The horror of the thing held David speechless.

"The town is after me," continued Carbanac. "At the last minute, when I was almost lost, I thought of you. I got up here. No one saw me climb through the window you left open in back. What are you going to do with me?" Even then, with all his agony, there was something whimsically appealing in the terribleness of his smile.

David had no time to answer. Peter came in.

Twenty minutes later Carbanac was hidden in a storeroom at the back of Peter's lodgings.

[1] This remarkable duel was "fought" near the spot where Dorchester Bridge now spans the St. Charles River, late in the afternoon of December 1, 1754.

CHAPTER XVIII

Carbanac's presence, his story, and now the fact that he was a fugitive from justice in the house, with a half of Quebec on his track, had not disturbed the black look of despair and melancholy in Peter's face. Behind this, when he found himself alone with David, flamed a coldly white passion which he found it difficult to subdue.

"Poor devil!" he said, referring to Carbanac. "I know how he feels—hopeless—like myself. Outside this house iron bars and a hangman's noose are waiting for him, and ruin scarcely less preferable for me."

"I can understand the first, but not the last," said David.

Peter looked at him pityingly. "No? Then let me tell you. Never since the first white man came up this river has a more damnable or disgraceful trick been played on a gentleman than this that has been played on me today. Any other man on earth I would have shot dead where he stood, and the situation it has put me in is humiliating and vile, one so degrading and shameful that I would almost change places with Carbanac himself—for in killing Nicolet he only did what justice would have refused to do for him. Tomorrow my name will be the gimcrack and chaff of every tongue in town. I will be the jest of the Province. Think of it—jilted, tricked, robbed of honor, all by the same woman—Nancy Lotbinière!"

"Yet Nancy does not look at it in that way," said David.

Peter glanced at him sharply. "What do you know about it?"

"I rode home with her after the—er—fight," said David. "She was the slim young man who stood beside the taller one in the edge of the open."

"Good Lord!" gasped Peter.

"Yes," nodded David. "And she was immensely proud of you. Happy, too, when it was all over. She said she knew you would never fight another duel, for you were a man of honor, and would keep your pledge like a gentleman. She emphasized that—your honor. She said that was why she loved you."

"Why she—what?"

"Why she loved you," repeated David. "She said this, Peter, 'Say to him that I have loved him for a long time, but that the passion of respect which I want him to have with my love could never be given as long as he lived only to fight duels and do nothing.' That was her message, just as she spoke it."

Peter walked slowly to the partly shuttered window that looked out on the street. His face was turned from David. From there he said, "David, under no pressure of circumstance would you give a false reflection to Nancy's sentiment? Can I believe you—absolutely?" His voice was tight and a little strained, and filled David with a desire to see his face.

"She spoke those words, and I swear that she meant them, or else I am deaf, blind and a fool."

Still Peter did not turn. But after a moment he murmured, "There are people in the street. I think they are hunting for Carbanac."

"I am sure Nancy will be happy if you see her tonight," persisted David. "The white anger and furious quarrel you told me about were only a part of her plot. And it is true about the kisses. She wanted me to tell you that. Her father and I——"

"Did you observe Carbanac's hands?" asked Peter, as if he had not heard David, and without turning an inch from the window. "A riverman's hands, were they not?"

"Yes," answered David, puzzled.

"And he said he had traded as far as the middle waters of the Ottawa, until his wife began to worry him?"

"Yes, he said that."

"He would be a strong man in a canoe," mused Peter, as if speaking to himself. "Too bad that a man of his virtues should be lost to the country."

David waited, still more puzzled at the meditative tone that had come into Peter's voice.

283

Peter shrugged his shoulders. "Do you know what would happen if they found us hiding him here?" he asked.

"I can only guess."

"They would hang all three of us. That is the law. Fancy it! Peter Gagnon and Lieutenant David Rock, hanged in the Lower Town Market! And with Nancy and Anne looking on! We could almost expect that climax, if our anticipations were measured from the exciting times you have had since coming to Quebec. Yet between this hour and our hanging, I think——"

"What?"

"That still more exciting events are in store for us, David."

Peter faced him then. A most remarkable change had come into his countenance. Strain, anxiety, passion and despair were gone. A tranquillity through which shone the warm glow of a subdued eagerness had taken their place. And with that tranquillity was something of strength and resolution which David had never seen in Peter. It was not the physical courage of duel-fighting. It was a thing farther back.

"Will you mind if I leave you?" he asked, and after he was gone David thought he was losing no time in going to Nancy.

David went alone to a coffee-house, and contrived to smuggle some food for Carbanac. The killing of Nicolet was already the chief gossip on people's tongues. Carbanac had escaped. Everyone knew that. At least, he had succeeded in hiding himself so well that no one had found him yet.

Later, David watched Carbanac eat. He talked a little while with him about the Richelieu. Carbanac knew the country.

Then David began reading one of Peter's books, or tried to read. But now that he was alone he could think of only one thing, the slowly widening breach between himself and Anne. He started and listened at every sound of footsteps on the stones and flagging outside. Until the last he was praying for a word from her.

It was late when Peter returned. He seemed a bit tired.

"Have you seen Nancy?" asked David.

"No. I have been astonishingly busy—for me. I have prepared a little surprise for Nancy. It will please her. And you must not ask me about it."

It seemed to David that Peter would never get through writing letters after that. It was midnight when they went to bed, in different rooms. He fell asleep wondering what they would do with Carbanac.

Morning found him dressed and waiting at an early hour. Peter did not appear. After a time he went to his room. To his surprise Peter's bed looked as if it had not been slept in. Peter himself was missing.

He went to the storeroom, Carbanac's hiding-place. It was a small room, dimly lighted. A glance told him that Carbanac, too, was gone.

Puzzled, he returned to the big room. From some isolated quarter, apparently across the hall, the black servant appeared and gave David a letter.

"Dear David," it began, and then followed, in Peter's handwriting, three pages of such an amazing nature that David scarcely breathed once while reading them. Peter had gone, and had taken Carbanac with him, blackened like a negro servant. They had stolen away two hours before dawn, when all the town was asleep. "It won't be difficult to get through one of the gates," Peter had written. "The guards know me, and Carbanac makes a good man slave."

But that fact, the escaping of Carbanac, was not the dramatic point of the letter.

"Use my house and my servant," Peter had continued. "The furnishings are yours. I will never need them again. If I return to Quebec it will be as a guest. I am done with it. I am going without seeing Nancy because I realize now what a pithless bit of waste paper I have been. Blind, like a bat, stupid, good for nothing, not worthy even to look at her or speak to her again until I can return with my stomach-line as small as yours, my face as brown, my hands as hard. I love her desperately, and I am trying with equal desperation to believe, as you said, that she cares for me. My ambition now is to form an independent band of fighting men on the Richelieu, and hold them in readiness for the great struggle which will surely break about us before we are much older. In this struggle, when it comes, I hope to win some merit, and Nancy's respect. God bless her for awakening me to my worthlessness at last!"

David found that he was becoming accustomed to unexpected and astonishing events. His first thirty-six hours in Quebec had been crowded with them. And now the climax that Peter had added did not startle him.

But he was calmly, quietly thrilled. Even Peter's letter with its amazing declaration of change and intent, added to his steadily growing belief in the inevitableness of his own struggle. He had, without realizing the depth of that fact himself, begun to accept the certainty of his fight in a fatalistic way.

Between the time he left the house and finished his breakfast he made a decision as definite as Peter's, and with an equally grim determination behind it. He would fight to the last drop of blood in him for Anne. To do that he must remain in Quebec. He would go on, as Bigot had planned, a protégé of the man whom he was beginning to despise, and in whom Anne had placed a faith that had already begun to wreck their plans and happiness. That faith, if wrongly placed, he must destroy. The nearer he came to Bigot, and the more intimately he allowed himself to be drawn into his plots and affairs, the surer would be his own information and action later on.

Of his own danger no thought came to him.

Returning to his rooms from the coffee-house, he relieved the pressure upon his mind by writing fully to Peter while waiting for Captain Robineau, who was to call for him at nine. Of course he said nothing about Carbanac, but did set forth his intentions in detail, and also his suspicions and his certainties.

Robineau arrived promptly. From ten o'clock until one he gave David his first lesson in military instruction. After luncheon he put him through sword practice. He was thorough and painstaking, and as unrelenting in his demands as he was conscientious. David's liking for him increased. He asked if Robineau knew of any immediate way of getting a letter to the Richelieu. Robineau did. Official mail was leaving that night for Crown Point. He would be glad to see that David's letter reached its destination.

That same afternoon Bigot was reading this letter. It gave him an immense satisfaction, and he thanked Robineau, who had delivered it to him. He made a copy of it. The letter was then resealed and sent on to Peter.

"Such little matters as this relieve you greatly from your obligations to me, Captain Robineau," said Bigot. "It must be a considerable satisfaction to see yourself progressing so splendidly!"

Robineau's set lips made no answer.

All through the day David had been praying that word from Anne would be waiting for him when he returned to the lodgings in Sainte Ursule Street. But no word had come from her. There was a note from Nancy, brimming with cheer and happiness, telling him that she had received a long letter from Peter, and urging him to have supper with her that night. Only her father would be with them, she said.

He accepted unhesitatingly, hiding the unhappiness which had settled upon him. Nancy, radiantly lovely, greeted him first. Her voice fairly trembled when she spoke of Peter. The day had not worn out her excitement. The blush of it was in her cheeks, the glow of it in her eyes. She had but one fear—that Peter might get too near the Indians!

David, first pledging her never to tell Peter, let her read the letter which Peter had left for him. Nancy's eyes grew misty.

"Precious Peter," she whispered. "It will be a long time before I see him again. But—I am glad."

Monsieur Lotbinière, who liked to have people forget his title of Baron, welcomed him like a father. More than that, like an equal. This tall, splendid, military-looking bulwark of the Honnêtes Gens, whose ancestors had begun the building of New France under the glorious Talon, impressed him more deeply than anyone he had met in Quebec. Confidence and respect sprung up swiftly between them.

David told of the Richelieu, the country south, the English forts, the Indians, and his host drank in every word with an almost avid interest. In return, he spoke about Quebec, its government, its politics, its strength and weaknesses, and of the men who were imperiling it. Truths fell quietly and surely from his lips. David could not disbelieve them. They made his own convictions more positive.

When David mentioned Robineau, Monsieur Lotbinière's face clouded for a moment.

"I cannot understand the reason for his association with the Intendant and his friends," he said. "The Captain is the best military expert in New France. He knows the conditions of the country even better than I. He comes of a race of loyal and honorable fighting men, yet a year has changed him so that we scarcely know him. He himself holds aloof from us now. He has become almost a recluse except for his military duties. I cannot conceive of the hold which Monsieur Bigot must have on him."

Until her eyes grew sleepy Nancy sat up with them, and listened mostly to their talk. When at last David was about to go, and they were alone together, she spoke for the first time of Anne.

"Have you seen her today?" she asked.

"I have not been that fortunate."

"But you have heard from her?"

"Not a word."

"I have heard enough for both," said Nancy, the softness of her voice accompanied by a sudden glow of fire in her eyes. "A long and bitter communication upbraiding me for poisoning your mind against Bigot. It seems unfair of me to disturb you, David, but I shall continue to believe it is my duty to do so until, between us, we have rescued Anne from this monster's influence. Bigot had Anne out driving again this afternoon, on the Sainte Foye Road. I am bewildered. There is something behind it all—something which we must discover if we can."

She stopped, with a little shiver, and tried to smile into David's white face.

"Why don't you speak what is in your mind, Nancy?" he asked, his words a whisper, his calmly terrible eyes burning into her own. "Why don't you?"

"I cannot. I cannot. My thought is too terrible—too untrue."

"You mean that Bigot wants Anne?"

She bowed her head. "Yes, that is what I fear, David."

"And you think——"

"I am only—afraid."

He said good night without a tremor. He walked with the straightness of an Indian through the door into the night. But in the street, alone, his feet stumbled. He did not see or care where he was going. Chance more than his own intention brought him to the convent walls.

He passed around them, shrouded in the deeper gloom of the very building where Anne was sleeping. Something sinister seemed to walk with him, an invisible, ghostly thing that crowded and suffocated him. Anne was just beyond the walls, almost within reach of his hand; she could hear his voice if he cried out—yet those walls seemed a million miles in thickness to him now, and Anne a vast distance away. Torturing visions rose before him—visions of Sunset Hill, of a golden bottomland filled with sunshine and flowers, of a red rose, a crumpled glove, Anne riding with Bigot.

He fought against them, and held his head higher. The sky was filled with brilliant stars. A little distance away he could see where they were shining on the Richelieu, on his mother's cottage and the secret paths and by-ways which his feet and Anne's had made. It seemed a long time ago, a year, even more, since he had come from there. He wondered where the Black Hunter was. If he could be here tonight, with him——

He set his jaw tighter. He knew what the Black Hunter would say. "A Richelieu man, David, never turns his back on a fight."

So at last, after weeks and months of blindness, the truth had come to him.

CHAPTER XIX

The third day after Peter's secret departure word came to David from Anne.

Her communication was brief. She called him dear David, and ended affectionately, but a lack of spontaneity and warmth lay between the lines. It was not the old Anne who had written them. She had been ill, she said. She would not try to see him until her condition was better, but meanwhile would be thinking of him every day. She hoped her messenger had delivered the commission to him safely, and that he was progressing in his work. Every night, before she went to sleep, she prayed for him, and she was confident that her prayers for his happiness would always be answered.

David seemed to have lost the sense of painful emotion. He felt the stab of the letter but it was dull and heavy and endured with a calmness that had become almost stoicism. His heart choked him a little, something thickened in his throat, far back in his eyes was for an instant a flash of anguish. But even Bigot would not have observed these things. He answered the letter, quietly and tenderly. But he did not prostrate himself either in one way or another. He did not even urge an early meeting with Anne, except to impress on her how unhappy he would be until she was recovered. He told her about Peter, and his training under Robineau. With equal casualness he spoke of the evening he had spent with Monsieur Lotbinière, and of his high regard for the man who had taken such a kindly interest in him.

After that, with a still grimmer resolution, he set about his work. For a week he received only an occasional note from Anne, who seemed to be having difficulty in coming round to her old self physically again. During this week his progress amazed Robineau, who reported faithfully to Bigot. It was a week filled to the brim with action for him. Three times Bigot had him at the palace, with Cadet, De Pean, and the others. He received his uniforms, and became accustomed to them. A light of professional pride came into Robineau's eyes when he saw him for the first time in one of these, wearing a sword.

If anything, Bigot devoted himself with greater interest to David. He personally presented him to the Governor and made him acquainted with the Councillors who met in the Castle of St. Louis. On a second occasion, when these Councillors assembled in a special conference, he had David present to give information about the wilderness country, and particularly the upper Richelieu. In a number of ways during this week he made David feel that he was actually rendering something in return for what the Intendant was doing for him. At his own Council, held in the palace, he questioned him closely about his journey to Fort William

Henry and the Pennsylvania country, and about what he saw and learned on that adventure. He also had him before the Bishop, to tell of certain matters relating to rival church activities in the south country where French and English influence met.

David, with the great question in his mind unanswered, was still more puzzled by this increasing friendliness and concern for his advancement on Bigot's part.

Bigot, watchful as a spider in the heart of its web, was exultant over their results.

From the tongues of De Pean, Vaudreuil, and Deschenaux fell carefully planted stories that found their way to the ears of all Quebec. They emphasized the depth and sincerity of the friendship which had sprung up between the Intendant of New France and this handsome young cavalier of the wilderness who had so fearlessly baptized him a few weeks before. Its dramatic picturesqueness caught a popular fancy. Romance was added to it. With each day that passed, David found himself a figure of greater interest in the city. He could see it, and feel it. He was marked with the favoritism of the most powerful man in the French dominions. His quiet and unexcited acceptance of fortune, his Indian-like aloofness, the picturesqueness of the background against which his past was painted in rich and varied colors, all added to the effect.

Meanwhile, Bigot was pouring out his soul to Anne in several long communications, the confidence of which, he said to her, he was sure she would preserve as she would her own honor. He entreated her to forgive him if he was taxing her strength, but she was the only one to whom he could speak regarding the welfare of New France in that frank and unguarded way, to which, it seemed to him at times, he must surrender himself or go mad. And, also, he was deeply troubled, and needed her sweet prayers and guidance in a matter that was touching more and more intimately the happiness of the two he loved most on earth—herself and David. He asked her to invocate in her holy way against the mysterious treachery which was seriously threatening his own efforts for the greater glory of New France, and to use her influence in keeping David from any further communication or association with the Black Hunter. His letters were the epics of a great soul. Their humility lent to them a touch of saintliness.

It was in Nancy that David found the source of his greatest courage in these days of mental trial. Her pride in him was positive and honest. There was no qualification in the way she and her father accepted him. He became acquainted with an increasing number of their friends, among them several of Monsieur Lotbinière's most intimate associates of the Honnêtes Gens. Nancy's eyes were brighter and her cheeks more prettily flushed when he was with her.

She was childish in her delight when he first appeared before her in his uniform.

A little at a time, but very surely, she crept closer to his heart. He saw her once, and sometimes twice, each day. Somehow, it seemed to him they were making a fight together—she for Peter, and he for Anne. He loved to see the light in her eyes when they were talking about Peter. It was a deeper, more holy light than he had ever seen in Anne's. He tried to tell Peter about it in a second letter, and, failing, destroyed the letter. This love of Nancy's, a steady, glorious fire revealing itself constantly to him, kept his own hopes alive when, at times, they seemed almost to have burned themselves out. She had no doubt about Peter now. And, also, inspired by her own happiness, she began to overcome her fears about Anne.

"It is inconceivable that she can make an error, except in her own opinions, while she is under the guardianship of the good nuns at the convent," she told David. "Heaven could not guard her more carefully than the environment she is now in, even granting Bigot the powers of a king. And before her school is ended next June she will have seen the truth so clearly, David, that she will entreat your forgiveness on her knees, and Grondin's Manor will be the most beautiful place in the world to her, just as Peter's home on the Richelieu is the one paradise I yearn for more than all else in this beautiful land."

That same day, Angela Rochemontier said to Nancy, "Anne is not sick. I mean it is not her body. It is something in her heart, in her mind, a thing that worries me more than a grievous malady that could be put to rout by proper medicines."

It was the next day, Saturday, that Anne at last sent for David. The message came to him early in the morning. He was to see her, alone, at the school that afternoon.

At first a wild and joyous flood of anticipation broke over him, so that Robineau, in the first hours of their work, observed the change in him. But a grim and compelling fact slowly deadened the excitement that had taken possession of his heart. It was not only fact, but duty. In his communications to Anne he had refrained from pressing on her his growing convictions regarding Bigot. But now that he was to see her, his conscience would stop at nothing less than a clear and definite announcement of what he believed, and what he knew. He must do that, if half a man. He would not go into any one of the sickening details of Bigot's life with which he had already become acquainted in Quebec. But he owed it to Anne, as well as to himself, to say what was in his mind, and to let her know that he was taking advantage of Bigot's favor simply that he might be better equipped to fight for the honor of New France later on.

He went to the convent and was ushered into a plain, low-ceilinged room, sparingly furnished and with an uncarpeted floor, where for several minutes he waited alone. He could hear, now and then, soft footsteps of the nuns, and among these, at last, he knew that he recognized those of Anne.

He was standing when she appeared. A little shock ran through him as she paused for a moment in the door. It did not seem to be a change caused by illness which he saw in her. Her face was without color and thinner than when he had last seen her. It was this whiteness, the utter lack of the softly beauteous glow and animation that had always been a part of her, that struck him first. The nun-like quietness of her dress, the barrenness of the room, its white walls, the stillness about them accentuated the effect her appearance made upon him. She was spirit-like in her colorlessness, except for her hair. That was radiant. Its soft masses glowed in the light from the corridor. It seemed the one thing about her that was still riotously alive.

Anne saw the shock in his eyes and the swift thought that followed it. It was only a moment or two, before he could either move or speak, but in that time she had closed the door and was smiling at him, with her hand reaching out. He knew, instantly, that there was something forced about the smile. He took the hand. He held it tightly in both his own, looking down into her face, fighting back the yearning desire to take her in his arms. Anne, too, was making a fight.

He could see that, and the knowledge of it made him bend his head, as if to kiss her.

Anne's hand pressed gently against him. "Not now, David," she said.

They sat down, facing each other, near a shuttered window. Anne's eyes went over David's uniform. She smiled again, making no effort to hide the pride in them. But it was an older smile, something that struck him a blow instead of giving him pleasure.

"You look splendid in your uniform, David."

"I am glad you like it," he said. He did not know how white and cold his face was.

"And Angela tells me you are making amazing progress and have become quite a figure in the town."

"Robineau says I am doing fairly well." Suddenly he sprang to his feet, and his eyes were ablaze. "Anne, in the name of Heaven, tell me what has happened? What is it that has changed you? I am in this accursed city because of you. I am in this uniform because of you. I am accepting the bounty and hypocritical friendship of a scoundrel and a traitor because of you! A little while ago you were glad to have me take you in my arms. You said you loved me. We were happy in our dreams and plannings. Now you avoid me. You keep me away from you. You seem to hate me. Why is it? What has wrought this change, if it is not Bigot? This monster who has blinded you with his fine talk, this fiend who had Carbanac whipped through the streets, and who has plotted and worked to take you away from me that he may have you for himself! Why is it——"

He got no further. Anne, too, was on her feet. The pallor in her cheeks was lit up by a sudden flush. She pointed to the chair from which David had risen.

"Sit down!" she commanded.

His passion had brought from him more than he had intended to say, until she herself had dragged it from him. He reseated himself. Anne faced him again, her eyes filled with a flaming glow.

"I beg of you to remember where you are, in this holy room of the Ursuline nuns. And—please—let me talk to you a little while without interruption, and tell you why I did not come into your arms, and why I have—as you so plainly see—changed in a way. Since a week ago my heart has been breaking, yes, since that day in the palace when you refused to kiss me. I have not been sick, except in my heart, and this sickness had grown to be so terrible that a little thing like that which I saw through Nancy Lotbinière's window seems pitifully trivial. I want you to take me in your arms. I want you to kiss me. I love you even more than in those hours when we were planning and dreaming, as you say. But three things love cannot rob me of, and never shall—my faith in God, my loyalty to my country, and my honor!"

She paused, looking at him as if she believed he must understand.

His heart pounding at her confession of love, yet bewildered, David said, "How can your love for me make you sacrifice any one of those three things?"

"You have just said that Monsieur Bigot is a scoundrel, a traitor, a monster and a fiend?"

"Yes, and in proof of which I gather more evidence each day."

"Then when you have heard what I have brought you here to tell you, David, your opinion of me will be vastly changed. We have each our duty to perform, in spite of love, and for days I have been strengthening myself, even as my heart grew sick, to speak plainly to you what is in my mind, and what I believe, and think. Bigot is honorable, in spite of the wickedly malicious stories you have heard about him. His enemies are threatening to destroy him—and with him, New France. He is the one loyal and splendid bulwark on which our future depends. His vision has been clear, where yours has been blind. And only because of his friendship for us does he withhold the hand that would destroy one whom you hold very dear to you.

"He has discovered one of the sources, and the chief one, of that despicable treachery which is strengthening our enemies at every turn. I know, now, the meaning of the fear and horror which filled me on the Richelieu whenever you spoke the Black Hunter's name. It was God warning me, even before the Intendant came. For there is no longer a doubt. This Black Hunter, who has so closely and so mysteriously attached himself to you and your mother, is a traitor and a spy, the deadliest enemy New France has ever had. His hands are red with the blood of French men and women and little children. His mission is to gather that information which will turn over our most defenseless homes and settlements to the scalping-knives. Through friends—and the Intendant has evidence that they were on the Richelieu—he has secured and given to the English military facts and secrets of priceless value. And of late, as you know, he has become more daring.

"Bigot knows that he came with you almost to the very walls of Quebec, and left you there, and then stole in afterward disguised as a trader, and two days later departed with information for the English. And Monsieur Bigot, this man you call a scoundrel and a traitor, this great-hearted patriot who has so sincerely befriended you and me, has let this menace to our country go free and unpunished because—because—David, you will hate me now!—because, if taken and hanged, the very death of this Black Hunter will so terribly involve you and your dear mother!"

David's face was ashen, his blood numbly cold, by the time she had finished. And Anne, even as she saw the effect of her words, seemed calmly and terribly inspired. She was speaking only what she believed to be the truth, and dully there flamed in her eyes the light which told him she had gone to the extremity of martyrdom in this prostration of her own love and happiness for the thing which, in her own soul, was a grim and inevitable duty with the command of God and the Church behind it.

Even as the crushing significance of her reference to his mother and himself bore upon him, he could not find it in his heart to regard with anything but a sense of amazement and pity the slim, white creature who sat before him, and who, as he wet his dry lips, bowed her head a little, and said, "David, I called you here to tell you that, even though you hated me for it. And now, with our happiness as the price, and your own future and safety at stake, I am asking you to repudiate and disclaim this man who calls himself Peter Joel, to cast him out of your life so completely that he will never see you again, and to urge your mother to do the same, even though—it is possible—she may refuse. For if Peter Joel is caught, and hanged——"

"I shall gladly take my place at his side, and hang with him," said David.

The effect of his words on Anne was startling. She stared at him for a moment with wide and unbelieving eyes, then covered her face with her hands, and from behind them came a strange and choking cry. He could see her little body tremble as if shaken by a chill.

He rose from his chair again and placed his hand on her bowed head. His fingers pressed into the velvety softness of her hair. Its warmth sent a glow into his heart. A bar of sunlight came through the partly shuttered windows and fell upon it, and the radiance and beauty it made replaced the tenseness of his lips by a gentle smile. More than ever, in spite of all she had said, he loved Anne St. Denis. And now, with his love, was a worshipful compassion—a knowledge tenfold stronger in him that it was she, and not himself or the Black Hunter, who was in danger, and that his fight for her had suddenly grown to be an epic thing.

Tenderness filled his voice. "All this you have heard is a lie, a monstrous lie," he said.

She did not move and scarcely seemed to be breathing now.

"In a little while you will understand," he whispered hopefully, bending lower. In another moment he would take her head in his arms, and kiss her—her lips, her sweet hair. "You will understand," he repeated. "It is Bigot, Anne. He is winning your confidence and doing these things so that he may turn you against me. He wants you. And he knows——"

He did not finish. Anne, too, was suddenly on her feet, facing him. Now he saw sharp pain in her eyes.

"David, do you mean what you have just said, that you would gladly die with the Black Hunter—if he were hanged?"

"Yes," said David. "That could not repay the love and debt I owe him."

"Then may dear God give me strength to bear what the future holds," cried Anne with sobbing bitterness. "You speak of the thought of another man wanting me as if it were dishonorable, and not in the holy nature of things—yet in that same breath you say you would happily die a traitor's death! Oh, why do you break down so terribly even the last of my doubts? Even you make me believe! And you have come to me straight from the Black Hunter, and will see him again today, or tonight——"

"You are mad," cried David. "Peter Joel is neither a spy nor a traitor. He is not in Quebec. I do not think he will ever come again, unless I urge him. He is——"

"In the city now. Waiting for you. Plotting his terrible work. And you—you—David, why do you look at me so steadily and so clearly and yet speak to me so falsely? The Black Hunter is here. Monsieur Bigot might have him in prison now, but he holds his hand, almost a traitor himself because of his affection and friendship for you—and his love for me, which I reveal without hesitation or shame, since it is honorable and rouses no spark of gladness in a heart filled only with love for you. But even this love seems doomed when you stand like that, with honesty in your eyes, and—and—dear Heaven, I must speak the words!—with such dark lies upon your lips."

"Anne—you believe that? You think I am lying?"

"It is not a thought. It is——"

Despairingly she turned to the darkened window, and her fingers almost mechanically opened the shutters wider. The cold winter sunlight streamed in.

For a moment she stood there, then swayed back, as if an unseen hand had suddenly thrust her from the window. She tried to speak, but only a dry sob came from her lips. She passed David, opened the door, and with another sob entered the long white-washed corridor of the nuns. The door closed again. A bolt clicked. Anne was gone, and an inviolable world lay once more between them.

Stunned, David heard that last faint sound of her footsteps. Then he passed through another door which led to his own world, the outer world. He was conscious of a sweet face smiling at him gently. The cold December air struck his face. Its sunlight filled his eyes. He stared ahead, to where—on that first black night—he had seen Anne get into a carriage with Bigot.

Now it was not that vision, but another thing, which drew his breath short. He saw what Anne had seen through the window. Advancing to meet him, joy and pride in his face, was Peter Joel, the Black Hunter.

CHAPTER XX

In her own room Anne felt that the last of the hope in her heart had died. In a sobbing, crumpled heap she lay on her bed, stifling the moaning pain that forced its way to her lips so that one passing the corridor outside might not hear her. In these first moments of grief she cried out softly again and again David's name.

And then those same tortured lips were praying for him. For it was something more than chance that had made the Black Hunter appear outside the window in that very moment when David had lied to her so terribly—when his eyes and face and voice had almost made her believe that he was speaking the truth, and that it was Bigot who had given her false evidence. Not chance, but God had brought the Black Hunter to convince and guide her then. And as she prayed for David, it was Bigot who forced himself into her mind. Bigot, from whom terrible truths had come to her slowly and grudgingly, through fear that they might mean unhappiness for her. Bigot, who had first warned and then had fought to save the David she loved. Bigot, whom so many hated, and against whom even the nuns had spoken to her gently—Bigot with his unselfish love for her, his still greater love for New France, his soul which he had bared for her to understand. Bigot at last stood triumphant in that little room in the convent of the Ursulines.

With this triumph a light seemed to go out in Anne's soul, leaving it in darkness. She sat up, and dully her eyes went about the room in which that soul had found its richest and most beautiful visions of life and of God. It was a room of dove-like purity, filled with the breath of love and faith and good-will to all living things. Its walls were white. The bed was white. Robes of sweet-faced nuns who looked at her from pictures on the walls were white, the crucifix before which she daily knelt in prayer was white. Gloom, blackness, wickedness could not enter here and find an abiding place. About her, breathing and vibrant with the spirit of God, dwelt two things above all others—hope, first of all, and after that, duty.

A hundred times Anne had laughed and talked into the gentle face and kindly, understanding eyes of Mother Mary of the Incarnation, who had died almost a hundred years before, but whose soul was warm and living to her in the picture on the wall. Upon her knees she now asked for her help and guidance. When she had finished she felt the comforting nearness of one in whom she had a great faith. It was as if the spirit of her own mother, strong and clear of purpose, had come to walk hand in hand with her. After that it was duty whose insistent whispering seemed clearest, while the voice of hope drew farther away.

David had lied to her. But it was not the mere utterance of this lie that terrified her. It was the purpose which lay behind it. He had lied to hide something. And that which he was hiding was what Bigot had so gently disclosed to her.

From their place of concealment she drew forth Bigot's letters, and with eyes dulled and filled with torture read again the long communication that had come from him that morning. It was the tenderest and finest, yet the most painful, that he had written her. What the final pages of his letter contained gave him the golden opportunity to tell her more fully than he had ever dared to tell her before how devoutly he worshiped her.

"For your love," he said, "I would sacrifice everything I have on this earth. For it I fear I would give up my God, my hope of Paradise. Strengthened by your love, there are no heights to which I would not attempt to climb. If God had so intended this love to come to me, your soul would have become the soul of all New France, and together we would have carried the glory of Church and Country to the uttermost wildernesses. I am writing you this, not to press my hopelessness and emptiness of heart upon you, but as an excuse, even a plea for forgiveness for the distress I am about to occasion you. I would rather strike my right hand off than cause you pain, I love you so dearly. Yet that very thing I must do—bring grief to the one for whom I would happily lay down my life. And humbly I entreat the blessed

Saints to plead with you for me, that I may be forgiven, and that you may understand I am writing this to you so that we, together, may save from destruction that very one whose success in your affections means my eternal unhappiness."

And then, with that same finesse and tenderness of which he was master in writing as well as in spoken words, he told her of the Black Hunter's presence in the city, of its significance, and—at last—of the convincing evidence which had come to him of David's increasing interest in the Black Hunter's plots of apostasy and treason.

David was in deadly peril.

For her sake, because for him she was the angel of all life, because her happiness meant more to him than even the safety of his country, he would risk his own name and honor—and struggle with her to the last dead-line to save David. But David must not see the Black Hunter again. And if David loved her truly, which surely was the case, then her influence could easily be made to bring about his salvation.

He ended with a final declaration of his consuming desire for her happiness, so tender and true and so exquisitely mellowed by his own renunciation that it was almost a prayer.

It was to Bigot, after all, to whom she must go in her final hour of darkness. The thought crept upon her, possessed her, overwhelmed her. With it came a great fear, for under the tenderness of the Intendant's letter she saw the monstrous thing which he was so splendidly trying to conceal from her. It was as if he had written, in letters which now burned themselves into her brain, "Save David. If you cannot, then may God help him. For the demands of the King, the law, the people are stronger than I. I am holding my hand—but how long can it be held, with the Black Hunter even now in Quebec?"

She found herself trembling. No matter what David had done or was doing, no matter if he had lied to her, or had even joined in treason, but one duty called upon her now—and that was to save him. Bigot had left her no doubt. The Black Hunter would ultimately be caught and hanged as a spy. And when he died, even when he was caught, David's hour of deadly peril, so strongly hinted at by Bigot, would be at hand. For that reason, knowing the menace was terribly near, Bigot had written her the letter and had urged her to drag David from the pit of destruction before it was too late.

As soon as she could get to him she must let him know that she had failed. In Bigot, all her hope, all her prayers were centered now. On her knees, if she had to, she would beg him to let the Black Hunter go unmolested from Quebec—for David's sake.

She did not try to think beyond that. She arranged her hair and dressed for the street. Three-quarters of an hour later Deschenaux carried word to Bigot, who was in his private apartment, that Mademoiselle St. Denis was below, waiting for an audience with him.

He came just as Bigot had finished with one of his informers, who had brought him word that the Black Hunter was with David in Peter Gagnon's lodgings.

It was some time before Deschenaux returned to his secretarial room. A look of anxiety had come into his face.

"Monsieur Bigot is not well," he said, in a cleverly puzzled voice. "I have noted an unusual change in him since morning, and have urged him to see a doctor. He is delighted you are here, and possibly your word may have some influence with him in that respect, mademoiselle."

Bigot's big room was empty when Deschenaux ushered her into it. The secretary departed and closed a heavy door behind him. Not until he was gone did Bigot come out from one of the curtained rooms adjoining.

Even after Deschenaux's words, Anne was surprised. Her own emotion, her heart struggling to keep itself from sinking, could not keep her from sensing that change which Deschenaux had spoken about in Bigot. It lay heavily in his face, in his posture, even in the droop of his shoulders as he flung back the curtains and paused for a moment in the doorway.

Inimitable actor of his day, despondency—a flash of despair—possessed him then.

Almost as soon as his eyes fell upon Anne he made an effort to throw off this mental sickness that revealed itself in his face. But not before she had seen it. Not before his clever mind told him that as she stood before him, pale and wide-eyed, she had understood the meaning of it.

His acting, more consummate in its skill than words, had said to her, "I know what has happened. The hour I have dreaded has come, and I can see no way out." Pity, tenderness, an infinite sympathy filled his gesture and his sad smile as he reached out both hands toward her.

Dragged by a force which she could not resist, Anne came to meet him, giving her own hands to him. Something was twisting in her head. The air of the big room seemed stifling. A dry sob came from her lips as she stared into Bigot's eyes.

"Poor little angel," he breathed softly. "Poor, poor little angel!" And then he drew her into his arms. Before she could realize what had happened, before the twisting thing in her head gave up its hold on her reason, she was lying against his breast, her face still raised to him, so that his kisses were crushing her soft lips before she had made an effort, or could make an effort, to keep them away from him.

And Bigot did not wait. He freed her, and stood back. Even in this one glorious minute of triumph and passion his satanic cleverness did not desert him. Before Anne could resist him there was no necessity for resistance. He had given her up gently, just as he had taken her in his arms. Hot flame leaped into her face, but, a miracle even to herself, it was not of shame or anger. Any other man's kisses, given like that, would have driven her into a fury. But she was not furious at Bigot. Even as her heart began to race like a little engine in her bosom she could find no words with which to punish the man who stood before her, humble and compassionate, yet as if he had done no wrong.

"Poor little angel," he breathed softly again.

With her hands at her throat, and the wild race of color in her cheeks swiftly fading into pallor, she struggled for words—intelligent words—which must follow an act like Bigot's.

But Bigot gave her no chance. "I know what has happened," he was saying, his voice caressingly gentle. "Since this morning the Black Hunter has been under careful surveillance. He is now with David, in Peter Gagnon's rooms. He plans to leave the city tonight, with the information and drawings which David has prepared for him. My poor, dear little girl."

He turned, a break in his voice, and for an instant covered his face with his hands. The twisting thing in Anne's brain made her dizzy. She sank into a chair. The wordless sob came again from her lips. Bigot bent over her, took her hand, held it and stroked it tenderly, and kissed the soft, hot little palm of it as he whispered his hope and cheer. Anne did not draw it away. He pressed its fingers against his cheeks.

"I have been thinking, thinking," he said. "Since morning, when I knew what was going to happen, I have been thinking until I have almost gone mad. And now I must do what my heart dictates, and in doing that must sacrifice my honor and my country. Anne, sweet little Anne, why is it that God doesn't make you love me only a little as I love you? Oh, the crime of it, the mistake of it!"

"My love—has all—gone to David," said Anne, and her voice came strugglingly. The hood of her cape had fallen back, and Bigot's lips pressed her hair. With a supreme effort he held himself in leash. In a few days, a few weeks, she would come to him, forever—of her own sweet will.

He dragged himself away from her. Something told him he had responded to the impulse at just the right moment. Anne's glorious eyes, more beautiful than ever in the feverish light of their fear and pain, were looking straight and wide into his. She forgot his kisses, forgot the caress of his lips in her hair.

"What are you going to do?" she asked. "What—what are you going to do with the Black Hunter—and—David?"

"The Black Hunter will go unchallenged from Quebec tonight, with his information for our enemies," said Bigot. "Once outside, he will be warned never to return again, on penalty of death. Tomorrow I shall send David on a mission among our Indian allies, in the Ottawa forests."

It was inconceivable that such calm, desperate resignation and despair as that which was in Bigot's face could be feigned. Even the suspicion of the thought did not come to Anne. She saw the man's soul suddenly torn and twisted by its own treason. For David, for her, he was sacrificing that which he held most sacred on earth. Yet, in the face of this agony of resolution and sacrifice which she saw in him, she could not restrain the joyous relief which his words produced in her. A little cry of gratitude came from the lips he had kissed a moment before. That same gratitude leaped to her eyes and cheeks, and trembling she thanked Bigot, and let him take her hands again and raise her gently to her feet.

There, for a moment, they stood, and much as if she had been a little child Bigot laid a hand on her hair and caressed its silken softness, smiling with such a sad and dreaming light in his eyes (as if looking and thinking far beyond her) that it seemed to Anne he was only partly conscious of what he was doing. But his lips said, while his eyes still gazed off into cloudy distance, "Always I am seeing you, Anne, night and day, awake and in my dreams, as I found you that afternoon in the bottomland with your beautiful hair afire in the sun. It does not seem to me that I can wholly lose you after that. Perhaps my faith in God is too great. Yet nothing can ever destroy that faith. Sweet little Anne, if there had been no David—could you—possibly—have loved me?"

"You are great and good," said Anne, something choking at her heart. "But—there is a David. I think—God—intended me to love David—and him alone."

"Yet, if there had been no David," mused Bigot. "Together, you and I, giving our lives to Church and Country, hand in hand. The glory of high resolution and achievement—of a thing even greater in God's eyes than love itself. It is a beautiful dream which brings light into the darkness of my heart, Anne. And—might it not have happened?"

Anne bowed her head, and he saw the tremble of her slim shoulders, and did not press the question.

But half an hour later he was saying to Vaudreuil, who had answered quickly the summons of Deschenaux, "There is no need of further delay. All that is required now is the coup de grâce. After that, very soon, Mademoiselle St. Denis will come to these apartments—to remain."

"No time will be lost," said Vaudreuil. "Pardieu, but you were always a lucky devil, François!"

The haunting nightmare of fear in which she saw David lost through the treason of the Black Hunter was less terrible in Anne's brain as she returned to the convent. In the dark shadows of this coming night Peter Joel would leave the city, and tomorrow the great western forests which she had once dreaded, but which she now welcomed and blessed as a sanctuary for the one she loved, would claim David. This respite, comparatively brief though it might be, lighted for her once more the star of faith and hope. She believed in Bigot. She believed in prayer, and even as her feet carried her back to the Ursulines she was praying again for the boy who had so suddenly grown to be a man, praying that God and the blessed Mother of Mary would help her to bring him out of that path whose end she saw in a black pit of ruin, dishonor, and death.

That she had suffered Bigot to touch her lips and body she had almost forgotten. Bigot's love, filling her ears with its repressed but passionate earnestness, seemed insignificant and trivial to her compared with the mightier thing that had happened—his promise to save David from the fate which this very night might have seen descending upon him. All other thoughts but those of David found repelling forces in her mind as the cold gloom of evening fell about her and the convent bells tolled their vesper anthem.

On her knees she prayed for him. In her bed she prayed. Another dawn she awakened with prayer in her heart. And in that dawn, with the sweet music of its bells, the gray promise of its sun, a thrill undreamed of last night came to warm the hope in her breast.

If David would come back to her—she would go with him—go forever. She would give herself to him—now—

today—that she might stand constantly between him and the Black Hunter. That she might fight for him, and with him. That she might save him from those final acts which, unless she gave up her soul to eternal condemnation, would separate them for all time.

Her hand trembled as she wrote her message, entreating him to come to her at once. "I have found a way," she cried to him in those few precious lines. "Oh, my David, I have found a way, and I have been wicked and blind not to have seen it before!"

She was happy. Song rose out of her heart as she measured the seconds and minutes it would take her message to reach David. She watched for him. She saw the messenger returning. And into her hand, suddenly robbed of warmth and feeling, her own writing was returned to her.

She was too late. David had left the city an hour before her note reached Sainte Ursule Street. It was as if an omnipotent hand had reached out of Heaven to strike her, answering her prayers with a blow.

That day she received word from Bigot. He had lost no time, he said. David was safely on his way to the forests, empowered to make a new war treaty with the Ottawas. His companion was one of the Intendant's most trusted runners. Peter Joel, the Black Hunter, had also gone—undoubtedly on his way to the English with his ill-gotten secrets of Quebec's military defenses.

Devoutly Bigot thanked God that this situation which had frightened him so was over. A little longer, with the military in possession of their secret, and the present Governor his enemy, he would have been helpless. He was sure that by the time David returned the Black Hunter would be settled with, so quietly that no one would ever hear of it. He was buying a hundred masses to show his gratitude for the good fortune which had remained with them thus far. He was hopeful, tender, comforting.

But the shock which had come with the return of her own message to David left its effect on Anne. Fear again took the place of hope. And with this fear came another emotion, a seed that had sprung into life, a thing growing slowly, steadily, insistently. The friend she loved most dearly, Sister Esther, had planted this seed, and innocently, with only the highest and most glorious of thoughts in her gentle mind, she had nurtured it. "God intends you to be one of us," she had said to Anne many times. "I feel it. A voice in my soul has whispered it to me from the beginning."

Sister Esther would have given up her life for Anne. Yet, with the holiest of desires for her friend's happiness, she unconsciously brought into life the soul unrest which began to torture Anne. Was Sister Esther right? Did God intend that the physical attainment of her love for David should give way before a higher and nobler duty? And this duty? Was it, as Sister Esther so truthfully believed, that she should consecrate her life at the feet of Jesus, and take her place among the nuns? Or did that duty have to do with a greater glory for God, a greater New France—and Bigot?

For days the torture burned within her, unseen by others, unobserved even by Sister Esther.

Would God give her some other token—some surer sign to guide her?

And would that message come to her through David— David and the Black Hunter? Would David be sacrificed that she might be made to see?

Thoughts that were at times almost madness possessed her. Yet those thoughts were the product of her day, of its illimitable faith in the inexorableness of divine guidance.

Priests were dying at the stake, singing the glory of God. Martyrs were sacrificing themselves with joy, because martyrdom in its holiest sense was pleasing to the will of Heaven. The hand of God was seen and felt, His voice heard.

Anne waited. Days grew into weeks, and no word came from David. Christmas passed, dull, heavy, terrible for her. Events happened, events vital to the future of the world. In January the Marquis de Vaudreuil became Governor of New France, and on his staff was a place for David—when he returned.

In the middle of a black night she awoke, dreaming, whispering those words—when he returned.

And now, digging itself out of the secrecy with which Bigot had enshrouded it, rumor poked forth its head and stalked the streets of Quebec as ugly fact. There had been spies and traitors in the city. Treason! The word warmed itself as it passed from tongue to tongue. Monsieur Lotbinière and others of the Honnêtes Gens smiled grimly, but the populace were blind—as populaces usually are—to what greater and keener minds could vision clearly. Treason gave promise. It was lurid with possibilities. It roused avid interest in a city shut in by the walls of a wilderness and a terrible winter.

The King of France was made to proclaim loudly an old and established fact—that traitors should die. Vaudreuil, the new Governor, flung the musty news abroad from the mouths of the town criers, and had old and ponderous laws read aloud before all gatherings of the people, so that—like the thrill of a scandal that never dies—it came to be dramatic and new again to those who heard it.

But Bigot was silent. Always he was letting Anne see the fight he was making—the fight to keep that ugly thought from the tongues and the consciences of the people. If he had merely posed as a god before, he seemed like one in truth to her now. In Bigot, and in him alone, she found the last of her comfort and hope. With her he waited and watched for word from David. She could see his unhappiness, caused by her own. At times she was ashamed because of this infliction of her grief upon him. At others she was swept by a great pity, a sympathy so sincere, so tender, that once or twice Bigot found himself fighting desperately to hold himself back until that final day of triumph which he knew was swiftly approaching.

The short, black days of February came and passed. March roared out of the wilderness. The twenty-second of that month brought with it wind and storm. A blizzard howled out of the west.

It was beating and snarling against the windows as Anne stood for a moment, preparing for her bed, before the small mirror in her room. A little while before she had wiped the frost from the glass. In the candle-glow her breath was white. Yet in that cold, biting through the white gown she wore, something held her eyes upon the mirror—and the reflection she saw in it.

Because of the cold she had not braided her hair. Its thick warmth about her neck and shoulders was comforting on a night like this, in a room wherein the only heat came from a tiny candle-flare. She stared at herself, and her eyes were not the eyes of another Anne who had looked into a mirror at Grondin Manor months ago. She stared because something in the eyes was frightening her, making her forgetful even of the cold.

That afternoon, late, she had gone to Bigot again. He, too, like the eyes in the mirror, had frightened her. He was like a man in a fever, hiding something from her—something that he dared not tell her, something—about David. And, when she left him, he had thrust back her hood, and had called this hair of David's his hair, and then he had kissed her, and a moment later was pleading with a bit of madness in his voice for her forgiveness. She had come away sobbing, for deep in her heart she knew that Bigot had heard about David, yet would not tell what he had heard. And Bigot was changed, utterly changed. Hope in him, too, seemed gone.

She extinguished the candle, and, shivering, lay for a long time wide awake in her bed. The watchman passed, calling the hour. She could hear his voice faintly in the storm. At times the wind came in fierce gusts, assaulting her window as if determined to break it in and clutch at her soft throat. Then it would grow quieter, and she could hear weird meanings outside, and cautious whistlings from the capsheafs and cornices, as if ghosts were signaling to one another.

Deep in the bed she snuggled her little body, and fought to tear out of her mind the thoughts that seemed bent on driving her mad. But the wind, filled with its little devils, kept her awake. She heard the watchman again. And then again—twice in the two hours that seemed longer than a night itself. And at last all sound, even the wind, the whistling, the beating at her window, seemed to bear in it one word. David. David. David.

Exhaustion brought her sleep—a sleep that was not restful, but filled with the distress of uneasiness and of mental agonies. Subconsciously she sensed the torture of this sleep, and struggled to rouse herself, just as hours before she had struggled to find relief in its embrace. But she could find nothing—no one—to help her out of it. It held her with chains that stretched and gave way but never broke.

It was the watchman who helped her at last. She could hear him coming toward her, giving her courage. It was he who broke through the black barriers that shut her in. She sat up in her bed, wide awake. She had gone to bed in storm. Now it was very quiet, and a pale light was filtering through her frosty window.

The storm was over. That was her first thought. Then, in the stillness that had followed it, she heard the watchman's voice. It was distant, coming nearer. That was strange, she thought, for it was the watchman's voice that had awakened her, very near, seeming to shout in her ears. She thrust back the thick masses of hair from her face and listened.

Moments of silence followed, and she heard the clack, clack, clack of the watchman's stick. He was near—near her window.

Something held her heart still.

Then came his voice.

"Thrr-e-e-e-e-e o'clock in the morning, and a traitor has been caught! God bless the King—and death to all traitors!"

From Anne's lips came a choking, answering cry. The man stood under her window, shouting the words. They rolled out through the night with a booming, triumphal note.

He passed on, but his voice came back and thrust itself through her window, piercing her heart.

"A traitor is caught—death to the traitor—and God save the King!"

A third and a fourth time she heard the voice before it died away.

For many minutes she sat in the bed. Then she dragged herself from it. She did not feel the cold, for her body and her heart were as cold as the night outside.

A traitor had been caught!

She lighted a candle and in the light of that candle her face was whiter than the face of the blessed Mother of Mary in the picture on the wall. Life seemed to have gone from her, except from her eyes and her hair.

Unhurriedly, even mechanically, she began to dress for the street. Then she waited—at the window.

She was not reasoning or thinking. Something more irresistible than either reason or thought possessed her. In her, colder than death, was certainty.

In a little while the watchman would be returning with his terrible cry. But before that——

She even expected the footsteps which came at last in the hall. She opened her door before the one outside could knock gently at it to awaken her. The Mother Superior was there, and Sister Esther. They were surprised to see her fully dressed, and she tried to smile, as if to let them know without words that she understood why they had come for her.

The tranquil faces of the nuns, usually undisturbed by any vicissitude of peace or war, revealed faintly the signs of an emotion which they were struggling to repress as they greeted her. Sister Esther, forgetful for a moment, kissed Anne's cold lips, and seized her still colder hand.

"Monsieur Bigot, the Intendant, has interrupted our night with a request which we find ourselves unable to refuse," said the Mother Superior, in a gently comforting voice. "He asks for your presence immediately at the palace, on a matter of importance to both the Church and the State. Sister Esther will go with you. But, dear child, how does it happen that you are already dressed?"

"Because, Mother——" Anne said no more, but went with Sister Esther.

A carriage waited for them. And as this carriage bore them through a cold and dismal gloom down the frozen slope of Palais Street Anne heard once more that far-reaching, terrible cry, "A traitor has been caught! Death to the traitor—and God safe the King!"

CHAPTER XXI

In his apartment Bigot waited. With him was Vaudreuil, Governor of New France. Beyond them, about to depart through a door, was Brassard Deschenaux, the secretary, who looked as though he had not been in bed that night, and whose crafty countenance glowed with an almost feline satisfaction at things happening or about to happen in his master's affairs.

Vaudreuil, silkier and smoother than ever, his woman's wig glowing in the candle-light, wore no appearance of having been disturbed in his rest or of having come through a cold and ugly night at this unusual hour of three o'clock in the morning to keep an appointment. As a matter of fact he had slept in one of the Intendant's chambers. The governorship had gone well with him. His egoism had increased. His innumerable conceits had multiplied. He was puffed up more than in the days of promise and believed himself to be the greatest man that had ever represented the King in the western world. His dreams were filled with visions of Fontainebleau and Versailles, and Bigot had petted and nursed these visions and a hundred other weaknesses until the Governor of New France was his tool, body and soul, without knowing it, and even the destiny of the military power of the Canadas lay in the hollow of Bigot's hand.

It was Bigot, the super-artist, who alone bore the marks of travail and distress. With a woman's cleverness Deschenaux had helped to finish the work a few minutes before. His clothes were crumpled, his hair untidy, his face made pallid and lined by Deschenaux's delicate skill. His appearance was that of one who had gone through mental agonies and who had not slept for a long time.

He was ready for Anne.

Even Vaudreuil had been amazed at first. Now the Governor was twisting about his fingers one of the curls taken from an Englishwoman's head. His short stature had seemed to grow taller and to swell larger at the words of praise which the King's Intendant had just bestowed upon him.

"I told you this is what would come to pass," he said placidly. "Is our little lady on her way?"

"She is coming," said Bigot.

"Then nothing more can be asked. The game is as good as finished. I have brought you a beautiful dove, François."

"Almost too beautiful to be true," said Bigot. Then he laughed and his dark eyes glowed with a fire of passion. "I am a fool for saying that, Vaudreuil. But I shall not tell you what I have asked La Pompadour to do for you until the last great hour comes. Tonight and tomorrow you have your biggest part to play. And after that, very soon, you may have to attend to Captain Robineau."

For the first time since entering the room Vaudreuil's face clouded. "He would dare——"

"I think—he might," interrupted Bigot. "The thing has been wearing on him for a long time. When he sees what comes of it all he may prefer to——"

"Die like a gentleman," nodded Vaudreuil, dropping the curl to fall into the other habit of twiddling his thumbs over a fat stomach. "We shall find little difficulty in satisfying him, François. I have in mind Captain Jean Talon. I have advanced him another ten thousand francs and he owes us a duel whenever we ask for it. He hates Captain Robineau and would like nothing better than to put a bullet through his heart. The affair can be brought about very quickly."

"Good Lord, what a brain you have for defeating the unexpected," exclaimed Bigot, this time in unaffected admiration. "Occasionally you make me afraid of you, Vaudreuil. Yes, if Robineau rouses my suspicion much more I shall give you the word! One shot is all that devil of a Talon would require with which to ease Robineau's conscience forever!"

He walked with Vaudreuil to the door through which Deschenaux had passed, accompanied him a few steps beyond it, and then returned alone. Anne, when she came, would appear through another door.

It had been a busy night and one of sleeplessness for him. But he was not tired. Since ten o'clock every nerve in his body had been at its highest tension. Of all his dreams and passions and ambitions this which was now arriving at fulfilment was his greatest. In a few minutes more the supreme drama of his life—his epic love-drama—would be enacted in this room, with Anne facing him alone. Once more he knew that he must fight to maintain himself a god in Anne's eyes. Even then there was a chance that his victory and her surrender might come a few hours before he had planned it. But against this thought he tried to harden himself, crowding it back so that Anne would see no sign of it in his face.

As the hour of his triumph approached, his meditations possessed him pleasantly, and he paced slowly back and forth over the deep and faintly perfumed rugs of the room. A touch of humor curved his lips as his mind leaped over the sea to La Pompadour, the King's mistress and his own best friend. With a quizzical smile he wondered if the magnificent Louis would jerk his head from his body if he knew just how much had passed between himself and the beautiful favorite; and with a wryer look he meditated upon La Pompadour's reactions if the truth of his passion for Anne St. Denis should ever become known to her.

His affairs with Catherine and Charlotte, so tragic in their ending, and his amours with Madame de Pean and a score of others had entertained and amused La Pompadour, whose wide knowledge of life made her understand that men must have their little pleasures; but this that was happening between himself and Anne would, he knew—if the whole truth became known—cost him both power and favors, if not his head. The others he had adored for a time because of their beauty; he had given them up easily after a certain length of play, as La Pompadour would have him do—but his passion for Anne had become a fixed and indestructible thing in his life, and this the King's mistress would resent even to the point of his destruction.

So not for an instant had there come into his mind, even in the most favorable moments, a thought of marrying Anne. The idea in itself was so preposterous that it made him grimace. He had not married Catherine, yet she had been helplessly a part of him until she killed herself. The others, even those encumbered with husbands, had remained his chattels until the humor came upon him to drop them. Anne St. Denis would be bound to him more closely than Catherine had ever been when his hour for forging the connecting link between them came. Possibly in some time to come, if La Pompadour should die or her influence over the King wither with her fading beauty...

But this was as far as his mind traveled toward a vision of marriage with Anne.

There came a quick and excited rapping at the door through which Vaudreuil and the secretary had disappeared into the lower halls of justice and of state. The interruption snapped Bigot back into action. The moment had arrived and the knocking at the door was the signal for the curtain to rise. Anne St. Denis had reached the palace and was coming up by way of the private stair and passage!

Bigot threw open the door. De Pean stood there, while two of the huge guards from below thrust in ahead of them the shivering figure of a man whose big, round face was white with fear. He was the watchman of Upper Town—the man who had widely and loudly cried out the news that a traitor had been found. Bigot drew back into the room, and the men advanced with their prisoner and stood before him. De Pean's eyes had shot to another door—the door through which Anne would come.

Even as he looked a tap, tap, tap came at that door. Bigot, with his ears keyed for the sound, heard but gave no evidence of it. In a voice which trembled with subdued fury, an inimitable pretense of anger which he appeared to be holding in leash with an almost godlike effort, he loosed the quiet but terrible condemnation of his tongue upon the cowering watchman and whoever else was responsible for advertising to the city that a traitor had been caught. Without turning, Bigot knew that Deschenaux had opened the other door and had quietly thrust Anne within. He knew she was standing there now, with the door closed again behind her, and that with white face and swiftly beating heart she was listening to his words.

335

His voice rose, filled with the tremble of his anger and his despair. "Take him away, De Pean," he said at last, "and mark me well the man who has betrayed my commands by giving to the watchman the news of our prisoner. He shall be punished, even if the informer is the Governor himself and my own hand must be called upon to administer it. Go!"

The guards led the prisoner out. De Pean followed. The door closed. Bigot, looking after them, seemed stricken the instant they were gone. His shoulders drooped and he bowed his head. "God help me now!" he sighed.

He heard soft steps behind him but did not turn until a voice came.

"Monsieur!"

Then he faced Anne.

Even she in her whiteness, which was almost death-like, scarcely presented a more terrible picture of suspense and agony than did Bigot himself. He seemed shocked into speechlessness by her unexpected presence. From under her hood Anne's great eyes looked at him. He could hear something beating, his watch—or Anne's heart.

As if words could not come to him he held out his hands toward her. Anne did not appear to see them. Her eyes did not leave his own.

"It is—David?"

Her voice was a dry whisper. It made Bigot think of the dryness of the corn-husk he had helped David gather. He wet his own lips and nodded. "Yes, it is David."

Anne swayed a little. Her face could go no whiter. But her eyes seemed to grow darker until the flame in them was almost madness. Then she caught herself and was steady. Bigot's hand was on her arm. He led her to a chair and seated her, and with gentle hands loosened her hood and drew it back from her head. He did not touch her more than that, but his eyes blazed behind her. Suffering in a beautiful creature, when that creature was a woman, always stirred him to ecstatic depths. As a Caligula he would have given himself untold pleasure in that way.

He stood a little behind her. "Have I done right in sending for you?" he asked.

Anne was looking straight ahead. She did not move or answer, but Bigot saw her hands trembling and twitching in her lap. Her nerves were gone. She was broken—broken as he had intended that she should be.

So he bent lower, and said, "Spies of the military council caught him two days ago. I did not know until tonight. He was taken red-handed on his way to emissaries of the English. In his coat were plans of Quebec's defenses, maps and drawings and every detail of our strength, together with instructions to the commandants at Fort Edward and Fort

William Henry telling them of the way up the Richelieu, and of the fighting men between."

If he had whispered a scurrilous thing to her she could not have sprung to her feet more quickly, facing him with dilated nostrils and eyes that struck him like twin flashes of lightning.

"There—you lie!" she cried, and her hands clenched as if to beat at him. "They all lie when they say David is a traitor, and you—you—most of all—when you say that—about—the Richelieu!" She swayed again and her hand caught at the edge of the table to steady herself. "If David is a traitor—then—there is—no God," she finished, and even in Bigot's breast came a passing touch of pity as he looked upon her hope and beauty dying before his eyes.

But he did not speak. He dragged himself like a sick man to another chair and sat down with his face buried in his hands. He heard Anne crumple into the chair from which she had risen. And then her dry, terrible sobbing filled the room. That was what he wanted. He looked up. Anne's head was buried in her arms on the table. Her heart was broken.

He went to her side and for a few moments spoke words which she only half heard. God alone could bear witness to the effort he had made to save David, he said. But it had been impossible under the circumstances. When the paroxysm of her shattered nerves had passed, he let his words fall like pointed knives in her ears. The military and not his own friends had caught David, he explained. Vaudreuil was at the head of that, and Vaudreuil and all his council, embracing the highest officers in the land, had nothing but death in their hearts for the treachery that was imperiling New France. So bitter were they that preparations had already been made for a court martial and David's fate would be known very soon. In a voice that trembled with emotion he entreated God to favor him in his last great fight for David.

In that same voice he spoke of hope. There was always hope until the very end. Every shred of power and influence he had he would exert for David. He would sacrifice everything, even the Intendancy of New France, if that sacrifice could be made to save her happiness.

To Anne's tortured brain and body his voice was like a soothing hand—the voice of her greatest friend on earth, the only friend who could save David. She felt a strange sense of something that was more than hope passing over her again, and involuntarily her hands found one of Bigot's and clung to it. Her sobbing ended. "I must see David," she whispered.

Bigot's free arm had closed gently about her. "That is why I had you come, dear. In this hour I knew that David would want to see you."

She was conscious of his lips pressing hotly against her forehead and something in the touch of them seemed to raise her out of the chair so that she was free from his hands and stood facing him. The flame under Bigot's skin was hidden by Deschenaux's skill. The lights were shaded. It seemed to Anne that heart and soul he was a man of God as she looked at him, his pale and haggard face almost like that of the martyred saint who looked at her out of the picture in her room. If she had ever doubted his love it would be unthinkable to doubt it now. And it did not revolt her nor did it frighten her. For in Bigot she saw now more clearly than ever the three great things which were the foundation of that love—his faith, his honor, and his friendship for David.

Her mind cleared strangely. Where a few moments before she had felt a weakness in her limbs and body came a sudden strength. Bigot saw the change and reacted to it even more quickly than she. The slump went out of his shoulders and a new light came into his eyes, as if by sudden force of will he had thrown off his burden of hopelessness.

"I must see David," Anne repeated, and her voice was no longer atremble. "Where is he?"

Bigot could not have asked for a better development of the situation. Anne herself had suggested the step which would take her into the trap he had set for her.

"You must be brave," he said, brightening at her changed appearance. "The fight is not yet lost. David's fate at present hangs in the balance, and when the council has surveyed its evidence and is ready for a decision I shall appear before it with a request and demand for leniency. Meanwhile, if you can persuade David to accredit his present position to the influence of the Black Hunter, and get him to give evidence against the scoundrel who has ruined him, it will help his case so much that the council can refuse quite gracefully to pass the judgment of death upon him."

"Death!" The word broke in a startled gasp from Anne's lips and the room seemed to swirl about her.

"Yes, it is that bad," said Bigot, and for another moment his voice seemed to come to her from beyond the walls of the room. Then again all was clear and she was staring into his eyes. After all, it was that very thing—death—which she had visioned from the hour the watchman had cried his terrible news. But the sound of the word on the Intendant's lips came as a blow which stilled for a time the beating of her heart. Bigot was continuing. "Some enemy of mine told the watchman to proclaim the news to the city and that makes the verdict almost certain. That treachery has weakened us against our enemies is common knowledge in every home, and to catch the traitor, then show him mercy, would bring revolution around our ears. If David's capture might have been kept a secret among ourselves———"

"You believe that David Rock is guilty?" Anne's voice cut in upon him sharply and her eyes blazed amazement and indignant challenge. "You believe that?"

Bigot bowed his head. "The evidence was found inside the lining of his coat," he replied gently. "No matter what I believe, unless he betrays the Black Hunter the council and all of New France will condemn him as guilty. I know, like you, my precious Anne, that in his heart David is clean. To save himself he must sacrifice that other who is at the bottom of his ruin. Just that much you must urge upon him, while I, with every atom of power at my command, shall work to free him from the terrible fate which suspends itself by nothing stronger than a gossamer thread above him."

Anne made no answer. She waited while he called Deschenaux, who was conveniently near in the outer rooms. Then he walked with her, holding her hand tenderly in his own, to the door through which she had entered his apartment. The secretary opened it for them.

"Deschenaux will go with you," he said. "I shall return to the council room. The minutes are drawing near when action will be taken.[1] Be brave, dear heart, and win from David the evidence which will help so much to save him."

When she had gone he straightened himself with a gesture of relief and his face flashed with a triumphant smile. To be alone with Anne in his own apartment at this hour, and under conditions which might have been used to place her almost helplessly in his power, had subjected him to a terrific strain. But he knew that he had acted well. One more chapter in his little drama—the meeting between Anne and

David—and his still greater moment would arrive. Dawn, the thick and ugly dawn of a day of gloom, would bring him that happiness which, when he dared to think of it now, fired his brain with a sudden drunken madness that seemed to fill the room about him with dancing flame.

Scarcely had Anne and Deschenaux disappeared through one door when De Pean entered through another. Bigot turned toward him. An odd smile lay in De Pean's face and he seemed for a moment, even as he smiled, to be looking beyond Bigot—to something else. Possibly he was thinking again of Madame de Pean, his wife, whose loveliness he had sold to this monarch of New France under rules and stipulations entirely satisfactory and friendly, and whose affair of the heart—and of the purse—was now arriving at such a tragic end. Possibly he was not displeased. But he was of the kind to smile in that wry way when he reflected upon the humiliation it would bring to his lovely Angélique.

Bigot's voice trembled with the emotion roused by his own visions when he greeted the other.

"You have cared well for Sister Esther, who came with Mademoiselle St. Denis?" he asked. "She knows what has happened, has seen the evidence, and——"

"Has been told to the minutest detail how you are fighting to save David Rock," De Pean cut in, with a half-mocking inclination of his head. "She is praying not only for Anne but also for you, François. She has seen David's coat and what was found in it, and though she is as gentle as a bird she cannot find forgiveness in her heart for such a red-handed traitor to her country."

Bigot's face shone with joyous satisfaction.

"Have her kept comfortable and commend her praying," he said. "And do not by any chance let her see Anne."

[1] It was not uncommon in these days of Bigot's régime for the Intendant's plotters to assemble at night to plan or perform those hidden acts of moral and political rottenness which meant the ultimate destruction of the nation.

CHAPTER XXII

From the moment Deschenaux led the way into the candle-lighted murk of a corridor that was new and strange to her, Anne felt herself smothered in an atmosphere of gloom that seemed to press to her very heart. The candle-glow was ghostly, the silence death-like, and as her escort opened door after door into other halls and corridors, the grimness of the thing which threatened all her future lay heavily about her. The cold stone walls of the passageways were naked of paint or paper and upon the stone flags under the dully burning candles lay the accumulations of their drippings. The air which she breathed was thick and musty and more than once Deschenaux wiped away the floating ends of cobwebs which the opening of the doors disturbed and sent with clinging insistence against his face.

These things of gloom made Anne tighten her lips to keep back the crying agony which was in her heart. Beyond the last door of the arched and seldom-used tunnels of rock she knew she would find David, for Deschenaux had said, at the beginning of their journey, "We are going this way because it is the only passage by which the lower floor and the dungeons may be reached unobserved."

Even then Anne's senses had caught but dully what he said, for her mind was a flaming torment of thoughts and visions of her lover. David a traitor! David, the boy she had worshiped and the man she loved! David, the son of Marie Rock, the idol she had set up so far above herself on a pedestal of love and faith and pride—David—her David—a traitor—lying in a dungeon.

Before Deschenaux had come to the last door her soul rose in a revolt of protest, of denial and of disbelief. No matter what Bigot had said and no matter what all the world might say David was not that! Something had happened, something which might look bad for him now. Whatever it was it would easily be explained away. Hope within her, fighting itself into a paroxysm that was almost an exultation of certainty, rose triumphant for a little. When Deschenaux turned to her at the last door he saw her eyes filled with a strange eagerness and her breast rising and falling quickly. She stepped out ahead of him into the gloom of the vast, candle-lighted hall through which Bigot had first brought David on his way to the inner and hidden magnificence of the palace. And then Deschenaux saw the miracle of a flush in her cheeks, and her lips were no longer tight-set and white.

He loved the thrill of a struggle—the struggle between a woman and a brute before the woman finally surrendered. It was his reflected pleasure, the spice of his knavish trap-setting and of subtle deeds without a name for his master's entertainment. His face shone with approbation and satisfaction as he closed the door and locked it and led the way quickly down the great hall.

Anne was conscious of the presence of the guards, but conscious without looking at them. They were mere shadows. But at the far end was a flood of light, and with it, life; and Deschenaux whispered in a low voice, "We must pass the chamber in which the council has assembled to pass sentence upon Lieutenant Rock. If we keep close into the shadows of the farther wall we can go unobserved."

To pass sentence! The three words pierced Anne's brain. She quickened her steps so that she went ahead of her companion. She had no thought or desire to remain unseen. The wide double doors of the council-chamber were partly open and the unusualness of this fact did not strike her. A brighter light poured from the room out into the hall and through this light a figure hurried into the chamber as she and Deschenaux approached.

She recognized the figure. It was Cadet, the commissary-general. An overwhelming impulse seized her to follow him in, to fight for David, to declare his innocence before them all and demand his freedom. For a moment she hesitated with the light streaming on her, and Vaudreuil saw her from within. Deschenaux held his breath in this moment of intriguing possibility. Then his ferret eyes noted the shiver that passed through her and the giving way of something that for an instant had almost forced her to act with all the sudden fury that had gathered in her being. A fury against Peter Joel, the Black Hunter—the mad desire to cry out to these men in the council-chamber the guilt of the man her own hands were ready to kill if that act would save David, and to call down upon them the curse of God if they dared to punish the one she loved because of the treachery and guile of the other. She saw her chance, or what seemed for that breath or two to be her opportunity; the great room with its big oak table, the men gathered about it with faces ominous and stern, and Vaudreuil, standing, leaning over the farther side of the table. There were no smiles among them now, no bantering lightness of tongue, no countenance of cheer or promising humor as they listened to the military governor of New France, whose voice she could hear, but not his words. Yet something held her back, a hand within her stronger even than the impulse to begin her fight now with the men round the council-table. It dragged her away from the door and toward David. She must see him first. The soul of David, his innocence, and his own story must come back with her to that room and the men who were in it. Then she would win! She would not need Bigot. She would need only herself—and the truth from David.

As they continued into the more dimly lighted extremity of the hall she did not notice Captain René Robineau, who had entered from the outer corridor, and whose face was grimly set and white as he watched them disappear.

Into another and narrower tunnel-like passage and down a flight of steps to the lower level of the labyrinth of secret underground storerooms and dungeons under the palace Anne followed the steps of Deschenaux. There was little time for the horror of the cold and ghostly walls to creep upon her, for scarcely had they taken a score of paces beyond the steps when the corridor opened into a rock-walled room filled with the light of burning candles. One half of this room was divided into two barred prison-cells. And in one of these cells, facing her as she entered, stood David.

In that same moment Deschenaux's footsteps were retreating rapidly down the passage, and before Anne's lips had formed a word or sound the upper door had opened and closed and he was gone.

It was David's attitude and his terrible appearance as he looked at her which held her speechless and almost powerless to move, now that she was alone with him. Somehow, it seemed as if he had expected her and was waiting like that, grim and motionless, for her arrival. His coat was gone. His shirt was torn so that one shoulder gleamed naked in the candle-glow and his long hair was tangled and uncombed. But it was what lay in his eyes, his motionless contemplation of her, his unamazed notice of her coming that shocked her.

She advanced toward him. "David!" she greeted. "David!"

"Mademoiselle St. Denis," he replied, and his voice was so cold and unlike the David she had known that it chilled the blood in her veins.

She reached the iron bars and thrust her hands between them but he made no movement toward her. He was like a man cut out of stone. His silence frightened her. David himself frightened her. No sight of love-light or joy in his eyes, no gladness and no emotion that might betray more than dispassionate and uninterested recognition of her! He was like the boy who had stood in the hall at Grondin Manor when Colonel Arnaud had condemned him to be punished with a hundred lashes on his naked back, only he had changed into a man. And it was herself, Anne St. Denis whom he was looking at now—and something in that look, calm and unexcited though it was, terrified her.

Her hands gripped the rough bars. "Dear God, why do you look at me like that?" she entreated. "I have come to you as quickly as I could! Sister Esther is with me. She is out there—now—waiting. I came to tell them that they lie, that it is all false, that you are not a traitor and never could be one—that it is all a terrible mistake———"

She wanted to cry out her love first of all, but the smile which came to his lips stopped her as suddenly as if he had struck at her. He bowed a little. She had never seen cynicism and mockery in his face before.

"Yes, a mistake," he said quietly. "The mistake, mademoiselle, of allowing yourself to become François Bigot's toy."

If a drop of blood remained in her face it went out then. The agony of his blow might have sent her swaying from the cell if she had not gripped fiercely at the bars. A dizziness overcame her, yet through it she heard clearly David's voice.

"De Pean told me Bigot had sent for you and that you were coming," he was saying. "You see, they wanted the show to be complete—wanted you to see me like this so there could be no doubt left in your mind as to my guilt. I asked De Pean to have you kept away from me, but I knew they would not do that. And now that you are here I am not sorry. You already believe me a liar because I told you honestly that I did not know Peter Joel was in Quebec the day you saw him from the convent window. Now I want you to believe I am worse than that, a criminal and a traitor. Of course Bigot showed you my coat in which the papers and maps were concealed. They can leave no doubt can they, mademoiselle, when I confess to you that the coat is mine and the papers were found on me? You, like Bigot, must surely agree that I should be hanged."

"David—David—this terrible thing that has happened has made you unlike yourself," moaned Anne. "Come to me! Let me touch you! Kiss me—let me know it is you—you—and not someone else who is speaking to me in this strange, mad way——"

Again she reached her arms through to him, but David did not move, and she saw in his face a thing which never in all her life had she seen there before—something which struck out at her in all its bitterness, almost like hatred.

She tried to speak again and her palsied lips whispered, "David—my David—I love you—love you——"

"So it would seem." And through the mist that blinded her she saw David coldly incline his head again. "So it would seem, from the day you succeeded in getting me to follow you from Grondin Manor that I might be hanged as a traitor in Quebec. So fools might think, after knowing how well you have played the game with Bigot. But I, knowing that I am here because of you, refuse to believe it. Go back to Bigot, for whom you have sacrificed me. Please do that. You made your choice a long time ago—years and years ago it seems to me—and you cannot change again even if it were in my heart to let you. I choose to be alone. I am not afraid or lonely for I have with me one splendid consolation. It is the knowledge that some day you will know the truth of Bigot's friendship. And then—what a monstrously funny thing it will be for you to think of all the rest of your life!"

David, with his ears trained to the falling of wilderness leaves, had caught the sly returning of Deschenaux' footsteps after the opening and closing of the upper door, and now in a louder voice he cried, "Deschenaux, you may come in from your eavesdropping and assist Mademoiselle St. Denis back to your master, where you may report fully on what has passed between us. Give my compliments to Bigot, and tell him that you are almost as great a blackguard as he. Come quickly, for mademoiselle seems a little faint at hearing so much truth so honestly spoken!"

And Anne, in truth, felt that the world had slipped away from under her and that she needed a hand to keep her from falling to the floor. She had come to see David—had come to bring him comfort and love and hope—the promise to return to Grondin Manor with him forever as soon as he was free. And this was not her David! The husk of him was there, but all the old David was gone and in his place now was a man—years older—who hated her. Her grief came in a sob which scarcely reached David's ears, while her body and brain were numb with the blow. Still she struggled to break her way through the darkness that was shutting her in, to reach David and fall upon her knees at his feet, entreating him to unsay the words with which he had so terribly crushed her. But no sound came from her lips. Her hands slipped at the bars. Dizziness swept over her, and as she fought against it, her lips forming unspoken words for

David, she knew that someone had come to help her—and that it was Deschenaux—and that very soon she was walking unsteadily at his side, back through the corridor and then up the dungeon steps, her weight bearing on him heavily.

Deschenaux heard the sobbing in her breath. His own heart was beating faster. He had not expected this, nor had Bigot. He looked at her eyes, wide open and staring straight ahead of her as if she was straining to see, yet seeing nothing. She made no effort to look into the council-room when they passed. She did not observe Captain Robineau, still standing in the edge of the deeper gloom of the outer corridor. But Deschenaux saw him. Deschenaux noted the dead-white face, ghostly in its thinness, with eyes which were filled with something more sinister than the reflected glow of flaming candles.

Why she was going with Deschenaux and why she was returning with him to Bigot's inner palace was a thought which did not press itself on Anne's confused senses except that in a physically mechanical way she was doing what she had expected to do. Deschenaux, measuring the situation by the fact that she would have crumpled to the floor had it not been for the support of his arm, was praying that Bigot would be in the inner chambers when they arrived, and that Sister Esther would forget the passing of hours in the devotion of her prayers. If he could have added to the blow that had stricken the frail and lovely form at his side he would have done so. Gladly he would have borne it an utter weight in his arms if he could have achieved that unspeakable triumph for his master.

He found Bigot's apartment empty when they entered it.

"Monsieur must be in the council-room," he said, as he relieved himself of his half-fainting burden. "Remain here, mademoiselle; I shall bring him."

His voice roused Anne and she made an effort to call him back to tell him that it was not Bigot she wanted, but Sister Esther. But the door had closed before she could rise or her lips could form a sound. She swayed to her feet and stood fighting desperately to get her balance. She knew that something unusual had happened to her and that it was monstrously weak and inexcusable of her not to be able to speak or to see clearly when she wanted to. She had never fainted and had never before been subjected to this sickening force of great shock. It was like a blinding cloud before her eyes, and she put out her hands to thrust it away. Slowly the dark blot went out of her brain. The room grew larger, the lights and its appointments clearer, and her eyes strained to find the door through which Deschenaux had gone down into the passage-ways again.

She took a step toward it and caught at the edge of the table to support herself. Only one thought possessed her and that was to return as quickly as she could to David. In a dazed way she was wondering why she had left him—why it was that she had let Deschenaux bring her away. It was not because she had wanted to come. For surely David had not meant what he said, or in this strange sickness which had overcome her she had not heard him truly. He did not hate her. He did not believe she was wicked. He was David, her David, and he loved her. He had not intended that Deschenaux should take her away and he would tell her so if she could get back to him. He would put his arms around her and kiss her, and she would tell him what was twisting round in her mind now—something she wanted him so terribly to hear—that she loved him more than she had ever loved him before, and that she knew he was innocent and that it was all the Black Hunter's fault—and that with her own hands she would kill—kill—yes, kill Bigot even!—if Bigot should cause harm to be done him.

The dark cloud came back a little, confusing her, and a step at a time she fought against it toward the door. And then the door opened suddenly and Bigot came in and closed it behind him.

In a moment he was at her side with his arms about her. "Dear little Anne!" he cried. "It has been a hard night—a hard night for you. You are faint and sick. But we have won, dear! We have won!"

The note of triumph in his voice seemed to her like a shout of gladness.

Won!

She swayed against him. She was not conscious of his arm drawing her more closely to him. They had won— and David would be free! And he would not hate her now because of Bigot's friendship, for it was Bigot who had done this—Bigot...

She wanted to cry out in her joy. How horrible it had all been, yet how easy to clear away! She thrust against the dark cloud so violently, in her desire to see and to reach the door which led to David, that Bigot let her go. Deschenaux had spoken to him swiftly in the corridor, and he wondered if his secretary had misjudged the moment. Then he saw what Deschenaux had seen—and felt. She was praying on her feet even as gladness lighted up her face.

He caught her arm again. "It might have been death," he said slowly and clearly, his face aflame with a purpose which Anne no longer had the power to see or shrink from. "That was what they wanted, even Vaudreuil. To be broken with iron bars and then hanged before the eyes of the town that it might be a lesson to all of New France. At last they gave in, but not until I had threatened Vaudreuil and a few others with political and social ruin. Do you hear me, Anne? David is saved. He is not to be hanged. He is simply to be drummed out of the army, and after that whipped through the streets of Quebec at the tail of an ox-cart, like Carbanac."

With a little cry Anne reached out, her hands seeking to find something in the empty air. The strain of months of suffering and unhappiness crowded upon her, driven by the pitilessness of Bigot's final blow. David to be whipped—whipped through the streets of the town—tied to an ox-cart—like Carbanac! That was her last thought as the dark cloud blotted out her consciousness. Yet even then as Bigot caught her in his arms her lips moved in an effort to speak David's name.

Of all the monstrous hours of his life this which had come to him now was Bigot's greatest. For a brief space he was stunned by its completeness as he looked into the beautiful face that had fallen back from his breast. With a cry that was almost savage in the intensity of its passion he crushed the limp form in his arms until if there had been consciousness left it must have fled. Never had Anne stirred his desire for her—never had she seemed half so beautiful—as in these moments of her utter helplessness. She was worth life, death, anything—the mere possession of her, even if it was a possession bound by chains. No thought of future, no fear of tomorrow, no wakening sense of pity or honor could have held him back from the thing that had become the consuming want of his existence. How slight she was, how like a lovely flower—a child—as he raised her in his arms! Even death, if it had to be such an impossible thing as that, would not be too great a price to pay for what he held within his reach!

He turned with her to the door through which he had come and locked it. The click of the key filled his face with a demoniac joy. Its metallic voice assured him of his happiness. Then he faced the opposite door, through which Vaudreuil had gone. But before he went to it he carried Anne to a couch and placed her upon it. For a moment he stood over her. His fingers had loosened the shining coils of her hair, and their brightness streaming about her shoulders and throat added to the deathly whiteness of her face. He bent down with a guttural, brutish cry and kissed the silent lips and closed eyes.. She belonged to him now! She would belong to him forever if he chained her closely enough this night—or day. For the day was breaking in a pale and sickly dawn as he turned to lock the other door.

His hand was reaching out when to his amazement the door swung in. He had heard no sound and no voice. Captain Robineau stood facing him. And a little behind this man of sinister fortune was Sister Esther.

For half a dozen seconds the eyes of the two men met, and then Robineau's hard face relaxed and for Bigot alone his thin lips twisted in a smile of understanding.

"Sister Esther has come to say that it is time for Mademoiselle St. Denis to return, monsieur," he said, and bowed stiffly but without giving the military salute due to the representative of the King.

With the maddening fabric of his happiness crashing about him Bigot still had sense enough to hold back the storm of fury that possessed him. Robineau had beaten him. Robineau, who yesterday had lain so helplessly in the hollow of his hands. Beaten—and by him! Yet he smiled. While his heart and brain reeled under the blow of his disappointment and the surge of his hatred, the cleverness which never deserted him revealed itself in the swift transformation of his face—its change from astonishment and shock to solicitude and gladness as he greeted Sister Esther. He was that very moment on the point of seeking her presence, he said, because he was alarmed about Anne. He was sorry now that he had sent to the convent for her, as the shock of seeing and talking with David and of hearing the sentence that had just been passed on him had been too great for her. She had only a moment before fallen in a faint. He had carried her to the couch, and prayed God that nothing was seriously wrong with her.

Now that his work was done Robineau had departed. So Bigot brought water and smelling-salts for Sister Esther, and when a few minutes later Anne sighed and opened her eyes his happiness was so great that it impressed itself deeply upon the good and trustful nun. It was then Bigot knew that Robineau had betrayed none of his suspicions to Sister Esther.

He called assistance, and Anne was borne tenderly to a carriage that took her to the convent, held securely in Sister Esther's arms.

Before the gloomy thickness of dawn had given way to a brighter glow of day Vaudreuil had received his instructions. Captain Jean Talon, the duelist, must instantly reopen an old quarrel with Robineau. Bigot had another ten thousand francs for Talon if the affair could be arranged within twenty-four hours. And Robineau must die.

CHAPTER XXIII

At the end of March, 1755, the beginning of that change which had been slowly creeping over New France and which in the end was destined to rot the very foundations of the nation was making itself felt in Quebec. For some time there had been a feeling of unrest and of uncertainty throughout the wide domains beyond Quebec's frontiers in spite of the apparent successes of French arms and diplomacy. The people, the sixty thousand men and women pioneers who kept these domains for France, were beginning to lose the pride and courage which go with a conviction of security and power behind them. War had not yet been declared. Mirepoix, the French ambassador to London, was teaching the English how to dance, and Lord Albemarle, English ambassador at Versailles, was reciprocating by teaching the French to play whist. Madame Pompadour had risen to her highest power and was not only the King's mistress but also his procuress and a sort of feminine prime minister.

The courts of both nations were smiling at each other, eating, drinking, dancing, and making love together, in March of 1755. Yet General Braddock had already arrived in the colonies with the forty-fourth and forty-eighth regiments to fight the French, and Baron Dieskau, with eighteen ships of war and six battalions of La Reine, Bourgogne, Languedoc,

Guienne, Artois, and Béarn, three thousand men in all, was sailing after him to meet him in a mighty duel in the wildernesses of America.

Such was the situation, without a parallel in the history of the world, on the day when Anne St. Denis, crushed and broken, left David in the dungeon-cell of Bigot's palace—a spectacle of two great nations—the two mightiest courts in Europe—dancing and playing whist like loving friends while each sent out armies and fleets to wage war upon the other across the seas!

And thirteen months were still to pass before these players would drop their masks, pick up their games, and declare war—thirteen months during which armies were to be annihilated, and the colonies run red, while Mirepoix fondled the curls of a favored lady in waiting, and Albemarle made his conquests with Chesterfieldian manners and graces at Versailles.

The English colonies with their million and a half of fighting people could stand this dalliance, but New France, with less than a hundred thousand including her Indian allies, could not. Albemarle, playing whist in Versailles, had half won the war before it started; and Mirepoix, because of soft curls, a pair of pretty eyes, and a red mouth, had performed his part in half losing it.

The people of New France, bred of warrior stock and loving their wilderness country as they loved their lives, had put up a loyal fight and were destined to make a still greater one. But a little at a time the truth of their situation had pressed upon them, until in this early spring of 1755 a panic of restlessness and uncertainty had begun to possess them, and many foresaw and dreaded the unavoidable and terrible calamities ahead of the nation. Rumor had followed upon the heels of rumor through the wildernesses, and seigneurs as well as the common people were asking themselves questions which had never troubled them before.

And among these rumors, persistent and frequent in Quebec of late, had been the one which spoke of treachery. This rumor, encouraged by Bigot and his ring, had spread like a disease in the blood of the populace. Added to facts and fears that had been steadily increasing it gave a new and fiercer impetus to the demand that something be done. The great fortified city on the rock, positive in its faith of invulnerability only a few months before, was beginning to have its doubt about the rest of the world, and its own world in particular, in spite of last autumn's victories and Dieskau's coming. Discussion of events took on a different tone in coffee-houses and on the streets. People were worried and eager for something to happen.

No time could have been chosen when the populace was readier for a sensation than on the twenty-third of March, when it learned that a traitor had been caught red-handed in the act of carrying precious secrets to the hated English, and that this traitor was Lieutenant David Rock, a favorite of the Intendant.

The news spread swiftly. By midday it was known that a military council, called together the preceding night, had lost no time in taking action and condemning the prisoner. That its judgment had halted a step short of death was openly ascribed to the influence of the Intendant. But Bigot's victory for the stranger he had brought in from the wilderness to honor with his favors was not in itself a very great triumph, many thought, for to a gentleman of New France, or an officer in the army, hanging was preferable to the infamous ox-cart and whipping parade through the streets of the town.

Various emotions swept the populace as the day lengthened. There were many, jealous of David's swift ascent into popular favor, who were filled with satisfaction. Others were shocked that treachery should have found itself so close to the person of the Intendant and the inner secrets of state. A few, like Monsieur Lotbinière and his friends, held their judgment in abeyance, either suspicious or disbelieving. But above these mental impressions—whether they were bitter or tolerant—and in the minds of all except a few of David's most intimate friends swept a fiercely growing conflagration of sentiment that demanded and anticipated the punishment of the traitor, and which was only relieved by a strong undercurrent of pity for Anne St. Denis.

Anne's beauty and her goodness of heart, together with her vivacity of mind and many lovable qualities that had endeared her to the high as well as the low, had won for her a place of gentle worship in the hearts of the town which, as Mother Mary Boucher afterward wrote in her diary, was "a sweet consolation and pride to the sisters who had been privileged to teach her." So among those who knew of the relationship that had existed between Anne and David the sensation aroused by the latter's crime and debasement, with the certainty of its horrible ending, was tempered by the romance that had been so cruelly shattered in the girl's heart. In some way which no one seemed bent on questioning, the more intimate details of the preceding night's tragedy in Bigot's palace began to pass from mouth to mouth. It became known that Bigot had sent to the convent for Anne, and that her visit with David, and subsequent happenings, had proved such a grievous blow to her that she was now too ill to rise from her bed. And Bigot, according to the few who had seen him, was so deeply grieved and shocked that he had refused to leave his apartments.

The storm of popular opinion gathered more darkly as the hours passed. The unrest and suspicions of weeks and months found their vent in an increasing sentiment against David, and many began to condemn the influence which had saved him from the death which all traitors deserved. This was what Bigot wanted. With the powerful human machine at his command, answering his every beck and call, it was not difficult for him to add to this whispering dissatisfaction until it became a dominant note in the voice of the city. That he had lost Anne in an hour when she had seemed to be hopelessly his prize had not lessened his certainty of possessing her. In a few days, and possibly in a few hours, his opportunity would come again, and this time there would be no Robineau to stumble like a fool between him and his desires. He was confident that Anne and Sister Esther were free of any suspicion of his thoughts and intentions, and Captain Talon, who was already on the trail of his man, would see to it that Robineau's lips were sealed.

Therefore, he spread fearlessly throughout the town a condemnation of his own efforts in saving David, for he knew this talk would come quickly to the Ursulines and to Anne. And what could appeal more deeply to the girl he was determined and mad to possess than a public arraignment of the act he had performed in his apparently self-sacrificing effort to save her happiness?

There was one heart in Quebec in which grief and despair were overwhelmed at times by a smoldering fury and that was the heart of Nancy Lotbinière. Only her father's restraint and his grim assurance that she had no proofs of the things which she might say restrained her from disclosing to the public the suspicions which for a long time had been so insistently a part of her. It would be far better that David should go through his experience, and then return to his wilderness, than to make Anne St. Denis' name a common thing tossed from mouth to mouth throughout New France, the Baron said. And Nancy conceded this was true. But she was determined to fight for David. First of all she was determined to see Bigot. Without mincing a word she would face him with every thought and conviction that was in her soul, and demand that he discover David's innocence or fight to his own social destruction the almost irresistible feminine influence which her beauty and personality exerted over the gentler sex of Quebec at this time. In such a way, she thought, could she strike a deadlier and more effective blow at Bigot than even her father and all his friends, for as yet she had not completely guessed the monster's passion for Anne or his willingness to sacrifice anything that was now within his grasp for possession of her.

Her first disappointment, in spite of the almost peremptory tone of her request, was her failure to gain an interview with Bigot during either the afternoon or evening of this twenty-third of March. Neither was she successful in getting permission to see David. And then, in the early evening of that day, came the climax to the tragedy. Through the streets and in the public places the town criers read in loud and official voices the news that Lieutenant David Rock, traitor to the King, was to be drummed out of the army and whipped through the streets of Quebec at high noon of the following day, the twenty-fourth of March, in the year of Our Lord and His Gracious Majesty, 1755.

When Anne St. Denis heard that news it seemed to her that death would be a welcome deliverance from her agony.

In the late hours of the night she rose from her bed of sickness, dressed, and waited for the dawn. And scarcely had that dawn given way to the clear sun and bright sky which heralded with almost a touch of spring the twenty-fourth of March, when another shock ran through the city of Quebec with an even swifter thrill than that which had been roused by David's capture.

A duel had been fought in the first light of day, a duel between Captain René Robineau and Captain Jean Talon. Talon, notorious for his killings, lay dead at the Intendant's palace. And Robineau had gone—no one knew where.

CHAPTER XXIV

By mid-forenoon of the following day the ancient city of Quebec was prepared for one of those unhappy spectacles which were not infrequent in New France at this time, and which persisted in official and popular favor until nearly half a century later.

With their own social structure resting on a foundation of tragedy and martyrdom, the horror of punishment in its most agonizing forms had not struck deeply upon the consciences of a people who regarded crime of almost every kind, even to petty pilfering, as something punishable by death or near death. Rompu vif, or "breaking alive," in which a prisoner's bones were broken one by one until death came to ease his torture, was not uncommon under the French régime; and the killing of a condemned person by disemboweling him in public was a method of execution carried out as late as 1797, when Chief Justice Osgood, at Quebec, demanded this punishment for David McLane, convicted of high treason.[1]

But no punishment of this kind, with all its terrible and sickening detail, aroused the curiosity and interest of the people as did a public whipping through the streets. This was an event to be anticipated by women and children as well as men, and especially by the common people, though the whipping—like the passing of a circus parade—was viewed by the grand monde from many windows and outside vantage-points, and not infrequently parties of thoughtless young people were formed to join in the crowd. The whipping at the tail of an ox-cart was supposed to have its humorous as well as its distressing side, and, because of this degradation of being made a laughing-stock and a creature of shame, men of spirit preferred death rather than suffer its indignity.

David Rock, upon whom this punishment was to be inflicted, stood in a different position from that of any of those who had recently preceded him, as his case was a military one rather than of civil authority, and was attended by certain preliminaries which could not fail to leave an abiding effect. His crime and the punishment which was to be its price were loudly heralded by public criers; military officers were commanded to have their companies and regiments on parade at the "drumming out"; and a special guard was detailed to escort him outside the city, from which he would be forever banished when the infliction of justice was at an end.

In his cell David knew of the show which was being prepared as the grand finale to his ruin. From the hour in which he had spoken his last words to Anne, and had seen Deschenaux take her away white and half fainting, his resentment and despair began to give way before an inversion of feeling which left him strangely and stoically calm. This calmness at times became an almost half-mad exultation at the thought that not only he, but Anne St. Denis as well, was about to suffer on this day when the monstrous plot of the man who had so successfully posed as her friend arrived at the culminating point of its triumph. For the motive of Bigot's plotting was now as clear to him as the flare of the candles in his cell. With himself a traitor, whipped, and banished, degraded and condemned in the eyes of all New France, what could lie in the way of the Intendant's wooing of favor from Anne St. Denis, who must thereafter regard him with the contempt—even though it might be mitigated by pity and a spark of love—in which the rest of the world would hold him? But in a little while, even more than today, Anne herself would suffer. In these bitterest hours, when all sense of charity and mercy and love were burned out of him, this thought was his chief consolation.

For it was Anne who had brought this shattering and unforgivable tragedy into his life. Anne and her insistence that he come to Quebec, her lack of faith in him later, her willingness and unreasoning trustfulness in accepting more and more favors from Bigot even after David had warned her against him and had let her know of his own unhappiness at the increasing intimacy between them. For Anne, on this morning of his punishment, he found no excuse, and no spark of the passion which had been the soul of his life.

At least he told himself it was dead. And the futility of protesting his innocence, and of fighting to save himself from the ordeal with which an unbelievable travesty of justice was facing him, had become an equally determined thing within him. If he told the truth he would not only be punished as a traitor but would be laughed and jeered at on the streets as a coward and a liar.

As the hour set for his torture drew nearer he began to seize a little more disquietly upon the crumbs of comfort which he could find for himself. He thanked God that it would all be over before his mother or the Black Hunter could hear of it, and by that time he would be in his forests again. In those forests were men and women who would believe him when he told the truth. And after that, some day, would come the time when drop by drop he would make Bigot's blood pay for its monstrous perfidy, and when Anne, accursed by the part she had played, would suffer even more than he was suffering now.

He was not afraid of the lash. The lash itself had scarcely entered his thoughts. What was there about pain to shrink from? Only men like Bigot and Vaudreuil and most of the others in this rotten city of Quebec feared physical hurt. He thought of Peter, who had fought duels with smiles on his lips; of the Black Hunter, who was gentle and humorous in the face of many deaths, and of an Indian he had seen die in agony down at Fort William Henry without so much as a flitting betrayal of pain in his heroic face. The forests were not afraid of either hurt or death! But they shrank—shrank in horror and fear—from the debasement of that thing within them which was called the soul of man. It was this soul that had writhed in David until the truth had come like a revelation that only the guilty could be debased. Only the coward and the liar. That was why no amount of torture or vilifying could rob dignity and pride and defiance from the face of a brave Indian dying at the fire stake of his tormentors.

And then he thought of Carbanac—Carbanac the murderer—who had walked so like a god through the streets of Quebec, his back torn by the lash, because there was no guilt on his conscience!

Could Carbanac with his heart crushed by a wife's faithlessness do more than he, who had all his forests and all the open skies of the world waiting for him?

At last the hour came.

And David was given a military coat with glittering buttons and fine appointments. It was brought to him by two guards who were accompanied by an officer and an escort of half a dozen soldiers. One of the guards unlocked his cell and the other helped him on with the garment while the soldiers formed in two stiff and wooden files. He did not look at them as he stalked between.

The thought came to him even then that it was Carbanac who was doing this over again; Carbanac, the honest man, the man whose calloused hands had choked the life from Nicolet, and his lips set in a grim and mirthless smile as he looked straight ahead to where the spirit of Carbanac was leading him.

For the first time in days he saw the sun when he came up the dungeon steps into the great hall. It was this sun which struck him first, the way it came through the narrow windows which faced the south and then scattered itself brokenly in golden warmth over the stone floor. And in some unaccountable way, along with this sun, a tatterdemalion of a dog had found his entrance into the proscribed limits of the palace. He was a very beggar of a dog, a vagabond with wiry hair and uncouth tail and joints, and yet there was something in the manner he held his head and in the bright directness of his eyes as they looked out of his whiskered face that made David think more than ever of Carbanac. For this dog, like Carbanac, was not a coward though he was in a strange place and pursued by enemies. A moment before David had heard his howl as a guard struck him; and now, in passing, he held out a hand and before he could withdraw it the mongrel was at his side and had given it a swift and friendly touch. Then came a kick from behind, and after that other kicks from the guards in the hall, until the animal was driven to an exit which took him from the human enemies among whom he had come quite without criminal intent and with all the good humor and comradely curiosity of his humble breed.

The dog and the sun, but especially the dog, had robbed David's face of the extremity of its bitterness, and like a flash of strange warmth the unexpected caress of the animal's tongue had passed through him and left a glow behind.

They were approaching the main doors of the palace, which opened on the parade, and David allowed himself to look about. No need of keeping his neck so stiff, he began to think.

There were only guards and a few soldiers in the hall. From outside he heard a murmuring commotion which could only come from a great crowd. Then he passed through the open doors and stood on the stone square at the top of the palace steps, with the city of Quebec looking at him.

Even then he did not at first sense the spectacular setting of Bigot's drama or the overwhelming conspicuousness of his own figure, for coming toward him up the steps, courageous and undaunted, seeing only him, wagging his disreputable tail only for him and blind to all the power and pomp and threat of dire calamity about him, was that pariah of a dog again!

Standing alone on this palace stage six feet above the crowd, as Bigot had planned that he should stand, his scarlet coat a vivid mark for all eyes, his wild blond hair shining in the sun and his face alight with a smile of welcome for the dog, no thought of the immensity of the scene occurred to David. Bigot's deadliest enemy could not have conceived a completer anticlimax to military glitter and pompous strut, for in these moments the people were not thinking of the whipping-cart and the lash but only of a dog and a man. And many years were destined to pass before the scene wiped itself out of the memory of the city, for as they looked, and as the soldiers held their breath in wondering speculation, the vagabond dog laid himself down at David's feet and gazed with unexcited confidence out over the heads of the assembled host.

A breath ran through the crowd, a great sigh of movement and voice, a thrilling, growing unrest of scarcely expressed thought, and then the momentary spell was broken by the closing in of a thin cordon of soldiers, and when the cordon opened again the dog was gone. But David was no longer the man who had come up from the dungeon cell, any more than the crowd was the same crowd that a few minutes before might have been roused into shouting itself hoarse for his death.

He was amazed at his own calmness and at the interest rather than fear and horror with which he looked down upon the closely drawn lines of soldiers and the people packed in the streets and square beyond them. Immediately below him at the foot of the steps were the ox-cart and the ox. The ox was a big and lazy-looking animal that chewed its cud placidly as it waited. David shrugged his shoulders. That ox would set him a slow pace through the streets of Quebec, he thought. But the reflection did not make him nervous. He was strangely free of that. Slowly his eyes traveled over the sea of spectators while a red-faced and blatant-voiced officer half-way down the stone steps read aloud the brief details of both his crime and his punishment. He scarcely heard a word. He was looking at the women and children, hundreds of them. Why should they come to see him whipped, he wondered. He could excuse the small boys. As a small boy he would have been there himself. But the women!

Yet deep in his heart he was praying, above all other things, that Anne St. Denis was among them. He wanted her to look upon his degradation and punishment. He wanted this picture and all that was to follow to burn itself so deeply in her brain that it would remain with her all the days of her life.

The voice on the step had stopped and now came a slow beating of drums. It was a solemn and terrible sound and sent a shiver through David. It was like the melancholy sobbing of the tom-toms in a wilderness camp where there was mourning for the dead. And it was for the dead, the sombrous lament of the drums, which he had heard more than once as they led the way to a military grave.

Adjusting their own movements to the gloomy booming of the drums two officers advanced up the steps toward David. They were like important owls, he thought. They paused, one on each side of him, and stood for a few seconds like wooden images until at a sudden signaling crash of the drums they began to take methodical and deliberate turns at tearing the brightly polished brass buttons from his coat.

Curious turnings and twistings came in David's brain. He wanted to laugh and he wanted to strike out with his two fists. There was something childishly funny in all this ostentatious play, this ripping off of buttons, as though it were a mighty religious sacrifice to some god or other. He pitied the buttons. He saw them rolling one after another down the stone steps, bright and glittering in the sunlight. He heard the coat tear where bits of cloth came with the buttons. He noticed that one of the officers had short and stubby fingers and the other long and bony ones. All this struck him as funny. But at the same time there was something growing in him which made him want to smash out with his fists, something which he held back with an iron grip. His coat was taken off after the buttons were gone. Then his shirt, and he stood naked from the waist up before the crowd. And all the time the drums were beating their slow and solemn death-march.

Still he did not so much as clench his hands. People looked at him and wondered. He was a splendid figure on the steps, finer in the strength and youth of his unclad shoulders than he could ever have been in a uniform. His hair was blond and his skin as white as a woman's. He was not afraid or cringing. Many swore afterwards that there was a smile on his lips and in his eyes as the officers tugged at his buttons. Others said the smile was still there when he walked down the steps and allowed his hands to be tied in the iron rings in the block at the tail of the ox-cart.

David did not know he was smiling. He was forgetting the crowd and the sun and even the dog. He was fighting. Fighting to crush a monstrous spirit within him which wanted to cry out to all these people the truth about what was happening. He knew this inclination was roused by the coward in him trying to find its way out. It would make a better show for Bigot. The Black Hunter would not have surrendered to it. Even Carbanac had held the thing in leash.

Suddenly he found that he had company at the tail of the ox-cart. The vagabond dog was there.

The dog scurried under the wagon when the ox began slowly to move, and continued to travel under its protection, so that David could see a part of his angular and half-starved body at times. The man who said the dog was not thinking would have been a fool. He had found a friend. In the friend he had found a master. And in some very accurate way he had reasoned that he and his friend were alone in all this crowd, except that the ox and the cart were not inimical to them. His sharp ears heard the first falling of the lash on David's back. But he heard no word or cry from the man he had adopted. The sound of the lash was not new to him. It sent him farther under the cart and nearer to the plodding heels of the ox. Undoubtedly that swishing beat of thonged leather was intended for him and he was of a strong mind to keep out of its way. Now and then he glanced back to see that David's legs were following.

The cart jolted and creaked over cobblestones and frozen ruts and climbed a long and winding hill. The crowd was a streaming mass on both sides and behind, and many of those nearest the cart pointed out the homeless cur tramping along under it; small boys began to call to it and throw bits of frozen earth. A new kind of curiosity and with it a sense of antagonism began to seize the dog. Rock-like clods fell about him, one or two struck him, and when a boy ran in close and poked at him with a long stick he bared his fangs and snarled and dropped back nearer to the legs of his friend.

He began also to take a new and keener interest in the whip. There were intervals when it was still and when he could hear only the jolting of the cart and the growing voice of the pursuing mob; and then it would start again, with sharp cracking sounds which seemed to be reaching out for his own quivering flesh. Something happened after a little which turned his brain red. A heavier and more accurate clod struck him and he dodged back quickly, and in that moment he saw the whip. Its snarling lashes cracked like breaking sticks in mid-air and fell whistling and hissing upon the back of the man who was his friend. For an instant he hesitated, and in that instant the black man who was wielding the whip sent his arm backward and forward swiftly and the red-hot tails of the scourging thing wrapped themselves about the body of the dog. They were no swifter than the mongrel himself. The crowd heard the sudden horrified yell of the negro. Many saw the dog leap. And when the animal had been kicked and beaten and furiously lashed until it was lost in the mob those same people saw blood running down the black man's arm, just as it was running from David's back.

For an interval there was rest for David, until they reached the streets of the higher town. He had felt his nerves beginning to crack. But now they were set again—and the dog had helped. The dizziness which had begun to cloud his brain disappeared. No one had seen him flinch and his chin was higher as the ox-cart lumbered into the fashionable streets of Upper Town. Here would be his friends. Openly as well as from behind curtained windows they would be looking at him. The lash was falling again when they passed Nancy Lotbinière's house. But there the curtains at the windows were drawn tight. God bless Nancy Lotbinière! It was her little message for him, letting him know that she might be praying for him but that her eyes, and no eyes of the Lotbinière house, should look upon his shame.

There was a horrible and sickening pain to the fall of the knotted lashes now. They seemed to burn through his flesh and bones into his very soul. Hot flames racked his body, yet like an Indian he stalked in his torture.

Down St. Louis Street into the great square in front of the Governor's palace plodded the ox at the head of the cart. A thousand people had gathered to witness the end of the barbaric circus which had begun with the common people at the end of Palais Street.

Here, as with Carbanac, would come the last scene of the whipping and in this instance the banishment of the criminal from the city. David wondered why he felt no shame, no sense of sweeping humiliation as he stood calmly with the eyes of the Upper City on him, so straight and unfaltering that no one guessed his brain was dizzy or that his nerves were strained to the edge of the snapping point. He was facing the west, and illimitable distances lay before him, miles upon miles of forest terrain which one can see to this day from the top of the big rock. Of all the hundreds gathered about the square only he saw the forests or was thinking of them, his forests, his home, where lay everything that he loved or ever would love from this day on. When the lash fell again he did not take his eyes from them. Something

383

seemed to be reaching up out of the dark masses of the far wilderness to comfort and strengthen him, and while many grew sick and turned away as the black man's arm rose and fell he stood like the heroic Indian he was thinking of, with all of that Indian's glorious heritage of life and freedom filling his staring eyes, in which vision, in spite of his last supreme courage, was slowly but surely fading away.

And he was standing thus, his back running red in the unclouded sun, his blond head still high, the lash cutting its last marks upon his flesh in a crescendo of furious vindictiveness, when Anne St. Denis saw him from the open inner edge of the square.

The crowd had made way for her. It had parted, amazed and speculative at this slim, furiously fighting slip of a girl who forced her way through them. Many recognized her. But the news traveled more slowly than did the girl herself, and not until she had darted through the thin line of soldiers which guarded the square did David hear the sudden murmuring of voices which came like a great sigh from the crowd.

For a few seconds Anne hesitated in the open space which was the heart of the crowd as if blinded by what she saw, and now the eyes of the people were on her and no longer on David. The black slave and his victim were unconscious of this fact. The whip rose and fell, and to give his final assault a more spectacular effect Bigot's merciless barbarian made each back-lash of the whip snap with a report that was as loud as a pistol shot.

His ebon skin, naked to the waist like David's, gleamed with a shining perspiration; his thick-lipped face was twisted in a paroxysm of joy as he inflicted the climax of punishment on one of the white skins he hated, and David's back was redder in the sunlight, so red that a scream such as the ears of Quebec had never heard until this day came from Anne's lips as she hurled herself upon the black monster and his whip.

It was a cry not only of horror and madness but of rage and vengeance. Her hands caught the curling lashes of the whip, and so furiously and unexpectedly had she come that the weapon was torn from the black man's grip. At the cry David had turned, and now he saw the whip used even more furiously than it had been employed on him, and the terrified slave was fleeing from it. The sigh that had passed through the crowd grew into a low rumble. Bigot's executioner stumbled and fell, and Anne overtook him again, lashing his face until he screamed in agony. The crowd's rumble grew into a roar. Its edges swayed, its mass undulated in a great wave. Where the black man darted into it the people closed in like a destroying avalanche. But it opened for Anne St. Denis—Anne and her whip. It made a path for her, and the people who forced themselves back from the edge of this path saw the strange madness in her eyes and heard her panting breath as she passed them, clutching tightly to the whip that had stained her own white hands with the blood from David's back.

Even those who knew her made no effort to assist or stop her, nor dared to speak. But outside the farther edge of the crowd a man was waiting, a man with the collar of a long coat pulled up about his throat and wearing a battered hat that almost covered his eyes. He ran toward her as she appeared, and, with the girl clutching at his arm and still holding the whip, they hurried down the cobblestoned slope of the hill past the Golden Dog, with the more curious and less sensitive of the crowd beginning to follow. But at the turn of the street a carriage was waiting, and into this the man thrust his companion, following her quickly, and the carriage disappeared at a swift pace in the direction of the Ursuline Convent.

There were those who did not follow the whipping who saw the carriage go down Fabrique Street that day at a gallop; there were others who saw it turn on Saint John, and continue again at a gallop down Palais, until the horse that drew it was halted where Nicolas and Lacroix came in at an angle near the Intendant's palace.

Five minutes later Bigot alone in his apartment heard a knock at his door, the door which only a few used, and with that knock the voice of Anne St. Denis asking him to let her enter. Joyously he unlocked the door and Anne came in—Anne with the whip in her hand, the whip that was red with David's blood; and behind her, no longer hidden in the long coat and battered old hat, closely followed Captain René Robineau.

Only in rumors and strange stories that crept out long afterward did Quebec or New France know of what happened in Bigot's palace that day. When Anne had finished, David's vengeance had been paid in full. Three times Bigot seized the whip that was in her furious hands, and three times Captain Robineau's sword pierced his clothes and entered his flesh until in mortal terror he gave up his grip. At last one would not have recognized his face, and not until then did Anne sway back against the wall and sink sobbing and broken to the floor, her strength gone. It was Robineau who picked up the whip and completed the work, and could Quebec have seen his face when it was done, alight once more with the flame and pride of the ancient Robineau honor, it would have marveled at a second and greater miracle which had come to pass with the whipping of David Rock.

[1] "For punishment of which I require for the King that he be condemned to have his arms, legs, thighs, and backbone broken, he alive, on a scaffold, which shall be erected for that purpose in the market square of the city, and that he then be disemboweled and his face turned toward the sky, to be so left to die."—From His Majesty's Attorney's requisition for the death of Jean Baptiste Goyer, done at Montreal, the 6th of June, 1752.

CHAPTER XXV

The world might have changed again for David outside the city wall if he had let it. As the gate closed behind him, and the crowd was held back, he found Doctor Coué on the other side waiting to meet him. There were several others in his company but David did not know them. He accepted their presence in a cold and unemotional way, and in a small house a few steps distant his lacerated back was dressed by the little surgeon who had come with Monsieur Lotbinière to play their trick on Peter in the dueling-wood many weeks before. The more poignant of David's emotions had snapped. He felt his pain dully. He was not conscious of a thrill at the significance of the unexpected scene which had occurred in the square. Anne was no nearer to him than when she had left his prison cell, and her act had not inspired him with hope, regret, or gladness. He had only felt for a few swift seconds an immense and overwhelming satisfaction that God had answered his prayer and had let her see him at the tail of the ox-cart.

Even that emotion had burned itself out now. It was not the first time the little surgeon had witnessed this numbing of senses in the body of a strong man fighting against a mental inertia which in a weaker spirit would have meant physical collapse. He performed his work quietly and gently

388

and with the thoroughness of a master. It took him the better part of an hour and not until he was finished did he offer advice or give instructions. David was to remain where he was for a little while, until friends called for him. Monsieur and Mademoiselle Lotbinière were coming for him at four o'clock and would see to it that his journey up the river was a comfortable one. Mademoiselle was preparing now and wanted him to know that she was planning to accompany him the entire distance to his home on the Richelieu.

This intimation of Nancy's plans sent the first shock of interest through David. It was an unpleasant shock. It did not show in his face as he thanked the doctor and watched him depart. But as soon as he was alone he began to act. His belongings had been brought to the cottage, which was apparently tenantless except for himself. He saw that a few necessary things were in a small pack, put on warm clothing, found his powder-horn and bullet-pouch, seized his old rifle and sought the rear exit from the cottage. He moved quickly, and all the time a warmer glow was growing in his heart for Nancy, the first reawakening of the soul which had been lashed out of him.

It was she who had done all this, not Anne. It was Nancy who had thought of him, even to bringing the things she knew he would want most—the things he had borne with him when he came a stranger to Quebec. In his heart he was blessing her. But he did not want to see her. His one desire, consuming all other thoughts in its demand, was to get away—alone. Even the Black Hunter or Peter he would have shunned. He wanted the woods to himself, the trails where he would meet no one and hear no voice. To be compelled to talk, or listen, or even to know that pity was near him in these hours appalled him as a possibility that was unbearable. Nancy could not help him and it would be impossible for him to make her understand.

If he had been guilty of the crime which Bigot had fastened upon him he could not have stolen away more cautiously, and that the shame of transgression might be acknowledged by the manner of his going did not for a moment trouble him. He experienced no anxiety as to what Nancy Lotbinière or any others who had been his friends might think of him. Whether they believed him innocent or guilty neither added nor detracted from the coloring of his world at the present moment, when every energy of his mind and every ounce of strength in his body were inspired by the desire to get away from Quebec and everything that it held as quickly as possible.

Striking back from the cottage and away from the gate through which a few years later the dying Montcalm was to be carried from the Plains of Abraham, he experienced little difficulty in reaching unobserved the neck of woods which fringed the old meadows of Abraham Martin's farm, and thence achieved the brush-grown ravine which so successfully sheltered Wolfe's Englishmen on that fatal September day, 1759. From here his descent to the river was easy, and Sillery Forest lay ahead of him, and beyond that the hidden trails of a wilderness so vast that as yet no man had found its end. But until he had passed the mission at Sillery, hiding himself well in the woods in circling it, he did not feel himself safely beyond the environs of the place he had grown to hate.

A last time he looked back, standing on a forested pinnacle which in a few moments more would blot out from his eyes forever the city on the rock. In the bright sun undimmed by mist or cloud he could see the battlemented heights, and his eyes rested where he knew the convent of the Ursulines lay hidden behind the grim, dark streak which marked the fortress walls. It seemed years ago that he had come in the cold and melancholy gloom of evening, and had listened to the welcome of the bells. Since then hope had lived and died for him. An eternity had passed and what he had dreamed was scattered dust. He had found, at last, what he had truly expected to find and what little old Fontbleu, the miller, had told him that he would find.

The city which he hated now with a smoldering fury had robbed him, beaten him, dishonored him, just as it had done these things for Carbanac, and he gave voice to the curse which was in his heart. The city—and Bigot. The city—and Anne. He clenched his fists. It had been his hell and its people had swarmed like devils to see him suffer. A traitor! He was that now, if never before; its deadliest enemy, an avenger praying for the power to destroy, vindictive, implacable, malevolent in his bitterness.

And then something broke in him which was not the man who hated with a passion born of despair. It was what was left of the boy, a broken sob, a great breath of grief and frailty, which came from him before he could stop it.

It was the boy of Sunset Hill, the boy of the flower-strewn bottomlands and of Grondin's Wood, the boy who had listened to the stories of the old mill-wheel and his mother's prayers, the boy of the Richelieu struggling in him again and finding its voice in that sob which came as he looked back and cursed at the great city on the rock.

And then, looking down, he saw something coming up the steep path which he had followed, a creature with its head close to the ground, nosing his footsteps with the surety of a four-footed hunter—the dog.

He waited, and stood without sound or movement until the animal was very near. The lash, the boot, hunger, and a wild yearning were all in the story of the dog's approach. David noticed these things now. The dog might have been a powerful beast if his body had not been thinned by starvation. But there was a ferocity of desire in the way his loose muzzle nosed the scent of friendship in the snow and frozen earth, which was greater than any hunger of the body. Not only a dog but a dog's soul was coming up the craggy ascent, and unconsciously David named him then and there by calling softly, "Here I am, Comrade!"

They went on together, striking into the untrailed depths of the deeper timber where there was no chance of meeting people he did not want to meet. Now and then they came to little opens and on the sides of sunny knolls the snow had begun to soften in the warmth of the sun. This was the year of the early spring of 1755, when birds returned to their northern haunts a month ahead of time and the first wild-flowers bloomed when in other seasons their awakening roots had scarcely thrust green shoots out of the earth. It was the year when praises were sung in the churches of New France because of "a miracle of early spring prophetic of God's love and weighted with fair auguries for those who had continued their faith in Him through a terrible winter." And its first warmth came with the dawn of the day of David's whipping.

In the forest there was life. It had begun to stir out of hidden nests and deep retreats. Squirrels chattered and scurried from tree to tree in the hardwoods, and David saw occasional stranger wings among the plucky birds who spent their winters at home. An hour ago he would not have noticed these things. A little at a time they began to interest him, and by mid-afternoon Quebec seemed more than a few hours away. His back hurt him, but its hurt was not comparable with what was building in him. His mind was

393

clearer and the torment of hatred that had scourged him like a fire was softened by the stillness and sunshine and softly whispered confidences of the forest, and by the pat, pat, pat of the friendly feet always close at his side. He began to talk to the dog, and Comrade listened with a keenness of interest in his whiskered face and answered so promptly with his battered tail that David found increasing comfort in his company. He shot half a dozen squirrels, and the familiar voice of his rifle added to the slowly mounting readjustment of his nerves. Toward evening he found a hollow so densely filled with the lacy tops of spruce and balsam that the snows of winter had failed to penetrate to the cloister-like refuge under them, and here he prepared to spend the night.

With this night, its cheery camp-fire, the thickening of darkness and the sighing and whispering of the hundred tree tops that made the roof of his shelter, an easement of mind stole over David such as he had not known for a long time. Through many weeks past, while on his bogus missions for Bigot, his heart had eaten itself out with suspense and yearning and dreams of Anne. But tonight there was no longer a cause for any of those things. And now he began to understand why it was better to suffer a blow and have done with it than to see it endlessly impending. Anne was lost to him as he had a thousand times feared that she in some way would be lost. He had dreamed and planned and hoped, and the fabric he had built was level with the earth again. He was back in his forests, not transiently and without purpose but steadfastly and forever. The thought was a solace. It made his grief less acute, his desolation of soul and body more bearable.

He roasted the squirrels and divided them with Comrade, and after their supper made a hollow in the unfrozen balsam needles and folded his one blanket in it, ready for a bed if he grew sleepy. He gathered firewood and fed it to the glowing coals as their flame died down, and in these flames and the coals he saw his future painting itself step by step ahead of him. And soon the thought grew on him, as if it were something new and strange, that everything the world had ever held for him was still his own—except Anne.

Slowly and at times illogically his mind struggled to convince itself, and in doing this began to conceive its plans. And David, the physical, gripped tenaciously at the straws it presented until he felt himself buoyed up by a force greater than the one which was bearing him down. He would go home, of course. And then, when his time came, he would do what he had always wanted to do, explore the unmapped and unknown mysteries of the farther wildernesses. Quebec might die and rot on its rock, and even France herself might be driven into the sea, but all that could not change by so much as the weight of a hair what lay beyond the western frontiers. He would join the Black Hunter. He would see the world as he knew that world. And there would be fighting to do, such fighting as Peter Joel had told him this land had never seen in all its ancient past. In time would come his day of triumph. For westward were vast worlds to conquer, and names to carve as great as any that had gone before. Memory of Anne should drive him on, for in his vindication and success would she reap her most enduring bitterness.

Yet he was not thinking now in the same terms of vengeance with which he had last looked back on the fortressed town of Quebec. Nor was he hating in the same way, except when he was thinking of Bigot alone, or of the monsters who played with him. For them no power could ever wipe out the settlement which some day he would demand. But the red fire, the coals glowing as if filled with thinking life, the darkness, the stillness about him all brought truth to him as well as the immensity of his aloneness. Bigot was not New France, nor was Anne the beginning and the end of the world.

He slept a few hours and when it was light enough to see he was traveling again with the dog. His back did not burn as it had last night, but it was stiff, as if Doctor Coué had covered it with an unbending board instead of soft bandage. This stiffness wore away, and with the warmth of another sun he felt infinitely better than yesterday. Not until midday did they find themselves something to eat, when David stopped at a habitant's cottage at the edge of a broad seigneury, whose great buildings he could see several miles away, and purchased supplies to last to the Richelieu.

With calmer reflection he still did not regret that he had stolen away from Quebec without waiting for the support and consolation of the friends he had left. His desire to be alone was a growing one, and Nancy would understand and forgive him when in time he explained to her.

This day, struggle as he would against it, Anne returned to him again and again, and a hundred times he saw the white vision of her as she lashed the black man and ran with the blood-stained whip from the square. She had pitied him, pitied him to such an extent that she had allowed a moment's madness to drive her to that unexpected act. Tenaciously he kept that thought in mind, telling himself that it could be nothing more than pity—and yet he had effort in keeping back another thought, the thing he was trying to destroy and believed he had destroyed, the consciousness of truth in the words of love and pleading she had spoken in the dungeon chamber.

The second night his restless sleep was filled with dreams of Anne, and always his visions of her were not of the glad and beautiful Anne of Sunset Hill but of the white-faced, death-stricken Anne whom Deschenaux had taken from his prison-room. He awoke troubled and mentally unrefreshed. But his physical body responded more and more each hour to the clean, strong blood in his veins, and the third day he made thirty miles between dawn and dusk, and at night, for the first time, tried to make himself whistle cheerily as he prepared supper for himself and the dog. But in his sleep Anne came to him again, and he saw her as she had stood with the soul crushed out of her beyond his prison bars.

As one day followed another his fight became a slow and deadly thing. It was the forest, with its heritage of unbreakable mettle passed on to him, that made him win in the end, if his achievement could be called a triumph. Definitely he cut himself away from everything that might have drawn him back to Anne. Rock by rock he built up the barrier between them and enshrined his old and sacred love in a temple which he knew he would never enter; and with this defeat of his hopes and triumph of his convictions a pride was born in him which was bound to endure to the end of his days. A pride in the thought that he had followed the Black Hunter's admonition to "go clean to the end," though Anne herself believed him guilty of a monstrous crime; pride in his strength, pride in the vastness and glory of his forest world. Now he was able to measure it with the littleness and pompous fatuity of those who conceived that the city on the rock, and the King across the sea, were the guardians as well as the possessors of its farthermost horizons.

He was coming home at a time that was ripe for the releasing of the new and harder passions for physical achievement that were born in him. The storm was about to break, a storm that was destined to twist the histories of the nations of the world, a storm that had been smoldering like a great fire in the American wildernesses, awaiting only the final impetus that would send it in an avalanche of fury and destruction over half a continent. And while it gathered, Mirepoix and Albemarle were still at play; Versailles was the bawdry show-house of a dissipated France, a swarming-place for silken nobility, a gilded rendezvous for princes and princesses, dukes and duchesses, and the great ladies and gentlemen of a nation, while the King—a weak and dissolute wretch, mocked at by the common people on the streets—ruled at the beck and call of his mistress, Pompadour. While New France was dying, Old France—still in that hour the mightiest nation in the world—was bleeding herself white through the weaknesses and passions of the flesh.

That England was only a step behind her was England's luck and not England's pride. For these were also the days of the "unwashed and unsavory England of Hogarth, Fielding, Smollet, and Sterne; of Tom Jones, Squire Westers, Lady Bellaston, and Parson Adams"; and as Saxe, one of the many bastards of Augustus of Saxony, King of Poland, had ruled the debaucheries as well as the armies of France, so in England was the fame of Beau Nash more envied and greater than that of king, philosopher, or statesman. While the men of the New World, inured to the pursuits of war and adventure, were ready for a mighty struggle, their higher-caste brethren of the Old World dressed like women, wore beauty patches, and carried muffs. Selfishness, fanaticism and a morality lower than the iniquity of a dissolute Rome had honeycombed Europe with its rottenness, and Rousseau, crying his first half-mad alarms, preached the doctrine of a world about to vomit its spleen. Honor, if not courage, was dead in the courts that ruled the earth; and nations, like men, were struggling to deal death-blows in the dark, like common thugs.

These were the conditions which in March of 1755 had set rolling throughout the New World the plans for a monstrous war which had no official recognition, and of the two tricksters England was a step ahead of the stupid court at Versailles, where there was no longer a Condé, a Turenne, a Vendôme or a Villars to guide its destiny. Before Dieskau and his French regiments had reached the St. Lawrence, Braddock and the Governors of the English colonies had made their schemes and set them in motion. A gigantic four-fold blow in time of peace was to be struck at New France. An army was to move on Fort Duquesne. Another was to reduce Niagara. A third was to attack Crown Point, and a fourth was to smash Acadia. New France was to be ground into dissolution like a kernel of wheat between the upper and the nether millstones—before war was declared.

It was the Richelieu, with its protectorate of fighting barons and its ears always open to the winds from the south, that learned the truth first, but only a part of the truth.

Word came that the English were preparing to move against the French in Pennsylvania, but no news or rumor of the avalanche of death about to descend upon Crown Point and the Richelieu had crossed the frontier.

So when David came at last to his home he found a new Peter at the head of twenty stalwart men preparing to leave for the great adventure at Fort Duquesne.

CHAPTER XXVI

For a week David remained at the Seigneury St. Denis, and in that time no word came from Quebec and no intimation or sign that Nancy Lotbinière was on her way to the Richelieu. For each day that ended free of the two things he dreaded, the story of his whipping and Nancy's arrival, he gave thanks at night; and because he knew that even his mother would plead Anne's case, and point out lovingly all the folly of his own, he kept his secret—except that he told it to Peter one afternoon when they were alone in Peter's room in the lower seigneury.

The same months that had dealt so heavily with himself had also changed Peter. The forest glow was in his face, a new light lay in his eyes, his lethargy and plumpness were gone, and his muscles were hard and grown swift to act. "Ten hours a day in the fields and forest, and half my nights spent beside camp-fires with the frozen ground for a bed, have partly done the work—but mostly it is Nancy," he explained to David. "And now I pray God that Fort Duquesne and whatever may lie between will make me worthy of her when I return."

This was before the night when David showed him his back and told the story of the whipping-cart, and of Comrade, the dog. Then, to David's amazement, Peter

402

unlocked a letter which had come from Quebec by a swift messenger, and which Nancy had written and dispatched even before the hour of his torture and banishment from the town. "I am planning to come to the Richelieu with him," Nancy had written, after she had told him about David and Anne. "And before I come I would like to kill this monster Bigot."

Peter had already worn out his fury, and was now so coldly calm and placid over the matter that David found him a pillar of strength and not a tribulation. "We are brothers—here," he said, and placed a hand over his heart. "We both have lost, and we both are going to win. I am glad you ran away from Quebec, so that Nancy could not come with you, for I do not want to see her until I have passed through a test greater than the hardening of a few muscles and the training of a score of men. When I face her again I want it to be with a strength born of experience and not alone of dreams; and when that hour comes I think you will find the old Anne waiting for you at Grondin Manor."

"Such a thing can never be," replied David coldly. "The gulf between us has grown too wide."

Before this David had learned all that was to be known about the Black Hunter. Twice in the last five months he had come to the Richelieu. But now he was gone, and had left no word behind except that it would be a long time before he returned. "He went away in black from the crown of his head to the toes of his boots," his mother said. "Something was in his heart of which he said no word to me."[1]

That David was to go with Peter was very soon settled, for there was no excuse now by which even a mother could hold him. New France was about to begin the desperate fight for its life, and Marie Rock herself would have gone with a rifle over her shoulder if she had been a man.

The few days still necessary for Peter and his men to make their final preparations were ones of grief-filled memories and bitter reflections for David. He terribly missed Peter Joel, for it was the Black Hunter's calm strength and fatherly comradeship he needed, and if there had been one chance out of many of finding him in the trackless wildernesses he would have set out alone on the quest. Not an hour passed that he did not find himself in some spot hallowed by the presence of Anne; her spirit was with him wherever he moved—on the trails they had traveled together in the golden glow of sunsets; on secret paths which only their own feet had made; in the frozen opens where flowers had grown, in the deep woods and on the naked hills. Ghosts rose up about him where he had told Anne the story of the powder-horn, and where she had forever plighted him her troth, and he felt no shame because of the sob which rose to his lips.

And now he found that the love which he had so bitterly tried to destroy had only covered itself with ash, and that he must carry the smoldering fire of it within him forever. Never would it die, the memories, the sweet voice whispering and laughing and promising him out of the past; visions of childhood loveliness all his own for a time, and now dead, just as Anne must remain dead for him. For even to Peter he did not reveal the fatal depth of his hurt, or the poison that had made a horrible scar of the wound. For what Bigot had possessed he could not and would never take again as his own, and of that one thing his bitterness had made him certain—that Anne, if for only a little while, had forgotten her love for him that she might give her favor to the Intendant of New France.

Once he was away with Peter he would never again return to Grondin Manor. Of that he was surer as the last days came, so sure that he talked to his mother of the amazing beauty of the land beyond Lake Champlain, and told her it was his dream to make their home there when the English were driven, as they surely would be, far beyond the frontier which they had so brazenly usurped.

It was the eighth of April when David and Peter marched away with their twenty men to the beginning of a great war. And it was little old Fontbleu, the miller, gripping his hand in parting, who made prediction once more.

"I've seen something in your face which you haven't put in words, lad. But you'll be coming back soon, an' when you do, something tells my old bones the millwheel will be singing fairer than ever in the wind, an' Grondin Manor will hold a message for you which will last long after I'm dead an' turned to dust. Yea, lad, dreams tell strange truths, an' I've been dreaming of late with my eyes no tighter shut than your own are now." And as David left it seemed to him that the ancient miller was more than ever like a ghost, so old and thin and frail that the winds which turned his mill might lift him up and blow him away.

It was Kill-Buck who gave up for a time his charge of David's mother to guide these free rangers of Peter's down into the land of his fathers, and the old Indian with his stoical and uncommunicative love for the boy he had watched and guarded from babyhood was a consolation to David. Next to Kill-Buck, even before Peter, for some strange reason came Carbanac.

These two had lived tragedies so much greater than David's that at times he felt shame creeping over him when he saw their strong, heroic faces in the glow of the forest camp-fires. For something of nobility had grown in the face of Carbanac, the murderer, and, looking at his mighty figure, his great hands, and the cleanness of his eyes, David thought of the giant spirits who had come many generations ago to blaze the first trails in New France, and wondered if Carbanac was one of the unsung brood they had left behind them. Between Carbanac and Kill-Buck there had sprung up one of the strange affections which are born of the forests, and the old Delaware's love for David was scarcely greater than that of the man for whom David's friendship and sympathy had opened the way to a new life.

As day by day the little war-party drew nearer to the country of their enemies David watched these two with increasing interest, and what he saw in Kill-Buck's face—a book which many years of intimacy had made it possible for him to read—added steadily to the strange, wild thrill which was beginning to possess him. This wine in his blood was the knowledge that for him, as well as for Kill-Buck, the adventures of peace had come to an end; that this was no adventure with the wilderness alone, but that for the first time in his life he was on that most thrilling of all blood-stirring hunts, the quest for men to kill. And at last, with an almost dramatic shock, Kill-Buck drove this fact home. He disappeared one evening, and David did not see him again until dawn. And then he was a new Kill-Buck. The head on which he had allowed his hair to grow during many years of peace was cleanly shaven except for the scalp-lock which he had left with an Indian's courage and honor for the enemy who might vanquish him. In this war-lock were three eagle's feathers dyed red and a string of wampum. His face was lined with streaks of vermilion, white, and yellow, like gashes made by a knife, laid on with the help of a little tallow, and in the center of each cheek was a round black spot made from the scrapings of a pot. In his ears were rings of copper wire, and wampum collars swathed his neck. His shirt was daubed with vermilion, and a large knife which David had never seen hung on his breast. And in a strange belt which engirdled his waist was a bleeding scalp.

This scalp dangling at Kill-Buck's belt filled the day with a sinister quiet. It needed no questioning to know its story. Late the preceding afternoon the Delaware had pointed out a strange trail crossing their own, undetected by the white men's eyes. During the night he had followed and killed, and had bedecked himself with his spoils. It was a Mohawk scalp. They were in the land of their enemies, even now breathing the air of the red and white plague which was always threatening to inundate New France.

Kill-Buck's eyes were no longer the eyes of the guardian of a woman. They blazed with the light of an eagle's on watch for its prey. He was young once more, and his blood was flaming with the thrill of ancient and glorious days when his own race had been a dreaded power in the wilderness. Hatred lived in him again; lust for the blood of his hated enemies; desire and passion and a mercilessness that sent a stir of horror through David, all held in leash under the cold, calm mask of the warrior's countenance. This fire was reflected in the weather-beaten faces of the hardened rangers whom Peter had gathered in his little band.

Death was about them now. It stalked in the darkness, breathed in the whispering winds, shivered in the crackling of every twig; the stars seemed to shine with a different light, and the shadows made by the cold glow of the moon were filled with mystery and omen. There were no fires at night, no campings in the chosen places, but only sleep stolen in deep and hidden fastnesses, with keen and watchful eyes and ears, trained to catch the flight of an owlet's wing, on guard over those who were slumbering. And in day men walked with steps that fell as softly as the steps of a padded cat; there was no laughter, no voice that rose above the murmur of the tree tops, no firing at the deer and turkeys that frequently crossed their path.

In these days and nights when every hour he expected to hear the crack of rifles and the yell of attacking savages life measured itself swiftly for David. What had happened in Quebec seemed a long time ago. Anne faded out of his dreams in time of restless sleep, and hatred and bitterness died out of him, trivial now with the ominously throbbing pulse of life and death like the stirring of air about them.

Only a master like Kill-Buck could have found the way through the Mohawk country without paying deadly toll to their enemies. Three times in as many days they crossed the trails of war-parties, and always with these bands the old Delaware pointed out the presence of white men. Twice they saw the smoke of Mohawk camp-fires, and twice David looked from ambush on the warriors of their enemy, while at his side Kill-Buck's breath came swift and fast in his desire to fling anathema and defiance into the teeth of the forest scourge who had destroyed his race. But Peter, and back of him the rangers, held Kill-Buck in leash. Always the thought was to reach Fort Duquesne, though white fingers as well as red were itching to pull the triggers that would have set a furious host like wolves at their heels.

Through the edge of the Mohawk country, guarded by the warriors of its northern castle, Kill-Buck stole his way to the beginning of the twisting French frontier that ran in jagged lines down to Louisiana. David had felt death; now he saw it. They came one day upon the charred remains of what a week before had been a group of pioneer cabins. Here had been a show of strength, a concentration of human souls strong in their conviction of safety with French domain about them and a French fort scarcely twenty miles away. There were five men dead, with their heads scalped clean. Three women lay on the frozen ground with their faces to the earth, and a sickness came over David as he looked at them and thought of Vaudreuil, with his woman's hair. It was dusk when they chopped shallow holes in the thawing ground for graves, and that night through long and sleepless hours David thought again of Grondin Manor, and of Anne and his mother, and of the Black Hunter's prediction that this same scourge of death would one day sweep the Richelieu.

The next day they came to what had been the fort and found it a mass of ruins, and here there were mounds in the soil which showed that white men had been with their Indian allies.

Then Kill-Buck headed west in a great detour, for he counted that a hundred enemy rifles had been in this assault, and so recently that from deep down in the debris of the fort he dug out ash still warm with the warmth of fire.

Spring came now in its fullest glory. By the sixth of May the open meadows and sun-filled hardwoods were carpeted with flowers. The birds had come, and robins greeted the dawn and sang their evening pæans to the setting sun. The earth itself was bursting with life; tapestries of green lightened the dark passageways of the forests, the sweet smells of growing things drifted softly in the air, and through woods, and hills ran the droning music of a thousand streams and rivulets pouring their flood-time waters toward the lower levels of the sea.

Everywhere, it seemed to David, were the auguries of friendliness and peace; peace on the earth and in the sky and the soft air between; cheer in the call of the wild turkeys at evening, gladness in the song of the thrush and the catbird and the play of the spotted fawns; hope with the sunrise, benediction with its setting—peace everywhere except in their own slinking and stealthy march through the wilderness.

If his own eyes had not seen the desolation of fire and massacre he would have doubted that a hell lay ahead and all

411

through this world. He was beginning to doubt, when like a shock came Fort Duquesne.[2]

It was the afternoon of the fourth of June and Braddock was already well on his way to the Monongahela with 800 horses and a host of 2,200 men. To Contrecoeur, in command at Fort Duquesne, had been steadily dribbling in the savage forces of New France to meet the British invasion, and in the hands of his captains, Beaujeu, Dumas, and Ligneris, the blood-thirsty warriors of twenty tribes were being mobilized from a restless and heterogeneous horde into a compact fighting strength. Eight hundred savages were camped about the log stockade and fort when Peter and David came out of the woods with their rangers. Eight hundred red wolves gathered for a feast of blood, painted, half naked, drunk for the promised slaughter. Among them were baptized savages from the distant Canadas—Caughnawagas from Sault St. Louis, murderous Abenakis from St. Francis, and Hurons from Lorette, whose chief bore the name of Anastase in honor of that father of the Church. The rest were unbaptized heathen—Potawatomis and Ojibwas from the northern lakes, Shawanos and Mingos from the Ohio, and Ottawas from Detroit, commanded by Pontiac himself. No distance had been too great for these allies of France to travel, and the camps they made, each separate from the other, were so many smoldering volcanoes of impatience and fiendish anticipation.

For many days Beaujeu, Dumas and Ligneris, almost like Indians themselves, had held the red host within bounds, and that first night David witnessed why it was that the white men's faces were thin and drawn and their eyes sunken under the strain of their sleepless struggle. Before the sun was down a war-party of Abenakis came in from the English settlements with thirty scalps, mostly of women and children, and while the Abenakis' camp was a carnival of joy and triumph a storm of passion and excitement that was almost a tempest of fury broke loose among the rival tribes, chained like wild animals to the inactivity which they hated. A saturnalia of tumult and confusion began with the darkness of the night. Twenty great fires leaped to the skies, and from about these fires the shrieks and war-cries of the rival tribes filled the wilderness for miles about with a blood-curdling din.

A horror seized upon David and the exhaustion of a long day's travel did not make him think of sleep, even though he might have closed his ears to the barbarous discord that racked the night. The Black Hunter's words kept recurring in his brain—that some day this same red death that was yelling and whipping itself into dancing furies about him would sweep up the Richelieu. There would be no difference in that holocaust of fire and hatchet when it came, for under their skins the Mohawks, Oneidas, Onondagas, Cayugas and Senecas of the English were the same as these allies of

413

the French. And with his horror came a sickening sense of revulsion and disgust.

"The Indians are what the white men have made them," Peter Joel had told him so many times that those words, too, were burned indelibly in his memory. And here, for the first time in his life, he was looking with his own eyes upon one of those boiling caldrons of passion and hatred for which his own race was strictly accountable. And as the French had done, so the English were doing. Building hotter and hotter the fires of rivalry and hatred. Paying blood-money for dripping scalps. Sending into the wilderness shiploads of liquor to finish what lies and subterfuge and God-given brains of superior mentality had begun—training the Indians to be demons instead of men, and to hate with a mad hatred wherever the white man's more powerful will directed.

He thanked God that the English were moving against the French frontier in Pennsylvania and not the Richelieu. And yet a grim dread began to possess him. At what hour might not that other thing happen even with Dieskau's powerful army just inside the gateway to the Canadas? He did not speak his fears even to Peter, for Peter, like all the others, believed the road to the heart of New France to be invulnerable. Fort Edward and Fort William Henry trembled at the end of it, and soon it would be these English strongholds, and not the French, that would be laid in ruins.

So all of New France thought, or Peter would have held his men at home to guard their own threshold.

But the seed of doubt, once planted, began to grow in David. Excited like hounds by the sight of the Abenakis' scalps, a hundred savages deserted the fort that night for the scattered homes of the English frontiers, and the next day, and all the days that followed, David could not keep visions of doubt and fear from his brain. In just that way, some day, a red and masterless horde would go up the Richelieu.

Continually now he was thinking of his mother and Anne. And as day after day he saw the savages come and go, and looked upon their mad revelings at night, and listened to the exhortations and briberies and pleadings of the white officers to hold them, it was the old Anne who filled his heart again; the Anne who had never been to Quebec, the Anne who had listened to his story of the powder-horn, the Anne of the old mill-wheel and its legends. Now that at last the wall he had built up against himself had fallen there grew in his heart a great yearning to return to Grondin Manor—a yearning that was only half desire, and the other half that strange and pressing fear of which he spoke no word to Peter.

Events developed swiftly as this fear increased its hold upon him. Each day the older and more experienced forest men sent out as spies brought in news of Braddock and the approaching enemy. They were advancing slowly and tediously, a long and attenuated red, blue, and brown line of horses, wagons, and men that often extended over four miles. They traveled so slowly that at times they progressed no more than three or four miles a day, and the sound of their axes, the shouts of the wagon-drivers and the playing of fife and drum could be heard with the wind for a long distance ahead.

By July first the humor of the Indians about Fort Duquesne had changed. They had expected to meet a mighty enemy and in place of that a huge sacrifice was slowly marching their way. In anticipation of it they made hundreds of little hoops on which to stretch the scalps that were coming so gaily to the music of the fifes and drums, sharpened their knives and hatchets, and danced around the fires at night, swinging and tossing the hoops as if scalps were already attached to them. Beaujeu and some of the other whites dressed and painted themselves like Indians and danced with them. But the Long Rifles from the Canadas, 146 in all, held themselves more and more aloof. The horror which had grown in David was beginning to find itself in them. They had come to fight, and this which lay ahead of them was butchery.

Even David, as yet a stranger to the physical clash of war, could see why this was so when he looked upon the advancing army for the first time on the fifth of July. Foolishly clattering and smashing, unprotected and strung out, and with its musicians fairly bursting their drum-heads and lungs now that they were near Fort Duquesne, as if to frighten their enemy by a last supreme exhibition of confidence and bravado, Braddock's line was open night and day to the destruction which awaited it. Only George Washington and his 450 Virginians, "those slothful and languid fellows unfit for military service," as Braddock had written, kept a part of the line in form against the death which the wilderness on both sides was hiding.

Even then it was not until the eighth of July that Duquesne emptied itself of its killers, 900 men against Braddock's 2,200, and of these, 637 were Indians. Band after band, the warriors of the different tribes stole off into the wilderness, stripped almost to nakedness, smeared from head to foot in war-paint, and now so still that no ear could have caught the sound of their passing through the dense shelter of the trees.

That day, with the sun shining out of a clear sky, with masses of flowers blooming about him and birds singing in the forests, David looked upon a scene in which every tree and log was transformed suddenly into a pitiless, shrieking, maleficent spirit of death. Here he saw in flesh and blood what had come to him so often in that ugly dream of his boyhood.

With Peter and his twenty forest men he had crept to the edge of a stony coulee, and down a little valley they could see half a mile of the straggling enemy line, the red-coated British, the blue-coated Virginians, wagons and tumbrils, cannons and howitzers, with banners flying, officers mounted, and music playing. From where they lay, these twenty men from the Richelieu, unerring and deadly masters of the rifle, might have stretched out crimson carpets of dead below them. But David, who had come prepared to fight, could not raise his gun or fire. Men near him hesitated, gripped their gun-barrels tighter, and waited. That pause, passing like a spirit from man to man, held every rifle among the Canadians about them silent. In later years history was to call them cowards. French officers and men, despising the quiet and lean-limbed trailers of the wilderness, and themselves slaughtering from ambush with the passion and joyous exultation of their red allies, were destined to paint them blackly for the future. And Dumas, dressed like a savage himself, except that he wore the gorget of an officer, was to write for posterity, "They fled shamefully, crying, 'Sauve qui peut!'"

But Dumas lied, and history has lied, as it has lied in so many other ways. In place of cowards the forests bred men; men who were destined from their cradles to be examples of the survival of the fittest; men of a heroic age, builders and defenders of homes, killers by force of circumstances and environment, but not murderers. There were exceptions, as there are exceptions among men of every age; dark souls under white skins that reveled in the slaughter of that eighth of July, 1755, but for the most part the escutcheon of the Canadas was clean on that day, for which Canada—in spite of written history—may be proud and not ashamed.

Between the two wilderness walls of death Braddock's army was melting away like snow under a sun. Out of the tumult of rifle-fire and the wild yelling of the Indians came clearly the swelling sound of drum and fife and of English voices shouting "God save the King!" as Braddock's men, at first dying bravely, fired volley after volley at the enemies whom they could not see. Only the Virginians fought back in the wilderness way, for when some of the red-coated British sought the shelter of rock or tree their officers drove them back into the open "to stand with the others and fight like men." Their dead lay in piles and it needed no Canadian rifles to spread the crimson rugs upon the earth.

At last no human soul could stand the strain; lines and squares began to break like vivid autumn-colored leaves scattered by a wind, guns were thrown away, and, like the herds of cattle and pack-horses that had stampeded at the first assault, men turned and ran. David and the tensely breathing, white-faced men about him were looking upon only a sixth of Braddock's line, but its horrors were sufficient to fill a world. From their hiding-places, from rock and tree and hollow, the savages burst forth like starving wolves, shrieking with the madness of demons, and every savage with a knife in his hand. What happened then filled David with a strange and gripping sickness, yet he could not take his eyes from the horrible scene. From man to man the allies of France ran with their dripping knives, tearing their treasure of scalps from the heads of the wounded as well as the dead in the frantic haste of each to beat out his fellows in securing the gruesome plunder.

Staggeringly David rose to his feet and turned away. Most of the Canadians were gone. But behind him stood a figure, with a rifle in the hollow of his arm, strangely and sadly contemplating the scene below. Now he looked at David, and with a sudden wrench at his heart David found himself standing face to face with Peter Joel, the Black Hunter.

For a silent space of a moment or two the man and the youth looked into each other's eyes, and then Peter Joel said, "David, I am glad you did not fire."

[1] General Braddock reported that late in June, 1755, an "uncouth personage" known as the Black Hunter had appeared before him to warn him of an "impossible massacre" of his army in the wilderness. Peter Joel, foreseeing the tragedy, was probably on that mission of humanity when David arrived at Grondin Manor.

[2] Where the city of Pittsburgh now stands.

CHAPTER XXVII

What David had witnessed at the head of Braddock's line was but the beginning of a pandemonium that reigned in a frightful orgy of pillage and death through all that afternoon of July 8th, 1755. As the front ranks of the doomed army telescoped in mad flight upon the miles of its strung-out line behind, its defense became so pitiable that the Indians no longer sheltered themselves in ambush but rushed out openly and dragged down the frantic men who had thrown away their arms, scalping them while they were yet alive. The trail for miles was a path of dead and of half-dead; of cannon and wagons and abandoned baggage; a litter of rifles and coats and articles that might impede mad flight; but mostly, from the point of attack to the river, it was a long red ribbon of the slain. In that distance sixty-three out of eighty-six officers and 914 men lay dead; and among those who had fallen mortally wounded, a gallant but foolhardy and blundering bulldog to the last, was Braddock himself; and his was the only body carried across the river and buried beyond the reach of the Indians' scalping-knives. Had the savages been less drunk with the desire to despoil their victims of their scalps as they fell, there would have been no survivor to recount the tragedy of that day.

Scarcely could the presence of even Peter Joel relieve David from the shock to which his soul and brain and body had been subjected. He had looked on such scenes as he had never dreamed of, and their torment and horror were burned like great scars in his face and eyes as the other put his arms about him in the old and gentle way, as in the days at Grondin Manor. As they stood, saying no word in their greeting, they could hear the shrieks of the dying and of those about to die, and, even more terrible, the agony of the horribly half-dead whom the savages had scalped and left to expire by inches.

Hardened by years to the spectacle of death Peter Joel led David back through the forest to the great clearing and log stockades of the fort, and David gripped hard at himself, listening to the Black Hunter as he told how he had come to Duquesne in the very hour of the thing they had seen, and was on his way to the Richelieu.

What a few weeks before he would have confided in this man he now kept locked in his own breast, for everything that had passed in his life had become trivial compared with the happenings of that afternoon—his disgrace in Quebec, the whipping, even his break with Anne, inconsequential matters not to be talked about until the darkly shadowing possibility of another tragedy, even more terrible than the one which they had witnessed, was cleared from his brain. Of this fear, which he had hidden from Peter Gagnon, his broken nerves now made him speak to Peter Joel. Day after day it had throbbed in his head, last night he had dreamed of it, and now, with an almost hysterical effect, the ghastly torment of it burned in every drop of blood in his body—the fear and thought that this same Moloch of savagery and slaughter might be sweeping down the Richelieu while they were away. He was unrelieved by Peter Joel's assurance that Dieskau and a powerful army were already on their way to Crown Point, and that Braddock's fate would be an added deterrent to any concerted British and Indian movement in the direction of David's home.

The coming of evening added to the haunting oppressiveness of the misgiving which remained with him. Not until then did the completeness of the French triumph force itself upon him in a manner even more repellent and shocking than that which he had contemplated from the edge of the coulee. The savage warriors began to return to their camps, and not one of them but had a load of scalps hanging at his waist. If their whoops and yells of defiance and anticipation had been fearful the day before, their shriller screams were more so now, as each camp worked itself into a blood-drunk frenzy of rejoicing. Even this madness did not reach its climax until sundown, when eleven English prisoners were brought in, stripped naked, with parts of their faces and bodies painted black and their hands tied behind their backs. As darkness fell these men were burned to death at the stake, one by one, on the bank of the Allegheny, opposite the fort. That Contrecoeur, the Commandant, made no effort to save them from their terrible fate, and that the French soldiers gathered to view the spectacle as if it were a show, twisted at David's brain until, half mad himself, he plunged into the depths of the forest and did not rest until the screams of the unfortunate wretches dying in the flames could no longer reach his ears.[1]

It was dawn when he returned to the fort and it seemed to him that in one sleepless night he had lived an age. A strange quiet had fallen over the scene about the stockade and at first he thought that the Indians, exhausted by their revels, were asleep. Then he saw that most of their camps were empty. One by one during the late hours of darkness or in the earliest dawn the war-parties had stolen away, eager to return to their friends and families with the spoils and proud tales of their prowess.

Scarcely had he made note of these things when the Black Hunter found him, anxiety deeply settled in his eyes. "Don't do it again, boy," he entreated when David had explained his disappearance. "Some of the redskins who have gone are not too squeamish to add a stray Frenchman's scalp to their bag." Then, after a moment in which he drew a deep breath of relief, he added, "A party of new Indians came in late, Ottawas from Canada, and with them a white man who says he has come all the way from Quebec to find you. He appeared to be half dead from exhaustion, and I don't know him. Traveling with the Ottawas is no easy matter unless one has buckskin feet."

"Where is he?" asked David.

"With Contrecoeur. They evidently know one another, and the Commandant has given instructions for you to present yourself immediately on your return. But there is time for our breakfast, which you clearly need to set up a stomach somewhat out of place. Older heads than yours went sick with last night's doings, lad. Even I——" He stopped with a grimace and a shrug.

"I cannot eat until I have seen this man from Quebec," David said, trying hard to hide the emotion stirred in him by the other's announcement of the presence of one who could be nothing less than a messenger from Nancy or Anne.

But the throb of it was in his voice and the flame of it in his eyes, so that Peter Joel without appearing to discover it led him in the direction of Captain Contrecoeur's quarters and left him in charge of one of the guards at the gate of the fort.

There were voices in Contrecoeur's room, and when the door opened to admit him David saw a man sitting before a table on which there were remnants of food, with the Commandant opposite him. This man rose from his chair when he entered, and David's breath drew itself short in shock and amazement. He was dressed in rough deerskin;

his hair was uncouth and unshorn, his face weathered by wind and campfire and covered with a scraggly beard. For a moment David disbelieved his eyes. Then he knew, despite these changes, that the messenger from Quebec was Captain René Robineau!

But what a different Robineau!—not alone in the strangeness of his dress, his unqueued hair, the untrimmed beard, but in the man himself. Could this be the old Robineau of Quebec, that beau ideal of military dress and manners, the man whose skill in the science of war was scarcely greater than his perfection of deportment and personal appearance? Could it be the Robineau so mysteriously somber, so uncommunicative and unsmiling, with the shadow of a deeply buried tragedy always weighting him in gloom? For this Robineau he was staring at now, exhausted from long and unaccustomed travel, was smiling as he rose to greet him— smiling in a way David had never seen him smile before; and he came quickly to greet him with two outstretched hands, like a comrade and a friend instead of the man whose hand had never before gripped his own, and whose lips and face he had never seen with that look of cheer and gladness upon them.

In that same moment a flash of understanding came to him, and with it a sense of disappointment so swift that it was like a blow. Captain Robineau was not a messenger for him. He had without doubt come in that way that he might not be suspected of bearing precious military orders and secrets to Fort Duquesne; and by chance he had learned that the boy he had tutored was at the fort, and had inquired for him. But why this show of friendliness, this gladness of greeting to one who had been discovered a traitor in the eyes of Quebec and who had been whipped from the city?

Robineau's hands had closed about his own. "Thank God, I've found you!" he cried, and in his voice also he had changed. It was buoyant and enlivened by a thrilling freedom as strange in David's memories of him as the transformation in his personal appearance. He turned to Contrecoeur. "Captain, this is the David Rock I have been telling you about—the lad to whose affairs I owe more than my life will ever be able to repay, and who, in that strange way I told you about, set me the task of killing your old friend, Captain Jean Talon."

Contrecoeur was reaching out a hand now. "For which I thank you, Lieutenant Rock," he said. "Captain Robineau is a better shot than I, and I must surely have met this fellow Talon on my return, because of an affair between us, and undoubtedly with dire results to myself. I am going to leave you now, for Robineau has much to talk to you about which is better for four ears than six." As he went David wondered how this pleasant-faced man, so apparently a gentleman, could have looked so stolidly upon the burning of the Englishmen last night.

No sooner had the door closed behind him than Captain Robineau motioned David to a chair beside the table, and, seating himself opposite him, drew a pistol from his belt and placed it in the space between them. A smile lightened by its new touch of pride and humor trembled on his lips as he saw David's eyes rest for a moment upon the weapon.

"For weeks I have promised myself this bit of melodrama, if I found you," he explained. "The pistol is for you. It is loaded. If a little later you want to shoot me, do so without hesitation, and Contrecoeur, who is an old academy mate of mine, is bound as a gentleman to say it was an accident. Thank God, a man's honor is sometimes only sleeping when it appears to be dead, and because mine has awakened I have followed you through the wilderness for no other reason than to make what restitution I can for as heinous a crime as a man who calls himself a gentleman can possibly commit."

"I fail to understand," exclaimed David, staring at the other. Then his tongue added the words which he could no longer keep back, "You have some message for me from Anne St. Denis?"

Robineau shook his head. "So far as Quebec is concerned I have disappeared from the face of the earth. No one knows where I am, not even Mademoiselle St. Denis. I have no message from her, but I have some few things to tell you about her. Which will you hear first—about me, or about

Anne St. Denis?" There was a light in Robineau's eyes which told David he knew what the answer would be.

"About Anne, if you please."

"Because, like a fool, I was made to be a part of the plot which was to destroy you, I knew what might happen in the palace that night Mademoiselle St. Denis came to see you," began Robineau, and his face darkened as he went on, telling the story of the hours which David did not know: of Anne's return from the dungeons with Deschenaux, of his fear for her, and of his interruption with Sister Esther and Anne's return to the convent.

"Then Bigot tried to kill me by setting that scoundrel of a Talon on my heels, but fortune favored me and I put a ball through his heart the next morning," Robineau continued, and after that he told of going to the convent, only an hour or two before the whipping, determined to tell Anne all that he knew about Bigot and his plot, and in what manner the papers which had proved David a traitor had been put into his coat.

"They told me Mademoiselle St. Denis was sick and that they feared something had happened to her mind," said Robineau. "Even when I persisted they refused me admission. I could not drag myself away from the convent gate. I knew when the whipping had started, knew when it was coming up the hill; I could even hear the crowd, but something held me to that place. I made another effort and was refused a second time, but scarcely had the door closed when it opened again and Mademoiselle St. Denis ran out, with a nun protesting vainly behind her. She recognized me at the gate. At first I believed she was mad and that I must return her to Sister Esther and the Mother who were following her. She was bareheaded and her face was whiter than death. We could hear the crowd gathering in the square, and I thought she was going to shriek. But she didn't. She caught my arm, and said, 'Bring a carriage as quickly as you can near the Golden Dog!' That was all.

"Even I could not have caught her then as she ran toward the square. I followed and lost her in the edge of the crowd. I found a carriage, fastened and deserted by its driver, and waited. You know what happened. She came back a little later with the whip. I was frightened. It seemed to me her heart must burst, and then I knew what she wanted the carriage for and why she had brought the whip. 'Take me as quickly as you can to Bigot's palace,' she commanded. And I did."

Robineau no longer remained seated. He stood with his face blazing exultation. "If you could have seen what happened then, New France might die under your feet and there would yet be some joy left! We found the monster in his apartment, and what that whip had done to you was nothing compared with what it did to Bigot in the hands of Anne St. Denis. When he tried to get away from her or catch the leathern lashes in his hands I went after him with the point of my sword, and when mademoiselle's strength gave out you could not have recognized his face. Then I took the whip and finished the work until Bigot lay like a dead man on the floor, and I had to carry mademoiselle back to the carriage, for she was in a dead faint. But on our way up Palais Hill she roused herself enough to tell me not to return her to the convent but to take her to the home of Nancy Lotbinière. It was there, a little later, I told her all I knew, and how the papers had got into your coat; and for three days, while Monsieur Lotbinière kept me in concealment and I was preparing to follow you to the Richelieu, we thought she was going to die."

David, too, had risen to his feet. Words unbelievable were pounding against his senses, and he stared at the man who had brought him this cataclysmic news of Anne, unable to speak, almost unable to breathe as the significance of it beat upon him.

Robineau was continuing, "Mademoiselle Lotbinière wrote you about all this when she found you had not waited for her at the cottage, and sent the letter by messenger to the Richelieu; so to tell you these things is not what has brought me all this distance. I have come to clear my honor by confessing to you my own weakness and crime, to ask your forgiveness and to make restitution if I can."

At last David spoke. "I received no letter from Nancy Lotbinière," he said, and Robineau seemed only now to notice the strange whiteness in his face.

"No word came to you on the Richelieu, telling you that Mademoiselle Lotbinière and Anne St. Denis were hurrying to Grondin Manor as soon as Anne was able to make the journey?" he demanded.

"No."

"Then I have another sin to be forgiven for," exclaimed Robineau. "Even Monsieur Lotbinière had no idea of my intentions when I left Quebec. I might have carried Nancy's letter, but my desire was that no one should know of my movements. I traveled slowly, and when I came to Grondin Manor and found you were on your way to Fort Duquesne I thought you had received the letter and were purposely running away from Anne St. Denis, as there had been more than sufficient time for the messenger to reach you. When I found you gone I—almost—refused to follow. I thought you were even worse than Bigot had tried to make you out; that you were a—a man whose thoughts made you unworthy of the love of Mademoiselle St. Denis. If you hated her, if you could believe her bad——"

"What do you mean?" cried David. "Who told you that? Why should you think——" He stopped, the dryness in his throat choking him.

"Why?" asked Robineau. "Because as she lashed Bigot in his room that day, she kept crying over and over, 'You have made him hate me, you have made him hate me—and you have made him think I am bad!' I tell you it wrenched my heart as I stood there! And those words were the first and last I heard from her lips——'He hates me—he hates me—he hates me!' And when I found you gone——"

A bitter cry interrupted him. David had covered his face with his hands. When he took them away Robineau saw a countenance twisted between the agony caused by this knowledge of the great sin he had committed against Anne, and a joy which, even through his wretchedness, revealed itself like a glow of fire.

"Where is Anne—now?"

"I think she must be at Grondin Manor."

"But you said she was sick—so that you thought—she might die." And his voice trembled as he looked at Robineau.

"Monsieur Lotbinière told me she was better on the third evening, when I left. It is not death I fear. It is——"

"What?"

Robineau turned his eyes away from David "I am afraid—when she finds you are gone from Grondin Manor—that she may return to the convent—forever."

"Dear Mother of God!" cried David, and his voice broke in a gasping cry. "If that should happen—I—I——"

"Will go on living, as I have lived," interrupted the other in a low voice. "Fifteen years ago the doors of the convent closed behind a girl I loved as dearly as you love Anne.[2] A thousand times I would have died to undo the act that drove her there. Yet I live. And I would die now, gladly, if I could undo the part I played in the tragedy which may make a nun of Anne St. Denis, sweet and holy though she would surely be."

A sickness which made him dizzy had seized upon David's brain.

"I thought to tell you of this fear of mine as a punishment merited by you for running away from Grondin Manor after receiving Mademoiselle Lotbinière's letter," Robineau was saying. "As it is, I can only urge upon you the necessity of returning as swiftly as you can. I speak brutally, because I have come to tell you the truth. I am afraid, even with all the haste you make, that you will be too late, for no sooner was Anne in Mademoiselle Lotbinière's home than she regretted her command to me and wanted to return at once to the Ursulines. What has happened since I do not know. But the Lotbinières were firm in their decision to take her to Grondin Manor first. Five months will have passed before you can again set foot on the Richelieu, and in that time many things can happen."

David raised his head and stood back from the table. The blood had gone from his face leaving it gray and hard.

Robineau saw the mighty effort he was making, the stiffening of his body, the strange fire that was gathering slowly in his eyes, and he reached out his hand again, and took David's.

"You are going?"

"Yes, as fast as my strength will carry me."

"And there is nothing more you want to hear from me?"

"Nothing, unless it is of Anne."

Robineau's fingers closed more tightly. "There is one thing you must hear. It may be foolish of me, but I have devoutly sworn that my conscience shall be cleared by confession. I was one of Bigot's chief tools in helping to ruin you."

"If God gives me back Anne I care not a snap of my fingers for all that has happened," said David, unmoved.

"But I helped to make you lose Anne."

"No," denied David. "All that which happened was but a small test under which I was not man enough to bear up. My own folly lost Anne, my blindness, my jealousy, my own unworthiness. I drove her away when she came to me in the dungeon, believing that she had come out of pity, and because she had given me a sacred promise, and not because she loved me. You need not tell me what part you played for Bigot, for you have more than repaid by coming to me as you have."

Still Robineau did not free his hand.

"You must hear me. I shall not trouble you with the details of how Bigot got hold of me until our ancient pride, the Robineau honor, was completely in his hands. I will only tell you that I knew you were to be ruined when you came to Quebec, and that my own hopelessness and despair were so complete that I did not care, and followed the commands of the man who I thought was my master. I trained you and helped to place you in public favor, knowing you were to be sacrificed; I drew the maps and plans while my heart and soul were still of stone, and when I gave them to Bigot he sneeringly told me I had done a consummate piece of work because they would some day be found on your person and prove you a traitor. He loved to torture me, confident I would never rise again to strike back.

"But not until the last did I know he was doing this to win Anne St. Denis from you. Yet I did know the papers were in the lining of your coat when you left on the wilderness mission for Bigot. I might have warned you. I might have saved you. Yet I made no move until I saw that monster's trap yawning only a step ahead of the unsuspecting feet of Anne St. Denis. Then something roused itself in a soul that Bigot thought was dead. I saved Anne from a fate worse than death, that dawn you drove her from your dungeon. I defied the man who had shackled me. I killed Talon. And now I have come to you. These acts my pride commends, but they cannot wipe out the unforgivable darkness of the others, and for them—if so you choose—you may kill me without a qualm of conscience."

David's hands were tightly closed about Robineau's when he finished. "If forgiveness from me will ease your mind then you have it freely and in full," he said. "I still hold myself in debt to you, and if God wills it that happiness is to come my way once more through you, then I must love you next to just one other man in all this world." And this time Robineau did not hold him with further words, but saw him to the gate and through it.

In the morning sun David saw a great commotion before the fort and many men together as if a new and startling thing had happened; and out of this crowd Peter came running suddenly toward him with a face which betrayed unusual tidings before his lips had spoken them.

"You have heard?" he cried.

"Heard of what?" asked David.

"Men from the Mohawk and the Albany country have just come in and bring with them terrible news. The English are moving against Canada by way of the Richelieu, and Sir William Johnson has eleven hundred Indians behind him. My God—twice the number that we had here—and we are four hundred miles away!"

[1] "These screams were more terrible than anything I have ever conceived of in hell," wrote James Smith, an

English prisoner at Fort Duquesne, and eye-witness of the scene.

[2] Antoinette de Vitré, of the Isle of Montreal.

CHAPTER XXVIII

This was the alarming information which came to Contrecoeur the morning after Braddock's defeat. With his victorious Indians and a part of the Canadians already gone, leaving him with less than a hundred French soldiers and officers, he saw the second most important road into New France open and almost defenseless before the enemy if they should return in force. His dread was that Dunbar, advancing with a fresh division, would pick up the remnants of Braddock's troops and resume a contest which, under swiftly changed conditions, must inevitably end to the disaster of France. Had he realized the completeness of his enemy's demoralization, and that Braddock was dying, his worry would have been less.

As it was he went even further than the prerogatives of his command could legally justify and issued a command that none of the free rangers from the North should leave the fort. While this authority might easily have been ignored by the Long Rifles, who had sworn no allegiance to military rules or regulations, there was no inclination to take advantage of their freedom. They had come to fight, and now that the Indians were gone and there was prospect of man-to-man contest instead of wholesale massacre, they were generally eager to remain.

This sentiment, as well as Contrecoeur's command, included Peter's little force, so that when David's homeward race was finally planned its personnel was limited to himself, the Black Hunter, Peter Gagnon, Carbanac, and Kill-Buck. While others from the Richelieu would gladly have accompanied them, unnerved by the news from the Mohawk country, it was Peter Joel's decision that a party of five, all trained to the forests with the exception of Peter and Carbanac, could steal their way through the heart of the enemy's country while a larger force would be compelled to make a detour hugely expensive in time, or, in all probability, fight. Under cover of darkness and unknown to all but Contrecoeur and Robineau they left Fort Duquesne on the night of the ninth of July. There was no attempt on the part of any member of this little band to conceal from the others the seriousness of the situation or the fears which were inspiring such haste. Peter Joel, to whom even Kill-Buck now looked for leadership, expressed in a few words what lay in the minds of all.

"Never has such a war-party of Indians been gathered for the purpose of slaughter in either the French or English dominions," he said, "and for skill in surprise attacks, fearlessness of death, and savage cruelty none can compare with the Mohawks, the Oneidas, and the Senecas. If Dieskau holds them back the danger to the northern waterways will be less; but even then, in the face of English defeat, these hordes of scalp-hunters will sweep around the French defense, unseen and unheard, to fall upon the unprotected homes behind. That is Indian strategy, as you have witnessed here by more than a hundred and eighty scalps of women and children that have been brought in. If Dieskau should fail to hold the English, and the savages know that a victorious ally is behind them, then may God have pity on a doomed land to the very shores of the St. Lawrence."

His face betrayed openly the depth of his feelings, and knowledge of the truth he had spoken lay as clearly written in the dark and sinister countenance of Kill-Buck, who carried at his waist seven scalps taken from the English dead.

"It is a good six hundred miles to Grondin Manor by wilderness trails if we follow the safety of French frontiers," Peter Joel had said, "and four hundred as a crow might fly, not making allowance for the barrier of lakes and swamps on the way. We can make it in that distance by piercing straight through the heart of the enemy country south and west of Lake George."

And this was what they set out to do.

Confiding in no one the dread intelligence which Robineau had brought to him, and not alarming Peter by telling him that Nancy Lotbinière might be at Grondin Manor, it was David who bore the heaviest burden of distress and fear as they began their long journey through the wilderness. Deep in his heart was an agony greater than that which visions of death and physical disaster could breed. In these first days it seemed to him that death, its possibility and its horror, had become of less importance than the other thing which was dragging at his soul, a thing which grew in him and devoured his waking hours as well as his restless sleep until it seemed at times that the mere weight and gloom of despair would set his brain reeling with the darker clouds of madness. His own crime pressed upon him, the unforgivable crime of his thoughts against Anne, the wrong he had done her, the terrible blow he had struck at her through his prison bars; and gladly, as one reaching out for a precious thing, he would have died if through death he might have recalled the acts and words and lack of faith with which he had so terribly destroyed what years of love and trust had built up. He was no longer thinking of Bigot, except that he had been a pigmy whose futile efforts were unimportant now when confronted by the proven love and loyalty of Anne. Even more shameful than Bigot's plotting had been his own weakness and cowardice, an unworthiness which possessed him more completely with each new thought of the one whose happiness and whose pride and confidence in him he had so utterly destroyed.

Yet this burden of grief was less than the more poignant and consuming fear which was eating at his heart and mind, the fear that Robineau's half-prophecy had come to pass, and that Anne St. Denis, carrying out her promise of immolation that she had made to him that day on Sunset Hill if his love for her should ever fail, had buried herself forever in the cloisters of the nuns. That her mind, more than once inspired by Sister Esther, was sweetly conscious at all times of the glory and holiness of a life dedicated to God and the Church, she had never tried to hide from him. To give herself as a bride to Jesus, as so many of her friends had done, would not for her be a sacrifice inspired by a broken heart, and burned-out hopes alone, but a duty which she would perform with that gladness and richness of spiritual obligation which only her love for him had held from an earlier consummation.

This David knew, now that the truth was beating at his very life. It seemed years ago that the fear of losing Anne in this way had come to him first, and like a drop of hot iron it had burned him that afternoon of the powder-horn story on Sunset Hill, until almost word for word he had recalled the holy letter of Sister Esther pleading with Anne to give her body and her soul to God. And now every hour he heard Anne's words of that day, spoken with soft voice and eyes filled with a misty sheen, "But I shall become a nun only if you are untrue to me, David."

And he had been untrue. That was the appalling and monstrous fact that struck at him as day after day the little band stole with moccasined feet and bated breath through the forests. Each night something harder and deeper shone in his face, and sleep, when it came, failed to wipe away the scars of grief and hopelessness which he could no longer keep from the eyes of Peter Joel.

"We will find our people safe," encouraged the Black Hunter, guessing only partly at the cause of what lay in David's face. "All of the Richelieu will have good warning even if Dieskau's army fails to hold."

Vainly and desperately David fought within himself against the mental sickness which had seized upon him. He struggled to vision hope again and to think of Anne waiting to forgive him for his wretchedness. But gloom settled more sinisterly where he prayed and reached out for light, until at last something which he could no longer combat told him that the thing he dreaded had come to pass. It was like a whisper out of the air, a spirit coming from Anne to breathe the message to him, telling him that because his love and his faith were gone she had pledged herself to the Bridal Veil of God. And now he knew that she was not at Grondin Manor, and that from the home of Nancy Lotbinière she had gone to the cloister and not to the Richelieu.

Stricken by a conviction which seemed imposed on him by the awesome power of Heaven itself he settled into a condition of dogged and unreasoning physical exertion. He demanded even of the Black Hunter that they rest at fewer intervals and travel longer ones, and that they follow the higher and clearer aisles of the forest instead of the lower, though greater danger lay there. But Peter Joel, with Kill-Buck grunting approval, still sought the hidden ways of the lowlands and the swamps.

It was hot. The midsummer sun rose in cloudless skies and seethed like a caldron through them to the sunsets. The swamps were moist ovens, with little running or standing water, yet not parched enough to destroy the multitudes of insects which day and night made life a torture. The glory and the beauty of the wilderness were overwhelmed by a triumph of discomfort over beast and man. Mosquitoes and black-flies had driven the deer to the hills and mountains; the foxes had sought the higher levels; rabbits were on the plains and plateaus; and even the black bear went berry-hunting in the uplands.

The Indians were on the open waters, with cool breezes filling their nights, or in the high hardwoods, where generations of savage feet had made trails freer from the torments of the Flying Up Moon, when everything is on the wing. "For that reason we are safe in the lowlands," said Peter Joel a score of times to encourage the spirit of his comrades; but even then it came to pass that Carbanac, with his face like a piece of beef, and David and Peter, scarcely seeing from swollen eyes, had to seek relief from the mosquitoes and black-flies or go mad. Not until the last hour of endurance did Peter Joel follow the beaten trails of the enemy country. Progress had been torturously slow in the tangled lowlands, and it was even slower now, inspired by the necessities of caution. Evidences grew about them of war-parties on the move; they came to an Indian village on a lake, and Kill-Buck, spying close, reported it filled with women and children, and warriors gone. They saw canoes, and fires at night, and several times Senecas and Mohawks passed so near to them that only the caution and skill of the Black Hunter and Kill-Buck kept them from discovery.

Then came another blow in the punishment which David believed he so fully merited. Carbanac, climbing ahead of him up the face of a cliff which had proved solid to the feet of Peter Joel and the Delaware, loosened a great rock which caught David in its descent and almost killed him. For many days the little band now lay in hiding unmindful of David's pleas that they leave him behind with Kill-Buck and continue as quickly as they could to the Richelieu. Against this both Peter Gagnon and the Black Hunter took firm stand, so that on the third day it was the old Delaware who, alone, left for Grondin Manor, and David's heart beat more freely. If by any chance Anne was there she would know that he was coming, and into Kill-Buck's ear he whispered a message for her which the grim-faced warrior promised to remember word for word.

August was well on its way before torn ligaments in one of his legs would allow him to travel. It was September before he had fully regained his strength, and they were near the safety of the French frontier. They swung eastward and traveled with lighter hearts. A French trader whom they met gave them news that Dieskau was moving against Lake George with a great army which was bound to annihilate the English. This trader had come up from Montreal and he said that along the Richelieu were peace and safety. A growing glow of happiness filled the countenances of Peter Gagnon and the Black Hunter; and Carbanac, returning nearer to the scenes of his own life's tragedy and the menace of the law, revealed a more subdued reflection of relief and thankfulness.

David struggled to exult with the others. His mother was safe and all the people of the Richelieu were safe. Yet the thrill of that thought could not wipe away the somber thing that had become a part of his being, or lighten a heart in which happiness was buried as if under a weight of stone. Kill-Buck had reached Grondin Manor many days ago, but he had grown more and more certain that Anne was beyond the reach of his message and was forever lost to him.

The day of September eighth, 1755, was gray with cloud and rain and filled with occasional intonations of thunder. Late in the afternoon the Black Hunter stopped a number of times and listened with a tense and puzzled face to something which he seemed to hear far away in the north and east. "It must be the thunder," he said. "Yet I have thought it might be guns."

That night the skies cleared and the stars came out, and a full moon rode up over the wilderness; and through this night the Black Hunter sat awake while the others slept, and still faced the north and east.

Near the dawn he heard a sound which he knew could not be the echoing of distant thunder over the hills. It came suddenly, and died suddenly, and a new shadow was in his eyes when the others awoke.

With no further hesitation he led in the direction his eyes had turned under the glow of the climbing moon, and at last David knew there was something in his mind which he had not spoken. It was midday when they came over the crest of a ridge where a great rock lay, and looked down on a shallow pond across which a strong arm might have thrown a stone in either direction. It was Peter Joel who saw first what was there, and a crying breath came to his lips, followed in an instant by a startled cry from Carbanac.

The pond, dried within a few inches of its bottom by weeks of drought and heat, was choked with the bodies of dead men. They lay at its edge, and in the mud, and some farther out with white and sightless faces turned up to the sky. No sound save the song of a bird and the chatter of a red squirrel broke the somber stillness of that pond of death. [1] No human voice came with the whispering air and the droning song of honey-bees; no crackling of twig, no cry, no stir of life or groan of agony. Yet death had but recently passed, so recently that the water at the edges of the pond where the dead lay thickest had a reddish coloration in the light of the sun, the stain of blood.

Down into the dread place Peter Joel led, and where their feet trod were moccasin prints from whose little pockets of water the mud had not settled into earth again. Then they saw that not only death had been here, but the red scourge with the scalping-knife, and with this horror came another, swift and terrible. There were no English among the dead.

No words were needed to tell the story. Those who lay in the pool and around its edges were French and allies of the French; men in the gray and homespun of the seigneuries, in brown and weathered deerskin from the forests, and Indians half naked, without a Mohawk, a Seneca, or an Oneida to keep them company.

Peter Joel spoke no word as he skirted the pool and took to the ridge again, and lips were set hard in the white and stony faces of the others. And scarcely had they come to the thick brush beyond the ridge top before an object crawling slowly and painfully out of cover stopped them. It was a man. He wore the bedraggled and blood-stained uniform of an officer, and in his face and eyes was the shadow of death. So ghastly was his appearance that at first David did not see the still more shocking thing, that his scalp was gone. The Black Hunter dropped on his knees beside the dying man and supported him in his arms as he pressed the mouth of his water-flask to lips that were already stiffening with the palsy of death; and, in answer to his questioning, words came brokenly and in a sobbing whisper.

Dieskau had been defeated. What was left of his force was in mad flight. The big fight had happened yesterday, hours before the massacre at the pool, which had only occurred last night. He, and Captain Folsom, and McGinnis—had returned—to hold the Indians. Surprised there—at the pool—and slaughtered like sheep. Mohawks, mostly,—Senecas—Oneidas—hundreds of them. Hendrik—chief of the Mohawks—was killed—and his warriors—mad—for vengeance. Dieskau himself was wounded—and a prisoner—in the enemy's hands——

The man made an heroic effort to say something more. It was about himself, something in the pocket of his coat. He died before the words could come. But Peter Joel had guessed the message, and he found a letter addressed to Madame Henri Bernac, in Three Rivers. After that, while David and Peter were on guard, the Black Hunter and Carbanac dug a shallow grave and buried the dead man, and the four then united their strength to roll a huge rock over the place where he lay.

Even now there were no words between them. Their hearts were suffocated by the same thought. With Dieskau beaten the way lay open into the North for the red hosts of their enemy, and the war-parties of the savages were ahead of them, racing like wolves toward the settlements and the isolated homes of the pioneers. Peter Joel said this much at last. The French forces would reassemble near Crown Point; they might hold the English back, might even beat them there—but this would be too late to fend off the peril behind. Here, if ever, was opportunity for that Indian strategy which he had always dreaded when he thought of the Richelieu— war-parties stealing swiftly through the dead of night, unexpected attacks, massacre falling suddenly out of calm and peaceful skies, men surprised in their fields, women in their homes, children at their play. The blow would come first at the far end of Lake Champlain, a place so safe that no soldiers would be left on guard. That was always the way—a blow as swift as it would be sudden, passing in a night or a day, when the grim wilderness would swallow its red children again so that all the power of France and the Canadas could not find them.

So it happened that the Black Hunter once more began a race against death like the one of many years ago, when he had carried David in his arms and Marie Rock had traveled at his side. And now, as then, it was the sweet soul of the woman that urged him, her white face calling to him from beyond the far horizon, until even Carbanac in all his mighty strength found growing weakness in his limbs.

And pace for pace with the Black Hunter strode David, knowing that an hour had come when even for Peter he could not stop. Night did not halt them, for now Peter Joel knew hidden trails that led straight north. Between the beginning of darkness and moonrise there was rest for Peter and Carbanac, then the journey began again. It continued as the moon climbed upward and still went on as it sank into the west. Gray dawn found the Black Hunter and David tirelessly breaking the way, with faces white and wan; and behind them, like two ghosts who had passed beyond the physical strain of exhaustion, followed Peter and Carbanac.

Flesh fell from their bones that day, and hollows that grew steadily deeper and darker settled under their sleepless eyes. Yet no word for mercy came from lips that were bloodless. But Carbanac groaned and rolled face downward like a dying man when Peter Joel at last called another rest.

For three hours they slept, then ate, and went on. Stiffened limbs responded to the fight again, and with the coming of another dusk it seemed to David that something had clubbed his feelings to insensibility. He no longer recognized Peter as the Peter he had known, and Carbanac's face was a mask with wide nostrils dilated by the strain. And now he saw in the Black Hunter the strange and mysterious spirit, neither ghost nor flesh of man, that had made the borderlands shiver at the mention of his name, for only a superman could have stood that test so like a god beyond the reach of exhaustion and physical pain.

And Peter, looking at David, wondered if his eyes were tricking him, or if it was the real David he saw, with deep, gaunt lines in his face, and neck muscles that were straining to burst like pieces of overtautened rope.

They rested again at midnight on a bald hilltop that looked northward into the country of the Richelieu. Peter and Carbanac slept like the dead men back in the pool— David uneasily, striving to keep himself awake to fight with the Black Hunter against the peril of total oblivion for all. An hour passed, two, and three, and almost four. The moon went down and the world lay in a pall of darkness that preceded the dawn. Out of that darkness came a loud and awakening cry from the Black Hunter.

David leaped up, clutching at his rifle. Peter and Carbanac followed, swaying dizzily and rubbing the thick sleep from their eyes. Peter Joel was standing, a black shadow in the black night. And off there, where he was looking, miles away, was a great red glow of fire in the sky!

It was broad day when they came to the mellow bottomland from which tall red flames had painted the sky. Tonteur, adventurous, a fighting man, had owned it. Now Tonteur was dead. He was found with his face turned up, which was the Mohawk way of leaving their victims when they were men; the women, because they were servants to their slain lords, they turned face down. And there were women and children among the dead at Tonteur's. The farmers' cabins were piles of ash and coals, and so was Tonteur's big log home, which he had called a castle. And about this place so recently filled with the shrieks of women and children, the cries of dying men and the triumphant yells of bloodthirsty savages was now a terrible and awesome silence. The scene sent choking fingers round David's throat. The women were dressed as they had gone to bed. Death had come in deep sleep, and men had scarce had time to clutch at weapons or use them. And here, as at the pool, there was no time to bury those who lay so crumpled and still.

The Black Hunter had come out on the Richelieu half-way between the tip of Lake Champlain and Grondin Manor, and from what had been Tonteur's place they could see the blue haze of sky and forest where Grondin Manor lay.

Even into Peter's distressed limbs and travel-shattered body there leaped the strength of madness, and the Black Hunter led on at a pace which was almost a trot, their moccasined feet making not a sound in the smooth trail which lay between the ash of Tonteur's castle and the oaks of Sunset Hill.

They passed Old Paul's, where so long as people up and down the river could remember there had lived the mysterious old wilderness hermit who was known only by that name, and they found Old Paul, face up, like the others, with a long-limbed, fiercely snarling dog on guard at his side.

They could hear the turkeys calling in the morning warmth of the sun, and squirrels were chattering in the oaks, which they passed like grim and vengeful shadows. They looked like death. They felt death. And in their hearts was death.

In David it was a volcano of desire. Never had he felt that maddening passion to kill which overwhelmed him now, and with that passion was the primal urge to open his mouth and shriek through the miles the warning of his coming. He could see only one thing, above him, ahead of him, everywhere—the women with their faces to the ground, the children near their arms. Their unseen faces haunted him—he could see his mother as he had so often looked upon her like a lover with her hair unbound about her—and her face danced with the others in his brain; and Anne came and went, and the little children he knew, and Peter Joel could hear the sobbing agony in his breath as step by step he forged ahead until he, and not the Black Hunter, was leading in the last lap of the race to Grondin Manor.

They came to the place where out of a dense pocket in the forests Henri Taschereau and his two sons had carved a home that had bloomed with the promise and joy of two sweethearts coming soon from the Isle of Montreal. And here the three lay in a lifeless heap, the father, strangely, with a cold and yet unstiffened arm over the shoulders of each of his boys.

Then the waterfall where David, a long time ago, had once brought Anne.

And after that the mighty stub of a lightning-blasted pine that could be seen on clear days from the top of Sunset Hill, and the red cliff with its pair of ancient eagles that were older than the seigneurs themselves, and the Chestnut Plateau where wild turkeys were always thickest, and the break between two great hills where David got his choicest venison.

And here, coming to them faintly, they heard the firing of guns.

For only a moment the terrible lines in the Black Hunter's face relaxed in a sudden expression of joy. "Thank God they haven't caught St. Denis as they caught Tonteur," he cried. "Those are the guns of the men at Grondin Manor!"

Again David felt an unreasoning desire to shriek out that they were coming. They ran, and rested when they walked. Each minute seemed an hour, each mile a dozen leagues. Never had distances seemed so far, and not once did a thought come to these four of what small avail they might be against the overwhelming numbers of a savage enemy. One yearning filled the bursting heart of David, and of them all—to die at Grondin Manor, if die they must, so that their eyes would not behold there what they had looked upon at Tonteur's.

456

The firing ceased, and in the awful stillness which followed it fear gripped their souls.

And then, a golden radiance of oak and chestnut color, came Sunset Hill.

They climbed it, sobbing for breath, and passed where David had stood beside Anne with his powder-horn such a long, long time ago.

They sped under the oaks and out through their rim, where in the golden glow of the evening she had given that glorious freedom to her hair.

They came to the little hollow with its spring and flowers where they had heard the voice of the farmer's wife singing at the supper hour in her cottage, and David gave a moaning cry when he saw the little home of grouted stone. Its windows were broken, its door burst in, and close to the threshold lay the singer, her slim little body twisted, her arms reaching out as if still seeking in death the man who lay a few paces away.

And now it came all at once to David why no smoke and fire had risen from Grondin Manor, for the cottages were built of stone, and would not burn.

And he saw, looking away, no smoke rising from the farmers' chimneys in the bottomlands.

But from beyond the screen of Grondin's Wood there came suddenly a sound that made the blood thick in his veins, a yelling and howling tumult of savage voices, a madness of triumph that drove lightning-flashes through his brain, and with it a weak and scattered—pitifully scattered—response of rifle-fire.

No deer ever ran more swiftly than the Black Hunter ran now, with David touching shoulders at his side—past the spot where Bigot had first looked on Anne, through the thicket, up the trail, until at last they stood in the farther edge of the wood itself. And Peter and Carbanac, like grim death tagging behind, were at their heels.

Here Peter Joel laid a fierce hold on David's arm, and stood swallowing and panting for his breath. And with his tightening grip he said, in a moment, "Do as I do now—do that or we are lost!"

David's eyes were for an instant blinded by a veil of horror, for it seemed to him that they were looking upon a mad carnival of fiends, and that they had come too late.

[1] Known to this day as the Bloody Pond, with the date of its tragedy carved in the big white stone.

CHAPTER XXIX

All in a glance, with the yells of a savage foe splitting the air, he looked upon the place of ruin and death that a little while ago had been the peace and security of Grondin Manor.

The great house was cold and lifeless, its windows battered in, its doors torn down and from the upper and lower openings its contents had been hurled to the ground, a grim and terrible evidence of the completeness of its fate. And the thick oaken door to Fontbleu's stone mill was gone, and the mill itself was a ghastly corpse that had been robbed of its life, for close to where the door had been lay a little old crumpled figure with a dust-whitened coat, which was all that was left of Fontbleu, the miller.

Over him the wheel at the top of his mill was turning— turning as if the hands of spirits were there at work, for the day seemed empty of wind.

More than this David did not see, for what life was left at Grondin Manor had found a refuge in the old stone church across the green; and about this building the savages were swarming in their final triumphant assault as Peter Joel dug his fingers into his arm. Two or three shots rang out above their cries, but that was all—shots which told of the pathetic weakness within; and with these shots came the crashing of timbers against oak and iron doors, and a fiercer outburst of cries from the naked and painted demons as the barriers began to give way.

In these unforgetable seconds life lived itself in a thousand tortures for David. They were too late. The Great House was gone, and with it all that he had loved on earth, for there his mother had been, and Anne if she had come from Quebec. His brain grew black and the day seemed suddenly filled with the redness of fire, and only the voice of the Black Hunter speaking again at his side held his hands.

"Wait!" he said. "Fire only when I do, and see to it that each of you kills one of the Indians at the door. We have come in time—just in time!"

He drew in a great breath, threw back his head, and out of his throat came a cry, and with that cry Peter Joel was no longer just a man but that black and mysterious spirit of the forests, half human and half devil, who came and went with the winds, a creature of darkness and omen, a shadow of death—the unearthly Black Hunter of the border-lands. Never had David heard that fearful cry, and never had Peter meant that he should hear it, for it was not only a thing of madness, but madness itself—a wailing and terrible cry that began as a sobbing moan and grew in volume until it seemed to fill all space and to stir with vibrant horror the earth itself. Men would have sworn—as hundreds along the borders had done—that it was cry of neither beast nor human, no belling of the forest, no brawl or moan of wind or water, but rather the mystery of some Gargantuan monster of space, beginning in a whisper, rising to a scream, and dying away at last in a plaintive sob that seemed to lose itself in distance. And the man who sent it forth was once more the Black Hunter and no longer Peter Joel—the Black Hunter of the burning cabins and red death of years ago, the creature whose twisted brain had sent him with the shifting moons, forever wandering, never resting, seeking a face that was dead.

With his eyes drawn by the maniacal sound David looked on that madness of which his mother had told him and of which strange and gloomy whisperings had troubled the soul of Anne.

For Peter Joel had lost again the sanity which Marie Rock had won for him. A demon of madness and vengeance he stood as the last echoes of his cry died away, and the air was yet trembling with their horror when his rifle cracked. David fired straight through the heart of one of the savages before the door. The rifles of Peter and Carbanac crashed at his side, and they could not miss, for as if stricken by a sudden palsy the Indians had stopped in their assault and stood like wooden images as the Black Hunter's cry fell like a scourge of doom upon them. Had it been night not a warrior there was so brave that he would not have fled for his very life from that sound which in all the teepees of the border wilderness was feared as no other thing of either the living or the dead.

"Load again!" David had cried. "Load and fire as fast as you can!"

But this day was another day of sixteen years ago for Peter Joel, and as he had leaped with a club and his naked hands to wreak vengeance on the slayers of his wife and children, so now he ran, a mad and shrieking fury, upon those who had come to rob him of another woman he loved—Marie Rock.

Even then the Indians might have broken before that black and terrible figure, as others had broken in the valley of the Juniata, but behind this spirit of vengeance descending upon them came a man, and behind that man two others. And the sight of men—men with white and ghastly faces—broke for some of them the spell which had bound them with its horror.

David could see only death ahead, yet he would have faced a hundred deaths rather than desert the Black Hunter. Madness raced suddenly in his own flaming blood, and to Peter Joel's inhuman screams he added the savage and malevolent cries which had almost forced themselves from his lips miles back. A form raced up beside his own, the mighty body of Carbanac—Carbanac transformed into a monster, and out of whose lungs came bellowings that were like the roarings of a beast. If sound was madness, then madness smote the air of Grondin Manor, for even Peter was shrieking his fury and his hate. What eyes beheld through the shuttered windows and slit loopholes of the little church will never be seen again, and for a generation the story was to pass among the Indian tribes from the Upper Canadas to the far Ohio of how four fiends of madness fought half the Mohawk nation.

Like Peter Joel, the other three had dropped their guns and gripped their keen-edged girdle-axes, and those of their enemies who stood first before them broke in sudden fear and horror. And now David thought only of himself and of what he had to do, and the strength of ten men seemed in his body and arms, and with each stroke of his ax a scream as wild and as terrible as Peter Joel's followed from his lips. His ax turned suddenly red as he clove a shaven skull from crown to shoulder; he buried it to the head in a back that was turned in flight; it fell in crushing death against a naked breast. He felt no fear but only a superhuman power to kill. If blows fell upon him he did not feel.

Even then, filled with the insanity of a single desire, he was like a child beside the mighty Carbanac. For Carbanac had come to that hour of glory which was a heritage in his blood—Carbanac, the common man, a man thrown aside by a shameful woman, changed now into an appalling and magnificent god. His roars rose triumphant with the Black Hunter's screams. Right and left he clove his way, leaping with the fury of a panther, striking with lightning swiftness, invulnerable and merciless, towering head and shoulders over the head of the greatest of their enemies.

Fighting now not to conquer but to live, the Mohawk warriors enveloped him. Through them David went and for a moment the Black Hunter was at his side, and it seemed to him that the ax in the Hunter's hand was a glint of lightning so swiftly it moved in the sun. He no longer recognized the Hunter's face, for through the blood that stained it blazed the disordered soul of a man he had never known before. He saw Peter fighting like a tiger, and then he was alone, slashing and cutting, until the ring of death broke from around Carbanac. And as the ring broke another figure leaped beside the fighting giant, and David knew why the Mohawks had given away behind, for it was Kill-Buck with his battle-ax who had leaped from the shattered door of the church to join them in the fight.

For an instant David saw that door. The Mohawk assault had broken it so that it hung crossways of the opening like a wedge, and behind this breast-high barrier over which Kill-Buck had leaped there were deathlike, bloodless faces staring out—faces of women whose wide eyes were filled with a flaming horror in the semi-gloom of the ancient church. In this moment a thought flashed into David's brain a hundred times swifter than spoken words—where were the men of Grondin Manor? For he heard a woman's cry, and only that, and eyes and faces which he saw through the broken portal were not the eyes and faces of men.

Then the cleared space between him and the faces suddenly filled, and half a dozen naked savages maddened by the sight of the helpless prey leaped to the fallen door, but not quicker than David himself. He was an arm's length ahead and struck so furiously at a paint-daubed face that the face was obliterated in a sudden blur of red. He felt blows now. Naked steel cut his flesh. Death hemmed him in, close and panting, ferocious and without mercy.

And then through the dimming radiance of the day came a woman's cry—a cry from within—a cry from out of a hell that was transformed for him into a heaven.

In that cry was his name.

"David! David! David!"

He shouted back an answer. He rose to the mightiness and the glory of Carbanac. He fought as no living eyes along the Richelieu had ever seen a man fight before. A tomahawk buried itself in his shoulder, and he stood against it and sent back death to the one who had given him the blow. The Mohawks wavered before the devil-spirit which they could not kill, and as they wavered he set upon them like a blood-reddened monster that was immune to death. They turned, and in turning met the Black Hunter, and not one of the six returned to his comrades.

David fought as no living eyes along the   *Richelieu had ever seen a man fight before*

David fought as no living eyes along the Richelieu had ever seen a man fight before.

And again that cry out of heaven came to David: "David——David——David——"

It did not stop him, but urged him on. He was like the Black Hunter. He shrieked, not in fury now, but in triumph. The Mohawks were beaten, stricken to the soul at last by a fear that was greater than the fear of man. Devils had been sent against them, devils they could not harm or destroy. Their dead covered the ground, so many dead that a generation would pass before their places were filled again.

They fled, the Black Hunter a ravening death at the heels of the last to go.

In the center of a pile of the slain stood Carbanac. Something in the mighty man's attitude brought David to his side. At Carbanac's feet was Peter, unable to rise, but smiling through his blood and wounds. Close to Peter lay Kill-Buck, gone at last to join his crucified people in another and better Hunting Ground.

Carbanac, the god thrown away by a woman, was moaning, as if singing a strange song under his breath; and his eyes were wide and staring, as if he saw that woman coming to him with outstretched arms from the forest. And through eyes that were beginning to grow dark David saw the great rents in Carbanac's breast, and the terrible hole cleft by the blade of an Indian ax in his head.

Thus Carbanac stood as the Mohawks fled, and a smile came to his dying lips as he dropped his own red ax and reached out his hands toward the thing which no other eyes could see. After the smile came a little moan, and he sank down gently, making no sound as his great soul went on its way.

In the moment Carbanac died, a vast and smothering darkness swept over David, and he seemed to be falling gently through a space without end; but faster than he fell came the voice again, the voice of Anne, following him, overtaking him, until at last it was with him, and he could hear it crying and sobbing his name so near to him that it seemed to be a part of his soul. For in the last moment of his consciousness Anne was kneeling with her arms about him in that pile of the dead.

CHAPTER XXX

Hovering in a vale filled with the darkening shadows that drift between life and death, David for many days knew no more than his own eyes had seen of the tragedy which had come to Grondin Manor. But from the beginning, even in a moment when those about him thought he was dead, he knew that Anne was with him. Never for an hour through days of grief-filled gloom and nights of blacker hopelessness did either the spirit or the body of Anne leave his side, and in those brief and swiftly passing moments when the clouds broke their smothering prisonment about him it was always Anne's white face he saw, like an angel's above him, and Anne's great eyes and tender voice calling him back to life. Through all those days of one long prayer that God might give him back to her Anne guarded the hacked and twisted body, dividing that precious privilege only with David's mother; and Marie Rock, with a mother's love which knows no selfishness nor fear of sacrifice, knew that Anne and not she would hold David for them all if any power on earth could bring about that miracle.

For David's body had suffered a martyrdom of torture, and when she was alone with him Anne's lips kissed the scars which his back and arms would always bear from the lash of Bigot's whip, and hot tears fell upon them as she breathed her never-ending plea to the Mother of Christ that she might be forgiven for this thing that she had brought upon him. More terribly than the deepest wounds of the Mohawk hatchets were these marks seared in her soul. If David lived he might forget them. The marks themselves might disappear, but for her they would always remain, like the Cross itself, a part of her life, a part of her prayers—even of eternity when it came.

And always feeling this spirit-hand of Anne holding him from sinking deeper into the shadows David came at last entirely up over the edge of the pit into which he had been dragged; and one morning, opening his eyes to that same Algonquin Indian-summer sun that had warmed them with its promise just a year ago on Sunset Hill, he saw Anne—the old Anne—standing in its glow, and joyously spoke her name.

It was after that, through days of growing strength, that he learned of many things which in darkness he had yearned to understand. Peter came to him, his face scarred, and with a broken arm in a sling, and with him was Nancy Lotbinière. It was Anne, first of all, who told him that only through God's great goodness to them had the Mohawk assault come on a Sabbath morning when most of the women and children of Grondin Manor were already at the church, and that Nancy had looked with her upon that terrible fight, through the slit loopholes first and then over the top of the fallen door.

But it was of the grimmer things that his heart ached to know, and these came from Peter, and from the Baron St. Denis, whose gray face had aged and in whose eyes lay a deep and tragically slumbering thing that would never thereafter be quite wiped out. Carbanac was dead. Kill-Buck was dead. And little old Fontbleu, the miller, was dead, and along with him three other men, seven women, and four children of Grondin Manor. Most of the men, feeling their homes secure, had gone with Dieskau to fight the English. In the church that morning, sacredly kept there for many years by the curé, were six old guns, but scarcely half a horn of powder and less than a score of balls. All but a spoonful of powder was gone when the Black Hunter's cry came out of the edge of the forest. Ten minutes later it would have found only the red winds of death hovering over Grondin Manor. The Baron's face was still of clayish whiteness as he told of the miracle which had happened at the Big House. On that morning of the attack Anne was oppressed by the strange sickness which had overcome her so frequently since her return from Quebec, and Nancy was staying with her. All the others, including the black slaves, had gone to the church. At the last minute Anne got up from her couch and with Nancy came across the green. God must have sent them, for scarcely had the church doors closed behind them than the Mohawks swarmed out of the woods like wolves.

The Black Hunter was gone. No eyes had seen him after he had followed the savages into the forest. He had not returned for the rifle which he had dropped in the open and had disappeared as completely as though the earth had opened somewhere to receive him. Peter and St. Denis had searched every trail and thicket where his body might be found. He was not dead—unless he had continued at the heels of the Indians beyond the boundaries of the seigneury, where they might have killed him.

But something in David's heart made him refuse to believe that Peter Joel was gone forever. Anne strengthened his faith. "He can't go away—not like that—until God has given me the opportunity to get down on my knees at his feet and plead for his forgiveness," she encouraged him, her voice atremble with the bitterness of a grief which had come to find its place for all time with her happiness. "God will not let that happen, David, for I love him—I love him— and I have wronged him even more terribly than I wronged you. If he is dead, and I have helped to drive him back to madness when I might have brought him happiness, then in the end I must answer for it at the feet of Our Dear Lady in Heaven!"

David could only fight back the choking thickness in his throat and hold Anne's face so close that she could not see the scalding thing in his eyes.

"He will come back," he said, and those words he kept repeating through the days, and often to himself. Marie Rock said nothing, and her eyes told only a little of the story that was passing in her heart—a heart in which had settled a loneliness greater than any that had ever been there before.

"The tragedy in our lives has come," the Baron St. Denis said to her gently one day, looking yearningly at her bowed head. "But sunshine and happiness are ahead, and if—some day——"

But he went no further than that, for in his heart, too, was a hopelessness which had long abided there. If the Black Hunter was gone, then Marie Rock's heart was gone with him, and not only for a time, but forever.[1]

And, in truth, it seemed as though the tragedy which the Black Hunter had so long dreaded and presaged had come and passed, and that the Baron's prediction of sunshine and happiness was very near to its greatest fulfilment, for Sir William Johnson's Indians had deserted him, his forces from the colonies were breaking up and leaving for home, and nearly four thousand French were strongly entrenched near and beyond the pass at Ticonderoga. In spite of the first French slaughter and defeat the word went swiftly throughout New France that the English attempt against Crown Point and the Canadas had been a dismal failure, and that never again would their enemies on the south attempt to break through by way of the Richelieu.

Death for a time spread its pall of sadness over Grondin Manor. But a glorious October followed September, and while a few of the homes lay in cold and forlorn gloom life in its old way began again. Smoke rose softly in the autumn warmth from the chimneys of cottages in which men and their families were together again. There were light and laughter and occasionally song in the Big House, where Anne and Nancy and Marie Rock made their brave struggle to bury the scars of grief under the joys of living once more.

Happiness and sorrow walked hand in hand, yet each day happiness grew a little stronger and sorrow mellowed itself a step at a time. The call of the turkeys came out of the woods at dawn and sunset, dogs barked and played in the clearings again, and children took up their games, forgetting with the ease of childhood the red horror which had stalked so short a time ago in the edges of the forest they loved. The wilderness itself, as if exulting in the coming of an eternal peace, was clothing itself in the red and gold and yellow glories of the sharp night frosts, until they reached out for unending miles in vast tapestries of color which only the Great Artist which is God knows how to paint.

And the old mill-wheel continued its song again, and there was something about the manner of its singing which brought a great sob from Anne's breast and a choking cry from David now and then when it seemed no power within him could hold it back. For only they could hear the soul and the voice of little old Fontbleu, the miller, in the turning of the wheel; and only they knew that Fontbleu was still there, though they could not see him, and that his spirit hands were at work about the place he had loved, just as they had worked for so many years in the flesh.

Upon the top of Sunset Hill, in the very spot where David had told to Anne the story of the powder-horn, Fontbleu, and Carbanac, and Kill-Buck were buried. "I had them taken there," said Anne, when she first told David, "because that is our hallowed ground, David, and because there, through all the years to come, we will go so often together."

And one beautiful autumn day they stood beside these precious graves, and David was almost strong again, and Anne was as she had been a year ago, with her hair in a shining braid; and she was so very much like the Anne of that day, except that she was paler, that David fell curiously wondering, until, out of the shawl she had brought with her, she drew her powder-horn.

And then, with voice trembling a little, and head bowed so that for a moment he could not see the glow of the tears in her eyes, she said:

"David, I am here, just as I was the other day such a long, long time ago. It is the same dress, the same ribbon in my hair, the same"—and she choked a little—"the same heart in here." And she placed a hand on her breast. "And

I want to hear the story of the powder-horn again, David, just as you told it that day, except that you must leave out the talk of fighting which frightened me so, for that is done with now. But I want you to tell me again about these words you carved, and of the shrine in the forest with two angels kneeling, and of the boy, who is soon to be my husband, who stands disconsolately with the fish-pole in his hands."

And David told the story, close over the graves of Fontbleu, the miller, and of Carbanac, the god-man, and of Kill-Buck, the Delaware, with that same great world of glory and promise spread out before their eyes. And as he told it a four-footed beast came up from the trail behind them and stood wonderingly, then listened intently, as if he, too, understood—the mongrel dog.

[1] There are times when fact insists upon drawing a somber cloud between romance and its fulfilment. As the Black Hunter disappeared from the eyes of Grondin Manor, so he disappeared from the world. David never saw him again. But in 1772 a strange, wild recluse dying in the wilderness of the Juniata revealed himself as the Black Hunter, and was buried at the foot of the lonely mountain which today bears his name.

THE END.

www.ingramcontent.com/pod-product-compliance
Lightning Source LLC
Chambersburg PA
CBHW031025030726
47497CB00004B/1014